# THE CHEMIST

# THE CHEMIST

## LEWIS HASTINGS

This edition published in Great Britain in 2022

by Hobeck Books Limited, Unit 14, Sugnall Business Centre, Sugnall, Stafford, Staffordshire, ST21 6NF

www.hobeck.net

Copyright © Lewis Hastings 2022

This novel is entirely a work of fiction. The names, characters and incidents portrayed in this novel are the work of the author's imagination. Any resemblance to actual persons (living or dead), events or localities is entirely coincidental.

Lewis Hastings has asserted his right under the Copyright, Design and Patents Act 1988 to be identified as the author of this work.

All rights reserved. No parts of this book may be used or reproduced by any means, graphic, electronic, or mechanical, including photocopying, recording, taping or by any information storage retrieval system without the written permission of the copyright holder.

A CIP catalogue for this book is available from the British Library.

ISBN 978-1-913-793-58-6 (pbk)

ISBN 978-1-913-793-57-9 (ebook)

Cover design by Jem Butcher

http://www.jembutcherdesign.co.uk

Printed and bound in Great Britain

❀ Created with Vellum

## BY LEWIS HASTINGS

From the Seventh Wave trilogy:
  *Seventh*
  *Seven Degrees*
  *Seven of Swords*

Jack Cade novels:
  *The Angel of Whitehall*
  *The Chemist*

Autobiography:
  *Actually, The World Is Enough*

# PRAISE FOR THE CHEMIST

Hobeck Books has a team of dedicated advanced readers and other reviewers and readers. Here is what they have said about *The Chemist*.

'A brilliant, searing thriller you'll read in one go and then look for more by the same author. Better murder through chemistry!'
Brian Price, author of *Fatal Trade* and *Fatal Hate*

'I have followed Lewis Hastings' Jack Cade crime thrillers for some years now. I have always admired his attention to detail, original storyline and the substance of his characters...Lewis has definitely matured in his writing career. Five stars from me. Well done, Lewis.'
Claire Borlase

'*The Chemist* really did keep me up late into the night! I loved it and I can't wait for more.'
Alex Jones

'Lewis's stories are so well researched and would be great for TV... [he] never fails to keep the reader gripped.'
Sarah Leck

'I will never play roulette again without thinking of this book...all in all a riveting and good read.'
Lynda Checkley

'There's thrillers, and there there are Lewis's books. Excellent!'
Carole Gourlay

'Lewis's best action-packed, darkly twisted book yet.'
Louise Cannon

# ARE YOU A THRILLER SEEKER?

Hobeck Books is an independent publisher of crime, thrillers and suspense fiction and we have one aim – to bring you the books you want to read.

For more details about our books, our authors and our plans, plus the chance to download free novellas, sign up for our newsletter at **www.hobeck.net**.

You can also find us on Twitter **@hobeckbooks** or on Facebook **www.facebook.com/hobeckbooks10**.

*To my growing family – with love.*

*Would put your hand in the fire for someone – to vouch for them.
In Romania there is a premise that everyone is trustworthy,
until proven otherwise.*

## PROLOGUE



HE CLOSED THE BOOK WITH THE YELLOWED PAGES AND TATTERED cover at a shade after nine.

That its pages were crinkled was unusual, given that its contents were hardly likely to attract the attention of many in that institution. That it had found just one temporary owner in the last six years was surprising enough. The last few pages had both enthralled and amused him. Was it really that simple?

He sat nodding his head, making mental notes, staring at the wall and considering his future as he digested the paragraph, rote learning each stage until he could quote it ad nauseam:

*Those that were kept in captivity were far less deadly than their wild counterparts.* The irony amused him greatly.

He slid the book back against the wall, standing it up next to the other two he was allowed to keep for the week. Turning, he looked at the green metal door with its oversized keyhole, listened against it for a short while, wondering who the others were and where they all slotted into the hierarchy – the eternal power struggle of a modern prison. On that front, he had no concerns whatsoever.

He lay on his modest green mattress in his modest green cell, in the anonymous wing of Belmarsh, a Category A prison near the River Thames in South East London.

Belmarsh housed them all. If you allowed yourself a moment to consider what lay beyond its walls, you might find the grey, empty, desolate faces of child murderers, kidnappers, torturers and terrorists. If you thought about it for too long, you might not sleep again.

These were the faces of men from which the spirits had long departed. Their minds irretrievably lost, islands of despair in a sea of misery. Whilst many were institutionalised and had little recollection of anything else, it was a long way from heaven. In other words, it was hell.

———

They were all there: the misunderstood, the lowest of the low, the psychotic, sociopathic and just plain, old-fashioned evil.

There was that nameless individual who had hacked that poor and defenceless British soldier to death. They would always remember Fusilier Lee Rigby. That's how society worked. But what was the offender's name? Who really cared?

———

Locked away. That was all that mattered. With any luck, and the words of a strong judge, he'd bloody well stay there too, for good. He understood that, the man lying in the modest green bed. It made sense, completely, utterly.

As compelling cases went, it was almost without peer. There were other prisoners too, with their ideals, that were often far from ideal. They should throw away the key. They could all burn in hell for all he cared.

But he was different. His case was a miscarriage of justice; investigations where the authorities had knowingly steered a case in the direction that suited them, the system and the court of public opinion. The decision makers were bastards, all of them.

———

It was Tuesday. He could almost gauge each day by the wafting and slightly nauseating aroma of steamed vegetables.

This was the Hilton. It was the Intercontinental. Perhaps it was even the Hyatt. But the food lacked something. Wednesdays were his favourite. A shame he wouldn't be there to enjoy the light grey meat in gravy that they said was beef. He'd only just got used to the taste of his meals and the stares of the other prisoners, the trustees, those that manned the kitchens that had spat in his food, morning, noon and night.

They watched him constantly. They had nothing better to do. He just mixed it in with his fork. Everything had a nutritional value. The only thing that didn't were the negative thoughts that pecked away at his imagination. Tap, tap, tap…

He laid there, looking up at the ceiling, occasionally staring at a point so infinite that he nodded off: read and learn, learn and read. For now, that was all he could do. That is all they would allow him to do, but not for long.

He decided not to read another chapter. If luck was on his side, he could pull the pillow over his head and try to suffocate himself.

It hadn't worked yet, and it never would. Nor had his attempts at hanging himself with his Tyvek paper suit worked, the type they gave to the upper echelons of the worst inhabitants of one of Britain's most contentious prisons. It was almost cruel.

———

He laid back down on his exquisite plastic mattress. It was one fit for a king, compared to those that he had endured in his past; a past that saw him survive in the run-down, dark and desperate govern-ment building in the middle of Southern Bulgaria, where it always seemed to be winter.

This was the place with the name that made him heave; forcing bile into his mouth, in which, if he was lucky, he'd find some substance. The food in that place, or lack of it, was simply appalling.

Picking silverfish and weevils out of his lunch was considered entertainment.

The minute you entered the place, all you could ever do was pray for the night, and that with luck you would be dead by morning. The overpowering stench of the cell and the distant moans of a human voice invaded his mind, and somehow accompanied him through the night: over and over until the morning, when sadly, he was still alive.

A song drilled deep down into his sub-conscious: *wake up, wake up. It's time for you to step back into hell.*

In comparison, Belmarsh was heaven. To think that everyone else complained about the place. They complained about everything: the food, the beds, the facilities, the officers. They even complained about the 'bloody weather'. The irony that some of the people in his wing would never get to touch, hear or taste the true freedom of a single raindrop again did not escape him.

Belmarsh. Even its name was attractive. 'Bel' meant beautiful, didn't it?

Here, they laughed for no reason. They laughed at themselves, but rarely at each other. They saved their crying until after the lights had gone out, unlike Pazardzhik. Even the name made him cry. It made him shudder. When he closed his eyes, he was there again.

Tap, tap, tap, on the window.

He kept his eyes open, where and whenever he could. The drugs helped, when he could get them, which in prison was always. He traded the tobacco that he despised for drugs. It was a filthy habit, but worth more than gold, beyond the vicious razor-wire.

His mistress, heroin, hadn't visited for a while. One last adventure was how he sold it to himself. *Now look at me*, he thought. Never again. He said that about prison too, and look where that had ended? He was back inside, at the hands of two British police officers who had made it their goal to hunt him and his misunderstood people down.

———

He sat in his cell, focusing on the walls, the skeletal remains of past inhabitants scrawled on the brickwork, only to be overpainted, layer after layer of misery. Yet this was indeed heaven, Britain, in the year of someone's Lord, 2016. A few more weeks and then he would be out. They didn't want him to be out; he was never *supposed* to be.

If ever there was a compelling case about who you knew, this was it.

He wrote on a piece of notepaper with an old, and deliberately shortened, pencil, pressing down harder with each word. *You just watch*. He pressed harder still. *You. Just. Watch*.

Then, with his wrist trembling under the pressure, he carved the names of two men into the paper, ripping the surface.

*Jack*.

*Jason*.

Until the pencil snapped.

## CHAPTER ONE



### THE SANCTUARY PUBLIC HOUSE, LONDON

FIVE PEOPLE WERE SAT AROUND THE DARK WOODEN TABLE, UPON which were the fingerprints and watermarks of a hundred years, blended into one slightly sticky permafrost.

A typical London 'boozer', the Sanctuary had chosen to allow an eclectic group of men and women to call it their own. The villains had their pubs, as did the shiny, suited businessmen. The workers from Smithfield and Billingsgate markets practically owned theirs. That left the doctors, nurses and other emergency workers to themselves. The Sanctuary was a police pub.

That said, anyone was welcome there. That is, if you upheld the law. The Sanctuary had seen its fair share of robust debates, and had even seen a couple of fights, when alcohol had taken its toll and rank had won in the endless game of scissors, paper, cop.

The landlord was a man called Roger. Most people had no idea what his surname was. As long as he served them their drink of choice, an occasional meal and a place to switch off, that was all that mattered.

Roger was a good bloke. He was salt of the earth, an ex-copper. He was doing alright, for a Black Rat.

The Black Rats were the traffic police. Despised by the public until they turned up to drag them out of their ruined cars. The Criminal Investigation Department also considered them beneath their own unit. That is, until they needed them and their consummate skills in a pursuit. It was a dog-eat-dog workplace at times.

"Evening, Jason. Usual?"

"No. Do you know what, Roger, let's head out into the wide blue yonder, shall we? It's been a bloody big week."

"Of course. If you can perhaps give me even so much as a fighting chance to know just what the hell you are on about, you daft sod! What's your poison, Chief?"

Jason Roberts laughed and tossed a twenty-pound note at the landlord. "Just surprise me, OK? And whatever that lot is having. And, Rog, have one yourself."

"Oh, ever the generous soul. You'll need more than twenty quid for that round my son."

"Twenty not enough? I thought we'd locked up all the robbers in this city. Christ, there's plenty of other pubs we could go to, you know. I'll have you know, this is an elite team, hand-picked. Hand-crafted, you might say. We would be welcomed anywhere."

Roger scratched at his beard as he squirted some ginger ale into the Canadian Club. "What about the Blind Beggar?"

"Well, not without a warrant anyway." The two men laughed at the notion of Detective Chief Inspector Jason 'Ginger' Roberts ambling into one of the most notorious London pubs and ordering a lager shandy – worse still, a half.

The Beggar was where one half of the much-feared Kray Twins had come to notoriety. It was the very epitome of East End criminality.

It was fair to say, warrant or not, Roberts would not have been welcomed in that pub.

---

As Roger served a couple of cops in their half-blues, Roberts walked back to his table with a tray of drinks, slagging off a couple of detectives from another team, who had just arrived after their shift had ended.

"Alright you muppets – you timed that badly, I've just bought a round."

"First time for everything, guv."

"There is. On that note, I'll have another one of these when you are ready. Can't stand cheeky kids." He winked at the younger detective, a man he actually had a lot of time for. Married to an anaesthetist, he'd done well. This explained what he wore and what he drove. He certainly couldn't do it on a copper's salary. Either that or he was bent. There was a time when that would have been true. Back in the day. Some of his ancestors were as corrupt as the villains they frequently locked up.

"Dog eat dog, boss."

"No thank you. Strict vegetarian, bordering on vegan these days," Roberts said aloud.

He sat down and passed the drinks around the table, ladies first, along with a couple of bags of crisps. They were welcome to the smoky bacon. Roberts was happy with the bag that fashionably announced itself as vintage cheddar with shallots.

He spoke. "Roger only tried to suggest we relocate to the Blind Beggar, the disrespectful bugger. I wonder what it was like policing back then. JD, you must have some stories."

"Bloody cheek. I'm only a few war stories older than you, a few more than Jack, quite a few more than Carrie and a fair few more than Bridie. But, yes, they were quite some days. I worked with a few now long-retired coppers that actually did go to the Beggar without a warrant. In fact, they went to most places without one. My first ever inspector arrested Reggie and Ronnie. Can't recall what for, but it won't have been for shoplifting."

JD, or John Daniel to his friends, was best described as an articulate, suave and extremely knowledgeable boss. He'd risen through the ranks the hard way. The uniform had led to a suit, and in time he was famed for his particular liking for Aquascutum clothing, and an old green sixties Jaguar. Stereotypical, he wasn't though.

'You get what you pay for,' was his by-line. Another was, 'Treat people as you expect to be treated.'

He had a past that had a few shadows. One, to be exact. He referred to those years as his wilderness years. Shoulder-tapped by the men from Whitehall, he had learned quickly who to admire and, importantly, to this day, who to trust.

JD had retired early. His wilderness years had seen some extraordinary overtime opportunities, during which he'd banked every spare penny. His wife Lynne, too, and she had a dream to retire in New Zealand. So that's where they headed, to start a restaurant by the sea and leave it all behind, just about as far away from London as one could ever go.

Theirs was a liveable dream. Embraced by the locals, they soon gained a reputation for good food and great company. JD knew a lot about food and drink, but had forgotten a lot more about policing – and had become a mentor to one of the group, through good times and very bad.

He had come back to England for a funeral this time. He had travelled business class to break the interminable journey, then gravitated towards his old team. What was it they said? 'You can take the boy out of the police...'

Sat opposite him was Detective Sergeant Bridie McGee. It was her real name; taking her great, great grandmother's first and last names was an honour. She liked its simplicity and its powerful nod to Ireland. Her accent, though, was anything but Irish. She spoke with a slower, deliberate, articulate, sensual tone, more at home in South Yorkshire than Southern Ireland.

She had started in a uniform too, learning the art of policing the hard way; out on foot, in all weathers, where to shelter, where to find a hot drink, and in her case, where to cultivate some outstanding informants. Her disarming manner and ageless looks helped in that department. She had a smile that could light up a canyon, filling any place with that first hint of golden sunshine on a summer day.

Even the criminals loved her. They asked for her when they rang the station – or the 'nick', as it was affectionately known.

Bridie McGee had everything. A great career and a nice little flat, just down the road from work. She had a spaniel that had a mind of its own and loved to socialise with other equally wonderful dogs on one of the many, and unexpectedly large, grassy spaces in the city. She had a new black Mini Cooper – de-striped.

She liked to be subtle and loved to drive. She had a penchant for a great tune, which she'd sing to her heart's content, in heavy traffic with the windows up and the heater on. Avril Lavigne was her go-to when things got particularly shitty, as they had, not too long ago.

She had been on a surveillance op, in the back of the obs van, hatches battened down, waiting. In the half-light was her partner and the unrealised true love of her life, Nick Fisher, another DS.

That he'd died in her arms before he had ever had the chance to tell her would forever haunt her. That he'd died at the hands of men who had only greed in their sights, drove her to become almost obsessed with work. 'Job pissed', they called it.

This had been her life since that night she'd worked tirelessly, and if she was truthful, she didn't have much else. She prayed that one day someone would be sitting alongside her, in the Mini, belting out the same tune.

She'd written a poem that she felt summed up her feelings so well. A poem no one but her would ever read. She'd folded it and placed it in her jewellery box. With tear-stained ink, she'd locked it away forever.

Smiling at the other woman sat in the bar, at the sticky table she spoke.

"How's your day going, Carrie?"

"Better than some, worse than many." Carrie smiled back. Actually, since she'd met the man to her left, life couldn't have been any better, or worse. She had some incredible memories of the two of them, right here in this frenetic city she called home, and her man called his second, or was that third home?

Her life had taken its own wrong turn. She'd missed a red light and lived to tell the tale. That it was someone else's fault was something she preferred not to discuss. Now very much ex-job, she hankered for one last pursuit, one last foot chase, to feel the tang of adrenaline on her tongue, the breathless commentary into the radio handset.

Where was she? How had she got here? Where was her back-up? How long until they arrived? These were all questions which at some point in their lives all police officers had later asked.

Scotland Yard had been her eventual sanctuary. Re-trained and very capable, she had become an intelligence analyst, and a bloody good one too. If there was a job running that required a woman's intuition, and one with a gob to back it up, you asked for Catherine O'Shea to be on your team.

She kept her age and middle name to herself.

She had a level of candour that some bosses feared and others found alluring. Those that got too close came to experience what the wise knew was her weapon of choice: a pencil. It was preferably a 6H – the hardest graphite; simple, honed to a point sharper than an osprey's talon, it had been known to wreak havoc.

*Step over that line if you dare.*

She had a 'look' which she saved for fools and the occasional misguided, arrogant male – and they did well to avoid it.

It was during one such day that she'd met John 'Jack' Cade. Since that morning, where he told her she *was* going to have a coffee with him, they'd been almost inseparable. Almost.

The look had said it all, as they both had sat there in that misty window café opposite the Yard, blowing steam off the top of their chosen beverage, a matador dancing around the bull, the teenage girl avoiding the question, like an unopened email, sat, with good or bad news within, but one you dare not open.

There's wasn't a tempestuous start. It was brutal. The sex was alarmingly good: any and everywhere, up against the window of a hotel room, in the office, the lift, if there were enough floors, the common hallway of her Old Queen Street apartment, overlooking the Queen's own parks, anything went.

They danced, they kissed, they drank, they flirted. They avoided anyone at work knowing, that is, until Alex came to town.

———

John Cade, or, as he was known to his friends, Jack, after the infamous and rebellious English folk hero from the 1400s, was a man that earned trust easily and exuded passion and professionalism. He'd also started, as all police officers do, in uniform, but a hundred or so miles north, in the city of Nottingham.

His own destiny had been mapped. His ex-wife Penny, an eager and experimental lover herself, had led to his move to the capital. The problem with Penny was that she had been too eager, too often, and with too many. One of those had been his boss and a friend at the same time.

He was a partly fractured shadow of his former self.

This quickly led to Cade rapidly de-cluttering his life and moving to the nearby East Midlands Airport.

This is where he met *her*.

'Her' being an exquisitely interesting, captivating and alluring Bulgarian woman called Niko who had wrapped herself around him: mistletoe to his apple tree.

She had told him a story. He had sat and listened, on that rainy morning, over a coffee or two. He had been the first man to treat her well since she had fled Spain and her 'husband', Alex Stefanescu, who had given himself the name 'The Jackdaw'.

As nasty went, Alex was up there with Jack the Ripper, just better dressed and with more of a taste for the finest things in life, including women. They had a daughter, Elena. She was pretty like her mother, and skilled too.

Niko was what the Bulgarian government called an 'asset'. Trained in the art of intelligence collections, she had been the strongest salmon in the river, vying for Alex's attentions. A salmon that knew how to look after itself, until it fell for its hunters' charms.

What followed was a heady mix of Stockholm Syndrome: fear and pure lust. What followed that, was another story entirely.

———

Cade was what he best described as 'forty something'. He had short hair, regulation length. The salt was overtaking the pepper these days, since the time in his life he called 'After Penny' – but his eyes lifted the colour palette somewhat. They were ocean blue.

That was how they'd been described: liquid blue, the sort that women liked to occasionally bathe in. Niko, Elena and O'Shea had been no different in that regard. His friends, those that he trusted with his life, spoke of him being one of the most grounded people they had ever met. The sparkle in those blue eyes was never that far away though. But lately it had waned, the pressure of the work, the endless sleepless nights and the damage caused to his team had taken its toll.

The problem, was that wherever Cade went, chaos followed. Jack had learned fast that sometimes taking the gloves off was the only way to meet fire with its twin.

He'd been *sent* to London. More a case of, he was the only one with a head start on a growing problem. It was a case of right place, right time – Eastern European bank offenders – ATMs, point of sale devices, skimming, scanning, stealing. It was all about the money. Cade became an expert at following it.

He met Jason Roberts at the Yard and they'd been colleagues, and moreover, mates ever since. The banter was endless. If you had never served in blue, you wouldn't understand it. Jousts by another name, verbal oneupmanship, never yielding and always looking for a subtle crack in the armour that you could prize open. Work hard, play harder, was their motto. Cade had come to enjoy life in the city.

When Alex had started to dismantle that life, one team member by one, it had become personal.

Cade had recruited his own assets from the darker side of life. He had flirted casually, and at times dangerously, with the woman who would become the British prime minister. He had gained her trust, and in doing so, rarely heard the word 'no'.

"Go get 'em Jack. There's a good boy."

The problem was, 'they' were always one step ahead, until Cade and the Operation Orion team had locked them up for good. Those that weren't dead, would die in prison. The team had visited the issue repeatedly, ensuring that their case was cast iron.

Cade's first patrol sergeant had said something to him on Day One, and it was etched into his law enforcement mantra: 'Lad, if you are going to put the lid on something, make sure it bloody well stays on.' Wise words indeed.

As far as Alex and his criminal syndicate, the Seventh Wave, were concerned, the lid had been put on rather well, allowing the Orion team to expand and do what their namesake did best: hunt.

Having firmly put the lid on with Stefanescu, a new target had arrived in the city. An old sailor had a story to tell. Cade agreed to listen. That in itself caused its own set of broken rules and drama. It was what Orion had been formed to do, target what Ronnie Kray would have called the bad bastards.

Right now, the Orion squad were clearing up old files: stamping paperwork, squaring away expenses and overtime sheets, stapling, filing, forgetting, and waiting for the next 'what if'. There would never be another Ronnie or Reggie Kray. They were villains, some even said they were honourable, some disagreed, but in the echelons of organised criminality they were a thing of the past. They were legends by any other name.

———

DCI Jason Roberts had joined the Metropolitan Police to chase, track down and lock up the bad bastards, the evil doers, those that preyed upon the elderly and vulnerable. In that respect, he was like almost every other police officer. There was only ever one person he held a grudge against, the criminal. He loathed them all.

Ronnie Kray was much like Roberts' own nemesis; a predator, a man he had learned to despise. A man he had hunted down, fought with, been bitten by and eventually, after gaining the upper hand, was able to convict and sentence to twenty years in a maximum-security prison. Latterly, that prison was near the River Thames, in South East London.

Unlike Ronnie Kray, this man was not a diagnosed and paranoid schizophrenic. He was, just never diagnosed. He was many things, to many people, but to the senior officer in charge of the team they called Orion, he was one man, a Romanian national from the city of Craiova, and his name was Constantin Nicolescu, and Jason Roberts, the man, and the detective, despised him.

———

Tomorrow, he would hopefully watch him twist and squirm, as the judge read out his enhanced sentence, the result of daring to challenge the legal system that had earlier condemned him.

---

# CHAPTER TWO

---



## HM PRISON BELMARSH

"Nicolescu. Follow me."

"It's Mr Nicolescu, if you don't mind."

"No, I don't. You'll be back in here soon enough. If I had my way, you'd appear on a video link, I'd keep you here where I could keep my beady eyes on you."

"And they are very beady, are they not?" Nicolescu smiled. It was best described as a fractured smile, one he had planned to correct as soon as possible. The years of heroin abuse had rotted his teeth, leaving its scars both mental and physical. The money in an anonymous bank account was sitting there, for when the chance arose to make those teeth shiny and white once more.

He was wearing a suit. The one he had arrived at Belmarsh in – having been presented to a custody sergeant still dripping wet on a frigid British winter's night. His legal representative had demanded a change of clothes, and the suit was what Nicolescu had ended up with, via an anonymous benefactor, handed over at the prison reception area.

He recalled the night when they marched him into the prison. As he had stood there on that thick black line, dropping his underpants and squatting down, in the vain hope that drugs, or better still, a cell phone would drop out of the void. He knew better than that. This was not, as the Americans said all too often, his first rodeo.

This was not his first time in a British prison either. He considered himself somewhat of a cherished and frequent flyer in that department.

He liked the suit: navy blue, white shirt, red and blue tie and Oxford brogues, handmade by Church's of Northampton. He had a pocket square to emphasise the tie too.

'Dapper', they called it.

'A raging piss-take', Cade had called it at the trial.

Constantin had mirrored what Cade was wearing to court that day, down to the laces on his leather-soled shoes.

The trial had been brief; it was almost, as far as British trials go, rapid.

The conviction was swift too; something about leading an organised criminal group. Then there was the Terrorism Act charge. Both falsified as far as Constantin was concerned.

Seven years, that was what his legal people had said.

At his sentencing hearing, which followed very soon after, he received ten years for each offence, to run concurrently. No parole. His time was to be served in a British prison, despite other authorities wishing to have a slice of the pie.

So, he knew where he stood. But for him, this was the beginning, not the end. There were always second chances.

———

"Left here. Then left again. When we reach the prison van, you wait until I tell you to move. Then when I tell you to jump, you ask—"

"How high? I think you have been watching far too many films, S.O. Chamberlain."

Rick Chamberlain was a senior officer. Twenty years walking the gantries and corridors meant he'd heard, seen, smelled, and at times, touched it all. There were some prisoners he actually had some empathy with: the murderers that had killed as a crime of passion, those that had lost their heads for a brief moment and lived to regret their decision for the next ten to twenty. But they were all in lesser prisons across Kent where he had worked and cut his teeth.

Belmarsh was so different. Here, as far as he was concerned, they were all evil; just varying degrees of evil in a great big melting pot, and this smug bastard before him was no different. In fact, when he stopped and thought about it, he really disliked him; wished he had put up a fight now and then, but he was always so self-assured, pleasant with everyone, they almost avoided him.

The cons hated him too because he shone the torch of attention onto Belmarsh, and they had the place running just as they wanted it to be. They knew better than to try to physically harm him though. With that newly blackened wave tattoo on his inner right wrist, he was left well alone.

It was more a case of what they didn't know about him that made them wary. Try though they might, even the notorious internal intelligence system had failed to drag up any sign of weakness, and it seemed he had a very low friend in the highest of high places, none other than Home Secretary Robert Cartwright. Among other things, Cartwright was responsible for the probation service and the prison service. The police, too. To a man and woman, they hated his guts.

Prime Minister, the Right and very Honourable Sassy Lane, went one step further. She kept him close, knowing there was something about doing that with your enemies. It didn't prevent her from despising him, with his diminutive slate-coloured eyes and a slightly suspicious, all-year-round tan.

"In you go, yours is fourth on the left."

Chamberlain made sure the door slammed, just loud enough to cause the other prisoners on board the custody vehicle to wince. If there was one sound they hated, it was that: liberty, or rather its ending, personified.

## CHAPTER THREE



"Court rise."

A phrase that some might consider inappropriate for this hearing, given the minimal numbers of people in the room. Rules were rules, and etiquette, particularly in the Court of Appeal, was to be followed to the letter.

Those present stood as the three judges entered the courtroom: The Lord Chief Justice and his two colleagues, a Lady and a Lord Justice of Appeal called Barrowby.

"In the matter of Constantin Nicolescu."

It was how all such cases started. This was a review. No need for a full re-trial. The defence was adamant that it would be a waste of public funds and somewhat unnecessary, given their findings. Given the higher-level support they had received, which was considered an exception to the rule, they were confident that the entire case could be heard and done during the course of the morning: an hour and a half for the defence; to offer parity, two for the prosecution; and then another thirty minutes to sum up. It seemed perfectly achievable.

The Lord Chief Justice said good morning, then asked for proceedings to commence, outlining that both he and his learned colleagues had read the skeleton disclosure provided, and they fully understood the case before them. This was standard stuff.

This was a case that needed to be heard behind closed doors. The media were notably absent and would remain outside: blissfully unaware, dashing from court to court trying to find the next headline.

This was a rare event: a hearing, that for all intents did not exist.

Any case that had involved, implicated or linked a criminal syndicate to the British government, and importantly, exposed them as lacking in judgement, needed to be locked and shut down; sealed and secret – until today. Today, only the people in the room, deep within the Royal Courts of Justice, would hear the outcome.

This was a case that did not appear on the daily list, nor would it ever appear on any live streaming or court records, not for fifty years, anyway. It would stay within the archives of the grand old grey stone building, which jostled for attention among similar period buildings. Built in the Victorian Gothic style, it made a statement difficult to ignore, being one of the largest courts in Europe. Located in the Strand in the City of Westminster, but a stone's throw away from the true City of London.

It was an area that Nicolescu had once run through, forcing tourists and city dwellers alike out of his path, as he ran for his life, clutching an old revolver, towards the tube station, pursued by two of the men who now sat at the rear of the court; one, amusingly, dressed just like himself.

Constantin adored British history as much as that of his homeland. A shame he had never really had time to stop and admire it. He had been in somewhat of a hurry since his hedonistic initiation into the organised criminal group known simply as the Seventh Wave.

Nicolescu stood in the box, waiting, watching; as caged tigers went, he was arguably the most relaxed, ever.

He gave a smile here, a nod to people there, nodding as if he were listening to music.

One by one, he looked from left to right. There they were, the little Englishmen with their smug grins and clashing fashion and their two whores, the jumped-up detective with her charm and dismissive questioning techniques, and the girl called Carrie. He had got to know her rather intimately, up close and very personal, with a scalpel, as it happened. But that was in their past. Surely?

*Forgive and forget.*

Cade sat there in his navy-blue suit, pressed to within an inch of its life. It was cut perfectly to his frame: style and understated British elegance, right down to his shoes; polished, just enough shine to see the face of your enemy.

Then there was his garish opposite, Jason Roberts. He was a detective chief inspector at a tender age. What was he now? Forty? He'd done well.

Nicolescu detested him. Just locking eyes with him made his stomach knot. He remembered that day, he'd handcuffed Roberts to a dull metal pole in a tube train, deep beneath the city, then stamped on his wrist until it snapped. It had been one of his finest moments.

That Roberts had repaid the favour not so long ago, still hurt. He had stamped three times until the radius had given up its fight.

At least the British taxpayers had to pay for his surgery. Touché.

*Look at him, with his bright green tie and matching skin tone. Insipid bastard. All blond hair, smiles and misplaced confidence.*

He hated him. Hated him. Hated him.

———

The defence and prosecution had outlined their differing points of view. Both could sleep at night knowing they had done their jobs well. It wasn't about always believing the client; it was about the process, and if that process was carried out according to the law of the land, then so be it. Tomorrow was always another day.

Lord Chief Justice Carlton spoke clearly and concisely, aware that this was no ordinary day in the office, one which could potentially create case law. He was cautious but also keen to conduct his court as he saw fit, as he'd seen fit for almost twenty-five years.

"Mr Nicolescu, it is incumbent upon me to remind you that in England and Wales, a person found guilty of the offences outlined is liable, on conviction, to a term not exceeding..." He was summing up the past. It didn't interest Nicolescu, who wasn't listening to the judge. Waffle, they called it in England. Blah, blah.

He stood, smiling, shaking his head along with each sentence as if it referred to someone else entirely. As far as the man from Craiova, the sixth largest city in Romania, was concerned, it did.

"It is apparently disputed that you are, or were indeed even a member of an organised criminal group, nor were you a member of a terrorist group."

Nicolescu shook his head and yawned.

"Furthermore, planning, assisting and even collecting information on how to commit terrorist acts are all crimes... need I remind you..."

"Do get to the end," Nicolescu hissed from behind his plexiglass screen, turning up the sense of anticipation, just a little.

"I beg your pardon?"

"My apologies, sir, I often talk out loud. I mean no offence by it. I have done it ever since my dear mother's death. A death at which I was present. Please, continue."

The judge rubbed his eyes, took a deep and audible breath, and did as he was instructed. For that was how it felt.

"Need I remind you, that it is I who should talk audibly in this court?"

"No, you must not. Forgive me."

"To reiterate, it is also disputed that you were the leader of an organised criminal group, Mr Nicolescu, that, despite your obvious involvement in attempting to bring terror and chaos to the city of London, you were just a minor player, a pawn if you like, in one of life's most interesting games of chess. A leaf caught in a gutter. Would you agree?"

"I would, sir. As chess games go, it was indeed most interesting."

"For fuck's sake, Jack, this is a royal piss-take," Roberts whispered to Cade, attracting a paternal glare from the judge.

———

After many hours of ducking and diving, swerving, negotiating and posturing, the hearing was coming to an end. Each player had conducted themselves according to the rules, politeness incarnate. They were actors on a stage.

The courts had geared up for many hours, potentially even days of debate and counter-debate, of questioning the location of a full stop within a sentence of inflection and intonation.

"My Lord, in conclusion, my client, Mr Constantin Nicolescu has admitted to being present, in a number of locations during the days and weeks leading up to the events surrounding the intended attacks upon one of London's most iconic landmarks. That he was merely present is and never would be in itself a criminal offence." She let that part hang in the air, like a waft of Chanel No. 5 in a sewer, it hinted at something better to come.

"In these days of widely encouraged terrorism reporting, heightened suspicion and overt suppression of such a vile offence as terrorism, it is very much incumbent upon us, to be the masters, or mistresses, if you like, of our client's destinies. That is the letter of the law, the law of England and Wales."

She looked around the room. There was no intention of performing a show, of enacting pointless theatrics. She was doing what a good defence counsel did best, merely putting her point across to anyone that would listen, and rather well too.

She was playing by the rules.

Like him or not – and in truth she found him all together disturbing – it was her job, as his last line of defence to protect his best interests. It was his *right*.

"My Lord, forgive me for attempting to encourage you to dine upon the proverbial egg here, but I must carefully and deliberately outline the one point that is the very crux of Mr Nicolescu's appeal – an appeal that seeks not only to overturn his sentence, but also to cast doubt upon the aptness of his convictions." She paused, looking at the judge, a man of immense reputation, a reputation for getting things right, and many of the more recent letters of the law had been written by him.

"Go on."

"Thank you, My Lord. Where a sentencing judge passes sentence without the assistance of a pre-sentencing report, where it was indeed appropriate to have done so, an appeal ought to be lodged, which it was of course. That report might have provided the judge with a far-reaching understanding that Mr Nicolescu was in fact merely a puppet in this case, a puppet, need I remind those present here today, of the late Home Secretary of England and Wales the Right Honourable—"

"Yes, there is no need to name the individual. Thank you. Please finish your summing up."

Nicolescu shuffled from one foot to the other. He had chosen to stand, stating that his back injury, sustained whilst members of the Metropolitan Police had arrested him, now prevented him from sitting for long periods.

The defence counsel concluded her appeal, skilfully avoiding a critical tone of the previous judge who had convicted her client and another who had sentenced him upon grounds that were, she said, both uneven and wholly lacking foundation.

Her prosecuting colleague had tried, but failed to enhance the judgement, had failed to counter the claims, and ultimately had failed to provide a reason to both uphold the convictions and therefore the sentence passed down in Nicolescu's previous trial – a trial that been in a similar vein – behind closed doors.

What had started many months before, almost immediately after the prompt initial trial had ended abruptly. It was rare, if not unheard of, for the Royal Courts of Justice to make a decision so quickly. Handing it down as quickly as they did was a benchmark in British legal history, and one that few would ever know of.

Somebody was driving this from on high.

The courts had several options in the case of *R v Nicolescu*. They could reverse the lower court's decision, a decision never taken in haste, as it could undermine the very core of the British legal system. It could reverse the lower court's decision based upon a review of evidence. It could remand the case back to the lower court with strict instructions to reconsider an issue that had arisen during the appeal.

That decision would take a while, as the three judges sat and decided each point on its merits, then, at a pre-determined date, the Lord Chief Justice would hand down his decision.

That he would do it quite so soon caused emotions to run high on both sides of the moral fence.

———

As Constantin left the court, heading back to prison for what would be a shorter than anticipated stay, he looked at Roberts and winked, accompanied by a loud and clear 'chick, chick' sound with his tongue, just as Roberts had done when the Romanian had been sent down.

It felt good; so wonderfully, marvellously good.

He couldn't wait to head back to Belmarsh and begin counting down the days when he would once more be a free man. It was, he decided, time that he would now spend at *his* pleasure, not Her Majesty's.

Whether he was morally free was to become the subject of the court of public opinion, and as Roberts had left the court, his opinion had got the better of him. Cade had tried to discreetly steer him out of the room, but the senior judge heard what the DCI had to say, and how he had said it.

———

In Commander Steve Payne's office the next day, Roberts was told in no uncertain terms what damage the outburst had done for his own professional reputation and that of the Metropolitan Police.

"We have clear organisational values, Jason, need I remind you of that?"

"No, sir. You needn't. Sir…"

"Be quiet. You were given two ears and one bloody mouth by Mother Nature for a reason, DCI Roberts. In future, may I suggest you use them in that order, keeping those lugs on the side of your head open and that cavernous void in the centre of your fucking head, shut!" He hardly took a breath.

"You can. Sir, I…"

Newly promoted, Payne sat back in his black mesh-backed chair, spun it ninety degrees and stood up. He walked over to Roberts.

"Jason, you and I go back a long way. For that reason and that reason alone, I'm asking you to take a bit of leave, go and do some gardening or something, take Mrs Roberts away for a romantic getaway. Lord knows it's probably been a while, given the hours you and the Op Orion team have been putting in. Agreed?"

Roberts knew he had little choice. "Agreed," he said stoically.

As he left Payne's office, he heard the first steel ball clash against its neighbour – Payne's favourite office toy, a Newton's Cradle was doing its best to sooth the Commander's frazzled mind.

It seemed to be a popular desktop addition in the Yard, a few command staff had added them. The chick-chick-chick of the steel on steel only sought to remind Roberts of that bastard Nicolescu and his arrogant farewell in court.

––––––

The week of enforced leave passed, as they always did, faster than any period at work. Before he knew it, the alarm started, a sort of synthesised whale noise bound to an incessant vibration, that as always rocked his phone off of the bedside table. He'd palmed it into some form of submission when five minutes later it started again.

An hour and five minutes later, he was sat at his desk when a text message arrived on his phone.

*Hey you. You left before I woke. Just wanted to say thank you for a lovely time away. I loved every part. I miss you already. Me xx.*

He smiled, saved it into his private folder, then began to sift through the mountain of files that had yet to gather dust.

He knew Cade and O'Shea had also taken the chance to get away for a week, up to his old stomping ground in Nottingham and then north to the Yorkshire Moors. They realised they needed the break, too. It had been a very long year, and something wasn't quite the same. To some, what had happened to her, in that place, the one where no one seemed comfortable about mentioning she had changed – there was a deepened sense of unease, one she tried to ignore, and in her quieter moments, alone, one she failed to comprehend.

John Daniel, not wishing to be left out and physically unable to return to New Zealand and back in a week, had headed off to find

old friends, golf courses and a few bottles of malt, one a favourite –
Talisker Dark Storm for old time's sake.

———

A few minutes later, Roberts looked up from his sea of paperwork,
having scanned over a hundred unread emails.

"Morning, you two lovers. Good break?"

Cade replied first. "Intense, in so many ways, DCI Roberts."
This earned him a harder-than-expected punch on the arm from
O'Shea.

"Glad to hear it. I think Cathy and I put a few demons to bed,
too. Long overdue. Funny thing is I can't stop thinking about her
this morning. Finding it hard to concentrate."

"Perhaps you are back in love with her, guv?" suggested O'Shea, a
long-time supporter of her old boss.

"Perhaps. I might give her a ring. I'll have mine black, no sugar,
and Carrie…"

"I know, a little plate of biscuits and no fackin' ginger nuts!"

———

Roberts smiled, held a thumb up as he dialled, with his phone
perched under his chin, he kicked the door shut as he rang his wife.

# CHAPTER FOUR



It was all they could afford when they first got married. Now, it had become a tastefully refurbished four-bedroomed semi-detached in Ashford, once a part of London that fortuitously now found itself located in Surrey. It sounded so much better to say you lived in Surrey than the 'outskirts of London'.

Despite the fact that he was earning a DCI's salary, property was extortionate in and around London. His wife Cathy earned a nice salary too, but they had young kids, and a young family ramps up the cost.

"They'll cost me at least a million quid by the time I'm done," Roberts had once said in the Sanctuary to a few of his single colleagues.

He didn't mean a word of it. To Roberts, family came first and he'd resisted the little buggers for years.

Cathy was a primary teacher. It was what she did best, and all she ever wanted to be – working, but with children. This way, she got to see her own too.

She'd met Jason when they were both still in their late teens. Theirs had been a whistle-stop tour of a romance. He'd worked in a bank and hated it, she was studying to be a teacher and adored it.

Then a career in the police came knocking and before she could say 'wife of a DCI' he'd accelerated through the ranks.

———

She was in a rush this morning, as usual: drop the kids off, wave, check the back seats for lunch boxes, check her phone for messages, drive, listen to Radio 2 and the Breakfast Show, sing along to a song – something by that lovely ginger lad Ed Sheeran. This time, it was called *Thinking Out Loud* and was coming out of all four speakers. It seemed so appropriate. She thought out loud a lot. She was doing it this morning.

"OK, when I get there, I need to check the paperwork from yesterday, mark up the just-perfect stories from Class 3 and…"

She swerved to avoid a cyclist who had strayed into her path.

"Arsehole!"

The cyclist waved back.

She checked her rear-view mirror, her make-up looked fine.

Jason told her repeatedly to keep her eyes on the road.

She braked. Avoided the rear end of a VW Polo whose driver signalled with only one part of his hand.

"No need for that!" She did it back.

She drove off again. Stop, start.

———

She checked her watch – twenty minutes. She was making good time. She thought back to the weekend and smiled, closed her eyes, for a blissful second. She was back there, with him, in the shower, hands against the glass, trying not to scream.

She braked harder. That was close. She recalled what he had said the night before.

"The car is filthy. A bit like you." He tapped her playfully on the backside. "If you get time, my love, why don't you drop into that new car wash – the one without the brushes?"

She saw it ahead. No queue. It was meant to be. The silver VW was behind her now.

"Arsehole. Didn't get very far, did you?"

She pulled off the main A road and onto the forecourt, the one with the fancy car wash; he was right, it was the one without the brushes, no chance of it tearing the aerial off of Jason's much-loved orange Ford Focus ST.

"Just the car wash today please."

She queued for five minutes with her token in her right hand. There were two washes alongside each other. A black Mercedes in her lane was being driven out, gleaming, and a shabby looking silver hatchback in the booth next to hers.

She checked her watch again. She had a quarter of an hour to spare. She could sit and close her eyes, listen to the Eagles, as the robot car wash sprayed and rinsed and polished.

Time to herself. A rarity for a modern working mum.

———

Roberts was at his desk in the office just down the hall from the lifts, the room with a questionable view and a black leather chair that had a history. Its former owner now retired and occasionally living in New Zealand.

He opened his emails again, blinked, rubbed his eyes, wished he'd been back in bed for the afternoon with Cathy. He hit *select all*, then *delete* with those he really didn't need to read. That looked better. There were a few that could be forwarded. The subtle art of delegation was a skill indeed, there were some that needed urgent responses and one that caught his eye. He marked it as unread and made a mental note to return to it. He even made a quick note in red at the bottom-right corner of his blotter pad that sat just so in the leather frame.

The phone had six voice messages. He listened, made notes, deleted, saved one and then rang the owner of another straight away.

———

Cathy had begun to edge forwards into the brushless car wash. She'd selected the executive programme; including the spot-free rinse. The latter never worked, and it annoyed her husband immensely, but it would be cleaner than it was.

He used to say: 'Spot-free my arse. In fact, my arse has fewer spots than that!'

———

He was now sat on it in his office.

"Yes, hello, this is DCI Jason Roberts. You kindly left me a voicemail whilst I was on leave."

He listened, nodded, doodled a shape of something on his jotter, drawing a circle around the note he had made earlier. The circle became thicker, the ink darker as he drew and drew until he stopped, almost snapping the cheap plastic biro in two.

"He's done *what?*"

They heard him down the corridor in the Operation Orion Situation Room.

DS McGee heard it first.

"I guess the boss has just learned about Nicolescu. May be time to go and ask if he needs another coffee."

She tapped on the door and mimed drinking from a mug.

He nodded. Mimed hanging himself, with his tongue hanging out of the left corner.

She was back five minutes later with a strong, hot cup of black coffee in his favourite mug.

He blew the steam away and sipped it, motioning for McGee to stay, pointing at his watch and indicating two minutes. Then he tapped his right shoulder and yawned, an indication that he was talking to someone important.

"Let me get this right. Lord Justice Carlton has seen fit to allow that worthless piece of shit out of prison, has agreed with the pathetic pleas of the defence... and has allowed him to walk?"

"Lord *Chief* Justice Carlton."

"Please forgive me."

"Watch your step, DCI Roberts. You've already had one reprimand. You don't want to end up in front of him, do you?"

"No, of course not, sir. But you have to see it from my side. The PM herself gave us a full mandate to deal with this group, and we did. Locking up almost the whole team was probably the pinnacle of my heady career."

"Jason, I do understand. I also know that only the PM herself is likely to push this case into the Supreme Court. And you and I both know that could take years. Let sleeping dogs lie, is my advice. You got the ringleader, you got half of his family too, used a sniper that wasn't endorsed by any authority in the UK and..."

"Respectfully, sir, I didn't use, nor did I endorse any sniper activity. That a key player in the operation was shot by someone other than a police officer, was neither my decision nor order. That it happened, was fortuitous."

"Best you don't let anyone else hear you say that. Right, he's out, you need to let go and focus on new things. Forget about Operation Orion's 'most wanted' of the past and go and look for some new bad bastards to disrupt. Understood?"

"One hundred percent, sir. One hundred percent."

"Good. Look, Jason, off the record and do not quote me, but bloody well done on that last op too. Shutting down that nasty piece of work tested your team, who I know were already on their knees."

"Thank you."

"I want you to know that their resilience will feature in a Commissioner's Commendation that I have endorsed. I'd like you to think about that instead of focusing on the past. The past is done, but you can change the future. Good chatting, now go and keep those streets clear of chaos. I retire in just under a year, I don't want any conspiracies, chaos or corruption – until at least December."

"You have my word. January it is. And, sir?"

"Yep."

"Enjoy that retirement, I doubt we'll speak again before then."

"Only if you end up causing any of the three Cs..."

It wouldn't be long before the current New Scotland Yard would be demolished, bought by a consortium, whilst the Metropolitan Police relocated to a more picturesque location alongside the River Thames.

By the time they moved in, ironed out the teething problems and fixed the revolving iconic sign for all to see, he would be done. Six years at the helm of arguably the busiest force in the country.

A few floors below him, Roberts took a bigger mouthful of the coffee. He placed his cup down over the red circles and spoke to the woman who was leaning against his office door, tapping away on her phone, a chance to clear the relentless tide of emails.

"I guess you've worked out what that was all about, Bridie?"

"Yes, guv. Sorry, but you know what Chinese Whispers are like. We had the heads up whilst you were on leave."

"Should have rung me, Bridie."

"And spoil your time away at the *pied-à-terre*, boss? No way. You needed the break as much as anyone else. I'll wear that one."

"I'm sure. But next time, yeah? No exceptions. When it's something of that magnitude, you have my permission to ring me immediately, even if Mrs R is performing the Reverse Cowboy to Elvis's *A Little Less Conversation*. Clear?"

"Waterford."

"Eh?"

"Crystal. Waterford crystal. It's a brand."

"Is it, indeed? Good, well, make sure that is what you get me when I retire, or get sacked, a Waterford crystal decanter full to the brim with a thirty-year-old Macallan and a dash of humility."

"Thirty-year-old?"

"Yes, Bridie, you tend to find it on the shelves between twenty-nine and thirty-one. Are we done here?"

"Boss."

She walked off down the corridor muttering.

"I heard that, DS McGee!" Roberts yelled, causing her to smile. Her eyes lit up when she smiled. For Roberts, that was often the highlight of his day. That, and when Jack Cade was dashing around London with his arse on fire.

They were good days. He wondered when the next one might be. He checked his calendar. He needed to set up a date night with Cathy soon. They were few and far between these days. He wished he could be back, where he had been a week before, in the Surrey Hills.

## CHAPTER FIVE



"Mr and Mrs Jason Roberts."

"Ah yes, sir, we have been looking forward to you arriving. Your room is ready. I will get the team to bring your luggage across to you. I hope the cottage is to your liking. My name is Samantha, if you have anything at all that you need, please just ask."

"Thank you, Samantha. We'll be just fine." He winked at his wife.

The country house was exactly as it had been described in the guide. Tastefully refurbished and in keeping with the period, Barnett Hill had once belonged to the Thomas Cook family – famous for travel of a more international nature.

Nestled in the Surrey Hills, it had revealed itself after a short drive along a tree-lined driveway.

"Jason, it's beautiful. How much is a room here?"

"If the lady needs to ask the price, she can't afford it."

"No seriously, Jas."

"Seriously, Cathy, don't ask. Please. We need this. Four days away – away from everything; the kids, the folks, the work, especially the work. I owe you this for all the shit I've brought home in the last year."

She looked at him, she had fallen in love with him so many years before. Their lives had changed, he'd changed, physically he resembled a slightly larger version of Sting; hair cut neatly, dapper dresser, as popular with the men as he was with the ladies.

The difference was, Sting was rich, and could sing. Jason was a cop and couldn't. And cops never earned what they were truly worth. But in his company, she felt safe, and that counted for more than money ever could. More than any singer could ever make.

Four blissful days. All he needed to do was relax.

# CHAPTER SIX

## NUMBER 32

It was forty-one minutes away, if you drove at the limit. That's all it was from their suburban home in Ashford.

They had left in the early afternoon, to make the most of the day – by the time they were wrapped up in each other's arms in the Gatehouse bathroom, the two-man team had entered their semi-detached home. The one with the large mortgage, aligned towels and the empty soap dish.

Their briefing had been clear. Their briefing had come from Belmarsh.

The place where the only accessible phone hung on a wall and was distinguishable by the long queue of men, using their credits and dialling home and telling their wives or girlfriends how much they missed them.

His call had been made from a cell phone. He laughed. Why queue with the lesser mortals when you could just dial out and pass your instructions from the horse's mouth?

It was another royally directed middle finger – first to the man who he felt controlled him, and secondly, and with more vigour, to the British government with its rules and regulations – the ones that had wrongly accused him of a terrorist offence.

To be fair, he *was* guilty of taking part in an organised criminal group, burglary, theft and fraud – an exorbitant level of fraud – he was party to a whole lot more too. But that was then and, as his eminent defence counsel had told the judge, he was a man of simple means and was easily led by the man everyone called The Jackdaw.

Easily led indeed. *Little did they know.*

He could get a cell phone by making one call. Drugs, too. Also, the commodity that was worth more than gold inside – tobacco.

Weapons? You wanted a weapon, what sort? They were rudimentary, but they did their job. He chose to ensure that other people watched his back. The black tattoo was all they needed to see.

In one week, Mr Rick Chamberlain could go and screw himself. Jumped-up boot boy that he was, with his precious bunch of keys, on that chain that wasn't quite long enough to throttle him with.

"Hello. Now listen. I have two minutes before their system starts to do its job and this phone needs to be hidden long before then."

In the following one minute and forty-six seconds, he told them where to go, what to do and what not to do. He finished by thanking them, telling them that reward for their loyalty would be generous and financial.

He could put a price on loyalty. In their case, one hundred thousand between them, a small price for a man who was to inherit much more.

He had begun to sing again: opera. Chamberlain hated it. He said it was for the rich or those 'affected types what ponced around West London with their la-di-da friends. Pretentious twots the lot of 'em'.

Constantin's instructions were clear. The men knew not to fail him. He would be out any day now and they wanted to do their part and disappear until he called them again. They were his lap dogs forever, whether they realised it or not.

First, they went to an internet café; anonymous and frequented by kids and a man who was an archetypal paedophile – far corner, watching the door, nervous.

One man stayed in the grey Transit van, hazard lights blinking and the amber beacon on the roof rotating. He was dressed in

Telecom clothing, whilst the other paid for fifteen minutes of airtime and accessed the email.

'Don't use your phones. It must be from somewhere where they will struggle to find you.'

He read the file, wrote down the basics, folded the piece of paper and took the piece immediately below too. These were professional men. There was no point in making the equally professional men's lives easier, was there?

Now they were outside the target address: amber beacon rotating, half on the kerb and one of those little tents on the verge just outside number thirty-two.

The driver walked up the short path to the side door. It was as described. The site survey had been conducted well. All glass, it would have lasted a minute at most, but he'd briefed them clearly, no mess. Not even a stray hair. Understand? They did. Completely.

Why break a door when you can defeat the locks in less time?

He was in.

Meanwhile, his colleague was sat in the tent, pressing the trigger on the powerful drill, now and then, back and forth, to the van and even waving to the old lady across the road.

'Would I recognise them again? No dear, I didn't have my glasses on. And if I did, they would have been the wrong ones, you see. I left my others at the library last Tuesday, or was it Wednesday?'

Hiding in plain sight, they called it: up close and personal.

Trained by the Romanian government, he was a man with exquisite skill; he could enter a house and add or remove without the owners having the slightest clue.

There were many things he could have done: install cameras everywhere, in the lounge, the kitchen and his favourite, the bedroom. Once, he'd sat for four days until his target and his wife had got down to it. He, sat in the apartment miles away watching on a remote screen. He felt bad about it afterwards, but not for long.

This place was different. This man had seen to it that the boss had been sent to prison, and not just any prison, a place that was full of very bad people, people his boss did not like at all.

The least he could do was have some fun at his expense.

This mission was different to the others. The boss had been very specific about his needs.

'I want you to go to his house as soon as they are both away – at work, whatever, it does not matter to me, you are taking the risk, not me. When you are there, I want you to be so very careful. This man is not a fool. He's an idiot, but no fool. You do the following and in this order.'

———

The man stood in the lounge, looked at the family photographs, picked one up, there was no dust beneath it so he carefully placed it down in exactly the same spot, aligning it to the next. Cathy would have been so proud.

There were elements of a young family: the photos, the toy box, the hand paintings on the stainless-steel fridge.

He wouldn't find it here. The house was immaculate.

He opened the dishwasher: one glass and a bowl, one spoon.

That was all he needed. He spotted the print on the top edge of the clean glass. The surface was perfect, glass always was – clean, hard and very smooth.

He carefully opened the pot of black granular powder and dusted the surface with a fine brush that gently brought the mark to life. In fact, there were two: one a thumbprint, the other a beautiful index finger mark. It really didn't get any better.

With the marks visible, he used a gelatine lifter to pick the mark from the surface of the glass. The gelatine allowed for the mark to be carefully lifted and not damaged. It was what the experts called a positive impression. The ones that were always found on detective programmes seemed to exist in dust, which in fact made things harder. These were called negative impressions.

He was feeling more than positive now. The survey team had indeed done their job well. They would never meet and that suited them both, as deniability went, it was certainly plausible.

The phone was exactly where the team said it would be: right-hand bedside table, second drawer down in the bedroom with its wooden headboard and fancy scatter cushions. There must have been twelve or more pictures of the happy couple.

Inside a grey sock he found what he was looking for – Roberts' work iPhone, the one Cathy had made sure he would hide away.

'Promise me you won't take that thing with us. I'll make it more than worth your while...'

He'd obeyed. He knew what was good for him.

The black-haired male with the calm, almost metronome heartbeat lifted it out with his latex-gloved hands and slid it into the soft shoulder bag he was carrying.

Now he needed Roberts' car keys: the orange Ford Focus ST. The one he never drove during the week, leaving it for Cathy, whilst he took her car, a rather battered Ford Mondeo estate, to work, or the nearest train station, where he travelled free to the city. The car they had taken away with them, a pair of mountain bikes in the back, just in case they fancied physical activity of a different kind.

He walked back downstairs to the kitchen. The hook by the back door was empty. They were in the cupboard above, between the spaghetti and the penne: two jars, one car key.

He went outside and opened the garage that ran alongside the house, out of sight. The car was there, parked nose in and rather dirty. It needed a wash. He put the key on the roof and walked quickly to the van.

In the back, he found his colleague. Another ex-Romanian government employee who had found things more lucrative on the outside.

They made a great team. One was the consummate professional burglar and former scenes of crime officer who had latterly learned a new trade, the other had forgotten more than most people he knew about how to hack computers and phones.

The iPhone was no different to the Samsung, or any other so-called smart phone for that matter. If you knew how, you could. It was that simple. No brand loyalty. No hard feelings.

The way an iPhone of this generation opened was via the fingerprint scanner. It was what the techs called a capacitance scanner. Put simply, the scanner picked up a signal generated by the seemingly innocuous ridges and furrows and whorls on the humble human fingerprint.

He'd been fascinated by them for most of his adult life. A finger print was a lot like a zebra's backside; it was unique. It was also one of the first things to form in a human embryo.

When that unique pattern is pressed gently onto the phone, creating the correct signal, it opens.

But in order to do that, you either need the owner of the print present or their finger. He was a professional. He didn't go around cutting people's fingers off with a bolt cropper. It was beneath him. They had other teams that could do that sort of work.

He handed the image lifted from the glass and returned to the garage with a black bag.

His teammate was able to work away in complete peace and quiet, in the brightly lit rear of the dull grey Telecom van with its forgettable number plate.

He carefully cleaned up the image. Treating it like an unexploded piece of ordnance, he inverted it and with the small laser printer ran a 1200 dpi image onto a transparent sheet using a heavy and dark toner.

The next part was arguably the most crucial. He carefully poured pink latex material onto the pattern and, with a fine tool, smeared it across the image and let it cure.

————

In the garage, the van driver was carrying out his own second task. Having already done this six times on an identical vehicle that the team had stolen and replaced without the owner having the slightest clue, he was relatively relaxed.

He teased the door panel off, careful not to break any of the fiddly plastic fastenings.

The tracking device was large, but clearly designed to be effective. Who was he to challenge his employers? It just fitted and that was all that mattered to the man who took great pride in his work.

He'd done what he needed to do, then eased everything gently back into place and even rubbed the door trim down with his sleeve. It was just right; without a trace.

The only thing that could go wrong was if they came home early, or a neighbour got nosey. If that happened, they left. Immediately. There was very little to carry or drop, they travelled very light. It was another reason why Constantin had hired them. You paid peanuts, you got monkeys. He'd paid for the very best primates' money could afford, and they spoke his language.

———

In the van, the thin latex layer was lifted from the sheet. He gently breathed onto it to moisten it, then placed it onto the sensor. He unlocked the phone. Bingo.

Now for the fun part.

———

The garage was an extension of the Roberts' family home. Everything in its place: polishes, dusters, garden tools hung up, and a clean mower on the floor, full of petrol, ready to go: a row of chisels handed down by Roberts' father-in-law remained sharpened and never used. A single-glazed window with a single cobweb allowed more light into the brick building.

The operator sat in the driver's seat with his laptop, one of the things he had extracted from the bag. The other was something that no doubt did something rather ingenious: a small screen and cables, with red and yellow and white plugs.

It was, for all but the most gifted auto electricians, a job beyond the scope of many. But for a man like Darius, it was fun. What he couldn't make a modern car do, which the factory had apparently ensured couldn't be done, was to override almost anything in its ECU. The engine control unit and the other black box gizmos that Ford had included were ripe for harvesting.

The Focus ST was a rapid car, so no point in making it any quicker. No, what Darius needed to do, had been instructed to do, was something far more devious.

*Fun*, that was the word that kept coming to his mind. If he had known why he was doing it, perhaps that word wouldn't have come up.

Half an hour later, with a few checks of his black Tissot, he was done: cables wrapped neatly, screen away, all in a plain black Pelican case. The laptop was stowed.

No need to check his work – he was an expert and his work here was done. It was now over to a totally new team. Move on, don't forget to wash your hands. Now forget all about it. Go.

———

In the anonymous grey van, the second operator smiled as he finished the last line of a batch of emails. They were timed to be delivered when he was ready. They were written in such a way that only one man could have written them. That man had knowledge, guilty knowledge, and clearly needed to purge his soul for what had happened.

The operator had already updated Facebook with a date-sensitive update that ensured that when or if the time came, Roberts had been in a certain place at a certain time. It would say so in the records. They called it a footprint.

The messages and date stamps were irrevocable information and there for all to see whenever they were ready to. Only the best people would be able to work out how it had been done. If indeed they even thought to check. The best people were working outside of government departments these days – earning what they felt they were truly worth.

Footprints: DCI Jason Roberts, of the Operation Orion team, had just left a few muddy ones all over the city of London.

# CHAPTER SEVEN



"Right, it would seem that the chaos that has followed us around has abated." Roberts smiled, sipped his Americano from his favourite cup.

"At least it had, until a certain judge had decreed that one of our most despised criminals was deemed worthy of some royal bloody decree that allows him to be exonerated, absolved, acquitted, or in true London street parlance, let the fuck off the very worst of deeds."

"You what? Is this for real, guv?" asked Detective Sergeant Del Murphy. "When was I going to be briefed on this?"

"Now, Del. Now. Just like everyone else." Roberts sighed audibly. "Look team, this is a load of elephant-sized bollocks."

He paused, sipped on his coffee.

"I know it, you know it, the great and general public of this fair city know it." He looked at Cade.

"Jack?"

"Thanks, Jason. Team, all I can offer is that the law, as we all know, is an ass at times. In this instance, Nicolescu has employed the right people to run his case, they found a loophole. I've sat and read through the notes. I was even there on the day of the appeal hearing. He remains as guilty as sin in my book. Him and anyone that aligns themselves to him. But—"

"The guv is right, it's bollocks," said a disgruntled detective, taking his third digestive biscuit and dunking it expertly into his tea.

Cade let him vent as only a good boss would. He was a frontline cop too, not that very long ago. Promoted quickly, but with full credit, he had landed in London after what had been an equally quick ending to his marriage.

"...as I was saying, but what we need to do is regroup, focus on what our new challenge is and deal with that. We cannot change what has happened." Cade looked around the room. It was full of people he had learned to trust implicitly: civilian staff with more experience in their little fingers than many uniformed officers, and some young, upwardly mobile men and women who thought nothing of working ludicrous hours to get the job done.

What they had done as a collective over the previous year had been nothing short of remarkable – and the public had no idea. Only the Prime Minister herself was able to commend them, and in private. It was, she said, how it had to be, and Sassy Lane was nobody's fool. Well-liked by the rank and file and adored by the public, she was a rarity in modern politics.

Cade finished, "You'll remember what the PM herself said not many weeks ago – Orion is my hunter. And as soon as I have someone new for you to hunt, I'll be sure to let your bosses know. Well, it looks as though we may have a slight resurgence of the Seventh Wave – let's call it the second wave but with a lower-case spelling."

"You really think that lot will have another crack at us, Jack?" asked Bridie McGee.

"I would have thought the message had been clear. You are not welcome here, don't come back." She sipped her own hot drink, a mix of ginger and lemon and a spoonful of acacia honey.

Cade looked at Roberts. He was well aware that, technically, Roberts was in charge. Still, the younger man valued Cade's every word. They'd come a long way since they'd first met and had an almost telepathic relationship at times.

Roberts nodded, finishing his coffee.

"I'd agree, Bridie, but as we know, one of the thicker-skinned rhinos will walk from Belmarsh any day now. So, I suggest we prepare for the worst. If nothing happens, then so be it. Dave, Carrie, let's keep the open-source checks running, Del, your section run the CHIS and let's see what falls out when we shake the tree."

Covert Human Intelligence Source — the mortar in the brickwork of the modern police force — had actually been around since policing had first begun, not a million miles away from the briefing room that the Orion team sat in.

Nowadays, it was almost a police system within another. Monitored, each sentence scored on a value scale — did we know the informant? How well had previous information been passed on, and importantly, was it accurate?

The Admiralty Scale, they called it, where F6 was the unknown, and A1 was as accurate as you could wish for. All CHIS holdings were guarded as if people's lives depended on it.

In Nicolescu's appeal case, the informant was the Crown, and the information that he was due to walk free any day was obviously accurate to within a few hours.

It was A1 then.

He was soon to step out into the fresh air, south of the River Thames, in London.

"Right, you lovely lot, turn over some rocks, pay out a few quid if we need to, but let's get one step ahead of the man who snapped my wrist a while ago." He rubbed his arm unconsciously.

"And the first person who can successfully slide his evil arse back into a cell will be treated to a slap-up meal at the Sanctuary."

"Bloody hell, guv, that's a bit stingy, I'd have thought Royal Hospital Road would have been more appropriate," mocked DS Dave Williams, one of Roberts' original shift members from a past life. Dave was of Jamaican descent and highly respected. He should have been at least a DI according to Roberts and others, but he wanted to stay on the street, connected to the people. Many coppers wanted that, and the organisation needed people like that.

"Royal Hospital Road! I can't afford Chef Ramsay's menu, superb meals though they are. I once took Mrs Roberts there for a rather special evening where we dined à la carte."

"I bet you did, boss. I bet you did." This earned a cheer.

Roberts' phone buzzed. An email. He'd read it later. Then a text. That, too, saved for later.

———

It was 17.1 miles, to be exact. That's how far Cathy Roberts was from her man when she dialled his private number.

"Hello this is Detective Chief Inspector Roberts; I am unable to answer your call right now as, frankly, I am still exhausted from a wonderful break away with my delectable wife..."

"Jason, stop it. You're a naughty boy." She was also back there in the Gatehouse.

"Is that right, Mrs Roberts?" he asked as he walked away from Cade, blushing slightly, then turning the other way as Carrie raised her brow suggestively.

"It is. Look, Jason, there's something wrong with your car."

"Oh, it's 'my car' when there's something wrong," he laughed. He was in a good place, regardless of that piece of vermin preening himself, ready for release just across the water.

"Go on then, what's wrong? I only had it serviced a few weeks ago so you could race around Surrey with all the other delicious and yummy mothers."

"It's mummies, Jas. I don't know, it's just being odd."

"What, like putting on a strange French accent?" He cleared his throat. "'Allo, I am a sexy leetle orange number zat goes very fast...'"

"No, you bloody idiot, weird stuff. Like when I indicate, the dashboard lights glow brighter. And I've just put the window down to put my car wash token in and now it won't go up."

He laughed. "Turn the engine off, wait ten seconds, then try the window again, madam."

"Yes, I will. This is like one of those help lines that never is!" She giggled. It was so good to be having fun again with the man she had fallen in love with. So, what if the window didn't work? The worst that could happen was that she'd get a little wet.

"OK, it works. Bye, my love, and thank you, big boy."

"I bet you say that to all the customer helpline people."

She cleared down before him. It was a game they had played for years. As the car rolled forwards, the underneath of the vehicle began to be blasted with a high-pressure wash, as the current track on her radio got turned up just a little. There were no cars behind her now and only one alongside in the other booth.

It was a silver VW Polo.

———

The occupant of the Polo looked across, checked the Focus, making sure there was only one occupant, just as he had been briefed.

'Make sure there are no children in the car.'

There weren't. He was OK to proceed.

All he could see was the driver, a nice-looking woman, probably in her early thirties. She was singing – oblivious.

He checked his rear-view mirror. There was nothing other than a grey van. Why would there be anything else? It was how they had planned it, down to the minute.

He is an idiot, but he is no fool.

———

Cathy was leaning back slightly, music turned up loud enough to let her escape from the constant tide of life. She watched as the second light on the electronic menu board lit up. This was the rinse that was supposed to rid the car of bugs. Jason liked this one. A strict vegetarian, he'd happily kill a fly, especially those that tarnished his bright orange paintwork.

———

The Polo driver hovered his index finger over the small screen, keeping it discreetly out of Cathy's vision.

Now.

The driver's window lowered, then the passenger one: lightly tinted glass, down into the doorframe.

The light bug spray was approaching. Its arm robotically re-aligning to the side of the car.

"Bloody great." She turned the engine on, then off again. She tried the window, nothing.

She looked across at the driver of the silver car, then took her seat belt off. His wash wasn't working at all. She gestured an embarrassed shrug of the shoulders and a slightly anxious smile.

He raised a thumb. She lowered hers with a down turn of her mouth. He got out and walked around as the light spray appeared to ease.

"Thank you. I seem to be somewhat stuck," she said in her home counties voice.

He looked at her, shrugged his own shoulders and mirrored the sad face. Then he put his hands gently into his shoulder bag and felt the glass vials. He counted them off, still a dozen.

The ones the man they called The Chemist had told him all about.

'Be *most* careful...'

## CHAPTER EIGHT



**HMP BELMARSH**

They called him The Chemist rather than use his real name. There was no point in doing that when the authorities listened to their every word, and read all of their mail. They probably even listened to his cell, twenty-four hours a day, hoping to trap him with a word here and there during a rare deep sleep.

He had earned the nickname many years ago. Skilled at making explosives, he had carved out a reputation back in his homeland of Romania, then Europe, demolishing bank vaults and latterly blowing up ATMs with a cunning mixture of gas and a simple spark, long before it was fashionable.

But enjoyable though it was, that was in the past, and as he listened to Rachmaninoff, whiling away the last few hours of his incarceration, he was imagining the chemical process, molecule by molecule.

The prison library had been marvellous, and studying advanced chemistry inside the prison walls had only reinforced his earlier knowledge.

The simple truth was, he just liked destroying things. He just liked destroying people too, as he had proven once before, often an eye for another was all it needed.

———

Stood in his cell, Constantin enjoyed watching the other miserable bastards ambling from here to there and back again – polar bears, longing for the pack ice, trapped in a zoo. His music was playing, quite loudly, attracting abuse from the lesser men who neither enjoyed it nor knew its origins.

SO Chamberlain walked along the gantry and made his way towards Constantin's cell. The door was open today – by order of the governor himself, and Chamberlain and his peers hated it. It was weak. What sort of message did it send when one of the worst criminals in recent history could stand next to the door frame, nonchalantly listening to that rubbish?

"Listening to that Russian shite again, Nicolescu?"

"Dear Mr Chamberlain, first things first, if you please. It is Mr Nicolescu now as I await a few minor administrative changes, and as you correctly identify, it is Russian, one point to you. But, as you so eloquently describe it, it is not 'shite', it is one of the most difficult pieces ever written for the piano."

"Then it's difficult shite. Now listen, when you are on my wing you do as instructed, and you are not leaving here yet, mate."

"Another point, if you can tell me which famous film featured this piece of music. If your frigid wife lets you visit the cinema."

"I'm separated. But at least she was a woman, not like you. I hear you prefer your women to be of the slightly, how can I put it, unusual variety?"

"Amusing. Piano Concerto No. 2 – last chance."

"*Brief Encounter.*"

Nicolescu looked visibly shocked.

"I am impressed, Ricky. I would shake your hand, but you don't know where I have been. I could have been doing anything with it last night. Perhaps I was even thinking of you. Now, did you know there's something about Rachmaninoff that might interest you?"

"He enjoyed people admiring his pianist?"

Nicolescu clapped his hands and laughed. "Such juvenile British wit. No, really, you are very amusing, Rick. But let me educate you."

"I haven't got time for this."

"But you must. If I remember correctly, you are the captain of the prison quiz team, are you not? Thursdays in the Red Lion."

Chamberlain had no idea how he knew this, and tried to shrug it off.

"That's a yes, then. You bleed the truth. Unlike me, I just tell the truth and then bleed. But what would you know about true suffering? Sat there in your red leather Danish armchair, the one in which you lay back and watch banal television programmes until you fall asleep with your mouth wide open, until your troll of a wife demands that you go to bed and stop interrupting her viewing pleasure."

"I told you. She's gone."

Chamberlain clenched his fists, tightened his lips over his teeth, classic signs. His nostrils flared, too.

Timing was everything. A man of Constantin's upbringing knew all about fight or flight.

He edged back. "Governor McIntyre, how delightful to see you. Do you like Rachmaninoff?"

Chamberlain backed down, recognising the opportunity to save face. Why destroy his career for one good clean punch. He was adamant the Romanian would be back inside before you could say 'lights out'. His day would come.

"Mr Nicolescu. As it happens, yes, I do. Number 2 Concerto for Piano, if I am not mistaken, one of his more common pieces."

"Common or commonly known, sir?"

"Commonly known, and you realise that within the next few hours you'll be a free man, no longer any need to call me sir. I will arrange for the team to hand back your possessions. Perhaps you might walk with me for a moment? I have something I'd like to run past you, you know, for the benefit of our longer-term patrons."

He gave Chamberlain a look that said simply: *You can go now.*

The two men walked along the gantry, flanked by caging, cells opposite each other, a floor below them, containing men in various coloured T-shirts that did their best to brighten up the plain walls and the grey faces that lined the corridors, watching the minutes tick by, minute after painful minute.

What next? Watch the man opposite, watching me, watching him? Where would it all end?

Minute after minute, day after bloody day. What was that saying? The devil makes work for idle hands?

———

For whatever their reason, they were there, on that wing and for a very long time, unlike Nicolescu. He'd served his time elsewhere; he'd learned the very hardest ways how to avoid punishment.

He'd been strapped to a bed for days. He'd eaten raw potatoes. He'd sipped at a pitiful supply of fresh water after being made to scrub toilet blocks with a toothbrush. Then he had been observed by the staff as he cleaned his teeth. He'd been locked away for week after week with no sunlight, in this beautiful home from home.

As much as Nicolescu was in a good mood, just like the rest of the unwilling patrons, he could turn in a heartbeat.

McIntyre was an experienced and career prison officer first and foremost, long before he had become a governor: after a few tours of the Midlands and North East of England, he had been offered the flagship prison where terrorists were so feared they were kept apart from the murderers.

He knew who to trust, and for him that meant the people in uniform – albeit he knew one or two were corrupt. They didn't arrive corrupt, it was just a case of the population getting to them; they turned their minds, with veiled threats about what their mates could do with the officer's wives when they were working the night shift.

McIntyre had heard them all, and for that reason, he let Nicolescu walk a half pace in front of him.

"You like Rachmaninoff then, Mr McIntyre? He's one of my favourite composers. You'll know that his First Symphony was an unmitigated disaster. But I still enjoy its dark undertones. Thank you for allowing me to have that old cassette player, it meant a lot to me. Did you know he wrote that piece from what he called a pit of despair?"

"No, I didn't. Is that why you enjoy it? Does it strike a chord? That you have also been in a similar place?"

"Belmarsh is so wonderful. I have thoroughly enjoyed my time here – a chance to think. In fact, if I were to return to a prison, it would be to yours. I really should write an online review." He turned and ran his eyes up and down McIntyre. The man, half a step behind him, had no idea who he was dealing with, but he had shown some compassion, so why harm him?

He continued. "He wrote it after a dark time in his life. *That* strikes a chord. One of his fiercest critics said, 'This music leaves an evil impression... with its sickly perverse harmonisation...'"

"Deep indeed." McIntyre tried to steer him back on track. He knew how easily prisoners in Category A prisons could flick a switch. He'd seen that all too often.

"It was a deep period of his life, but that one moment saved his career. He didn't write for three years, then he produced the piece that was so recognisable even your Neanderthal prison officer Ricky recognised it."

"I can assure you, Mr Chamberlain is a good man."

"I agree. If I were looking for a zookeeper, he would be my very first choice. Did you know that Rachmaninoff dedicated the second piece to his therapist? I should dedicate my acquittal to you really. Your support has been appreciated. I leave later today a free man. Not many here can say that, can they, Martin?"

McIntyre did his best to ignore the familiarity. Knowing what the Romanian was trying to do.

"No, they can't. Tell me, Constantin, why did you not leave first thing this morning, when you had the chance? Most people here would have run out of the door."

"Would they? Institutionalisation, I think they call it. When one has been locked away for so long, the simple act of leaving the main gate leaves some with a sense of terror. Where will they shelter? Who will shelter them? Those people that were once friends, would they be now? Where will their next meal come from? My food was always heavily laden with the foul-tasting saliva of my so-called inmates, my comrades, but I ate it because it was free and after a while you come to like the taste."

"Where will you go?" he asked, again trying to ignore the hook.

"To a place that I feel safe." He looked at the large clock on the wall, protected by a strong white metal mesh cage. "I'll be just fine."

"You do know that I had to put in a very good word for you – to help you get the acquittal?"

"I heard that, yes. Thank you. Trust me, I appreciate it. I have no intention of ever seeing the inside of one of these places again."

"Well, that's good to hear. I genuinely don't want to ever see you here again either, you know." McIntyre's words were clear, concise, almost as if he needed a witness. In a place like this, he had hundreds, all listening at their doors, pretending to read a poster on the wall, or talk to staff members, but all the time listening. Rumour had it the governor had been blackmailed. Actually, it was worse than that. He'd been threatened, and there really was nothing he could do about it. Other than write the report supporting the Romanian's appeal.

McIntyre spoke again with a hint of false laughter. "Of course, to do that, to come back in here again, well, you need to do something very wrong indeed. You need to become bad again."

"No, Martin, I need to get caught."

He smiled, then unconsciously looked at his bare wrist to check the accuracy of when he was about to become bad.

"Governor, I must pack up my worldly goods. I note your kind words about how you have helped me. It was the least you could do really, given the options before you."

He smiled a fractured smile and put his hand out.

"No hard feelings I'm sure."

McIntyre looked around. Don't show weakness here, of all places. That he'd given into a man such as this, quite so easily, was bad enough. That his family had been threatened quite so skilfully was another thing altogether.

"No hard feelings," he said, trying not to choke on the words. He took Constantin's hand and discreetly pulled him closer.

"This ends here and now. Today. Yes?" he hissed.

"Of course. I am a man of integrity. Our paths will never cross again and your lovely little family, Jenny, Katy and Toby, will never know a thing about their husband and daddy and just how pathetic he really is."

He picked a piece of skin from his finger and flicked it down into the floor below.

"The last prison governor I had to corrupt was far easier than you, that's for sure. I had the photographs to prove it too." He shrugged his shoulders in a slightly affected manner.

"Now if you don't mind, I have a date with Rachmaninoff, and a moment of me time, where I may hopefully reflect on the finer moments of my pitiful life. In fact, that time should be..."

He looked back at the clock, behind the white mesh with its black hands on a white background, as the large minute hand laboured into place. "Any time now."

He re-entered his cell and closed the door, just enough to allow him to recover the phone. Just enough to watch, eyes wide.

"My goodness. This is such a thrill."

---

# CHAPTER NINE

---

CATHY STRUGGLED WITH THE DOOR. IT WAS LOCKED. SHE TRIED to reach out and open it from the outside but the door remained sealed. She was confused. She looked at the man, standing there, his black boots in three inches of water. Somebody somewhere had pressed pause.

"Please, go and get the man from the shop. Tell him something's wrong. My car won't start. I can't put the windows up. I'm going to get wet." She spoke clearly, slowly.

He just stared back at her. Orders were orders. It was such a shame. What he would have given for a few hours alone with her.

"Hello, I'm talking to you. I'll climb out. Help me, before the bloody thing starts up again." She smiled a half smile, now becoming uneasy around the black-haired man of very few words.

He pulled the phone out of his pocket and tapped on the screen. The passenger window began to rise.

"Oh my God, I don't know what you did, but thank you!" She smiled again, this time it was natural. Her phone rang, connected to the car, Jason's voice came out of all eight speakers.

"Alright my love, I'm in the lift, a chance to speak properly. Do a bit of flirting..."

"Jason, shut up. The bloody car won't start. I'm in a sodding car wash, the window is coming down again, I'm fifteen minutes from being very late and I fear the wash is about to start. There's a man stood outside the car who doesn't appear to speak any English but he's trying to help me. He's doing something with his phone, bless him. The passenger window went up again. I can't get out because the doors are locked from the outside." She sounded slightly panicked, but not ready to have a full-blown panic attack.

"Just climb out, leave the bloody thing."

"But your car, Jason, it will get very wet. The machine is starting up again." She tried to laugh, then tried to climb out. It looked easier than it was.

Roberts was watching the lift descend, five floors to go, a meeting in six minutes.

"You still there?"

"Yes, hang on, the man is motioning for me to get back in. He's touching his phone again."

Two floors to go. His mind began to whirr. He looked into the mirrored panel and saw an infinite image of himself.

"Cathy, get out. Get out *now*!"

"What? Stop being so dramatic. I'm in a car wash in Surrey, this is not something from your world, Jason."

As the lift reached ground, he was telling himself to stay calm.

The doors opened, and he met Cade, stood in the foyer with two cups of coffee: one for him, one for O'Shea.

Roberts looked panicked. It wasn't his normal facial expression. This was personal.

"Jason, are you OK?"

Roberts was pacing. "Get a car, Jack! Please. We need to go."

Cade ran for the stairs, climbing them two at a time. He knew Roberts well enough to know when he was being serious.

———

The black-haired man watched as the windows closed. He stared at the woman, with her short, blue dress and matching shoes. He swept his environs like the well-trained operator that he was. He pressed his phone screen and lowered the driver's window, just far enough to fit his hand into, just a bit more, he needed a little more space.

He stepped to the driver's side and threw the first vial into the car, and a second, a third and a fourth. Three landed in her lap. Two landed in the footwell. One landed on the passenger seat with its contrasting orange-and-black trim. Two landed onto the back seats. Little glass vials.

She just stared at them, shaking her head, looking left and right and up and down.

Then the car wash started up again: the rinse cycle, water by the litre, hundreds of litres.

Constantin had insisted that the operator should be up close, and very personal. It needed to be a tangible act, a courageous one.

"Cathy!" Roberts shouted down the phone. She tried to speak, but her throat was rigid. She was unable to swallow. She began to breathe faster. Then the driver's window lowered, the passenger side too, and the rear windows.

"Jason, the water... I can't get out. This is ridiculous. There are things..."

"What? Cathy, sound your horn. Do it now."

He turned to Carrie. "Get a unit to the BP petrol station on Staines Road."

"What's happening, boss?"

"I don't know, just get someone there, please. Get someone there now, Carrie."

He switched his phone to hands-free and placed it on the public counter. Gestured to the officer behind the screen to pass his radio handset.

"MP, this is..." He ran his fingers through his hair. What was his bloody call sign?

"MP, this is DCI Roberts Operation Orion. I need urgent assistance."

He conveyed the location to the remote voice in the control room, then passed the handset back to the bemused officer who carried on with his enquiry.

"You still there, Cathy?"

He could hear something: a shuffling, rustling noise, breathing. She was alive.

"Cathy!"

"Jason. I can't get out, the water it's everywhere. I've tried pressing the horn. It doesn't work. He threw some glass things into the car."

She went quiet, then screamed. "Oh God, no!"

The water-soluble wax was reacting now. The jets of cold clear water were blasting into the cabin of the orange Ford, soaking everything. Cathy ducked down, trying to avoid the deluge, flicking the glass vials away from her lap.

The wax melted in seconds, and as the chemical reaction rapidly changed the material inside the vials from gold to liquid gold. They started to steam. The steam began to escalate until the material started to spatter: small staccato noises, like gunfire. Then, the first explosion, followed by a rapid set of similar explosions, firing the caesium across the cabin, screaming hot flames, gas, and white smoke.

Caesium sits in a part of the periodic table rarely visited except by the keen chemistry student, or someone needing it for industrial uses – extracting the vacuum from a light bulb, or inside an atomic clock, or drilling for oil. It wasn't something you would expect to find in Surrey. To find hardly anyone at a car wash, on the way to work was even rarer. But he knew she would be there. He'd heard everything.

———

Almost all known caesium is to be found at Bernic Lake, Canada. A soft silvery-golden alkali metal caesium has a melting point of eighty-three point three degrees Fahrenheit, which makes it one of only five metals that are liquid near room temperature.

That wasn't what Constantin found fascinating. It was how easy it was for him to source it, and what it did when it reacted with water. That is what genuinely excited him. Forget sodium or potassium, they weren't even the poor relations. This was special. It was beautiful, in fact.

A few years earlier, he'd thrown a larger amount into a pond. The explosion, the sheer power of it, rocked him and left a huge smile on his face.

It had been that day that made him see chemicals in a totally different light. It was too late for a man of his background to retrain and become a useful scientist. However, nothing could stop him experimenting.

Nothing should prevent him from becoming a chemist. Nothing could prevent him from becoming *The* Chemist.

He just wished he'd been there in person, not watching from a small screen in Belmarsh.

———

"Are you seeing this boss?" asked the black-haired man.

"Almost, just try to get a little closer. I want to see her."

The man edged back towards the car, as if he were trying to enter to help her. By now, the garage workers had heard the commotion. They couldn't see it; the car wash was around the back of their building: out of sight, and out of mind. They weren't paid enough to investigate. They could perhaps ring for the police.

"Hold the camera there. How beautiful, look at her. Such a shame. If you like that sort of thing. Women have to be of a certain type for me to ever find them attractive. Prison does that to a man, you know."

"Is there anything else I can do?" The black-haired man asked awkwardly.

"Has the excitement stopped?"

"Yes."

"Good."

"Boss, I need to leave here. People will come soon."

"Yes, you must. And remember, we have never met, in case anyone should ask." It was an unnecessary statement. They never had, and they never would.

"One last thing. Take the camera nearer, I just want to see what it did to her."

The operator walked up to the driver's door. He held the lens for his boss to see his handiwork. Then he turned his head away.

"That's awful. Just look at her. How could something so beautiful do that to a person? She must have burns to over half of her body."

"Hold the camera inside for me so she can hear me."

He spoke. "Hello, my dear. How are you feeling?"

He smiled. He knew exactly how she was feeling, wretched, just like he had, day after monotonous day when her smug bastard of a husband had seen to it that he would be locked away for the rest of his life, him and his blue-eyed bosom buddy Cade.

"Well, how did that go for your man, Cathy? I'll answer that because from the state of your lips you won't be able to form a word. I'm filming this, by the way, you know, for old times' sake. For Jason, in case I need it as a get out of jail card. Cathy…"

She was slipping away fast. But something he said made her scrunch her eyes, shake her head slightly.

For Jason? Why would he be so cruel?

"No words for me? Not even a goodbye for your man? Dear Jason will be distraught. Go on, say something. It might be your last chance."

Cathy Roberts turned her head slightly. It was just about all she could do. Her pain levels had exceeded anything she'd ever felt in childbirth. The skin on her thighs had been peeled back to reveal deep, creamy flesh. The vial that she hadn't seen in time had done its job. Ruthless, damaging and almost powerful enough on its own to kill her. The femoral artery had ruptured in her right leg, filling the orange-and-black seats with bright, red foaming blood.

"Who… are… you…?" she asked through each laboured breath.

"I… am… your… guardian angel," he mocked back slowly.

"I died a while ago when your husband took my life from me. I'd suggest you ask him yourself, but looking at you I don't think you'll last that long. No doubt he is fighting through traffic to get to you, the white knight, to tell you he loves you so very much. To hold what is left of your hand."

Her head nodded to the left. He was right. Not long now.

She lifted her head up to face him, to look him in the eye. Then whispered, "Come closer. I was told never to trust you…"

She sucked her cheeks in, drawing the blood from her around her teeth. Her final act was to spit a mouthful of the life-giving liquid onto the screen.

"That isn't very nice, is it? OK, I've seen enough. She's gone. Don't forget the little extra task you had."

The man with the jet-black hair removed a marker pen from his pocket and wrote a large letter C on the bonnet.

"All we need to do now is clean up any evidence. Just hold the camera there a moment longer for me. Just to the left... this might need the flash to go off, it's dark in there now that you've wrecked the place." He laughed a humourless laugh.

The black-haired man altered the phone setting, then pressed the button on the phone, which sent a signal that was quicker than his blink of disbelief.

The signal initiated a charge which activated the detonator, which in turn fired a booster. Now things were reacting fasted than any human could comprehend. A blink? That would never be fast enough. The main charge was now compressing and propelling a copper liner that had previously retained the explosive. The liner moulded into a screaming hot projectile that travelled at high speed through the door and into the operator.

The blast hit the operator with such force that he didn't have any last words or thoughts. He just blended with the interior of the car wash as a section of the driver's door panel hit him in the rib cage, punching a hole in his torso and the glass ripping his skin to shreds.

Had his mind had the capacity to think, it would have momentarily seen the package, the shaped charge behind the door trim. The one with the fingerprints wiped away, and those fiddly little fasteners all carefully back in place.

The irony that he'd actually killed himself probably never registered.

Cathy, her body already horribly damaged, watched the auto-glass flying around the cabin, the windscreen deformed under pressure, distorting it and the roof lining partially collapsed, bits of the dashboard broke away as the pressure wave sought a way out of the car.

What glass there was, was now in bits, thousands of tiny cubed pieces which hissed and popped with static.

With a hiss of hydraulics and powerful jets, the next wash cycle started, damaged, but still able to apply yet more fluid, its robotic arms danced and weaved around the cubicle, rinsing and hosing down the suds as it passed along the passenger side, around the back, before running alongside the driver's side, forcing water into the cabin, washing the blood and saliva from her face and swilling his down the drain where it formed a congealing crimson stream.

They heard it now, the staff in the quiet comfort of the petrol station. They saw the smoke too. Now they rang, and they panicked, and they asked for help and ventured outside, easing towards the car wash.

What did they see?

"Nothing, we just heard a loud explosion," said the manager.

"How many people?"

"A lady, I think, in an orange car. Hang on, there's a silver one too. Oh no, wait. There's a man on the floor. I think he's dead. He's not moving. Neither is the lady. She's covered in blood or skin or burns... I'm sorry."

He held the phone at his side and stared. He just stood there, not knowing what to do or say. Sirens were sounding somewhere as the anonymous grey van started up and left the far side of the station and headed east into the city with all the other onlookers.

# CHAPTER TEN

They'd heard it half way down Staines Road.

They'd all phoned: people at home, passing motorists, all saying the same thing, as if they were the first to ring the emergency services. All adding to the length of the event text that the control operator was rapidly creating, her fingers dancing across the keyboard.

She entered the job, pressed the button that shared it with the fire and ambulance control rooms then called for any free units near Staines Road. To be exact, for anyone near the BP petrol station.

Then she ran the two registration plates through the Police National Computer. One was a silver VW Polo with no registered keeper and no current alerts. The other, an orange Ford Focus ST with a confidential keeper from Surrey.

She was spinning plates on a unicycle. It was what the best operators did. She wouldn't want it any other way.

Directing two units to the scene and another to close the road, she then dispatched a unit to the registered keeper of the Focus. She did it all without turning or looking or even breaking a sweat.

She pointed to the screen. The control room manager spotted the gesture and opened the event on her screen. An inspector with twenty-three years under her belt, she'd seen most things, got more T-shirts than she would ever wear.

"Help is on the way," said the control operator.

"I'm so sorry, there's nothing I can do for them. Those poor people. I'm sorry... they look terrible. The car is still smoking. I can hear sirens. Is help on the way?"

———

He heard some of the update in New Scotland Yard on the radio too, strapped to the constable, who stood behind the desk, staring back through the glass screen at the man in the grey suit with the bright orange tie.

He knew. The tense nature of the message said it all. They both did. When you deal with sorrow most days of your life, you learn to judge just how deep it might be, whether people had reached the chaos in time, or moments too late; it manifested as a subtle gesture, a battle with a tear, the inability to even speak a single word or pure unbridled grief.

Carrie put her arm around her boss, the man who she considered to be a friend first and foremost, and one who had carried her many times.

"Don't go there, guv. Please."

Cade arrived. "Right, let's go."

O'Shea shook her head discreetly.

"Jason?" asked Cade. He'd seen the look before, plenty of times.

"Jack..."

"Talk to me, mate."

"I think we might be too late."

———

Cade drove as fast as he could. Nothing was said. He changed gear to keep the unmarked car at its fastest; braking, checking junctions, avoiding the lights, accelerating again. O'Shea was sending text messages to the team.

No, there was nothing they could do. She sent another to her teammate, the ex-military intelligence officer called Dave Francis.

*Dave. I need you to bring up the job on Staines Road. Take everything from it you can, and start scanning. I have a truly awful feeling about this.*

Francis replied.

*Received. The boss OK? Stupid question?*

The reply came quickly.

*No. And it's fine, we all ask them.*

The sirens and grill strobes made the journey faster, but it seemed to take a lifetime, of stopping and starting, onto pavements, around traffic lights, judging the behaviour of the rush hour commuters – some of whom panicked when they heard the chaos approaching.

Stay calm. Don't move. Let the trained driver do their job.

The road seemed to open up before them. He pushed now, almost knowing the inevitable would not change, but wanting to get his friend to the scene as soon as he could. Then what?

———

It was an interminable ten minutes later that they bypassed the road block and arrived at the forecourt. Two fire engines were present, an ambulance and an advanced paramedic, who had arrived on a motor-cycle. As luck would have it, he knew Roberts.

He walked over to the unmarked car.

"Greetings, Jason. Long-time, no see. How's things with you?"

Roberts stared through him, gently shaking his head, forcing back tears, his throat arid and painful.

"Bloody hell, mate, I know it's been a while but you don't need to get so emotional."

Cade stepped forward. "Mate, a word, please."

"Looks like your hired help's going to whisk me away for interrogation, Jason!" Normally, the banter would have flowed, with Roberts giving as good as he got.

"Send my love to your lovely missus, won't you? Long overdue for a catch up. How is she?" He was persistent.

Roberts walked slowly towards the cubicle. Daring himself to go any further.

"She's in there, mate. Why don't you go and ask her yourself?" He pointed to what was left of his car, made a noise that for a split second sounded like laughter, then he dropped to the ground, his whole body collapsing beneath him.

Desperate to hold her, even more so to stay away, to remember her face, as he had that morning when he'd closed his eyes in his office: the face of the girl he'd married, the mother of his children, the exquisite eyes of his lover, his friend.

"What about the kids, Carrie?" He sobbed into her neck and she held him, as if she was his mother, or wife or friend.

———

The paramedic fought back the bile. "Christ mate, I'm *so* sorry. I didn't know. Just gallows humour. You know..."

Cade held his arm. "You weren't to know. Talk to me. What are her injuries?"

"Catastrophic," he whispered. "Worst I've seen for a while. It looks like chemical burns to me, but then it looked like the car exploded. A bomb?"

Cade turned, looked at the emergency crews who were standing around the cubicle, at the shop workers trying to get a human nature view at what had happened, their phones poised to grab a discreet ten second video.

Then he yelled.

"Everybody back, back onto the road. You... go! You... move! Now!"

———

At over four hundred metres, Cade considered things to be as safe as they could be. He'd have been happier with further, but the houses that bordered the station made it difficult at best. He had to order the main road to be closed too. He wouldn't be popular. One of those 'damned if you did' things about being a police officer.

You made a call, and you stood by it. No place for second guessing. The court of public opinion could wait until the trial.

The petrol station tanks were deep in the ground and potentially as safe as they could be. His fear was a secondary device. He'd seen it happen once. In the old days of the Provisional IRA, during their UK mainland campaign, against the British government and anyone who chose to get in the way – innocent or otherwise.

———

"Jack, I *need* to be with her. I'm going. Please don't stop me." Roberts' eyes were scarlet. The levels of stress and fear and anger were compounded by the fact that the girl he'd fallen in love with so many years before, the one with the conversational eyes, and those freckles, was alone.

"She used to smell of lemons and sunshine, Jack." He was crying now. "Her skin was like porcelain. Her hair was always so shiny. Jack... *please*. You have to let me go."

"Jason, I can't let you. I'm not going to fight with you, and I won't stop you if you really want to be with her. But listen to me, mate. Think about the kids. It's not good. OK? Listen to me. There may be another device."

"It's hardly going to be wonderful in there, is it? You've got us stood over here because you think there's a bomb in there. I mean, how much worse can it get? What if she's..."

"She isn't."

"But what if...?"

"Jason. She's not alive, she's gone, mate. I'm so sorry, there's nothing I, or anyone else, can do about it." He knew his cold demeanour wasn't what Roberts needed to hear, but he also knew the last thing he needed was another casualty. Let the bomb squad deal with it.

The SO15 team had already been deployed. It would take them thirty-five minutes to get there from Holborn. Without the noise and cacophony of multiple sirens, flickering strobes, skilled driving, and the ability to carve through traffic – it might take them an hour and a half.

———

An hour later, the road was declared fit to open, just one lane. It was better than nothing. The crime scene remained cordoned off. It would be for days, regardless of the petrol station owner complaining about the loss of income. Now and then, he would be reminded why it was necessary, when the forensic team removed another part of the black-haired male and labelled another piece of the car.

———

When the scene staff had all done their jobs, Roberts was allowed to take the painful walk towards the cubicle, or what was left of it.

They walked, just the three of them, O'Shea holding her boss's arm, and Cade, sweeping the environs, feeling uncomfortable at best. This was going to be hideous in every possible way. He found himself remembering the girl he'd once held, on a quiet country road, dying and beyond help. They let their friend walk the last few paces alone.

He entered the cubicle, water was dripping from the roof, the only sound coming from the nearby traffic and occasional drops of water onto the roof of his car, which seemed to echo as they would in a cave: drip, drip, drip.

The senior CID officer held his hand out.

"Guv'nor, I can't let you in there. You know that. I understand, I really do, but..."

"You don't understand at all. Your wife been blown to bits lately, has she, Micky?"

They knew each other from the old days, and as much as the detective inspector wanted to be compassionate and offer some leeway, as the SIO, the senior investigating officer, he was in control, regardless of Roberts' rank.

"Jason, I'm here to help, not hinder. You know the drill. Sorry, mate, I've got a job to do that none of us ever want to have to but..."

"I know, Micky. It's OK. No hard feelings, just do your job, and Micky?"

"Guv?"

"Find who did this, and leave them cuffed to a train or something similar, will you? You know, in a deserted siding somewhere, down near Cricklewood Train Depot would do. Make sure it's dark and raining..."

Blacknall was a proper old-school copper and didn't care who knew it. He'd earned the right to be grumpy, and to utter, whenever the mood took him that the 'job was well and truly f...'.

He'd got four months left of his untarnished thirty-year career and he dreaded every day passing, as it had been a dream career for him. Thirty years. It felt like ten. What the bloody hell was he going to do with himself?

His father had been a DI too. It ran in the family, with Blacknall's son now following in the family footsteps, a young beat officer in Camden Town.

Blacknall's role as SIO was complex. More than just delegating, he needed to ensure he covered off many bases: initial response, crime scene management, cordons, logs, exhibits, forensics. That was just the beginning. Witness management was a critical phase if there was ever to be a successful prosecution.

He ticked them off in his head. He'd done this countless times, but each new case deserved the very best he could do. This case was somehow more deserving; you looked after your own.

The petrol station workers – what had they seen, or heard? Was their view blocked by anything? How long were they looking at the scene? Did they recognise anyone? Had they seen them before? When? Was it recorded?

His mind ticked off the essentials once more.

He knew that his team of investigators would do their level best to help one of their own. They checked every CCTV location, from five miles out. The boss wanted to know every car that had driven into that petrol station, going back a week.

"Send staff to knock on every door, every office, then do it again until the log is complete. No stone left unturned."

Then there were the victims, two in this case.

Were they connected? Was one the offender? Both? Neither?

He needed to ensure they were positively identified. He had the primary family member present for the female. Whilst it would never be classed as an easy task, the fact that Roberts was also an SIO meant he would know the importance of getting everything right first time. He wanted that more than anyone present, among the growing entourage of suits and uniforms that had taken over the scene.

Did they need a family liaison officer? No, Roberts had said firmly. Cade would make sure it happened.

Then there was the post mortem.

Blacknall needed to coordinate that, too. He'd send his best detective sergeant along for that role and make sure he did it by the book.

He would need to oversee everything – the marks of violence, their cause, and any obvious or unexpected cause of death. He'd insisted they brought their 'a game' – a hair or clothing fibre might make all the difference.

"Don't miss a trick. I want your undivided attention on this. Understood? Any questions?" It was rhetorical. The team knew what was required and as much as they tried to remain impartial, the fact that the female victim belonged to the police family made the job both harder and more intense.

Blacknall's phone rang.

"Mick Blacknall. Yes, thanks, if you can. I want an initial media release. No depth to it, just that we are investigating blah, blah, you know the drill. Social media too, same drill. There will be no press conferences today or tomorrow. Let's try to avoid that if we can. And no mention of bombs or terrorism – OK? None whatsoever."

He cleared his throat – acid reflux, the curse of a poor diet and endless shift changes.

"Whoever even utters the T word will find their balls... forgive me, in these days of equality... or fanny, in a vice before you can say Osama whatsisname. Cheers, and anything you are not sure of... Good girl. Bye."

Blacknall was tired of battling the new wave, fed up to the back teeth of political bloody correctness. No one was going to cancel him. He'd be long gone by then.

He walked around the scene, careful to avoid anything critical. It wasn't like police dramas on the television, where the senior officer rampaged across the crime scene, lifting up police tape and stepping across the body, smoking a cigarette and casually flicking a dog-end onto the ground. Everything had to be documented, photographed, mapped, measured, plotted, everything.

God help anyone who fucked up Micky Blacknall's crime scenes.

He was desperate for a cigarette. He'd given up a fortnight ago. Good job he was at a vulnerable petrol station with its myriad hazards or he might have succumbed.

Instead, he sucked on a Polo mint, trying to make it last, so it remained as a perfectly round sweet, his tongue probing the diminishing hole as his mind went through suspect management.

He needed to identify the black-haired man, what was left of him. Was he a victim, a good Samaritan? Did the petrol station worker say he was filming the female at one point? Why? Where was the phone now? What about the images? Did he *actually* see that? How good was his view?

Think man, think about the court case. Would that man, who thought he'd seen so much more than he had, stand up as a credible witness for the prosecution in a year's time?

If the offender wasn't at the scene, who was responsible?

How dangerous were they? What was the likely arrest strategy? The list was endless. Again, on the TV shows, it was all done and dusted and pints being consumed down the local pub before the end of the day. The reality was much harsher: extra hours, cancelled days off, no paid overtime, coffee, bags under the eyes and microwaved meals, if you were lucky.

He needed a fingertip search of the scene. 'Yes, make the call, get them here.'

The search group staff would do what they were trained to do; search, record and plot and secure every stray hair and piece of glass that hadn't been already kicked away or moved inadvertently during the initial rescue phase.

He'd need a major incident room. For this was an incident that was major – not just the fact that the primary victim was also the wife of a senior police officer, more the nature of the job.

Was it a bomb? If not, what was it? It certainly wasn't a normal event. There had been an explosion, that much was true.

———

Then there was staffing, overtime, allowances and logistics. Cops marched on their stomachs too.

This was just one of nine major incidents Blacknall was overseeing. Who'd be an SIO, he wondered?

"Can I do anything for you, boss?" asked a sharp-suited young detective, keen to shine.

"You know what, Marcus, you can. Here, go and grab me and the boss a coffee. He likes his hot and black. And some plain biscuits, nothing with ginger in them."

He looked at the remains of the black-haired man. It seemed that his lower half had been detached from the waist, yet he had somehow remained as one, only tendons and sinews trying their damnedest to hold him together.

A huge blast injury had ripped the contents of his torso out via a hole in his back and blasted them onto the plastic see-through cubicle. He appeared to be welded to the wall, half-standing, half-sitting, motionless, one eye open, the other God only knew where.

The car was intact but for the missing driver's door and the shattered windscreen. The fire hadn't taken hold – to a great extent it had been extinguished by the water, and what flames there were had peeled back the orange paint, leaving bare metal beneath.

———

"There you go. And, guv, I'm truly sorry, you know..."

Blacknall took the coffees and ushered the younger man away with a fatherly nod.

For a second, the normally jovial Roberts stood and shook his head. "How am I ever going to get that clean again, Micky?"

He nodded to his pride and joy as he pulled on a paper suit, gloves and overshoes.

He looked at Blacknall; it was a look that simply said please.

'Please let me see her.'

Blacknall could see that Roberts had taken every precaution as far as forensics were concerned, except the obvious, that it was his car and his wife. He took a sip of the scalding coffee.

"Bugger, that's hot." He took the lid off to let it cool.

"Be my guest, Jason. You want me to join you?"

Roberts shook his head. Then he placed his wallet and phone on the ground next to Blacknall.'

"Check my pockets if you like? I know this is wrong. I appreciate what you are doing, for me, for my kids."

"Won't be necessary to check your pockets, sir."

Roberts walked around the car, checking every panel. He knew deep inside what he was doing. He was delaying the inevitable.

"What have I done, Micky? What have I done to deserve this?" His voice echoed slightly.

O'Shea held Cade's arm. "We should be in there with him. I have a rough idea how he feels right now."

Cade tried to remove his 'job hat' and replace it with one of a more compassionate nature, but failed. Policing made people hard, either that or it consumed them.

"No, we shouldn't. It's a crime scene. You know that as well as any of us. He needs to do this without us. He shouldn't even be in there. The DI seems like a good man, steady head on wise shoulders. Hard as it sounds, Carrie, we'll know when to join him. That's if you even want to. It will be awful. How well did you know Cathy?"

"Summer barbecues, Christmas parties, that sort of thing. She always seemed so bubbly, apart from that one blip Jason had awhile back, their marriage seemed idyllic. Jesus, Jack, we've had some chaos lately, but this will finish him."

"Then we need to wrap around him as a team, stand him down to be with his kids. Get onto the commander and let him know what is happening. Don't take any bullshit from him. I want the full works here, Carrie. We both know this was no accident."

## CHAPTER ELEVEN

## FIVE HOURS LATER

THE FIRST EMAIL DROPPED SILENTLY INTO THE METROPOLITAN Police generic inbox. It was one a of a few hundred that day; some would be deleted, others forwarded to their respective units, and some would be answered by an automated system.

The system sent a reply to the sender, stating that the contents were important to the Metropolitan Police and that someone would reply very soon. It followed a reminder that if the message was urgent, the sender was to ring 999 immediately.

It wasn't urgent. It could wait. In fact, it waited for the second and third email to join it. Now there were three.

Blacknall had seen enough. The bodies were being considered for recovery. Cathy Roberts was to be last, as a mark of respect, left in situ for Roberts to say goodbye, alone.

"Should the boss be in there with her, sir?" asked Marcus Brown.

"Not exactly going to do any harm now, is he? We've done what we need to do, and in our defence, we've done it quickly. I've known crime scenes where bodies stay in situ for days. Always upsets the family and the press can't bear it. So far so good on that front. You've done well to keep them away – when we recover Mrs Roberts, I want a full tent in place. Do not let one of that bunch of vultures break through our cordon with a telephoto lens."

"Roger that, boss."

"And if you see a drone, you have my permission to throw something heavy at it."

He had things to do back at the station. He introduced Roberts to his DS and made sure that he had the contact details for both Roberts and Cade.

He liked Cade. He was some sort of hybrid between a copper and a civvie, according to his sources. He'd never seen him in action but had heard the war stories from the frontline. His references were exemplary, and rumour had it that the PM herself had endorsed his services.

Blacknall liked the PM – attractive in a fancy your first cousin way, with an inquisitive mind and someone who put the people first and foremost in her policies. She also loved the police and had a great sense of humour. Just a pity her latest Police Minister was a complete arsehole, just like the last one, and look what happened to him.

As a selector of complete arseholes, the current government had broken all recent records, it seemed.

"I need to get back to the ranch, Marcus. Let's leave a scene guard here overnight, then come back tomorrow, same time as the event today. I want every vehicle that passes this place stopped, half an hour before the first call. There's often value in doing that."

"We'll piss off a lot of commuters, boss."

"Yeah, we will, won't we? Make sure you keep the boss's phone and wallet safe and dry." He smiled, popped in his last Polo mint, and walked to his car. As he did, Cade called over to him.

Blacknall stopped, shielding himself from a rain shower that looked worse than it was against the bright sodium lights of the large station.

"Mick? Jack Cade. We didn't really get the chance to be properly introduced. I wanted to thank you for the way you and your team dealt with this, and to ask you to contact me if you need anything.

Here's my card, day or night, and that's not a throwaway statement. OK?"

"It's a date. Is it true what the boys and girls say about you?"

"Probably! Care to narrow it down a little?"

He laughed. "Fair enough. Look, I heard you single-handedly shut down the team that was looking to blackmail the government a while ago. Is that true?"

"No."

"I did wonder."

"I had help." He winked at Blacknall. "Couldn't have done it without them, including that lady over there and that man sat on the kerb with his trademark grey suit and the bright orange tie. The one who looks like his world has just fallen apart. I need to get him home."

"You do. Thanks for looking after him. Good to meet you, and Jack?"

"Fire away."

"Ballpark question, any idea who did this and why?"

"Yes, and yes."

"Then get in the car, I feel we need to talk a little longer."

———

The first of the three emails was being read by an administrator, as Constantin walked the last fifty-two paces to the main gate. He was counting them out aloud when someone in one of the blocks wolf whistled. It was a common tune, often heard in prisons, especially when the new arrivals walked in, wide-eyed and terrified.

In the staff car park, SO Chamberlain dropped his backpack onto the passenger seat of his knackered old blue Fiat, inhaled, started the car, and began to head home. It was forty minutes as the crow flies. He turned left, then right, drove for about two hundred metres, until he was passing the main entrance, where he normally exhaled deeply.

The door opened as one of the guards said something profound to the man in the suit – something about turning a corner and never coming back. It caused the Romanian to stop. He turned around and looked up at the sign.

Above him sat the Royal crest and the prison's name, the obligatory warning signs, the cameras. The brown bricks and the iron-oxide red windows, framing the simple exit to one of the world's most infamous prisons. The media called it the British Guantanamo for a reason.

Constantin called it home for an exact number of hours. He would never forget them – he had counted them out each day – it was his way of staying sane.

"Don't worry. I won't be."

He waved to the cameras. It was a shame, he'd miss the evening meal and the sideways and occasional eye-to-eye looks, and the tinderbox tension that existed in the wings for every minute that the men were out of their cells.

He looked at the car that had come to collect him: a dark grey Mercedes E Class with matching tinted glass and every conceivable extra.

Chamberlain drove slowly by, looking at the prisoner he had come to despise, with his slightly effeminate ways, his boring bloody music and, above all, his ability to avoid trouble, no matter how hard Rick Chamberlain tried to divert it towards him.

How he'd arrived where he was now, walking the walk of a free man, he might never know. Surely, he had committed serious offences against the British people? Some even said he'd committed treason. Yet, he was *walking*. It was clear that Nicolescu either had luck on his side, a superb lawyer, or, as further rumour had it, somebody deep inside the government looking out for him. But why?

His day would come. He must have been mouthing those words as he looked at Nicolescu – because the former prisoner mouthed some of his own back.

"No, it won't." He blew a kiss and climbed into the car, pulling the door shut with a comforting thud. He was free, and he had more alibis than he would ever need.

He checked the time on his moon phase watch. It was an heirloom of sorts. It was time for those emails to really sink in. It was time for Mr Roberts, as he would soon be known, to slip into the abyss.

————

Across the river, in an office behind closed doors, a well-dressed lady in her sixties read the three emails in unison. She took her glasses off, rubbed her eyes, slipped them slowly back on, and read them again. Then she pushed her chair back and walked along the short corridor to her manager's office.

"Ted, you got a moment?"

————

It was much later that night that Cade and O'Shea left Roberts at his in-laws, red-eyed and trying to explain what had happened, and how he was going to somehow tell the kids in the morning.

He'd sat with Cathy for what seemed like hours, not wanting to move her in case he added to her pain.

"What have they done to her, Jack?" he'd sobbed.

The damage to his wife was said to be unsurvivable. It was a word that didn't really exist in many dictionaries, but one favoured by police. It acted as a pre-cursor to the inevitable message that had to follow, when a uniformed constable would knock on the front door of an unsuspecting family member and watch as their face altered. It seemed that people often knew, just by the tone of the knock.

*I'll get it love; it'll be the grim reaper. I'd recognise that knock anywhere.*

————

As Cade drove slowly back to his rented Thames-side apartment, he held O'Shea's hand. It hadn't happened much lately. A distance had been created by a man Cade had grown to hate with a passion that made his heart flutter and his fists clench.

"Pull over here, Jack."

He slowed and tucked into a lay-by.

"You OK?" He knew she wasn't.

She leant across and kissed him, then squeezed his hand.

"I need you to take care of me." Her tears were flowing.

"I will. I do. You know that. What brought this on? Stupid question I guess." He knew the answer.

"Not stupid. But yes, today and the past. I'm lucky to be here, we both know that. Watching Jason today really upset me." She started to sob.

Cade sat there, holding her hand until it passed.

Ten long minutes. She let it all out, and probably some of her own demons, too. It was long overdue. What had happened to her would never truly leave her, the mere fact that she survived was a whole different story.

"I have a bad feeling about today. Call me paranoid."

Cade resisted the obvious. "Me too, Carrie. Me too."

"It's them, isn't it?"

"I think we can narrow it down a little."

O'Shea frowned heavily. "I'm not with you."

"I don't think there's a 'them' involved. More a case of 'him'. I think *he's* involved."

"Constantin?"

"Nail, meet head."

## CHAPTER TWELVE

## THE APARTMENT AND THE OFFICE

Cade liked to lie with the curtains open, watching the lights dance on the river, the occasional boat wending its way upstream. The constant movement of the river had long fascinated him. O'Shea used to enjoy a more physical nocturnal pastime, with the curtains open. But not now. It no longer felt right; not since they had taken her and he had carved his feelings into her stomach. It was as if no man made her feel safe anymore. Perhaps one or two. It was unfair, there were more good men than bad. She just had to remind herself of that, whenever she was ready to move on.

She had seen that moment most nights, or on the rare occasions she had drifted into a daytime sleep. His face staring at her, smiling his broken smile and the raw intimacy of her secured to a table and him leaning across her, gently carving a sign into her stomach.

He had no idea about a secret she held, why would he?

If he had had an ounce of compassion, it would have been false.

He still did it, cut into her flesh with the new blade, marvelling at how the blood appeared, then ran and how, as he pushed deeper, the colours changed.

Tonight, unusually, she had slept soundly, now and then jolting awake, trying to control her breathing, her heart trying to keep pace. She must have made a sound, one that probed her self-conscious state and woke her.

She sighed audibly. He was gone.

Cade stood in the window watching the river, aware of his reflection looking back at him, asking him questions he didn't know the answers to.

"How long have you been standing there?" she asked sleepily, pulling the duvet up around her. "The neighbours will talk."

He smiled. "Let them."

"Talk to me, Jack. What is it?"

"I don't know, today I guess. Watching a family torn apart. I can't prove a thing, but whoever did that to that poor girl wants stringing up, and I'd be happy to do it."

"It was a professional hit, wasn't it?"

"I didn't think I was an expert, but the last few years have shifted that opinion somewhat. Yes, no doubt. The fire investigators said the burns were not caused by heat alone, there was a chemical component. The CSI found a glass vial in the footwell. We've secured that and sent it for forensic exam."

"What about the post mortem?"

"Interesting development there. Jason asked if his old mate, Dex Hodgkinson, could do it. Apparently, he said yes and would travel to wherever he was needed. They go back a long way."

"There'll be an inquest of course."

"Sadly yes. Hopefully, we can support on that and get things moving." He stopped, looked back out along the river.

"Listen to me, Carrie. What has happened to me? I sound like I want to move this along as if it's a bloody inconvenience."

"No, you want to end your friend's suffering. That's different."

She laid her head back onto the pillow and watched the lights quiver on the ceiling. What they'd just had was a professional conversation, what she wanted was one that was so far removed from work. She could feel her throat tightening as she tried to stem the tears. It was every night now.

———

"Mick. It's Ted Charles over at the Yard. Yes, we are all well. Listen mate, I know it's well past our bedtimes, but have you got a moment to chat?"

Blacknall checked his bedside clock, its glowing red figures slightly blurry.

"Christ, Ted, you must be bored shitless ringing me at this hour. Hold on, I'll go to another room. If I wake Sheila up once more this week, she'll have my balls for peanut butter."

"Crunchy or smooth?"

He closed the bedroom door and walked quietly downstairs.

"Right, Edward, my son, I'm all ears."

The DI listened, grabbed a pad from beside the phone in the kitchen and started scrawling some notes. He looked at the biro. Red. Great, whenever he wrote anything in red, it meant bad news.

Ten minutes later, having made encouraging noises and written three pages of notes, he asked his first question.

"You believe this pack of old bollocks, Ted?" He was hoping the answer would be no.

"I was hoping the answer would be no, Micky. But that's why we've been here half the night. We've run all sorts of tests over the data. It comes back to Roberts. Clear as I'm sat in my office in the middle of the night on an exorbitant amount of overtime."

Blacknall exhaled loudly, then tutted as he stared at his fish tank. Most of his beloved and rather expensive marine fish seemed to be in a catatonic state, slowly moving about in the subdued lighting, all except one.

*Pterois volitans*. The Red Lionfish, and it was prowling.

Blacknall had kept the more exotic saltwater fish as opposed to what some saw as their poorer cousins for years. He had many: Clownfish, Blennies, Butterflyfish, Damselfish, and Dartfish, and Dottybacks. But his favourite was the venomous Lionfish. He loved to watch it swim, the others all gently avoiding it with its glorious spines. It was a loner and at the wrong time and in the wrong place, if you stepped into its territory uninvited, deadly.

His eyes were beginning to blur. He shook his head. The Lionfish had gone, darting away into a bolt hole.

He watched the tank for a second, staring into the darkest corners, 'where are you?' – it was an all-encompassing question.

"So now what, Ted? I can't pick this up as well as the investigation into Cathy Roberts' death."

"No one would be expecting you to. We will try to find someone independent."

"Any thoughts?"

"The only person we can find who isn't currently drowning in work is Phil Jenkinson." He paused, grimaced almost. The name did that to most police staff in London.

"Jesus, is there really no one else Ted? What about Genghis Khan, isn't he available?"

"I'm afraid not. I ran it past my boss, he said that I needed to follow protocols."

The humourless Chief Superintendent Phil Jenkinson was a product of the East End of London, and had risen quickly through the ranks. He'd lost almost every hair on his head in the process. Although there was a medical reason, it added another dimension of nastiness.

Jenkinson was despised by not only the rank and file, but the mid-level managers too, and no one hated him more than Jason Roberts.

When Jenkinson had answered his own phone in the middle of the night, he had done so quickly, as if he weren't even asleep.

"Really? Is that so? Well then, I had better get into the office and start preparing things. The early bird and all that."

Jenkinson had smiled each time he removed another rare whisker from his face with his ever-sharp razor. He ran it over his head for good measure. It was a habit he hadn't yet lost.

He was an Aries. Some say they are the most stubborn of all the astrological signs, independent too. There were only three people Phillip Jenkinson wanted to make an example of: his old headmaster, who said that being an East End barrow boy he'd never amount to anything; his ex-wife, the cold-hearted cow that she was; and last but by no means least, the jumped-up flyboy, with his bright orange ties, who had dared to talk down to him one day in a briefing, many moons ago.

"Best served cold, Jason. No hard feelings and all that, but these things come home to roost, and you, my friend, are going to the big house any day soon." He cut the last whisker away with the precision of a surgeon. "Bye-bye."

He pressed a red-hot flannel to his face, stemming the blood from one small cut, showered, dressed and headed out of the door in his new silver German hatchback. Nothing too flash, discreet almost, but like its owner, able to perform when it really needed to.

He was in *his* space at the station in eighteen minutes, with the coffee burbling away and the emails cascading into his inbox.

It was a shade after three thirty in the morning and he felt awake, and alive.

———

At eight thirty that morning, Jenkinson left his office with three staff. They had been briefed. Jenkinson had made one call to Roberts' manager, Commander Steve Payne, another man who Roberts could take or gladly leave. If he had heard the discussion that took place, he might have altered his thoughts about his boss.

"Need I remind you, Commander, that I am sanctioned as the head of the Metropolitan Police Directorate of Professional Standards to carry out investigations into our own people – those that have chosen to cross the line, and in the case of your man Roberts, someone who has done it spectacularly?" He hissed like a cornered alley cat.

"No, Phil, you needn't do that. But what I ask is that you afford DCI Roberts the same levels of respect as you would any other officer, or member of the public for that matter. Remember, the police are the public and all that. And Jason is a senior staff member, innocent until proven guilty, Phil. Let's not forget that."

"Of course. I live and die by Sir Robert Peel's Principles of Policing – you should know that."

"Phil. I'm deadly serious here. Carefully cross and dot them all or you will have me to answer to. Jason Roberts is a good man with very good people around him."

"Sounds like a threat, Steve."

"It's a promise, Phil. And it's Commander to you."

"Thank you. I consider myself chastised, Commander."

Jenkinson tapped the red icon on his phone. "Bastard."

The Professional Standards team arrived at Roberts' house an hour later. Hemmed in by early traffic, they had driven past the crime scene that had claimed his wife. Jenkinson paid it momentary attention and had then returned to his notes.

———

In the hallway of his expensive semi-detached, Jason Roberts stood, trying to focus, working out why he was holding a carton of milk instead of his phone, when it rang, next to him, on a white shelf over a radiator.

"Jack, how's things mate?" he said dispassionately.

"I should be asking you that, my friend. Carrie and I are on the way over. Get the kettle on. Do you need anything?"

"Looks like someone has beaten you to it. There's a car just pulling onto the driveway. Oh Jesus, no! Of all the people I don't want to see right now. How far away are you? I may need some back-up."

"Is this for real, we can make some serious progress if we need to?"

"Sadly, not the sort of back-up where you check your watch, swallow hard, and hope you get there in time. In this case, it's nothing more than that Judas Jenkinson and his merry men."

"Phil Jenkinson?" asked O'Shea.

"The same, Carrie, and he doesn't look very merry."

"That's a worry, the only time that man ever smiles is when he's about to piss on someone's parade," said O'Shea knowingly.

"Yep. And he's brought three other coppers with him. Listen, I'll leave the phone on hands-free. I trust this bastard about as much as I trusted Alex Stefanescu." He laughed a nervous laugh, still reeling from the day before, his head felt as if it was stuck in an old rusty vice that might never open and his eyes were still raw, sensitive to the light.

He opened the door and tried to gain the upper hand, grabbing some resolve from somewhere.

"Good morning, Phil. I must say you are an unexpected visitor. I take it you've heard about what happened yesterday? In which case, if this is work, can it wait?"

Cade began to accelerate a little more. He was known for his intuition, and as Roberts had said on more than one occasion, for his propensity to act as a complete and utter shit magnet.

"Jason Roberts," said Jenkinson in an ice-cold voice, as his three suited henchmen stood behind him, almost ready for trouble.

"Well, yes, the last time I looked. Look mate, I'm in no fit state to play games. I haven't slept and unless you've been under a rock, my wife was..." He paused, swallowed hard, could feel his eyes burning again: "...blown to bits yesterday." He began to cry.

Cade had heard enough. "Hang on, Carrie."

"Jason Roberts..." the chief superintendent continued.

"Listen mate, I think we've established what my name is. Now, unless you want to crack on with whatever it is that you've come here for, I'm going to close the door on you and we'll have a little chat about this when I get to work, from bereavement leave, you know, when I have buried what is left of my wife." Anger was over-taking the tears.

Jenkinson was emotionless. "I am arresting you on suspicion of the murder of Catherine Mary Roberts at Staines Road, Ashford on..."

Roberts could hear noises. Dates and places, but nothing made sense.

"I am also arresting you on suspicion of the murder of an unknown male at..."

He listed the full wording of the offence, then the caution.

"...it may harm your defence if you do not mention when questioned, something which you later rely on in court. And that anything..."

Cade yelled down the phone. "Jason, say nothing! Do nothing. I will be with you in three."

He turned to O'Shea. "Get Payne on the phone. Then the Federation. This can't be happening, Carrie." He dropped the car into third and accelerated past a fixed speed camera which flashed at him mockingly.

"...you do say..."

"Boss, it's Carrie. Do you know why Phil Jenkinson is at Jason Roberts' place, arresting him?"

"I do, Carrie. But I cannot discuss it with you over the phone. Get back here as soon as you can, bring Jack if he's listening. It's not good."

"...may be used in evidence..."

Jenkinson, ever the closet coward, moved out of the way as his two sergeants stepped forward to take Roberts into custody.

He pulled away, and yelled: "No, this is not happening. Not here, not today! My wife. My wife. Can you not hear what I am saying to you?"

The two sergeants were joined by the third as they took Roberts to the ground, applying one link of the speed cuffs to his wrist. Rather than fight anymore he lay there sobbing, desperately trying to inhale, his head turned away from the people he thought were his colleagues, looking across the road where the curtains twitched.

Cade pulled up outside number thirty-two and got out, leaving O'Shea to frantically dial the Police Federation.

"Yes, that's right, a DCI on our team. He's been arrested by Professional Standards. Yes. For murder times two. Yes, you heard me right. He's going to need representation and a good solicitor. Who made the arrest? Chief Superintendent Jenkinson."

O'Shea nodded. "Yes, him."

On the driveway, Jenkinson was smiling the smile of a hungry jackal.

"Mr Cade, you interfere with this arrest and I will have you locked up for obstruction. Am I making myself clear? Under Section..."

"You, of all people, do not need to quote sections and subsections to me, but you do need to explain what the hell you think you're doing. You three, this is a DCI from your own force, yesterday he...look at him... look at yourselves!"

"Oh Cade, do stop with your snake oil selling and get out of our way. He'll be at the central custody suite. I'll get him a cup of sweet tea. But right now, he's got a whole lot more to worry about. Out of my way."

"You can at least tell me what this is all about? You owe me that much."

Jenkinson wafted his hand in front of Cade's face, as if he were swatting a bluebottle from his freshly cooked lunch.

"Cade, I'm one of those rare people that has a long memory. It serves me well. As for my actions today, let's use an analogy. I'm also one of those people that can't walk past a piece of dog shit on the pavement without having the urge to pick it up and put it in the bin. Same rules apply here."

He stared at Cade, cleaning the gleaming caps of his brown leather shoes on the back of his trousers.

"Move, or else. And as for your rights? I don't have to tell you anything. Go on, go. Last chance."

Cade let him walk to his car, then blocked the path, held out an arm in front of the two DSs.

He whispered.

"Boys, just a second. I am still an inspector as far as the Prime Minister herself is concerned. And this man is a member of our team. I want ten seconds with him. That's all."

The older of the two said in an equally low tone: "As we walk, boss, but no longer, please. Our boss doesn't suffer fools."

"Jason, I need to know if you have anything to do with this?"

Roberts stared at him, his reddened eyes emphasising his own natural colour. "I can't believe you are even asking me that."

"That's all I needed to hear. Stay strong. I will move mountains to get this sorted. You have to trust me."

Roberts, head down, hands in front, rigidly cuffed, just sobbed. "I do. It's everyone else I don't."

---

# CHAPTER THIRTEEN

---

## ROOM WITH A VIEW

THE TIME-SERVED CUSTODY SERGEANT ACCEPTED ROBERTS INTO his care and read him his rights; told him things he'd told others for years.

Roberts nodded, and signed what he needed to sign.

"You have the right to notify someone that you are in custody, Mr Roberts," said the sergeant, trying to be as reasonable as he could. Innocent until proven guilty, especially one of his own with their reputation.

"There'll be no need for that, sergeant," said Jenkinson haughtily. "That's already been done. A civilian member of another police team is aware. They were present at the arrest."

Roberts lifted his head and looked at Jenkinson. What he'd give for a few moments in a quiet corner somewhere.

"I would like my wife's parents notifying that I am here please, sergeant."

"No. That will not happen. That is witness intimidation. He's had his rights. Cell Three looks available." Jenkinson began to walk Roberts towards a dark green door down the pale green corridor. "Sergeant?" said Roberts in as loud a voice as he could muster. "I didn't do this. I need you to write that down. I would not, and could not, have done this. My in-laws are not witnesses to this horrendous act. This man has no evidence against me whatsoever. This is a witch hunt. I lost my *wife* yesterday. You've no doubt read the papers. The mother to my two wonderful children. If you put me in that cell, I will do everything in my power to kill myself."

"Guilty admission if ever I've heard one," Jenkinson smirked.

"No. Just the words of a broken man. If I were you, sergeant, I'd put me in the suicide cell, where you can watch over me twenty-four hours a day – if you intend to keep me that long."

Sergeant Matt Ratana looked at Jenkinson. It was clear he didn't like him or respect him. This was a rare battle in the police hierarchy; a sergeant in charge of the custody suite, could almost outrank anyone in the system, except a superintendent and above. Jenkinson knew it.

Ratana was a solidly built New Zealander who had left the North Island some years earlier to work in the Met Police in a job he adored. He was good at it too, a natural people person, he was the type to stand his ground with people, especially those as disrespectful as the man trying to dominate him now.

"Sergeant, need I remind you that as per PACE I have outlined the reason for Mr Roberts' detention, that I wish to interview him soon and that any delay is likely to lead to interference, or harm to, evidence connected with the offence of murder?"

"No, sir, you needn't. However, Mr Roberts will, of course, require legal representation."

"I also consider that delaying that interview may lead to physical harm to other people, further serious damage to property, or alerting anyone else suspected of aiding and abetting that offence. Do you have any further comments, sergeant?"

"Not for you, sir, no, but I have one for DCI Roberts."

"Mr Roberts for now," Jenkinson grinned mercilessly.

"DCI Roberts, for my own records, are you happy to be interviewed about the offences alleged, without delay and without legal representation?"

"No. No, I am not, and I wish you to add this to my custody record."

Ratana carefully added every word. He ran a very tight team and did everything by the book, to the last full stop. The only complaints his team ever received were spurious at best – they came with the territory, and right now, if he could spend a minute with Roberts, he would be encouraging him to lodge one as soon as possible.

"Just get the paperwork sorted, would you, sergeant?"

"All in good time, sir, I'm sure even you would agree that this is somewhat unusual and that we should be seen to do absolutely everything to the letter of the law."

"I am trying to do just that. Come on, the clock is ticking."

"Correct. However, I am not happy that Mr Roberts is proceeding without access to legal advice, and as the record will state, neither is he. Therefore, under Annex B of PACE..."

"Do not proceed to outline Annex B, section A, paragraph 3 to me. I practically wrote the PACE Codes of Practice." Jenkinson's face was crimson.

Ratana, who was physically intimidating, stood his ground and gave him a confident smile. "Respectfully, sir, you didn't." He added in a soft kiwi twang. "And I maintain that Mr Roberts has the right – and should be allowed to exercise that right now, at any point during his detention and certainly before any court hearing."

"You are starting to test my patience, sergeant."

"Good, that means I am doing my job – I wouldn't want professional standards criticising me now, would I, sir?"

"I believe, sergeant, that Mr Roberts' solicitor is likely to inadvertently, or otherwise, pass on a message to parties that will interfere with evidence, cause harm to persons, et cetera. Need I continue?"

"Please do. I also know the section word for word, but I will be making notes in the record that you are declining Mr Roberts' right to legal representation..."

"Good." He cut him off abruptly.

"I haven't finished, sir. And I shall also add comments to the effect that you have declined such representation, despite the fact that Mr Roberts has yet to nominate any solicitor, let alone one you object to." He stared at Jenkinson, carefully placing the piece on the chessboard, watching his every move and facial expression.

"Mr Roberts, do you have a solicitor you would like to nominate?"

"No one in particular, I've never needed one apart from my will. The Police Federation on-call will be fine."

"Is that acceptable to you, Superintendent Jenkinson?"

The senior officer was biting his lip, so much so it bled.

"I'll take that as a yes. Mr Roberts, please sign here stating I have outlined your rights and that you wish a solicitor to be notified immediately, sir."

"Interview Room Four looks free, sergeant, book him out to myself and Detective Inspector Cooper, who has joined me for this interview." Jenkinson walked quickly, a man with a purpose. Then he stopped and theatrically turned around.

"Sergeant, my sincere apologies. Roberts, you need to hear this too. I'd also like this documenting, immediately below your last question. Then you can ask him again if he's willing to be interviewed."

"Go on, sir..."

"I completely forgot to mention that I am in possession of a series of emails that indicate that the murder of Catherine Mary Roberts was planned." He craned his neck and face towards Roberts – a grey heron to a goldfish in an ornamental pond.

"And that those emails were sent to the Metropolitan Police by Mr Roberts who it seems had decided to do the decent thing and save his former colleagues a great deal of hard work by confessing to the murder of his wife, and a poor unfortunate who happened to be in the wrong place. A kindly Samaritan, killed because he cared."

"Prove it, can you?" It was Cade who'd entered the custody suite with John Daniel.

"I suggest you take your Doberman back upstairs JD, you really have no dog in this fight, apart from him."

"He has a point, though, Phil. Can you? Given that you are railroading his rights to a fair investigation. If I were his defence solicitor, I'd be wrapping you up in knots by now."

"Yes, JD, but you see, you're not, are you? I'm not even sure what you are these days. And any disclosure to the defence will start, at the very beginning, with what I might be inclined to call, my ace in the pack. The one you hold firmly downwards on the card table – you must remember the first cough you got, JD, all those years ago? Such an empowering feeling. For the benefit of everyone here, the only person that can open a police-issue phone is the person who it's issued to."

"Not necessarily," offered Cade, fishing for time, praying the legal rep would arrive soon.

"Nice. Loyal to the end, Jackie boy. Jason, I don't want you to answer this. In fact, I'm being more than kind by providing you a chance to concoct some ludicrous defence, so best you listen. Jason Roberts' police-issued phone was only able to be opened by finger-print identification. Jason, hold up your hands."

Roberts lifted his hands in a manner that said he was already defeated, convicted almost.

"Two thumbs, eight fingers. Agreed? Good. Disclosure done. Interview Room Four please, DI Cooper after you."

Roberts stopped in the doorway of the sterile room and looked back.

"Find the answers, Jack. For the sake of my children."

The door closed behind him, the first of many over the next twenty-four hours.

———

"Jason Roberts, as bail is not an option, you are hereby remanded in custody on the two charges of murder. How do you plead?"

'How do you think?' offered Cade quietly to himself in the public gallery where the young media hacks were feverishly making notes.

"Not guilty, your honour. Not guilty in any way, shape or form."

"Not guilty is sufficient, thank you. Gentlemen?" The judge nodded to the two court security staff who led Roberts away.

He tried desperately to remain calm and confident, despite Jenkinson staring at him, barely suppressing another smile.

All he could do was nod to Cade, who nodded back mouthing: 'This is not over.'

———

Three hours later Jason Roberts was added to the system at HMP Wandsworth in South West London. Imprisoned, he felt stripped of everything he'd ever known.

———

Built in 1851 in the classic style of all Victorian penal institutions, it could house up to sixteen hundred men on charges ranging from dishonesty to murder. Divided into five wings, from A to E, there was a mix of single and shared cells. Each wing had its own canteen and showers.

Roberts was fully documented, asked the same questions as everyone else, promised a level of protection due to his role, assured of a phone call and asked what he wanted for his evening meal.

"Nothing, thank you."

The smell of overcooked cabbage made Roberts feel nauseous as he sat on his bed, staring at the walls.

———

Ten minutes north of Wandsworth, the smell of a very different meal wafted through a luxurious apartment overlooking Chelsea Harbour.

This apartment cost fifteen thousand pounds, per *week*. He didn't flinch. His lawyer had seen to the necessary paperwork. All he had to do was sign it and he could move in the next day on a short-term lease, or as long as he required it.

The Romanian chef was young and eager, providing exactly what the new tenant wanted in both the kitchen and the bedroom; in the huge all-white walk-in shower and steam room, too.

The apartment had two balconies: one overlooked the harbour with its collection of mainly white cabin cruisers and a solitary yacht; the other, the River Thames.

He had always admired the architecture in London. Parts of it reminded him of the grandeur of his home city, Craiova. He loved the apartment's subtle cutaways – the hints to other rooms, where the vaulted ceilings gave way to more glass and white detail.

The kitchen sat on gleaming white marble tiles, the cabinets were white, bordered by a row of black leather and chrome barstools. The dining table was vast, all glass, with white chairs, ten of them.

The detail was exquisite. Hidden flat screen TVs were just a remote button push away in the lounge, the bedrooms and the bathrooms. Day beds adorned the main balcony, where if he chose to, he could lie, having a deep tissue massage, watching out across the south and west of the river. All with a view of Her Majesty's Prison, Wandsworth.

He had chosen the apartment for its elegant and understated sense of luxury, for its use of white. He liked white. He considered it an underrated colour. He felt it offered an insight into his current state of purity. Sober, they called it these days: off the gear, away from the drugs, divorced from his endless mistress, heroin, clean.

Half a dozen white mice scurried in a cage mounted on a shelf in the corner of the room. He didn't like any other colour and while they were not pets, he nurtured them carefully.

His master bedroom suite, reached by a small set of steps covered in white deep pile, was a feature that made any visitor gasp in awe. A huge bed, fit for four, looked out across the river.

He had never been happier, and for the man who had walked out of Belmarsh only a short time before, it could only get better.

He dismissed the chef for the evening and walked up to his bedroom, stood on the balcony, behind the blue tinted glass.

He could choose the oversized bed, where he could retire for the evening, or the day bed where he could lie, hoping someone might be looking at him as he propped himself up and picked up the phone and dialled.

A minute later, it connected to the switchboard.

"Hello. Metropolitan Police, how may I help?"

"Ah yes, good evening. I was wondering if you could put me through to Mr Jack Cade. I think the team he runs is called Orion."

The operator noted the strong accent, then checked the name, then the operation name. It existed. He clicked on a couple of links and asked: "Who can I say is calling, please?"

"An old friend. Tell him, it's an old friend."

## CHAPTER FOURTEEN

## NEW BEGINNINGS

ROBERTS WAS LYING IN HIS NEW CELL, IN HIS NEW BED, THE ONE that had been a sanctuary to countless men before him. For all he knew, he could have been responsible for putting some of those men there. The only saving grace was that the receiving officer at Wandsworth knew of Roberts' reputation, and rather than have a wounding, or worse, on 'his watch', he'd put him in a single-bedded cell. He'd get his own toilet too; a stainless-steel affair without a lid, and a limited supply of paper. Just enough to wipe his arse, but not enough to flood the cell with, one of the oldest tricks in the book.

His eyes were raw, yet they'd become acclimatised to the dark. He could see the painted bricks. He could hear the bed frame creaking with his every wistful move. He turned left, then onto his right, onto his back, then finally face down, desperate to try to rest to face the morning, to show strength, but equally willing to suffocate himself – if only he could. Not even the bloody pillows were willing to allow him to die.

He got up and paced. Laid down again. Stood, stepped towards the glass blocks that were concreted in so heavily it would have taken months to excavate them – they provided a hint of natural light so he pushed his eyes up to them, trying to focus on the world outside.

But there was nothing. Everything was distorted.

He heard the sobs of men down the landing. One even screamed out in his sleep. Some laughed, and here he was, Jason 'Ginger' Roberts, a detective chief inspector, banged up with the rest of this desolate lot. He was a father of two, now a widower, charged but not convicted, on remand, but potentially not forever. Waiting. Waiting for one man to make a decision. One man, to change his entire future. As if the actions of one man hadn't already done just that.

No, he would elect for trial by jury. *Jason, what are you thinking of man? You will be acquitted. Free.*

He was awaiting trial, not suitable for bail, locked up – tonight, and tomorrow and the next day, then the bloody day after that, and then what?

He paced again. He laughed now, too. He'd once seen an old lioness at London Zoo, marching back and forth just like he was. He was looking for answers to questions he didn't even know, back and forth, forwards and back again. He closed his eyes, there she was again, her ageing limbs and scabby skin, signs that she was about to give up, far from the graceful big cat she had once been, but still pacing.

Somewhere a faceless man whistled and called out Roberts' name. They knew he was here.

"Jason... oh Jason..."

Up and down. Sleep. Wake. Stare. Cry.

———

"Yes, I will hold," the calm, accented voice said.

"Putting you through now."

"Hello?"

"Hello, Jack. It's been a while."

The smallest hairs on Cade's neck bristled.

"It has indeed. And how are you?" He was fishing for time, trying to allow himself the upper hand, trying to identify the voice. He waved to O'Shea, miming *get over here now, I need you to listen to this.*

She threw a dressing gown on over her pyjamas and sat next to Cade as he put the phone onto loudspeaker.

"Fishing for time, Jack? That's not like you. You always struck me as a..." He paused. "What's the word? A maverick. You know, with the name Jack Cade. He was a rebel, wasn't he? If memory serves me well. I read about him in the library. You know, the library? The place that has books?"

"Yes, I'm familiar with such a room. Now, how can I help you?"

O'Shea was pacing now, too. She knew it was him. She turned a bedside light on. She didn't want to ever be in the dark again with him, not after their last meeting. She could feel the tears welling up, waiting to flood.

She mouthed, *It's him*. She paced the same route on the deep carpet, backwards and forwards, each foot following the one before, around and around.

Cade nodded. "OK, so you found me, what do you want, Nicolescu?"

"A bit rude. I called you Jack, the least you could do is call me by my proper name. I've earned that much surely, even the British justice system has seen to it that I have been released. A free man."

"That's debatable. It's late. I'll ask you again, then I'll hang up, I've got a long day tomorrow."

"Yes, you have. No doubt it will start with Blue Mountain coffee, perhaps a run down the embankment to clear that head, a shower, with your lover. Hi Carrie, how are you, my darling?" He laughed.

"I find that Blue Mountain is not bitter enough for me, Jack. I like bitterness, it suits me. Nice flat, by the way. If you stand on tiptoes, you could almost see Jason's new room. Wandsworth, wasn't it?"

O'Shea shook her head. How did he know this? This was ludicrous.

"Anyway, I just wanted to say hi, see how you were doing. You know, Carrie, what happened at the old factory, it was just a bit of fun, I think you know that by now. Tell me, do you rub rose hip oil into the scar? You should. I use it on all of mine, just lightly massage it in, round and round..."

"What do you want?" asked Cade firmly.

"I want you to say sorry, Jack. Carrie has, she bears the beautiful kiss I left upon her. Cynthia said sorry too, just before she slipped away. And the man who stamped on my wrist and left me with this peculiar appearance; an affected man was how one of the guards at Belmarsh put it. Camp almost! He wouldn't know camp from David."

"Can I ask you a question, Nicolescu?"

"Absolutely."

"If I say sorry, can I go back to sleep and forget all about this?"

"Ha ha, you mean 'Can I have my girlfriend Carrie up against the window again? Oh, don't stop! That's so good darling, do it again! Oh, yes!' Yes, of course you may go to sleep. You will need to rest for tomorrow. You get to make the first decision."

"What?"

"Not what, Jack, pay attention. Who? You get to decide who."

"You've lost me."

"Then find a way out of the maze, dear boy. Leave a trail of crumbs, just like Alice. Three rules to this game."

"It was Hansel and Gretel. And I didn't say I wanted to play."

"But you have no choice."

"I have every choice." A cross court volley with spin.

"Well, yes, that much is true. You do have three choices. And your first will be tomorrow. Now, are you ready for the rules?" A plunging, lobbed reply that was almost unplayable.

Cade felt something tugging deep inside his stomach. Why hadn't he killed him when he had the chance? Why did he not brief his contact – the contractor, to fire the second round, when he had the chance on that rain-soaked night?

"Go on, it's clear I won't get to sleep until you have your little game."

"Little? Hardly, unless like mine you consider a life to have limited value? No, you need to be aware that these are the rules. Number one, no cameras. Wherever you go, I will go, and I will know. But your team must not."

"Hardly fair." He knew he was in danger of poking the grizzly.

"Number two, no cell phones. Not even one hidden up your arse. You know, I knew that happened in prison, but had never really considered it possible until I was sent to Belmarsh. But I was so glad it was. I would have been somewhat marooned without a phone in prison. Not a smell I miss though, but what is it they say about the devil?"

"Needs must when the devil drives, I believe," Cade replied.

"Spot on. On that subject, number three, no cars. Public transport only. Just like I had to that day when you all made me run through the city like a wounded lion."

"More a Manx cat, you know the ones with the very short tail." Bear, poked.

"Jack, I've missed you. If I had been you that night, I would have just dropped me into the river, let me wash up with the man who you thought was the boss. You have no idea, do you?" He laughed.

"Was there a rule four?"

"Oops, yellow card for Inspector Cade. You can only ask a question once."

"That's five rules."

"Is that a question or a statement?" He was enjoying this now, almost aroused, lying on his day bed staring upstream towards Cade's bedroom. He ran his spare hand across his body.

"That feels nice, Jack, please don't stop. Did you know your man had fantasies about being with another man, Carrie?"

"Well then, that wouldn't be with you then would it, you piece of worthless shit." She spat the words out, her breathing was shallower by the second.

"Ah, so you *are* there, I wasn't sure. I think the phrase would be *you worthless piece of shit*. I spent hours learning your beautiful language in the prison library. Lovely to see you haven't lost your fishwife persona, Caz. How's the hair looking, must have grown back by now?"

"Better than your teeth. And only my brother called me Caz." Nice shot by O'Shea, catching Nicolescu under the ribs.

"Wow, Catherine, that was rather cruel. I didn't know you had a brother. I shall add him to my list. I have a date with a dentist, she's going to sort them all out. Heroin, you see, it rots many things other than the mind. I can afford the work, now the will has been read. Right, I need to finish what I've started, lying here watching you two lovebirds has got me just in the mood. Catch you in the morning, John Cade."

"It's Jack."

"I thought that was only to your friends. I am honoured, Jack. Tomorrow, then, Westminster Bridge, nine a.m., and wear something red."

"Why, are you hoping for something nice from Santa?"

"Hardly. Moş Nicolae as we called him, stopped visiting me when I was six. He said I was naughty. No, red is just so that I can pick you out in the crowd." He made a noise like a high-velocity round. The last time Cade had heard such a sound, it had been up river from where he was now. It had been the end of a chaotic period in his life, a scab that had yet to heal. Constantin had just pulled the top off it, allowing it to bleed slightly.

"And don't bother ringing your team to trace the call... I'm so far ahead of you it's embarrassing. Now go to bed or give that girl what she wants, so I can enjoy it too. And the old couple across the water, you are probably the highlight of their dull and boring little lives these days. You really should be more careful, you never know who is watching, cameras everywhere. Just you, and no phones, and what was the last one, Jack?"

"No cars."

"Good boy. And no bread crumbs either. Consider me the wicked witch, Jack."

"Didn't she end up being pushed into the oven by the young girl?"

"You know your old fairy tales!"

"As far as you are concerned, yes."

"Naughty Jack – as they say nowadays, I see what you did there. Anyway, I've got something to do. Night."

———

The room went silent. O'Shea was standing by the window, tightening the dressing gown cord around her middle, shuddering slightly, a chill breeze making her shake involuntarily.

"Do you really think he is out there, Jack? Even listening to us now, watching?" she whispered.

"It's gamesmanship, Carrie. Come on, you beat him once before and together we can do this again."

"Did I? Really. I'm glad that's what you think, that time is already healing me, well trust me, it isn't, OK?"

Constantin watched, listened, stayed very quiet, a hint of paranoia convincing him they could both hear him. He was wrong, he had the upper hand, and from where he sat, it looked like Cade's world was starting to crumble. A few more weeks of pressure and the girl would crack too. Turn the screw, Constantin, and watch it bite into her skull.

He twisted the imaginary screwdriver, tighter and tighter until his knuckles were blanched and her head cracked open.

"But what about tomorrow, at nine, on Westminster Bridge? What was all that about?"

"I have no idea."

"But you'll be there?"

"No, not at all. Not unless I am given a compelling reason."

He looked at her, sat on the edge of the bed, knees together, fists balled. What had that bastard done to his once confident girlfriend?

She looked back, intuitive as ever. "You have no idea."

―――――――――

## CHAPTER FIFTEEN

―――――――――

## WITHOUT A TRACE

He showered, then left his Chelsea apartment. He'd moisturised, then sanitised. Prison did that to a man: an air of obsession and compulsion could easily become the norm – all encompassing. Sometimes he would sit in his new shower for an hour, the one with the rainfall attachment. It was a place of tranquillity for the man from Craiova.

He had chosen black: black chinos, black polo, black jacket and black shoes. He even wore a black Nike baseball cap, and carried a black backpack, which contained all he needed.

Black. Unlike his home, which was pure white. The contrast amused him. He plipped the remote, down in the garage, entered his charcoal black Mercedes AMG and drove out into the quiet London streets.

He knew he needed to set the tone for the next few weeks. There was never any point threatening to do something if you didn't have the means or the motivation. Constantin Nicolescu had both.

He needed to send a message. One that would make Jack Cade sit up, pay attention, and importantly, abide by the rules.

He didn't consider Cade entirely responsible for his misery. In fact, in one aspect, Cade had done him an enormous favour, had even led to him having the lifestyle he now had, which was almost perfect. He missed just one person in his life, but that had ended badly and not at all as he had hoped. He could at least blame Cade for that.

In the hour he'd sat in the shower and the steam room, he'd thought about what he was about to do, gathering his thoughts and means. Then, motivation in place, he'd packed what he needed, and now found himself listening to his most cherished Rachmaninoff piece, *The Isle of the Dead,* on the speaker system.

He liked the car very much. It was more than he could have ever dreamed of owning, growing up as a small boy in a strict home in Romania.

The C Class AMG was not his first choice. He wanted its bigger brother, the GTS, but it was too obvious, too 'look at me'.

The C Class provided him with comfort and performance if and when he needed it. With its three-litre, twin-turbocharged engine, it did exactly what he told it to do, when he told it to. In a city such as London, it was anonymous, all the time, even more so on cloned plates.

He tapped the destination into the onboard navigation system: forty minutes at the speed limit, which he would obey; no point in attracting unnecessary attention.

He diverted to an industrial area, finding exactly what he was looking for: simple, yet effective.

The car rolled to a stop in the next street. He parked under a tree, away from the amber street lamps, pulled the brim of his cap down, the collar up, wrapped a scarf across the lower half of his face, grabbed his backpack and walked towards his target.

———

Ricky Chamberlain was on early shift the next day. A creature of habit, he had showered and headed to bed bang on nine thirty. It was dark, and needing to be up at five meant he was already counting the hours before the wave sounds from his phone announced the start of a new day.

He lived alone; had done since his wife had left him. She took the kids, left him with the cat, and the knackered old blue Fiat.

He was renting his current place, but hoped one day to meet someone and start all over again. His job had become his distraction. Living forty minutes north of work meant that by the time he was twenty minutes away, he wasn't just halfway home, he was in a totally different mind space, where listening to true crime podcasts had become his go-to.

With a sleeping tablet on board, he was out like a light, bang on nine thirty. He didn't hear the back door open. The cat did, arching its back until the man in black calmed it with a soothing tone.

The small flat was in a larger Victorian property in Edgware. It belonged to Chamberlain's sister, Liz, who was abroad, living the dream.

Consisting of a lounge, kitchen, bathroom, study and one bedroom, Chamberlain found it ideal. It was a place to entertain if he should ever be so lucky, but also somewhere he could afford on his average salary.

He was a heavy sleeper, lying on his back with his mouth wide open, snoring incredibly loudly. He slept in boxer shorts and a T-shirt, on top of the bed, as he did every night.

Constantin crept around the room, his heart beating heavily, hooking one end of the orange-coloured ratchet strap to the side of the bed, then laying it gently across Chamberlain's inert body. He liked this part of his life very much.

He attached it onto the opposite side, then increased the pressure, leaving his victim lying on his back, with one arm up on the pillow and the other down by his side. The orange strap passed over his chest, pinning the top half of his body in place. When Nicolescu locked the ratchet, Chamberlain was secured.

Next, he ran a length of duct tape across his mouth. He was now awake. A second strap secured Chamberlain's thighs, a move Nicolescu had practiced until he could perform in the half-light of an unfamiliar room.

The curtains were drawn, and only a shard of light entered the room from the nearby street lamp.

Nicolescu opened a side pocket on the small pack and removed a leather device. He ripped the duct tape away, folded it in half and placed it back into the backpack, then wrapped the black leather straps around the back of Chamberlain's head and pushed the plastic tube deep into his mouth, forcing his tongue out of the way.

Chamberlain was motionless now, terrified: the captive and the captor. How their roles had changed.

When Nicolescu turned on the bedroom light, Chamberlain tried to shout out, to scream but instead made a pathetic gurgling sound.

"Shh. It's OK. I'm here now, Senior Officer Chamberlain. Relax."

He held his hand over the tube to quell the sound.

"Now stop that or I will squeeze your nostrils together too, and then you will just suffocate, and that will be the end of a wonderful evening in which I am your guest, you are my host, and we all just get along and have a lovely time." He affected an English privately educated accent, which added to the menace.

"Good. You have stopped. Discipline does that to a person. And I should know, as you disciplined me enough, you horrid man!"

He slapped him playfully on the face. "Not too hard, we don't want to spoil those chiselled good looks, do we, Ricky?"

He walked to the curtains and pulled them closer together, slightly aware of the possibility of someone looking in. He wanted to be alone with this man, but for reasons so dark and depraved they almost upset him.

"Now, listen, please, because we may only get one take here. I'm going to switch the camera on and we are going to send a lovely message to an old friend. OK? Great."

He pulled the phone from his pocket and tested it.

"Time to prepare a few things, then we can make a call. You stay there. Are you hungry?"

Chamberlain shook his head. Thought about screaming again, but knew that his captor held the advantage in every possible way.

Nicolescu removed the glass tube and extracted the piece of gauze with stainless steel tweezers.

Tape, ratchet straps, gag, two pairs of tweezers, two bottles containing gauze, a scalpel, a monopod, a rolled-up pack of white material, a number of white cylindrical devices, a marker pen and a bottle of cola, that was all he needed. He travelled light and left in darkness.

How he'd obtained what the gauze held was neither here nor there. That he had, for a price that would remain strictly between the seller and the buyer, was all that mattered to him. A steroidal alkaloid – it was chemistry, but chemistry at another level.

He placed the alkaloid carefully back into the container.

"*Phyllobates*. Or to be extremely accurate, *Phyllobates terribilis* is one of the most toxic creatures known to man. In layman's terms, the golden poison dart frog is deadly. Bred in captivity they are considered non-toxic and have become highly prized by collectors."

He spoke as if lecturing a room full of chemistry students who hung off his every word, whereas Chamberlain was a student who wanted to be a truant.

For Constantin, the relative toxicity of what he held was of paramount importance and the utmost interest. Why buy a Ford when you needed a Ferrari?

The golden poison dart frog, or terrible dart frog, was the finest model you could ever lay your hands on, even if that act alone could kill you.

He'd once spent a rewarding evening in the prison library, marvelling at how the native Pacific coastal Colombians would expose the frogs to heat from a fire, and extract the poison that is secreted on their backs, coating their arrows and darts before they set out to hunt.

Now Constantin was the hunter. The swab that he held and admired may have had secretions coated onto it many years before.

"I like alkaloids, you see, Ricky. Underrated. They began to fascinate me in prison many years ago. Alkaloids and explosives. Never together, you understand. That would be..." He thought for a second as he looked into Chamberlain's wide eyes. "That would be like the sledgehammer and the nut."

As he had mouthed the word 'nut', he had traced the word into his prisoners' stomach, marvelling at how Chamberlain had recoiled.

"Don't be afraid. I'm not going to torture you, Ricky. I'm many things, but not a torturer." He paused again, deep in thought.

"Actually, I think there are a few people that might argue with that statement. Do you know Carrie O'Shea? Now, there's a lady who would disagree. I clean forgot. I need to ring them. That was one of the reasons why I am here at your lovely home, that and to teach you some manners."

Chamberlain gurgled again, trying to swallow, desperate to lubricate his arid throat.

"Would you like a drink? We must be careful not to choke you. I can't sit you up, so you will have to have drops. Do you like cola? Of course, everyone likes cola."

He unscrewed the cap and very gently tipped a few drops into the plastic tube. They ran quickly to the back of Chamberlain's throat as he frantically tried to swallow. Constantin thought about tipping the whole bottle down the tube, just for fun, but as he had said, he wasn't there to torture his victim, just humiliate him.

He took a small amount of the cola and swilled it around his mouth, it tasted sweet and he needed the sugar.

"This is an experiment. I am conducting a study, Ricky, on the fundamental differences between batrachotoxin and tetrodotoxin. I may even write an essay, perhaps finally get my degree. Now, depending on the nature of Jack's answers, you will either get to experience the first one or the second. Fun, yes?"

He attached the phone to the monopod, pointing it at Chamberlain and then pressed the light icon. The LED lit up the tube, revealing the back of his throat.

Then, leaving the light on, he pressed the green phone icon.

He unwrapped the sterile scalpel.

"Shiny! So sharp. Won't be a second."

He lowered the tool into the tube until it was resting on the back of Chamberlain's throat, then nicked it twice, making it bleed, before adding a few drops of the cola down the slippery tube.

"Wash that nasty taste out of your mouth. I want a great review, after all. 'Constantin was a dream to work with.'" He laughed. It was genuine.

———

Forty minutes to the south east, Cade's phone began to tremble. It was a private number: FaceTime.

"Could be anyone. I'll leave it," he said, laid with his arm under his pillow, looking at O'Shea, who stared back, wishing they were somewhere else. New Zealand seemed like a good bet.

"It could. Or it could be *someone*..."

She smiled. "It's fine. Answer it."

He sat up and pressed talk. O'Shea shuffled up the bed so she could watch from an angle.

"Hello."

"Jack! Good of you to join us. I'm not alone, are you?"

"No."

"You know who this is?"

"Sadly, yes. What do you want?"

"A bit rude. Shall we try again?"

"No, we shall not. It's late and I have an important meeting at nine tomorrow morning."

"Well done. Yes, you do. Hi, Carrie. Looking good there, lovely cleavage, not my type, but I can see why Jack enjoys your company, after all, I do admire the finer things in life, but maybe you should go and put something on, we don't want Jack distracted, like he almost was last night, do we? Well, to put it another way, until you said no. Is everything OK with you guys? You seem a little tense."

O'Shea looked at Cade off camera, swore under her breath. He *was* watching them. She banged her fists together so the knuckles clashed and became sore.

"Look, Nicolescu, just do what you came to do and leave me alone," said Cade, one eye on the screen, the other on O'Shea.

"But you asked for a sign, a message, what was it you said? Yes, you wanted a *reason* to not be late in the morning. Well, let me introduce you to Rick."

He kept the monopod and camera facing the inert male, running from his chest upwards to his head. Cade could make out a bright orange nylon strap across the man's torso.

"Can you see? Good, then I shall begin. You may be wondering why I've rung you. Well, I can't ring Jason as he's in prison, and they don't allow prisoners to have cell phones. Well, not entirely true, the very naughty boys get to have them. Anyway, time is of the essence, so, watch and learn."

He never showed his face, but both Cade and O'Shea knew it was him. They'd both had their own close dealings with him, and both wished him dead, in differing but equally painful ways.

"Batrachotoxins and homobatrachotoxins are as you know steroidal alkaloids, and dear me, they are nasty. The rather beautiful golden dart frog that this was harvested from is known to produce enormous quantities of these compounds, nature at her worst. You still with me, Jack? Carrie?"

Cade turned his head towards O'Shea and whispered words in quick succession as they both stared out of the window, paranoid now that he was watching them.

"Get to work and start collecting whatever information you can on this bastard. See if he had a release address from prison. Work out who Rick is, then do your magic stuff. Find his home address. Call the team in. This won't end well. Do not come back here. Pack the basics. Stay at the office if you have to, and Carrie, take care. Please."

"Jack, I asked you a question."

"I'm here."

"Known to be at least twenty times more toxic than other poison dart frogs. You know the difference between poison and venom of course, Jack?"

"Yes, but I'm not sure of the relevance. Why don't you let me know why you are doing this and we can try to resolve things?"

"Textbook, Jack. Did they teach you that in Nottingham or down here in London? It doesn't matter. What matters is what you say next. So be very careful about your choice of words. Now watch."

He opened the jar again and extracted the gauze, that white sleeve again. It had a familiar look, but Cade couldn't place it.

"This comes from the Colombian frogs; I could drink it all..."

"Then why don't you?"

"Cruel, Jack. Nothing would happen to me, it's all in the delivery. You are amusing, but cruel, and you know I cannot abide cruelty. If we inject it though, or say Rick had a mouth ulcer, then the toxins would be racing around his body before he even had time to think about his friends or family. It irreversibly increases the permeability of sodium ions in the nerve membranes and soon he would be paralysed. His body would sweat, his heart rate would slow right down, barely keeping him alive. Now pay attention please."

He lowered his face towards Chamberlain's, avoiding the camera by staying just far enough away. The edge of a white sleeve was all that was visible.

"Rick, the other most poisonous creature known to man is, a, a spider or, b, a bird. Or is it c, an octopus?"

Chamberlain frantically made a sound that had two syllables. Nicolescu knew exactly which word he was trying to say. His eyes were wide open and fixated on the man stood in the bedroom.

"You wish to phone a friend? Hang on, I've got Jack on the line from London. Hi, Jack." He giggled. "Actually, more of a kidnapping really, it's your host from *Who Wishes To Die This Evening*? And we have Rick in the studio with us. He can't speak very well, so I'll ask the question. Which animal, after the poison dart frog, is the most dangerous, a spider, a bird or an octopus?"

"And what if I get the answer wrong?"

"Then you forfeit Rick's life."

"Why?"

"Why not? He made my life hell, and everyone who has made my life hell will slowly come to terms with the fact that whilst I am still breathing, I will make it my goal to reward them in ways that are incredibly unpleasant. I've nothing else to do. I don't need to work. I have others to do that. Take Jason, for example. I don't have to lay a finger on him. I leave that up to his new friends in prison. They were expecting him, by the way. Sooner or later, he has to be alone. For his sake, I hope it's sooner. The waiting can kill you. Will it be today, or tomorrow, or the next day? You soon wish it would be right now."

Cade wiped his eyes. He stared out of the window, down onto the dancing reflections on the river, wishing his caller had drowned there.

"What do you want from me?" he snapped.

"An answer. Simple nature question. Or would you have preferred one on geography?"

"I find myself wishing you were history."

"I love what you did there, Jack." He held the gauze in the tweezers and lowered it down the black plastic tube.

"The answer is a bird. It's found in Papua New Guinea. It's poisonous, I read it somewhere, in an airport lounge whilst waiting for a flight. Now just let me help that man."

"Nice try. You are stalling for time so that your playmate can get some back-up organised. I've seen the films, Jack. No, the answer is not any of those things. It is humans, the most noxious creature of all."

He gently rubbed the gauze onto the back of Chamberlain's throat and stood back and watched, left the phone recording.

"Keep watching, my friend. No ambulance required, not even a doctor, no one will help Rick now, and you had the chance to save his life. So very sad."

"Why didn't you just shoot him, or strangle him? Something quick. Set fire to the house, for that matter. Good arsonists always like to watch the fire brigade arrive." He was still desperately hoping O'Shea had made it to the office, doing what she did best, finding the needle where there was no haystack.

"Well, yes, Jack, I could have done that, but you see great arsonists don't get caught, as you know, and I wanted to see his eyes. He used to look through the little hole in my door every night. I was only able to see one eye, but I knew he was smiling, then he'd deliberately kick the door, turn the handle one last time, knowing all the while that it was locked, with its big brass key and that awful sound of metal against metal. Am I making my point?"

"Not really. If your grudge is against me and my team, why not target us?"

"Fear not, I will be picking off the weaklings first. The trouble is, your team is full of such strong characters, so I need to experiment with some lab rats, and Rick here makes a perfect one. This stuff is evil, Jack. Just a tiny part kills a little white mouse, can kill a monkey, dead as a door nail. Whatever that means. What does that mean, Jack? Do tell."

"You know, it's just a question of time before you are back inside, don't you?"

"Inside?"

"Prison."

"I *know* what you meant!" he screamed down the phone.

He quickly calmed again. Reversing the poles.

Cade knew he had gained an advantage for a short time.

"You'll leave a trace, a hair. Knowing you, your DNA will be everywhere. We'll find you, it's what we do best. In fact, this conversation, this gruesome pantomime that you've put on for us, is evidence enough."

"Your word against mine, Jack. You have no proof. No video, no transmission to the world via the internet, a mocking five-minute exposé on this tube or that tube – just an audience of one. And unlike your normal enemies, I really don't care if I do leave a footprint."

"Mark my words, mate, this will come back to haunt you."

"I am not your mate, Jack. Not even friends. And I am already haunted by so many ghosts that another one will make no difference. I hardly sleep, so nightmares aren't likely either. Life for me is one long waking dream that I hope, one day soon, will end."

"I can help with that."

"You've tried at least twice before. You really do need more practice. The true English gent, who just doesn't quite have the killing instinct."

As he spoke, he removed the ratchet straps, unbuckled the face mask and carefully opened the marker pen and drew a letter B on Chamberlain's forehead.

"You may be wondering why I am writing a letter on his head? Simple, I like to keep pace with who and where."

"Alphabet killing is a bit clichéd, isn't it?"

"Yes, absolutely. I don't do passé; I prefer letters to numbers. If you were interested, I could be up to J by now."

He then asked Chamberlain, "Rick, any last words?"

Chamberlain tried desperately to speak, he could hardly close his mouth, unable to craft a sound, let alone a word, he was prone, like a hapless inflatable doll, and he knew his time was over.

He looked around the room, his eyes seemed to be the last thing to stop working, he could feel his entire body shutting down, cell by cell.

"Cells, Jack. His cells are shutting down. Do you get the joke? I hope so. I've waited weeks for this. See you at nine. Do not be late."

"And if I am?"

"Then the next person gets to try another way of dying. Needless really, but such fun. Look, Jack, this is not about revenge, it's about education and..."

"Money?"

"You offend me. I don't need money; Alex saw to that for me."

"And look at him now."

"Indeed. Ashes to ashes and all that. No, this is about having a bit of me time before it's too late. Nothing more, nothing less. I enjoy my work and if the dice roll in my favour, then I'll achieve what I want to achieve and be gone from your city by the time your friend Jason learns of his fate at the hands of a very nice judge."

Then he turned off the camera and packed the bag, leaving nothing behind but a memory and a headline in the next morning's papers.

Cade now had his compelling reason.

———

O'Shea reached the office by taxi, leaving the long-term hire car in the basement. It was a rare thing to have in inner-city London; a nice apartment and a car to match, and yet working for the government. Her boyfriend's other income came in handy from time to time.

She turned on the lights, powered up the computer, then rang Dave Francis.

"Hi mate. Sorry. I know it's late."

"I don't have anyone to disappoint, Carrie. What do you need?" He rolled over and looked at the digital clock. "Dear God. You really do owe me a decent coffee for this."

"Pick two up on the way in. Soon as you can, please."

"Anything I need to know?"

"Loads."

She tapped in the password. It hadn't changed since she'd left the Yard to head back to New Zealand with Cade. Or rather, since the time she almost left England for the other side of the world; finally getting to step onto his favourite deserted beach and feel the spray off the tops of the Pacific waves.

She truly hated Constantin. No wonder his father had abandoned him with his drug-dependent mother and left him to fend for himself. She wished his mother had drowned him when she had the chance.

She grabbed a marker pen and began writing on the nearby whiteboard. The fumes from the pen transported her back to the last operation she'd worked. It felt like a week ago.

The main lights flickered on.

"Alright sweetheart, what dragged the cat out of bed so early?" DS Del Murphy asked, sipping on a take-away cup filled with instant coffee and far too much sugar.

"You on nights, Del, or just here fashionably early?"

"Neither, Carrie. Just came in to pick up some stuff for my holidays." He looked at her. "Don't give me that look. I've seen that bloody look before." He sighed, placed the bag and coffee back onto his desk.

"Go on. What do you need?"

———

Constantin began to walk out of the room, but decided to open the curtains, and saw a glimpse of himself in the window; over his shoulder, the man who had mocked him so often, now lay taunted, rigid, mouth wide open.

He wished he'd let him live longer, to try a few more of his experiments, a hint of something less exotic to give his former jailer a hit to remember, something short-lived but painful, the starter before the main course. He doubted he'd ever done anything illegal in his whole life. But then, why give him any pleasure at all when the alternative was sheer misery and pain?

They would find him soon, of that there was no doubt. Cade was nobody's fool.

———

The Chemist walked back the way he had come, on the other side of the street. It was a deliberate walk, not too fast, and not too slow, away from the amber street lamps, his cap pulled down, collar up, and before long he was back at his car.

Emboldened by what had happened back in Chamberlain's bedroom, he had two choices: go home, or find another victim. All it took was the wrong look, the wrong thing said and the game could begin all over again, with any luck.

After all, he needed the practice if he was to become truly respected.

However, he had another meeting to attend before that could happen.

# CHAPTER SIXTEEN

## NORTH OF THE RIVER

Sixteen miles due south of Edgware, he stopped, next to a stretch of the Thames. It was called Dan Mason Drive, a secluded lane on the outskirts of the city, lined with trees, and discreet parking spaces for late night clandestine couples who ducked down to avoid the headlights.

There was a golf course to the north and to the south the river, where a rowing club had made their headquarters, no cameras, he'd been assured. The fact that the route he'd driven was lined with them did not matter; the car would soon be a thing of the past, new plates, back to its old identity. Why take risks that weren't necessary?

He stopped at the rear of the rowing club, next to which was a public lavatory, which was still open, despite recent damage and graffiti. He'd long outlived his desire to meet someone in the damaged cubicles with their smutty messages and sordid tales.

Tonight was simple: exchange clothes with the faceless man in the next cubicle by handing them over the top of his own, then leave before he did.

The man, separated by six or seven degrees of separation, knew what to do. He took the black chinos, polo shirt, jacket and black shoes. He also got a new Mercedes for his troubles, black like the baseball cap.

He'd leave when he got the signal, not before.

Constantin carefully ripped up every piece of the white paper suit, the one with the long white sleeves, taking time to flush it all away. Then, the hairnet. No gloves, that was the part he liked best – the part that would confuse Cade and his band of merry men. He needed to take *some* risks or it just wouldn't be fun.

The flush was the signal. Wait five minutes, from that moment, and not a second too soon. Just five minutes, and the car was his, and he liked the feel of the chinos too, and the cap. Life had just got better.

It had taken Constantin much less time to dress when he had reached Chamberlain's home than it had to dispose of the evidence. Again, why take risks?

He stopped for a moment outside, looked up at the night sky, breathed in the cool night air, coughed as quietly as he could, the drugs had damaged his lungs and it was an endless battle to draw in clean air.

He walked towards a car at the far end of the parking area. With the keys still in his pocket, he pressed the remote and saw the orange lights of the old Toyota flicker.

It wasn't what he had become used to, but it was a long way from his first car back in Romania. As he approached the driver's door, he heard footsteps in the gravel. He knew it wasn't the new owner of his car – his briefing had been very specific: leave at the same time as him or risk being his next victim.

The footsteps were soft, as if their owner was wearing running shoes. He could hear the breathing, which was equally quiet, quieter than his own. He pushed the blade of the car key up between his right index and ring fingers and stopped, then turned around sharply.

"Hello, you here for the same reason as me?" It was a local accent, hurried and almost accusatory.

Constantin looked at him for a moment, the shadowy half-light created by the security lamps at the rowing club. He was white, probably in his late thirties, a little overweight and unshaven. He wore blue jeans which were tattered at the hems, indicating that they spent far too long dragging on the floor. Perhaps he had lost weight? Perhaps he needed a belt?

"I'm sorry, I have no idea what you are talking about. Be safe my friend, there are some strange people about at this time of night. Now, if you don't mind, I must get going." He'd hoped it was enough to ward off the man.

"But hang on, I received your text, it said be at Dan Mason Drive, near the rowing club, just up from the toilets, look for an old Toyota. I'm ready for this." He waved his cell phone about, its screen lighting his face. He smiled eagerly. "Please."

"I have no idea what *this* is all about. I really must be going. Goodnight."

The male grabbed Constantin by the arm. He was stronger than he looked.

"Nothing to be ashamed of, pal. We're here for the same reason, so let's enjoy it shall we? Then we can go on our way."

"Please, let go of me. I have asked nicely. Trust me, I won't ask nicely again. Pal."

The man detected an accent, fairly strong too.

"Are you Russian? Wait 'til my mates hear about this. Cottaging with a bloody Russian!" He seemed genuinely excited.

"Cottaging? But I don't have a cottage. Now, let go and go and find someone else to play your games." He pulled away and turned towards the car, which had now locked itself.

"Mate, you know damn well what I'm talking about. It's my first time. It's taken me months to pluck up the courage. Do me a favour and show me a sign that you're excited. Come on... or are you shy too?"

He was far from shy and also knew exactly what the Londoner was talking about. It was just the wrong place and wrong time – and besides, he was of little interest, at a push, in the dark, drunk, maybe.

One thing Nicolescu had become very sensitive to was being mocked. When his own people had done it, not long ago, considering him an also-ran, he'd made a pact with himself to deal with it brutally, and here, stood before him was his chance to try out something new.

He reached out towards the man and ran his hand over the flies of his tattered jeans. "Nice. I guess we could have some fun before you head home to your wife. Yes?"

"I'm not married."

"You're all married. That's why you are here, down a lane near a public toilet in the middle of the night. I'd prefer you to be honest, it will help later."

"Later?"

"You'll see."

"I think I might like that." He was growing in confidence. "Tell me, is this your first time too?"

"No."

"So, you were here for me?"

"No. Look, let me explain, and I am giving you a chance to go home – I often feel hungry, but it doesn't always end up with me going to a restaurant, does it?"

"I guess not."

"Last chance, you can walk away." He hoped he would, he had more important things to do.

"No. I want this."

Now the man from Battersea was swallowing hard and could feel his heart racing, his throat drying. All he could do was nod.

"OK. Give me a second. Go over there into the golf course, we'll get started there, then we can go home and show your wife what good really feels like. But I want you to drop your trousers and underwear. You can keep your top on as it is so cold. The first thing you will feel will be me. Close your eyes if it helps. Deal?"

"Deal... but know we can both stop this at any time. Perhaps a panic word?"

"Trust me, you won't need one."

Constantin put his fingers up to the strangers' lips. "This way or nothing. Are you shy?"

"No." he replied hurriedly.

"Then go and prepare yourself for something really different."

The male walked up to a gap in a hawthorn hedge, quickly

looked back, climbed over a small wooden fence and stood by the large bunker that bordered the par five eighth hole. He talked to himself as he reached the bunker, the vast amount of pale sand acting as a reflector and the half-moon gently lighting the area whilst keeping the margins in darkness.

Constantin scanned the area with his eyes, up and down the road and across to a young couple who were out of sight, lying down in the passenger seat, hoping not to be seen.

A male appeared, dressed in black. Constantin ducked into the hedgerow and watched, waiting for him to get into the Mercedes and drive away. Nice car, and no longer his to worry about.

Now there were just the four of them on Dan Mason Drive.

Time was of the essence; he had no idea when the next eager local would arrive. The place was like a market for sex, and he considered himself above it these days. His nights of dirty, fumbling meetings in shadowy alleyways were long behind him. This was different; this was research.

He walked through the gap in the hedge, climbed over the fence, lowered the backpack onto the damp grass and removed one of the white cylindrical devices, carefully removing the cap, he slipped it into his back pocket, holding onto the other one. Then he prepped the third.

He approached the male. Quietly stepping across the grass as a predator stalks its prey. Gently now.

"Do you still have your eyes closed?" he whispered.

He nodded.

"Are you getting excited? Do you still want to do this? Don't turn around if you do. Just say yes, or no." It really was up to him: lots of questions, rapid fire.

The man struggled to speak; his throat dry.

"Yes."

"Good, then just look down and see how the moon illuminates you, doesn't it look amazing? Don't *you* look amazing? Tell me, truthfully, is this your first time?"

He nodded. Unable to speak.

"So how long have you known that you are bisexual? Or are you still just curious?"

"I was married when I was young... I was only nineteen."

"And before that?"

"Just once."

"With a man?"

"Yes, but it wasn't..."

"They all say that."

"I wanted my wife to be here."

"Ah, I see. But she doesn't want to play? Then you have just answered your own doubts. Tell me, what should I call you?"

"My real name or is this role play?"

"You choose."

"I'd like to be called Steve. My wife likes to be known as Suzie. Is that OK?"

"Absolutely, Steve, but Suzie isn't here right now, is she? Let's forget about her for now. Can you feel your heart racing?"

"Yes."

"I'm behind you now." The man jolted slightly; he had no idea that Constantin was quite so close. It was confirmed when the Romanian ran his left hand around the man's waist, slowly walking his fingers downwards.

"Oh my, you are excited, Steve, I can hear your heart beating really quickly. Are your eyes open or closed?"

"Whatever you want."

"I'd prefer them open for the next part."

"Then do it. I can't believe this is happening."

Constantin smiled and shook his head. "Neither can I."

Then with his right hand he rammed the EpiPen into Steve's neck, hitting him hard, holding it there, allowing it to deliver the contents of the ampoule into his body before dropping it into the sand.

Steve was shocked, grabbing his neck, trying to turn, trying to pull up his trousers, trying anything to comprehend what had just happened.

"Trust me, Steve, it will just make it more enjoyable." Then he withdrew the second pen and rammed it into the Londoner's thigh. Now the lifesaving drug was working against him, rapidly. Time for the third.

He dropped to the sand, onto his back, writhing for a short time as his heart began to race out of control.

Constantin stood on the edge of the bunker and watched until his new-found friend stopped moving. He trod on something hard, deep in the sand.

"That's handy." He picked it up, walked towards Steve, and checked his pulse. "I wasn't sure it would work, but you are definitely dead, or beyond help, Steve. Was it good for you too?" He patted him on the face as he prized his lips apart and having cleaned it down, he placed the golf ball into Steve's mouth, before walking to his pack and removing the marker pen.

The white face of the ball was staring up at Constantin now, its maker's name proudly displayed. He had no idea whether it was a cheap or expensive ball, deciding that Mark Twain was quite right about golf. He carefully drew an A on the ball and pocketed the marker.

He knelt down, picked up the three EpiPens.

"I wasn't sure whether these would work or not. I was intending to use them on somebody else until you came along and wouldn't take no for an answer. I gave you a chance to leave; they worked really well. In summing up the case for the defence, may I suggest to the people of the jury that Constantin Nicolescu acted in self-defence, and in doing so rid the local area of a social menace?"

He looked at Steve – a half-dressed man, caught with his trousers down. He placed one of the EpiPens into each of Steve's hands and the other, where only a pathologist might find it.

"Not guilty indeed. There, now they'll think you at least tried to save your own life. Been smashin' meetin' you, mate," he said in a mock London accent, as he tracked backwards, raking the sand perfectly, just as the sign commanded.

"We must stick to the rules, Steve. Always stick to the rules."

He walked away, across the course, over the fence, and back through the hedge, exactly the way he had arrived.

He plipped the remote, opened the old Toyota, and stood for a while. Somewhere, a blackbird was singing its heart out. It fascinated him how birds seemed to stay awake in the cities with their daylong artificial lighting.

After thirty seconds of listening to one of nature's symphonies, he started the car. With a puff of blue smoke, it sprang into life. He drove back towards the city.

"I really should pop round and tell Suzie. I'm not sure she's missing him, though. He was hardly much to write home about. Mate." He laughed at himself.

He pressed the worn radio search button until he found Classic FM.

"Ah, now isn't this just wonderful?"

———

Cade had stood for a while, listening to a couple arguing in a distant dwelling. He was trying to clear his head when his phone rang. It was O'Shea.

"It's me. Did he bugger off and leave you alone in the end?"

"He did. But only after he had killed some bloke called Rick."

"Do you want the good news or the bad news?"

"Bad. Always start with the bad. Then, even if the good news is crap, at least it will be better."

"Rick is Richard Chamberlain."

"Should I know the name?"

"No. Not unless you are his boss."

"Go on."

"His boss is the deputy governor of Belmarsh. And..."

"Let me guess. Chamberlain was Nicolescu's pet prison officer?"

"Worse. He was Nicolescu's most despised prison officer. Hated his guts. Swore blind that one day he would repay him for making him suffer."

"And how was that?"

"Chamberlain used to go into his cell and turn off his music. Apparently, he adored Rachmaninoff."

"Some taste after all, then. I'm heading into the office. I've swept this place the best I know how. I can't find any trace of any obvious devices. A little out of my league, though. Can you see if you can put in a job for our techies to come and give it the once over?"

"But how did he know where we were living?"

"How did he know where Chamberlain was living, Carrie? How does he know lots of things? How, how, how? He's got an inside line on us all. What I need to know is why."

"Isn't that obvious?"

"We were doing our jobs. He's the offender, not us."

"We should have left for the beach when we had the chance. I don't want to be at the apartment anymore, swept for devices or not."

"I'll second that. No time to dwell on sun and sea..." He stopped, interrupting himself. "Find out the following for me. Where did Chamberlain live? Where do we think Nicolescu lives? Given what he said to us earlier, he can't be too far away. Get the team together soon as you can. We're a significant man down on this. He's banged up and still grieving for Cathy. And Carrie..."

"Boss?" It was just like old times. Quietly, she loved it but felt uneasy, it shouldn't be hard to love someone. For now, she'd be professional, the rest could wait.

"Run a scan on any suspicious behaviour in the last few hours."

"Pretty broad, isn't it? Define 'suspicious'."

"Very broad. You sort that little one out. I know how much you love the challenge. Keep asking 'so what' and you'll get there. First one to solve this buys the other lunch." He checked his watch. "Which at this rate will be soon."

———

By the morning, O'Shea had crunched every bit of known data. Francis, too. They had something, but not much. It was three hours until Cade was supposed to meet Nicolescu on the bridge.

All he needed to do was show up.

## CHAPTER SEVENTEEN

### THE EIGHTH

"THIS IS MOST UNUSUAL..."

He walked around the edge of the green. Scratched his backside, then his nose, then sniffed his fingers and ran his hand through his hair.

Inspector Michael Hawker was a man's man through and through. A few months at most from retiring, he still had a full head of straw-blond hair and boyish looks that had charmed a few ladies in their time. Yet, through it all, he'd been married to his childhood sweetheart, Lizzie.

Mick to his friends, he knew more about street coppering than most had forgotten.

He was considered by some of the newer blood to be a vintage officer, some called him a veteran; he was trained in rote fashion, learning every section and sub section, every should, every must, every could or every might. Like most of that era he could still quote the burglary definition from the Theft Act as if he'd learned it yesterday.

He'd stagnated at the rank of constable for years, enjoying the thrill of the chase, until one day, for a bet, he'd taken his sergeant's exams and had never looked back.

Hawker was one of those cops that knew everyone in his area: the good, the bad and the indifferent. Even the cons liked him.

He had a nose for criminals like an osprey has an eye for fish. Hawker by more than just name.

He scanned the horizon now as a developing shower did its best to send him back to his unmarked car.

He looked again, back up the fairway to the tee, then slowly drew his sights in closer, closer still, until he was staring at the bunker of the eighth hole, and the spreadeagled body of a white male, possibly in his forties, naked from the waist down, clutching two EpiPens and with a golf ball rammed unceremoniously into his mouth. Where the third pen was left little to the imagination.

He said it again: "This is most unusual…"

"Tell me about it, I've played this course before, boss, and probably lost a hundred balls, and I've never found one yet. But I reckon that ball was placed there, very carefully, for it to have the A showing like that. Probably got prints on it."

"Oh, you're a SOCO now, are you? And as for golf, I'm sure I would lose every one of my balls. Never did get along with the bloody game. Right, talking of balls, keep this cordoned or I'll have yours in a vice. The course stays shut until I give the go ahead. No doubt CID and the CSI team will be here soon and before you can say Portaloo, this place will have tents everywhere." He started to walk away.

"And boys, take some photos on your phone just in case this all goes tits up. Send them to me. And keep the log running. No one, and I mean no one, not even the great Eldrick Woods himself steps foot into that bunker, or anywhere around where those footprints travelled to, until myself or someone of a higher rank gives the green light. Clear?"

"Swarovski, guv."

"Do what?"

"It's a make of crystal, sir. Austrian. My Sandra collects it."

"Does she now? Right, I've got a date at Newens for one of their lovely breakfasts and coffee to die for. Present company excepted." He nodded to the still motionless Steve.

"I'd offer you both one, but they're not good for you. I might even grab one of their delicious pies for my tea. Ring me, yeah? Anything, anything at all."

The first constable turned to the second, brushing a film of rain away from his waterproof coat.

"Shame I didn't bring my clubs."

"Shame you didn't bring your umbrella."

"I wonder what the story is here then?"

"No idea," said the second, quietly trying to avoid eye contact with the body and wishing he was somewhere else instead. "But I could murder a cooked breakfast."

———

Sipping on a mug of her favoured Jamaica Blue coffee, O'Shea rested her elbows on the desk and stared at the screen in front of her, until all of the characters had blurred into one chaotic pile of letters and numbers.

"You need a break. Take five," suggested Francis, also taking a moment.

"It's too broad. I said this to Jack. Too broad."

"Then narrow it down. We know we are not interested in conventional dishonesty crimes, or traffic. Even a hair-raising pursuit across the county lines isn't going to raise much interest. So, what would? Think like you're the SIO."

"Me, a Senior Investigating Officer? I doubt it, Dave. But, if I was, then I'd want to know the big-league stuff, things that might make the headlines, even in a city as diverse as this."

"Then you've just narrowed your search down." He smiled, took a rapid gulp of his Yorkshire Tea and carried on scanning the open-source information: CCTV, the media, social media. Then he spotted it on a Facebook community page.

"Got to love this new software, Carrie. How about we look at bodies that have appeared in the last twenty-four? Fairly serious, wouldn't you say?"

"Go on."

"Well, it says here that the police are all over a golf club over Chiswick way. Putting tents up now, apparently."

It was the news she wanted to hear. Her own police instinct said it was a possibility. Possibilities had led to convictions more than once.

"Bloody hell, I did some of my early probation out that way. My old teammate is an inspector there now. He had the hots for me back then." She checked the time. "If he's on duty, I know exactly where he'll be."

It took her five minutes to dig out his cell phone number from the force directory; she dialled.

Stood at the counter and putting the world to rights, Hawker felt the phone vibrating in his trouser pocket.

"Here we go, Kimberley. Somebody wants me. I often wish I'd stayed as a simple bobby, not a care in the world. Hold a second – any chance of a top-up whilst I'm on the blower? Lovely stuff... Hello, Inspector Hawker."

"Well, well, well. Now, if I was a betting woman, which I'm not, I'd be looking to pin you down to one of three places. Looking at the time of day and the traffic, I'd say you'd be going against the flow, over the bridge perhaps, into Surrey, where the posh people come from, and rumour has it, they do a lovely fry-up." She paused. She knew his mind was whirring.

"Who is this?" he asked, intrigued.

"You're the copper, work it out, guv."

"Your voice sounds familiar. Go on, give me a clue."

"Hendon."

"Thanks. That really narrows it down a lot... the Met training school was a big place in its day."

"How about the WPC with attitude and great boobs."

"Jesus H... there's only one, or should I say two, of them from my days at Hendon."

"And you never did get her into bed, eh, Micky?"

"I didn't – not for the want of tryin' – bloody hell, Carrie, how are you, my darlin'?"

"I'm good, Micky." She was smiling. He was too.

"How long must it be, ten?"

"Try a bit more than that, guv."

"Oi, less of the guv, we were, and always will be, mates. Come on then, to what do I owe this rather lovely pleasure? You nearby? Can we meet?"

"What? And have those octopus-like hands all over my arse again, no thanks! Dirty old bugger." She laughed a genuine laugh.

"Cheeky mare. Mind you..." He moved away from the counter so he couldn't be heard, "You always did have a lovely arse. Tell me, what's a nice bird like you doing ringing up an ageing old git like me?"

"I want you for your brain, not your body, Mick. Have you heard of Op Orion?"

"Sure, some flash outfit up at HQ, they chase the big league, locked up a load of those Eastern Euro offenders not so long ago. Massive job, by all accounts. A little birdie told me their boss was Ginger Roberts. Didn't you once work together? Did you hear about his missus?"

"I did, Mick, yep. I did. Just awful. Listen, Jason was my boss and you know he's inside now on remand. They charged him with murdering his wife and one other who has yet to be identified, if they ever can."

"Bloody hell, that's not very clever, is it, sweetheart? Jason was a good bloke."

"Still is. Look, we know he's innocent, just a matter of time before we get him out."

"If he survives that long in there." It was every police officer's nightmare.

"Exactly. My other boss is a man called Jack Cade, you won't have heard of him, but we were leaving the UK for pastures new, when an old target of Orion's cropped up again. Fresh out of Belmarsh and looking for revenge."

"You reckon this geezer's got the dirt on Ginger Roberts?"

"Bang on. Can't prove it yet. Jack's adamant that our target is at the helm. You know DI Mick Blacknall?"

"Of course, Mick joined the year before me, due to go any day now. His lad is in the job somewhere. What about him?"

"He's running Cathy Roberts' murder op; he's not convinced that Jason is guilty either. So, the Orion team is re-grouping under the guise of hunting for the main suspect, hoping we can find him and use him as a lever to get Jason out, before the inmates or his people get to him."

"And what's your part in all this?"

"I'm Orion's analyst. Jack has asked me to do some deep digging."

"You speak of him in a fond voice. You get on well with him?"

"You never let go, do you, Micky? Yes, I do, in fact, he's felt my arse more than once. We're partners now."

"Lucky man. Well, any friend of yours is a friend of mine. What do you need?"

"Did you attend the sudden death at the golf course earlier?"

"Bloody 'ell! Big Brother is alive and well and watching over us, it seems. I did, yes. My boots are still soaking wet from standing on the eighth and trying to figure out what happened. It looked like an instant death if the look on the victim's face is anything to go by."

"You sure it wasn't natural?"

"Bollock naked from the waist down, clutching an EpiPen in each hand and a graffitied golf ball shoved down his cake hole. Yeah, about as natural as they come for Chiswick these days, Caz."

"Caz, crikey, I haven't been called that for a while. Who's dealing with the case? We may need full access."

"You think it's your man? What's his name?" He held his hand across the phone for a second: "Yes please love, brown sauce and extra bacon, I've just been to a horrid job and need the sustenance."

"You don't change, Micky. Still do a good all-day at Newens, do they?"

He laughed. "You don't change, still got the cheek of Old Nick, but spot on. Yes, I am currently at the famous Newens, home of the tarts."

"You'll be right at home there then."

"Damned cheek! I had an enquiry over the bridge. Listen, you'll get your access. Quote me. I'm the SIO until the men in suits get there – if they ever do get there with the budget cuts we've been dealing with. And even if they arrive, then quote me. This is my manor and within reason, what I say goes."

"You not married to Lizzie anymore then?" she sniggered, Hawker's voice taking her back to a time she had loved.

"Sorry, Carrie. I lost Lizzie three years ago next Thursday. Breast cancer."

"Oh Mick, I'm so sorry."

"It's OK, you weren't to know, love. The job is my life now. I got a small extension to my time. Let's meet up at some point, just for a coffee and a sticky bun. Until then, you let me know what you need and I'll sort it."

"It's a date. I don't suppose you know of any other murders or suspicious deaths on your patch or further afield, do you?"

"Nothing else on us, I heard Edgware had one. Only came in earlier. And there was some chatter about a weird event out east somewhere. Up near Gallows Corner. Ironic there should be a body there. Do you want the detail on that, too?"

"Please. Anything like this is really important. May not be any connection, but this man, Constantin Nicolescu is the loosest cannon you can think of."

"Then I'm just the man to shove a bung in his hole."

"Don't ever change, Mick. Speak soon."

She turned to Francis. "Dave, get onto Edgware. In fact, get one of the boys travelling to Dan Mason Drive. And another to Gallows Corner."

# CHAPTER EIGHTEEN

## HMP WANDSWORTH

HE'D MADE IT THROUGH THE NIGHT. THEY CALLED OUT HIS NAME until he finally fell asleep.

"Jason, we know you can hear us. Welcome to hell."

They started banging the doors with anything they could lay their hands on, rhythmically chanting his name.

He'd sobbed quietly from one to four in the morning, laid staring at the ceiling, waiting for the birds to start singing. He was okay for ten minutes, then his mind pondered the past few weeks. With Cathy, in that beautiful cottage, miles away, yet close enough to get home to the kids if anything had happened.

He closed his eyes and could see her face, smiling back, her eyes blurring as his were so close. She kissed him, whispered his name, held him inside her.

Then he would jolt awake, realising that he was in this place, full of the sort of people he'd made a career out of incarcerating. He was on the inside now, too. The wrong side. His wife was dead. His children, practically orphans, left with their grandparents, their mother no longer a part of their lives, and their father as good as dead too.

Then, worse, he sat up, shaking, his heart thumping so hard he could hear it.

"Cathy!" he yelled out. She was gone; leaving a void in his life that he feared he would never fill. Every time he stopped thinking about her, the same image came back; taunting, teasing, playing with his mind. That bastard had taken her, and he may as well have taken his children.

How were they? What were they thinking? Would there come a time when their school friends teased them about their daddy? Of course there would. Children could be so cruel.

He got off the bed, paced like the old lioness that occupied his mind, then lay down again, back up, walking in circles, punching the wall, making his knuckles bleed: crying. Sobbing, trying to breathe. Lost.

He heard a metallic rattle. His cell door opened.

"Roberts, you've got a call. The governor says you can have it as you've suffered a loss recently. He's good like that, and between us mate, the rumour is you're a good bugger, with any luck, you could be out of here in ten."

Roberts clung to the door frame.

Ten years? He could be dead in ten days.

"I can't do this. I can't take another hour in this place. I'm going to kill myself. Tonight, when the lights go out. You've had your warning."

"There'll be none of that talk, Roberts. Suicides are the last thing we need."

"Well, I'm sorry if I might mess up your impeccable record."

"You will be. Just make sure you don't – I've read your file, you've got kids. They'll need you one day."

"If you've read my file, you will know I'm a good man. Yes, I have kids. For crying out loud, I need to be with them or I have nothing left. Do you actually understand what I am saying to you? I don't give..." He stopped. "I don't care about your stats or your reputation, and it's clear you don't care about mine."

As they walked along the landing towards the office, the calls started again.

"We can wait, Jason." Then a wolf whistle.

He tried to stand tall, answering the phone, which he knew would be monitored.

"Hello?" His voiced quivered.

"Jason? It's me." A friendly voice.

"Jack, I need to get out of here, I'll top myself if I'm here another night."

"No, you won't and yes, we'll get you out. The team is working on a plan. Just stay strong. Now listen, I need a yes or no, I know they're listening so say the bare minimum."

"Go ahead."

"Did any of your neighbours have CCTV?"

"Don't know."

"Did you?"

"No."

"When you got back from your break... with Cathy... did you notice anything unusual about your place?"

"No. But Cathy said a picture frame had moved. Blamed the ghost cat."

"Picture frame?"

"Yep, the one of us two at our wedding. In the lounge."

"Anything else?"

"No, mate. Look, they've done all that. I need to get out of here. I mean it, Jack, I won't last."

"*Kia kaha* brother."

"And what the fuck does that mean when it's at home?"

"It means stay strong. It's Māori."

"Is it? That's nice, send them my best."

"They would kick your arse and tell you to lift your game. They'd say 'harden up, bro', and I need you to right now. We're in full flow and we *will* get you out."

"Roberts, time to go," the officer, hovering over his left shoulder, was tapping his foot.

"Need to go soon. Jack, please help me."

"I will, mate. Just sit tight."

"That's a shame. I was thinking of going for a walk around Kew Gardens or perhaps take in a show. Instead, I get to lay awake at night contemplating why my life rapidly ended up down the shit pan."

"Jason, listen to me. Do you trust me?"

"With my life mate." He held back the tears. "With my life."

"Good. Let's talk tomorrow."

Roberts had a sudden thought. "Get someone to go and see Daphne."

"Okay. And who's Daphne?"

"The old lady that lives opposite my place. She doesn't miss a trick."

"Wouldn't they have spoken to her during the house-to-house phase?"

"They would've tried, but she's deaf. She never answers the door. Get Carrie to go. She'll talk to her. And, Jack? Thank you."

"My honour, Jason. You know that."

"They're saying I have to go." He was racking his mind, trying to get out everything he needed to say, as if it was his last day on earth.

"Speak to Dex, see if he got anywhere with..." He could feel the tears building and a pain deep in his throat. "See if he got anywhere with Cathy. I've got to go."

---

# CHAPTER NINETEEN

---

## WESTMINSTER PUBLIC MORTUARY, LONDON

DEXTER HODGKINSON WAS BEST DESCRIBED AS A LOVEABLE BEAR of a man. He was forty-two, or was it forty-three? As was often the case, he was ever-so-slightly hungover from the night before. He saw a glass or three of a good Pinot or Burgundy to be life extending.

He was, he conceded, also slightly overweight, but only by a few pounds, since his wife Josie had put him onto some bloody diet beginning with a K.

Josie was first and foremost Dex's friend, but since the new mortuary facility had opened, she seemed to see him less and less. He was married to the job, like many police officers, but Josie knew he wouldn't be happy anywhere else. Happiness for Dex Hodgkinson was sewing someone back up after discovering just what had led to their demise.

The black phone, a legacy from the past that he'd refused to relinquish, started to ring in its cradle; a shrill tone that would wake the dead, he often said.

"Dexter Hodgkinson, Westminster Mortuary. How may I help today?"

"Doc? It's Jack Cade."

"Jack, how are you? I guess I know why you're ringing. Awful job, Jason's a good man you know."

"I do, and I'm pleased to hear you talking about him in the present tense. Some have written him off already."

"Never! Not whilst I have a pulse, which is a rarity in this place. I consider myself somewhat unique. Look, I'll cut to the chase, Cathy Roberts died of catastrophic injuries, it could have been one of three things that actually killed her, but the certificate will say multiple trauma."

"Okay, but what was the *actual* cause of death?"

"Fair question, and I know why you're asking it, but if you'd seen her in here, you'd be hard placed to make a call. Massive and extensive burns that would have almost certainly killed her within a week, and if that wasn't bad enough, the femoral bleed would have got her very quickly. The blood loss was huge, unsurvivable, not even a transfusion on site would have kept her alive."

"Poor woman."

"Yes, and she would have suffered. I found significant traces of caesium."

"What's that exactly?"

"Alkaline, an alkali metal to be accurate. Fascinating stuff. Place a vial in your warm hand and the metal will melt. Rather beautiful stuff it is. It is used in the most accurate clocks in the world and without it your car's GPS system wouldn't be able to triangulate its position."

"All amazing as ever, however..."

Dex held an index finger aloft. "You want to know its relevance to her death? When caesium mixes with water, we get one heck of a bang. It releases hydrogen, and as we know, hydrogen can be pretty explosive. Mix lots of vials with an abundance of water and you multiply things somewhat. The heat from the reaction ignites the hydrogen." He almost smiled as he imagined the process.

"My forensic colleagues know there were more than two bangs though."

"Count up what the witnesses heard and we know how many vials?"

"Not so fast, Sheriff Cade. The employees at the petrol station say they heard a series of explosions, all almost identical. Bang, bang, bang, bang and one more. And then, boom!"

"Bigger vial?"

"Possibly, except a vial of caesium, even wet through is not going to blow the door panel off a Ford Focus."

"Secondary?"

"Full house, Jack. Yep, the injuries to the unknown male, who by the way is absolutely Eastern European, possibly Soviet region, were altogether different. Blunt force, a heavy object hits a soft and pliable human and there's only one winner. Except in this case that blunt force was shaped, it would have hit him at a speed we cannot comprehend. Anyway, on a brighter note, I hear I may be getting a few more bodies today."

"You're ahead of the game on that one, Dex."

"Your Miss O'Shea, she's been coordinating, pulling rank or cashing in favours, turns out she's got some weird and wonderful character en route here soon, found earlier today, after a call from a greenkeeper at the local golf course located him in a bunker in a rather unusual position. And then when that one has been processed, she's located another, discovered by your colleagues up in Edgware. I've got a busy day ahead. Have you met my new anatomical pathology technologist yet?"

"No, but I'm glad you managed to replace the last one." Cade grimaced on the other end of the phone.

"Yes, thanks to your mob my last one ended up somewhat unwell, didn't she? You'll have to drop by and meet Kitty."

"Short for?"

"Short for Kitty."

"It's a deal. Can I ring you later?"

"How about I ring you if something catches my attention. Still not sure why O'Shea wants random bodies to come to me, I've got enough to do."

"Yes, you have, but you're the best in the business and if we can establish any links between them, and that leads to getting Jason out of prison, then I'll pay for your overtime out of my own pocket."

"Appreciated, but you can't afford me. Bit flush, are we?"

"Let's say I had some luck a few years ago and I've been frugal."

"You have yourself another deal. But Jack, you know I'd never charge you, and that there's no guarantee that I can find anything sinister with these other bodies or link them to Cathy?"

"I do. But can you at least link the one from the car wash to her?"

"Geographically. Physically. Evidentially I'm not sure. Was he the offender or a good Samaritan in the wrong place, wrong time?"

Cade sent O'Shea a text.

*Fancy a trip out to Surrey to interview one of Jason's old neighbours?*

She replied: *What's in it for me?*
Her phone buzzed with the reply.

*Dinner tonight and a possible lead to get your old boss out of Wandsworth*

She smiled and typed: *On the way.*

"Dave, I need to get a car and go to Jason's old place. You all over your tasks?"

"Like a pus-filled rash. I'll crack on with the open-source stuff until there's nothing left. See you later."

"Thanks," she called out from the corridor, already on the way. She loved nothing more than being in the midst of chaos, as long as she wasn't the victim. That game had become tiring over the last few years.

She found the one car that no one else wanted in the vehicle pool, then made her way west to Ashford: forty-four minutes door to door. She sat for a while and looked at Roberts' old home, looked around for signs of life, then saw what she needed to see. In the windscreen of a van parked next to Daphne Rose's home was a dash cam.

She knocked on the bright red door, ID card in hand, hoping the occupant wouldn't check the date. It had expired.

"Yes, love?" asked the well-built bricklayer, munching his way through a slab of toast and strawberry jam. "If it's for some charity or politics you can piss off, I've had enough of both and don't need any more."

"Carrie O'Shea, I work at Scotland Yard. Got a minute?"

Old Bill, were normally bigger and uglier. She'd caught him off guard.

"Sorry, miss. Kettle's on. Fancy a brew?"

"Could murder one. Talking of which..."

"You here about Cathy across the road? Jesus, what a mess. That poor girl, nasty car fire, I heard."

"Sort of. No sugar, thanks. Listen, you've got a dash cam in your van. Does it record and do you download the footage?"

"Have you seen the idiots that drive on our roads these days, darlin'? Yes, of course. Every few days."

"Any chance at all that it would have been running at..." She checked her notes and put a circle around the date and time, then showed him the paper. "Around then?"

"Let me check. What you thinking?"

"I don't know at the moment, I've got a meeting with the old girl next door, but spotted your camera, I'm guessing none of the door-to-door team did, too busy lost in the fog of war."

"I was out when they called. They left a card, but no one ever returned. And as for Daphne, she's Mutt and Jeff."

"Yep, I know, I can sign though, so I'm sure we'll be fine. Nice tea by the way."

"Cheers. Here you go, all yours." He turned the dusty laptop around. "See anything you like and I can download it for you."

She was already concentrating, sipping her strong builder's tea and waving away a biscuit.

"My God! You were actually filming! Your timing is exquisite."

"Smashing. I was probably loading the van up and had the engine running, as it's been playing up when cold. Always a chance that some toe rag would nick it, but between us they'd do me a favour!"

O'Shea held up a hand, pressed her index finger against his lips.

"Sorry, I don't even know your name."

"Robert Jones. Bob to my friends."

"And you're a builder?" She laughed, relaxed, for a change.

"Yeah, I know, but in my defence, I was a builder long before the TV show!" He smiled a broad smile and offered another biscuit.

She shooed it away. "I'm too fat as it is. Wait. How do I rewind this?"

"Like this." He leaned over her slightly.

"See anything that interests you, Bob?" She had her arms folded and her head tipped slightly to one side, trying not to smile. It was a worthy distraction from where her life had headed recently. For a second, living a normal life with a hard-working builder had its merits.

He blushed but countered well. "Only that bloke walking backwards and forwards from that telecom tent," he said awkwardly, hoping his observations skills would redeem him.

"And why is that unusual?" she asked, agreeing that the presence of the van outside of Roberts' home was indeed interesting, and was, to date, very new information.

He placed his mug on the worktop. "Fancy a walk?"

They walked across the road. He stopped and looked back at his van.

"Would you agree that this is the view in reverse?"

"I would." She was intrigued. Perhaps Bob had watched too many crime dramas.

"So, the tent was just... here. This was very recent, agreed?"

"Agreed."

"Look down. Look all around here. What do you see?"

"Grass, a grass verge. And tarmac and concrete. I'm losing you on this one, Bob. Sorry."

"It's simple, probably why I'm the tradesman and you're the copper. Why put a tent on the grass if you aren't going to be digging under it, or better still protecting anything with it? There's no telecom cabinet within a hundred metres of this place and there's certainly no cable pit anywhere to be seen."

O'Shea looked up and down the street. He was right.

"Bob, can you bend down slightly?"

"Sure," he said uneasily, lowering his six-foot six frame to meet her.

She kissed him on the cheek. "That's from me to you. You have no idea what this might mean. I'll send someone to get a statement off you later, is that okay?"

"Sure." He blushed. "Absolutely. Might this help Jason?"

"Possibly. And that footage is critical. I can take it now, or could you email it to me? Whatever you do, don't show it to anyone else and for God's sake, don't delete it."

"You have my word. And if your man ever leaves you and you fancy a proper walk in the woods then here's my card."

"I'll be sure to ring you. You are now officially my first refusal."

She left him grinning to himself and walked next door and knocked on the glass panel. She knocked again, then walked around the back of the house and waved at a sixty-something black woman who was pegging out her washing.

She held up her ID so it was nice and clear. Then introduced herself in sign language. She knew it would come in handy one day.

"It's OK. I understand you; I can lip read," replied Daphne in a clipped and slightly nasal tone. "Tea?"

"No, thank you. Bob made me one."

"I bet he did. Come on in." She smiled and held the door open, trusting O'Shea instinctively.

Ten minutes later and O'Shea had what she needed. She slipped her phone into her pocket as she shook the woman's hand warmly.

"Thank you so much, Daphne. A police officer will come later to take a statement off you if that's alright?"

"Of course. The Roberts family is so lovely. Jason used to mow my lawn for me. Such a terrible thing. He was a good man."

"He still is, Daphne."

"That's what I meant." She waved and closed the door.

O'Shea stood for a moment. Watching up and down the street that her boss once called home. A place he had strived to buy, a place for his girls to grow up.

It could all change in a heartbeat.

## CHAPTER TWENTY

SHE GOT TO THE POOL CAR AND RANG CADE.

"It's me. How did you get on with Dex?"

"Usual tales of entertaining woe and misery. No idea how we've managed to coordinate those bodies all going to him, it must be breaching some SOPs somewhere."

"They are called standard operating procedures for a reason, Jack. This is far from standard and I have friends in low places when it comes to breaking the rules. Where are you now?"

"I'm ten minutes away from the bridge, on foot. About an hour early. It's already been a long day. I'll need to clear down in case he's watching. I've been scanning the ground, using my old hostile reconnaissance training."

"Before you go, I have some good news."

"Fire away."

"There was a telecom van outside Jason's. My new favourite builder across the road had footage of it on his dashcam. It showed a man, black haired, and the way he walked, it was with a purpose, like he'd done it all before, like he was trained. And the old lady directly opposite saw the van too and the same man leave the van and go to Jason's place. Then I probably breached an

SOP... I'm asking for forgiveness here, not permission." She paused, waiting.

"What have you done, Carrie?"

"Kind of breached identification rules. I showed Daphne the picture of our car wash person of interest. She positively identified him as the same man from Jason's place."

"Right, well, let's just agree that it didn't happen that way around. This is really positive, Carrie. Great work."

"But it doesn't prove Jason didn't do this."

"No, but it does prove there was something else happening whilst he was away from home. Get the CSI on the phone, grill them until they are well done. Anything unusual I want to know, and ask if they checked every single thing in that house for prints. And when you've done, breach another rule and get one of the team at Interpol Manchester to flash that image off to Interpol Bucharest, Budapest, Moscow and Sofia."

He walked and talked. Looking down to avoid any cameras.

"I want to know who he was and soon. If and when he is identified, let's run his details via the border agencies, see if he arrived in the UK with anyone else. Time is against us. And when you've done that, try to figure out how I'm going to stay in touch."

"How long have I got?"

"Fifty minutes."

"Thanks. I have no idea what I'm going to do. I'll figure something out. Why can't you just get rigged up with a wire like they do in a good crime drama? And why do *you* have to meet him?"

"He's making the rules. He killed Cathy, no doubt. He's put Jason in prison. And the currently unknown body from the car wash is probably down to him too. I can't risk anyone else, especially one of our team. We've lost too many."

O'Shea looked at her phone. Another caller, this time it was Detective Constable Andy West, a younger member of the unit who'd joined them during their last operation.

"Can I ring in two? Andy's on the line."

"Yep. Speak later, but sort out my comms issue."

"Andy," she answered briskly. "I haven't got long."

"You'll want to hear this, Carrie. Belmarsh prison rang. Seems one of their officers failed to show up for work today. They called him and sent a few texts – usual protocols – but the governor felt that something was not quite right, so he asked for a unit up in Edgware to visit."

"And?" She was processing Mick Hawker's earlier comments.

"Turns out the officer was as dead as the proverbial nail. They put the door in when one of the patrol staff saw him lying motionless on his bed. Seems he'd been dead for a few hours. Possibly died in his sleep."

"Right, go straight to the scene, don't take no for an answer. I want that body sent to Westminster Mortuary. Pull rank, tell lies, quote some section from the Terrorism Act if you have to."

"You know me, I'd do anything for the boss, but..."

"But what? That man is innocent. You know it. I know it."

"Carrie, I'm on your side, I'm on the guv'nor's side, but have you heard who's investigating him?"

"Yes, of course I have, and that should harden our resolve to get Jason out of Wandsworth nick and back home. Whether he ever continues his career is secondary, right now I need to keep him alive. Now, unless you genuinely don't want to, get that body to Westminster – in the boot of your car if you have to. I'll square it away with the local commander – he's an old friend. Go! As soon as you can, notwithstanding the local team needs to do everything first. Just don't take your eyes off that damned body."

"But why this one? What has this body got that another hasn't? Are we diverting every corpse to Westminster?"

It was a rational question.

"No. Just those that are deemed to be unusual. If Jack is correct, then our person of interest is active and he's very good at what he does. Before you came on board, we had him up as the suspect for at least four, probably five, murders. He's very specific about who he targets. Your early morning golfer might have been an anomaly, but he didn't have a heart attack or get stung by a bee. I can just feel it in my water."

"Have you tried cranberry juice? My auntie swears by it," he laughed.

"Piss off, West, and ring me when you know something useful."

———

Cade walked at a pace that allowed him to cover ground but also remain vigilant. He had no idea what he was entering into. It would have been easy to get a taxi to Heathrow and head back to his waterfront home on the Coromandel Peninsula in New Zealand.

Tempting though it was, he was loyal, and loyalty was one of Cade's currencies, along with integrity, professionalism and good humour.

He had to do whatever it took to secure Roberts' release, on bail if it came to it, or on the offer of a large surety. Cade had the money. He'd pay it himself, given their friendship.

It was a crisp ten-minute walk along the road from New Scotland Yard to Westminster Bridge. But Cade wasn't prepared to be so overt. He wanted to blend. He trusted Nicolescu as much as the Romanian's own mother had; she'd been in control of him during his childhood, making his life hell. She was arguably his first victim.

He'd once broken a little girl's heart at the school he rarely attended, and took some graveside flowers to her as an apology, so he had an ounce of compassion, but he could have easily cut his own mother's heart out of her chest with a bread knife.

The bullied often became the bullies.

Cade moved slower now, but not so much that he caused a bottleneck. The streets were already busy: tourists and business people spewing out of the nearby Westminster tube station onto the street and into offices nearby, some grabbing a newspaper, others a take-away coffee, headphones in to avoid conversations.

None of them looked at each other; it was a human ballet, with no one particularly enjoying the dance.

People stood out, if you knew what to look for. Body language and it was the same the world over.

He walked alongside new brickwork and old, black railings and red and white cones, and then onto the bridge, the bronze statue of Boudicca and her daughters stood sentinel to his left, the queen of the Iceni tribe, defying anyone to cause an issue on her bridge.

Beneath her, a stall was being opened up; Union Jack flags fluttered, models of the Houses of Parliament, the London Eye and

Buckingham Palace were all vying for attention, as t-shirts emblazoned with red double deckers swayed in the breeze.

"I've only got that one in a large, my lovely. You'll take a large? Smashing. That'll be just ten pounds, my darling. There you go, have a lovely day. Get your souvenirs here folks, everything you could ever want!"

Cade moved on, sticking to the balustrades of the iconic bridge. Beneath him, the river was already alive with craft, a police launch was heading upstream, as the floating piers, home of the water taxis and pleasure boats, groaned and heaved against the tide.

Ahead, the enormous London Eye turned slowly, offering a relaxed view of the city, as two police officers, in yellow high-vis and shiny boots, made their way to an incident.

Further along the bridge, two men had drawn a crowd of about a dozen who were watching intently with wide-eyed innocence. Spotting the officers approaching, the men broke down their wares.

Once they were fifty paces past them, the two men once more played Find The Lady; their plant in the crowd winning all the time. Seduced, a father of three placed a five pound note down, ever the optimist. A fool and his money.

Further ahead, a large Coade stone lion stood guarding the South Bank. Shining white in the brief rays of sunshine, he weighed thirteen tonnes and was once painted red, and so legend had it, was saved by King George VI from demolition.

Cade was admiring it, lost for a moment when he heard his name, barely a whisper.

"Jack Cade."

He turned, looked back along the bridge. Nothing.

"Jack."

He looked down. There, almost at his feet, almost unseen, was an outstretched fingerless-gloved hand, holding an old coffee cup, still stained brown with a few meagre coins inside, probably put there by the beggar herself.

Her back was arched at an almost impossible angle, prostrated towards him, a long skinny arm with green-veined, pianist's fingers wrapped around the cup. An old trench coat covered her whole body, allowing her legs to remain hidden. A large headscarf concealed her head and face.

"Over here."

He stepped out of the foot traffic and leant against the railings as a barge sailed by beneath him, gulls flitting at its stern.

"Yes, I'm Cade."

Another hand appeared at the left side of the coat; it was holding a piece of paper. The insistent shaking signalling 'take it.'

The voice was accented, old, probably a beggar, most likely linked to a syndicate, and pooling her monies with the other homeless that were pimped out by rich men from the east. She had one of the best pitches in London, so she was being worked by someone.

"And what if I don't?" he asked, probably pushing his luck, knowing that the woman probably had no idea who he was or what the note said.

"Then another person will die in your name within the hour. And another at eleven and twelve, until you stop."

Clearly, the old woman had been briefed.

He slowly lowered himself down to her side, awkward at first, trying not to damage the suit, then onto his haunches, figuring it was easier to stand quickly if he needed to move or fight.

"Listen, I can probably give you more than you earn in a month if you tell me, right now, who gave you this note – and why."

"No money." The voice was tense, but it was clear that its owner had been given a limited dialogue

He opened the note. It read.

*Hello Jack.*
*I am watching you right now.*
*Empty your pockets.*
*Leave everything with her.*
*Be at Waterloo at 09:20.*
*Catch the 09:30 to Chatham.*
*Don't be late.*

He held the note, read it again, and checked his watch.

She spoke again. "Your things. Now."

He shook his head, and looked along the bridge in both directions: just a sea of people, a lion, Boudicca, two stall holders selling souvenirs, a camera hung from a pole, facing him. He moved, it moved.

He stopped, it stopped. *I am watching you right now.*

He placed his phone, an old one that he wouldn't miss, next to the coffee cup. She shook it again. He'd taken his bank card out and stuffed it down his underpants. He dropped the old wallet next to the cup. He'd removed every trace of ID from it too, just a few stamps, a recent receipt and some old loyalty cards remained. He was keen to comply, but a long way from being completely gullible.

"Every pocket."

He looked up at the camera and turned out the linings of each pocket on his jacket and trousers. He was travelling light anyway, now just a little lighter.

"The note." A single digit beckoned. The arachnid fingers waved him away. "Go." The hand pulled the note and the possessions under the coat as a fisherman hauls in his nets.

He checked his watch again. Ten minutes, fifteen if he was lucky.

He ran. Caught up with the two police officers, and spoke as he walked, trying to avoid any obvious attention.

"*Please* don't turn around, I'm police – an ally. How long to Waterloo?"

Remarkably, one of the officers carried on walking and spoke as if Cade wasn't even there. "Ten if you walk quickly. Where do you need to get to, mate?"

"Chatham."

"Then you'd better run, that's Waterloo East. Second left is York Road then onto Mepham Street and follow the signs. You sure you don't need anything...?"

He was out of sight in moments.

———

On the bridge, the old figure slowly stood up, stretching limbs, clicking knee joints and allowing the blood to circulate, leaning against the balustrades for a while before walking south over the bridge.

A smile began to develop beneath the headscarf.

*I am not watching you any longer, Jack. But I was.*

"And I was close enough to touch you."

What was it they said about keeping enemies close?

"See you later. Enjoy the ride." He tossed the phone and wallet into the river, before stepping into a doorway on York Road, then discarded the coat, glove and headscarf before climbing into a dark blue car.

"You know where to go?"

"Yes, Mr Constantin."

"Good, then let's go and see what we've caught in the net shall we."

# CHAPTER TWENTY-ONE

## THE 09:30 TO CHATHAM

HE WALKED ALONG THE CARRIAGE AND INTO THE NEXT. THE train was moving slowly as it left the city. He was pacing, but trying not to appear too obvious. He was here for a reason; the note had been very specific. That old hand, in a grey woollen fingerless glove – there was something about the appearance that troubled him.

The train was heading south east into Kent. There were only seven people in the new carriage, all head down, some reading, some listening, most uninterested in him.

A guard appeared.

"Tickets please." An accent?

He moved up the carriage towards Cade.

"You're a long way from home, my friend."

"Tickets please."

"I said you are a long way from home, Bulgaria, Romania?"

"And I said, tickets please." He looked at Cade through the darkest brown eyes Cade had ever seen, so dark they blended with the pupils to form one sphere. They weren't evil, but they weren't kind either.

He held his ticket out for inspection.

"You are on the wrong train. You need to get off at the next station and catch the one behind us." He moved on, quickly scanning the passengers and into the next carriage.

Cade had had enough. He sat next to a young man, a student probably.

"Listen mate, don't freak out, but I need to borrow your phone right now. I'm a police officer and I need you to make a call. You dial the number I tell you and keep the phone near you on hands-free, volume low, OK?"

The student looked at Cade. He had longer hair on one side and shaved on the other, he never once removed his headphones and only vaguely lifted his eyes away from his study notes.

"Sure, just don't be long, my account is running low."

O'Shea answered. "Jack, where the bloody hell are you?" she asked, slightly panicked.

"Carrie. I'm OK. I'm in Kent. Look, we've been played. I should have listened. I'm making my way back, all we can do is wait for the moment our friend plays his hand again."

"Jack..."

"I should have seen through this..."

"Jack!" She was pleading for him to keep quiet.

"I've got an awful feeling about today."

"Well, you should have."

"Talk to me."

"I'll tell you when you get back to the office. The boys have been out to the locations of the non-natural deaths that Dave found on the CAD system. One north east, one north west, one south west and..."

"Let me guess, south east?"

"Spot on. It forms a cross. Edgware, Gallows Corner, Chiswick and roughly where you are now, Bexley. He's drawn a bloody great cross over the city." She involuntarily ran her fingers over the same vivid red sign on her stomach, the nerve endings of which were still raw.

"Slightly lopsided, but it's a cross alright."

"OK, you and Dave start plotting what's at the centre of the cross."

"I'm a Londoner. I already know what's there."

"Well?"

"Whitechapel. East End. Much of it is being redeveloped, some of it is as it was well over a hundred years ago.

"Then start scanning the area for anything, 999 calls, unexplained calls, suspicious neighbours, noise, fire, Jesus, in any guise, just do your analytical stuff, Carrie, if anyone can find them, you can." He looked down at his ticket. The guard had disappeared behind a door. His sleight of hand was impressive.

"Listen I've been handed a note."

He paused to read it first, then said it aloud.

> *Jack and Jason went up the hill*
> *To search for Alex's daughter*
> *But rush as fast as they both did*
> *They couldn't stop the slaughter*

There was a word crossed out, then the rhyme finished.

> *So, ask yourself this my friend*
> *Who will come tumbling after?*

"What? That has to be the worst poem ever." O'Shea said irritably.

"You tell me, you're the cryptologist. I'm getting too old for party games, Carrie. It's a terrible piece of poetry. We agree on that, but are we agreed this is Nicolescu?"

"One hundred and one percent."

"She wrote it on the whiteboard, then repeated it, with Dave Francis listening on hands-free.

"Well, it sort of rhymes," he offered, feeling lost.

"Anything?" Cade asked, pointing two fingers at his wrist to the student who shrugged indifferently.

"No. But there doesn't have to be an answer."

"Agreed, what concerns me is not how we resolve this, but why he's doing it in the first place."

"Games, Jack. Maybe nothing more. How long have I got?"

"From the moment the judge decided to remand Jason in

Wandsworth prison. I'm heading back, get a car to the station, I'm done with his instructions."

"Jack..."

"Go on."

"Why don't we just throw everything we have at this? We've got resources for Africa, let's use them."

"We have, and the fact that I don't want to yet bothers me greatly."

# CHAPTER TWENTY-TWO



## WHITECHAPEL, LONDON

AN HOUR EARLIER AND NORTH WEST OF CADE'S POSITION, THE white DAF van pulled into the car park and reversed, its wake-the-dead alarm sounding, warning people of its presence.

Six minutes later, it was in the docking area as officers checked the undersides, using the large permanent and extendable hand mirrors. Quite why anyone would want to break in to prison was an unknown, but stranger things had happened.

"Just the five today," the driver announced, holding his clipboard for inspection as his mate opened up the side door.

"Business Class only." He laughed.

The Wandsworth prison officer walked along the black rubber corridor inside the van, four doors each side, all exactly the same, numbered, with safety straps and a pair of vents above each door. In each a vertical window, just enough to allow light in and for the staff to observe the prisoner, no more, no less.

The five prisoners all appeared from within the secure dock. One by one, they answered their names and were ushered forward, rigidly cuffed with the heavier duty manacles that were favoured by the prisons and courts.

"Name?"

"Wilson."

"Next?"

"Obeya."

"Next?"

He continued until the last man shuffled along. He looked drawn, grey, exhausted as if any fight that he had had left him.

"Name?"

"Roberts. Jason Roberts." He kept his head down and walked to the end of the van and into the small compartment, that somehow felt more homely than the cell he'd left. Perhaps it was because in moments he would be outside the prison walls, a victory for the little man, an escape of sorts?

The van pulled out of the dock exactly on time and began the forty-minute journey north east.

The driver looked at the passenger. They both smiled, as behind them and predictably, one of the prisoners began to kick the door and slam his palm against the glass.

"My money is on the door to win," said the passenger.

They drove along the A3, before crossing the iconic Tower Bridge, taking a quick glance down into the Thames and the boat traffic that brought the river to life, since it had before Roman times.

They slowed, indicated and turned off the main road, into Graces Alley. This was the East End, Whitechapel to be precise, and once the haunt of another person called Jack.

The passenger spoke, with a noticeable accent. "They say Jack the Ripper preyed on his victims in this area."

"Some say they were *her* victims..."

"A woman? No way, killing at that level is man's work!"

"Clearly you have never met my ex-wife! She could carve the heart out of any man."

They laughed as the large gate swung open, inwards, allowing them to leave the minor road.

As the van entered, it came to a halt under a large tarpaulin.

Wilson, in compartment three, was still kicking the door and calling into question the driver's parentage, as they hauled him out and into the courtyard.

"Hey, where are we? This don't look like no fuckin' court to me – and I should know." He said proudly as he pushed himself towards one of the officers, who struck him quickly to the neck with the side of his hand. The blow felled the prisoner in seconds.

"He's out. It does work, I wasn't sure, but I will use that one again." He dragged him by his feet into the main area, a large triple-height room with a vaulted ceiling and curved plaster panelling.

At the far end, away from the main doors, was a stage, bedecked with over-length, deep red velour curtains. Along each side, on the ground floor, were four red, twisted, wrought iron poles, each doing their utmost to hold the galleried second floor in place.

The main floor was filled with rows of timber and velvet seating. Above the doors the gallery continued and revealed more plaster cornices, each with their original Victorian patina, a mixture of deep ochre, tobacco tar and blood red.

The roof space and much of the ground floor was dimly lit, but at each pillar, and replicated immediately above on the gallery, was a spotlight, facing up into the roof.

Six oversized wooden ribs held up the main roof, at the centre of which was a large plaster rose, from which three strings of small lights hung, fanning out across the main hallway and ending at the beautifully carved wooden panelling that lined the gallery.

In the middle of the hall, equidistant from the galleries, was a round structure, a wheel, with a central hub, and to the left a table, covered in green baize. It had a familiar pattern on it.

The five men were hooded, then quickly taken into the main hall.

Recovered, Wilson continued to protest, kicking out at anything he could make contact with. One of his hands was released, but the pressure on his wrist made further resistance pointless. In seconds he was secured again, this time to the rear and with one of the twisted poles behind his back and his hands neatly cuffed beyond that.

Obeya followed, then the next two, until Roberts was led from the van – last but by no means least.

He was also cuffed to one of the red poles. He stood now, listening. Wilson was right, this felt nothing like a public building, let alone a court. He kept quiet. For now, his sole intention was to survive. He tried to focus on his children and somehow erase the images of Cathy, he knew they would return when he let his guard down.

The prison officers retreated back to the white van, checked the compartments, then changed into casual clothes before leaving the building and heading to a bolt hole in the north of the city.

Roberts was straining to hear.

There was certainly somebody there, he could sense it.

Then a voice spoke. It was low, with a hint of a foreign accent. Roberts' stomach churned. He knew that voice anywhere.

"Gentlemen," the voice announced. "Welcome to my latest acquisition. Allow me to let you know some of this lovely building's history. It was first noted back in the sixteen hundreds, when it was just an ale house."

He cleared his throat. "This building has more lives than a cat. And now, with me as its owner, it will be loved once more. I wish you could enjoy the architecture with me. It was very famous once, now, like me, it is just a faded star, isn't that right, Jason?"

Roberts bit his tongue. He was at a distinct disadvantage and knew it.

"This old lady used to be the home of musicals and opera, short poems called madrigals – a sort of complex and unaccompanied vocal piece, wouldn't you agree, DCI Roberts?"

"He's a pig?" asked Wilson indignantly. "Finish him off first, would you?"

"Quiet. No one said you could speak. In fact, you can go first, the audience should be here soon. Team, deal with him and see how his competitor is feeling. I need to mix and mingle."

Nicolescu walked along the galleried landing, meeting and greeting his guests; some were like old friends, others, new acquaintances, but they all had one thing in common. A deep lust for money.

If the seven deadly sins were on a shopping list, then this group was prepared for some retail therapy.

At the centre of the increasing vocal soundtrack was a man in a red velvet jacket, with a red shirt and a red bow tie. He wore black, perfectly pressed trousers that resembled those worn by a guard at Buckingham Palace. Where the similarities ended was at his feet. This Queen's guard wore high heels; black, shiny and with a heel that could have been considered an offensive weapon.

He also wore a mask, a death mask, or at least half of one. Crafted from latex, it had been cast from a plaster mould created in Victorian times. Then it had been painted in black and white. It was half and half: a harlequin in high heels.

His role was Master of Ceremonies. He was rather good at it. He checked for the signal that the building was secure. Those that had arrived had done so via an old network of tunnels that linked the place to another empty building on Cable Street.

"Gentlemen, welcome, you know the rules. There is only one rule – one value exists, and that is trust. Break that rule and pay the price and each of you knows all about that. It gives me great pleasure to reveal today's guests, brought here from one of Her Majesty's pleasure palaces, and I hope very much for your liking."

Roberts knew this voice, too. Couldn't quite place it, but knew it belonged to someone he had once met. If only his mind would allow him some space, some capacity to think.

He closed his eyes and she was there, sat in the seat of his car, bloodied and torn. He squeezed his eyes together, willed himself to think only of his children. He could see them, playing happily at their grandparents, he was a spectre, viewing from afar.

———

"Where's Daddy?" asked his eldest.

"He's gone away with work, dear," replied his mother-in-law.

"When is he coming home?"

"Soon darling, soon."

There was a knock on the door. Cathy entered, the walking dead, trailing parts of her life behind her, every injury visible.

———

He jolted. He'd actually fallen asleep, a micro-sleep at best, but long enough to see her. The man who he held responsible was just out of reach.

His heart was racing. He needed to breathe. He knew he had to stay in control if he ever wanted to see his children again. How would they ever forgive him if he didn't return? For that reason, suicide was no longer an option. He had to put faith in the few people he trusted.

"Shall we start from the first pillar and work our way along to our most prized exhibit today?" asked the masked host.

The dozen men who now gathered along the gallery said nothing, just nodded.

Wilson was uncuffed and told he would be zapped with a cattle prod if he chose to resist. He chose the lesser of the two options and walked when advised to. The three men reached the large wheel. Wilson was lifted onto it and then strapped down, his head facing the central hub. One of the team, clearly the lowest paid helper, removed Wilson's hood.

"What is this? What's going on? I demand to see my solicitor. This ain't no court room? Do you hear me?" They did. All of them. But nobody replied.

Having been brought up on an inner-city council estate and engaged in stealing from the age of seven, he was a survivor, but now, for the first time ever, he felt scared. Like Roberts, and the other men present, he knew he had to avoid showing it.

Wilson strained his eyes, looking upwards, he became aware of a row of men, mainly white, one dark-skinned, possibly West African and three South East Asian men, all wearing suits, some dark, some lighter, a few striped, one blue with red check and one a pale beige with an orange shirt.

He then became aware of another person. He couldn't see them, but he sensed the presence of a human being, its own head pressed up against the central hub.

"Seriously, I will knock you all the fuck out when I get off here. You listening?" Nobody was. In the great scheme of things, he no longer existed as a human being. Now he was a prop, a piece in a game played only by the rich.

"Gentlemen. You will refer to me only as the Master of Ceremonies. Hopefully, by now you know the way this is played. And please, will you place your bets, now?"

The men all indicated how they wished to bet by tapping on a small electronic tablet. Their choices were wide, which made it fair; to be invited to such a display of human repulsiveness took more than money. It took contacts, knowledge, power, reputation, capable people behind you, and of course, money, a lot of money.

"Allow me to spin the inner wheel." The Master flicked the central hub, part of the larger device which was bespoke-made and resembled a roulette wheel, at the centre of which was another smaller one with four quarters, four red, four black.

Wilson was lying on the red segment of the wheel, his counterpart, a man clinging to life, on the black.

The young man had almost given up hope. He lay motionless on the damp board, which was soaked in a mixture of urine, blood and vomit, washed down, after every contestant had left the building and by one way only.

He had nothing against the new person whose head he now felt pressed against his, but with what was left of his will power, he prayed for red.

It landed on black.

This roulette wheel differed from the norm; there were no numbers, only letters.

"Gentlemen, please place your bets."

They were gambling on something entirely different. How long the man strapped to the wheel would last, once the drug, chosen at random, was in his system.

It was, Constantin told them when he had first advertised in a far-flung corner of the dark web, a game of chance, played only by gentlemen and fuelled by the foolish, the lost and the unloved. Those people had chosen to walk towards the light, to leave their past behind them, hoping for something better.

Two men, dressed in black, approached the wheel. They stood at each side and heaved on the contraption, which began to spin, then faster. The men at its centre tried to stare at the ceiling at first, but the weaker one closed his eyes, lessening the chance of choking on his own vomit.

"No more bets," said the Master leaning across the table with a long pole, on the end of which was a grab handle, he lowered the roulette ball into the swirling wheel. It skipped and jumped, bucked, dropped into one compartment, then flicked up and landed in another.

"H – we have the letter H!" announced the Master.

"Heroin!" whispered the crowd, who were all, as per the strict rules, men.

In fact, a woman had never entered this building since it had been an old music hall, opened in the eighteen hundreds after a hundred years as an ale house, again a refuge for men only.

One of the helpers in black approached the green baize table and checked the alphabet section, finding the sample of heroin. He placed a sample into a solid silver spoon, only the best, heated it over a large church candle and drew up the liquid into a hypodermic syringe, the hollow point and sharp tip of which slipped easily into the man's vein, which bulged under the straps that held him fast.

The crowd edged forward and watched, fascinated, as the second man in black shone a stage light onto the victim.

"What you are seeing, my friends, is the heroin coursing into his vein and finding its happy place. Watch as he becomes euphoric once more. Now his mouth becomes very dry, his skin heats up and his arms and legs feel *so* heavy."

Constantin peered over the balcony. "Are your legs and arms heavy ,my dear?"

He laughed and a few of the audience, the regulars, joined him.

"Now he will either become drowsy or very awake. And his mind will begin to stroll through the parks and gardens of his life..."

The man didn't move. He was almost rigid. He no longer cared.

"Normally heroin addicts have a routine, they lay out their 'works' – everything is dealt with in strict order, a routine like no other, because the user knows that the next fix may be their last. As I know only too well, she is one of the cruellest mistresses, robbing us of our most treasured belongings; our cars, our homes, our families and most of all, our self-respect."

He paused for a moment. It wasn't theatrical, despite where he was, it was a genuine reflection, back to the night in Germany when he had first fallen under her spell. He called it her. It helped to personify it.

"But gentlemen, you are not here to have a lesson in social needs, are you?" One or two nodded, some made affirmative sounds.

"Is anyone willing to raise the stakes?" He let the sentence hang like a bloodied pheasant in a butcher's shop window.

He knew what was coming next. They were literally gambling with his life. The Taiwanese businessman took a long sip of his gin, then tapped something into the tablet.

"That is a generous bet, sir. Does anyone wish to challenge it?"

The bet was five minutes, but it depended on the next turn of the wheel. It might mean heroin again, or another drug, or water, or even an antidote such as Naloxone.

There were only a few such humane slots; the ball rarely landed in them. Why would it, given its chances were made even slimmer by the subtle re-shaping of the narrowed receptacle.

Constantin nodded to the male who reached across and turned the wheel, faster and faster. Wilson's eyes were wide now, bordering on frantic, he tried not to retch.

"Please let this end," he said to no one, quietly.

"Round and round and round it goes, where it stops…" The Master was theatrical. It was what he did best and when he wasn't at the old music hall, he ran his own gentleman's club, an exclusive place indeed, for men of a discerning and depraved nature.

"It stops on… K!"

The gallery whispered. One said aloud, "Ketamine!"

The others clapped politely. Would ketamine take the man over the edge, finish him off or end his days in a euphoric state that would shut down his heart first, leaving his mind to come to terms with the end of his fractured life?

It was actually his drug of choice. Many of the 'players' that were 'recruited' had habits. His was alcohol and ketamine, which meant that his urinary tract was already so badly damaged that he struggled to excrete the drug which caused its ill-effects after it had left the body.

As the man in black injected the drug into the same damaged vein, the victim responded, drawn out of his torpor, and into a world where what he saw, no one else did.

The man in black became the devil himself. The true deliverer of evil. The victim thrashed around like a salmon on a lure, screamed, became rigid, then dipped once more, seeing animals and people in their most vivid form, paranoid beyond his control.

Then the pain started and the intense headache.

He hadn't been so vulnerable since he left his mother's womb.

"Please... just do the right thing. Overdose me, now."

———

On the gallery, the businessman, originally from Taipei, checked his tablet, watching the time, pacing slightly, would he make it?

His grid, saved each time he played, was slowly becoming complete, a bingo card, with each letter of the alphabet crossed off, a loyalty card system the likes of which the city of London had never seen before. All done in secret, beyond the doors of a derelict Victorian building, shielded from prying eyes and the scope of the government, departments of which would dearly like to find this eclectic group of men under the same roof.

"Well, how is he?" asked Constantin, walking along the gallery. He never entered the arena, as he called it, during play, only later, when everyone had slipped back into the cracks.

The man in black held up his thumb, it was horizontal, favouring the downward. It wasn't looking good.

"Time to place those bets, my friends. Time is of the essence and the stakes have *never* been higher."

———

The winner gained a monetary sum that was a fraction of that which he could win at a casino, or by investing on the world's stock exchanges, or buying precious metals. The loser had an awful lot more to lose. It was all about the game.

---

# CHAPTER TWENTY-THREE

---

## HMP WANDSWORTH

Across the Thames at Wandsworth Prison, Principal Officer Dave Rowette, the man in charge of the reception area, stood and stared. He shook his head imperceptibly. Just how the hell was he going to explain this one away to the governor?

An ex-marine, his current posting was considered one of the best or worst in the British prison service. It all depended on your approach to work and life.

Escapes were a thing of crime novels and films. He stood and stared at the newly arrived white prison van. Then he walked around the dock area for a few seconds, composing himself, taking a moment to allow his heart rate to settle and his knuckles to redden once more.

"Tell me again, exactly, how this happened?"

"Sir, it's not as easy as it sounds. They put some real effort into this. It looked exactly the same; same number plate, even the officers were perfectly dressed," answered the senior officer, another ex-military man.

"More effort than we did clearly. I mean we wouldn't want to announce to the British press that a bunch of badly dressed prison officer lookalikes got away with blue bloody murder, would we?"

He walked around the white van, opened the rear door then walked along the black rubber corridor inside the van, four doors each side, all exactly the same, numbered, with safety straps and a pair of vents above each door.

"More than we bloody well did." He turned and kicked the door, harder than Wilson had, leaving a black boot polish smear across the white paintwork.

"Fuck off out of my sight until I work out how we sort this pile of shit out. And get the governor down here and the deputy and ring the police, now! And if anyone, any single one of you, leaks this to the media, I will personally lock you up and throw away the key. Clear?"

None of his staff answered, all busy, heads down, backsides up, hoping that someone other than themselves would get the blame.

———

"Carrie, interesting job just came in at Wandsworth Prison," said Dave Francis, busy scanning the social media and police systems, blowing the steam off his third coffee of the day.

"Seems that the prison van that arrived to take five prisoners to court was not the correct van after all." He laughed. "Jesus, imagine the report writing which that is going to create."

He leant back in the blue typist's chair, so far that he nearly fell backwards.

O'Shea also laughed, but felt slightly uncomfortable, but for the grace of God, she had never lost a prisoner in her years in the job. Not once. Not even close. You watched them like hawks and trusted them less than a cornered rat.

She took a sip of her own Jamaica Blue – saved for special occasions, yet being consumed at a faster rate than it used to be. She rolled a pencil around her fingers.

"Dave."

"Carrie?"

"I've got a bad feeling about this."

When Carrie O'Shea had a bad feeling at work, most people

took cover, hid the sharpened pencils, her favoured weapon, and did their level best to stay on her side.

It was what Cade once referred to as her charmingly ugly face.

"Can we get onto the unit that attends, or better still, ring Wandsworth and get the list of missing prisoners?"

"Don't tell me you are thinking what I am now thinking?"

"Probably." She looked around the room, which was quiet, just like Cade, who had slipped beneath the surface.

"We've been set up. He was right. They just wanted Jack out of the city. It speaks volumes for how much they rate his intuition. Get the team back in here now and ring Wandsworth before you do anything. I'm going to get a car and go and find Jack. This game stops now."

"Game?" asked Francis, none the wiser, dialling the prison.

"Long story Dave."

———

As O'Shea was gathering her most cherished possessions and hunting for a pool car key once again, Francis was writing down the list of prisoner names.

"Yep, thank you, I'll speak to the police staff later, but thank you. We'll treat this as confidential, but any change, any at all, you can get me on this number." He turned in his chair, catching O'Shea as she left the office.

"You were right to be concerned. Four Category B prisoners, mainly dishonesty, violence and drugs. All missing presumed escaped."

"And don't tell me, one suspended DCI?"

"Spot on. What's happening, Carrie?"

"I have no idea. But it's not good, that's for sure. It's him. I know it's him."

"Well, if it isn't, we've got an even greater problem."

# CHAPTER TWENTY-FOUR

At Westminster Mortuary, Dex Hodgkinson was eagerly awaiting the examination of the first body of the day, a person who hadn't obviously died of natural causes. However, if the Operation Orion team had laid so much as a little finger on it, he could almost bet his pension on there being something out of the ordinary.

They had told him that he was considered *their* pathologist now.

He wasn't sure whether that was a compliment or not, but as he had done a thousand times, he unzipped the white Peva human remains pouch, or as it was better known, the body bag. He favoured the new versions; they were non-porous, which not only made life easier, it also made it cleaner and altogether a nicer process.

"Right, let's see what story this young man can tell us, shall we, Kitty?"

He looked up at his new technologist, a fair-haired and always upbeat New Zealander called Kitty Hanson.

Hanson had arrived in Britain, like many Kiwis, straight into London and had never left; never even gone north to see the real England or beyond. She had trained in her homeland at Otago University and during her fabled overseas experience – the OE – had landed the job of her dreams. Working with any pathologist in a city of many millions was one thing, working with Hodgkinson was akin to a young actor working with Meryl Streep.

"Cutbacks, Kitty, they are the bane of our lives; us, the police, the NHS, this country needs a sharp injection of cash before we get a real test, there's one coming, just a question of when, not if. Why do I say that? Simple, if there were more police, there wouldn't be half as many people in that sixteen-person racking system behind you. Agreed?"

"Agreed?" She smiled from behind her mask, inquisitive eyes searching for clues, ears always alert to the next piece of wisdom.

Hodgkinson moved carefully; examining, seeking answers, taking samples, using as many of his senses as possible, recording his every word, watched closely by his apprentice.

"Thoughts?"

"Severe head injury and spinal damage."

"Eloquently put. Sadly, there was no way that young man was going to survive. Let's put him back together for his loved ones, shall we? Least we can do." The buzzer sounded, announcing the arrival of another guest.

The new arrival was booked in and the whole process started again. Each case could take hours, sometimes longer. For Dex there was never really any point in rushing, for the families perhaps, but for the victim, it probably made little difference. He had a phrase for the departed – 'work with me' – it meant tell me something I might not know, tell me *your* story.

That was how he treated them all, as a life story, chapter by miserable chapter.

It would be many hours later when he rang the Orion desk phone, not expecting it to be answered by Cade.

"Orion, Cade."

"Jack, it's Dexter over at Westminster. You got a moment?" It was the standard question in their world, similar to 'are you free to talk?' – no one ever was, but for a colleague who might have an answer, they always made time.

"Sure, fire away Dex, after the morning I've had nothing will surprise me." He switched the phone to handsfree so O'Shea and Francis could listen in, both sipping cups of Earl Grey for a change.

"I doubt that, dear fellow. You'll know all about the body brought in from Edgware, the one your team insisted I take a look at?"

"I do now."

"Well, if I were to say it was one of the more interesting cases I'd had this week, I would be a master of understatement."

Cade looked at his team, who had now been joined in the office by DSs Del Murphy and Dave Williams and a couple of youthful looking, chino-wearing constables on attachment.

"Go on, you have an audience, Doc, we're all ears, so fire away."

"Does the word batrachotoxin mean anything to any of you?"

Cade exhaled. "Yep. Why?"

"Impressed. Did you do A-level biology?"

"No, but I did learn a lot outside of the biology class. Her name was Debbie, she taught me a great deal about the female anatomy. I think we were thirteen. Do go on."

"As sardonic as ever, Cade. Look, let's cut to the chase. Your prison officer had an unpleasant ending. Not horrific as one would expect from something painful, such as a deep burn or even a thousand paper cuts, this was relatively quick. But he would have known what was happening, would have felt his heart slowing, almost surreal."

"Poison dart frog," offered Cade aloud, not really concentrating on the phone.

"Possibly. Nine out of ten for effort. Could be a bird, the Pitohui found in New Guinea, beautiful they are too, black and bright orange. They say the man who discovered their potency did so by accident. Tried to rescue one from a net he'd been using. It pecked him, he licked the wound and noted in seconds that his mouth was numb. The local tribe told him it wasn't a plant he'd touched but the bird's feathers."

"Fascinating."

"You did it again, Jack. Bear with me."

"Apologies, I'm tired, Dex. I've been made to look a right prat today, just like half the squad. We've got an issue with an old foe who is treating us like puppets."

"Then may I suggest you cut the strings?" It was the perfect line and settled in Cade's mind.

"You may. So come on, what else do you have to tell us?"

"Getting hold of this stuff is not as easy as one might think. I tried searching for it, Kitty's had a play around on the dark web, where it seems like anything is available at a price. You could buy a puffer fish and feed certain parts of it to your victim, same effect, especially the gonads, or the tastiest part, the liver, but your man is out to prove something. Any idea what?"

"That he's a complete arsehole," offered O'Shea.

"Articulate," replied Hodgkinson. "However, he's more than that, he's someone who's done his research. He's therefore a very clever arsehole."

"I hate to admit it, Dex, he seemed to know what he was talking about."

"When?"

"When he was talking us through the experiment."

"Whoa there. You actually witnessed this man's death?"

"Sadly, yes."

"How quick?"

"Quick."

"Did he cry out, as if he was in pain, or did it seem quite peaceful?"

"He couldn't say anything, he had a tube rammed down his throat."

"And there you have it, Kitty! That explains the mild trauma around his mouth. As I was telling you earlier, if the dead can't offer an explanation, you either need the right witness, luck, or the stroke of a fountain pen to sign off the cause of death. In this case, no doubt, whatsoever, he was poisoned." He wrote something down on his jotter.

"Or rather, he was subjected to a very capable toxin that completely buggered up his system, sent it haywire."

He wrote something else down in the margins, then circled it.

"I have to confess that I have a penchant for toxins. Don't get me wrong, we all have to deal with little Johnnie who steps in front of a train now and then, but the cause of his death is often not as complex as a poisoning, for example." He paused, thinking.

"And, as luck would have it, I have recently finished some further studies on the very toxins I suspect we'll find in your dear departed prison officer. It will take a while, but I'm putting all my money on evens."

"How do you prove that he died as a result of one of these tetra…"

"Tetro. With an o, not an a, Jack. They are evidentially recorded at only a few labs in this country, ones that have the equipment. I shan't bother telling you what that equipment is, but let's just say, one of the words would make a rather impressive Scrabble score."

He studiously checked a glass of water on his desk, then drank it all in one go.

"This wonderful chemical will one day find us the answer to opiate addiction and painkillers, once they synthesise the compounds, someone will make an awful lot of money. But not this man. He gets a funeral. On that note, I think your next victim is due here. How many more do you anticipate? I do have a home to go to."

"Thanks, Dex. Why not call it a day now? I'm sure this one can wait. As for predictions, I never was much of a soothsayer. Let's throw caution to the wind, shall we, and say three?"

———

Hodgkinson unzipped the next bag, stood for a while, composed his thoughts, then spoke.

"Got anything on tonight, Kit?"

"You asking me out on a date?"

"You should be so lucky… lol as they say these days. No, Mrs H is at her painting class this evening and I've got sod all to do, so I was thinking I might take a look at their second offering."

She smiled. "I no longer have a life since I came to work here, social, sexual or otherwise, so why not? What have we got to lose?"

"Apart from our sanity?" He laughed, then turned on the recorder and the process began once more.

He recorded the height and weight, conducted an external search of the body, looking for the obvious, the obvious that was often missed. He checked for scars and tattoos, all things that might help the police to identify the person.

Hodgkinson aimed for two to three hours. In this time, he normally found what he was looking for, the more gruesome or interesting cases could take half a day. His goal was to gather the facts, to provide the family with a reason, and ultimately to allow the person to start their next journey. His official report might take many weeks – but the answer was normally the same.

'She died of this. He died because of that.'

———

Cade gathered the team around him.

"Today is looking like a day of herding cats. Whilst we've been here, there and in my case, Bexley mental hospital we've been played. Nicolescu wanted us away from the city centre, he wanted us scattered to the four winds. He wanted me out of the picture. We need to regroup and think this through. Dave, you take the lead, it allows me to think. Talk us through what we know and where our intelligence gaps are, please."

Williams was the epitome of a career detective sergeant; he missed the chase but loved getting results at the higher level and with Orion he had been involved in some outstanding operations. But today, for the first time, he felt a little lost.

"Boss, I think I speak on behalf of the team when I say we are extremely worried for Jason. For me that's the first priority for this team. We need to find out where he is, who has him and why."

"I agree Dave, who has him is anyone's guess, but I have a strong idea. Why they have him is simple, good old revenge, where..." He was cut off by a voice from the door, it belonged to a man who had almost silently entered and had used his swipe card to gain access, which meant one thing. He had either stolen it or he was important.

"Where indeed, Mr Cade? Where indeed? I was rather hoping I might learn the answer to that from his loyal subjects." The voice was as cool as an autumn morning and as shallow as a summer puddle.

Cade struggled to see his face, standing in the unlit doorway and the office lights turned down low.

"Sorry, you are?"

"No need to be sorry," he said, almost compassionately, staying in the shadows. "And the rest of you should be standing up, it's what junior staff do when a senior officer enters a room, or at least it was when I joined the police."

Cade could feel his hackles rising. O'Shea saw it too, but she'd worked out who their unwanted visitor was. She nudged Cade's leg, but he ignored her.

"Team, stay sat down. When our guest introduces himself, then you can decide whether to pay him such a courtesy. Now, sir, I asked who you were."

"'Sir' is correct. You got that part right. Have any of you heard of Sir Robert Peel?" he asked frostily.

Williams had also realised who their visitor was. He answered for the team.

"Yes, sir, of course, respectfully we all have." In conventional terms, when a junior officer said respectfully, it was the last thing on their minds. If they truly admired a senior officer and felt they could challenge them, they would probably say with respect.

"Marvellous man. He's the reason you are all stood now, well, all except the civilians in the room. He created his Principles of Policing. Anyone know what the eighth one is?"

He looked at Cade. Fixed a stare on him as a cougar stares down a young deer, then flicked all the lights on at once, causing some staff to squint and Cade to exhale.

"Police should always direct their action strictly towards their functions and never appear to usurp the powers of the judiciary."

"Bingo. Which brings me to the reason for my visit. I am, by the way, for those not aware, Chief Superintendent Jenkinson – Directorate of Professional Standards. You may not like me, but you will respect me. I have one question for you, and as your civilian colleague alluded, none of us is above the law, none of us would ever be willing to usurp those powers, would we?"

He was stood in the centre of the briefing room now, bald as the day he was born, eagle-eyed, a faint aroma of an expensive after-shave, straight-legged navy-coloured trousers and a crisp white shirt, with French cuffs and FBI Academy cufflinks. The tie matched the cuffs.

"With my last point in mind, I want all of you to think seriously about what has happened today. Mr Roberts has gone missing and I suspect that someone, possibly in this room, but don't quote me, knows something about it. You could either talk to me now, in public, which is the right thing to do, or ring me later, I'll leave a few cards, or you could even ring Crimestoppers. Either way, do the right thing."

He turned, walked towards the door, and flicked all the lights off.

———

It was a full minute before Cade could say anything. He was glad he had waited a few seconds to speak, just at the point that Jenkinson had made his theatrical entrance. He'd done Cade a favour, a huge one, an ace card he needed to show to only a few.

"Team. You heard the man. Either go and stop him and tell him what you know, ring him, he left his cards, or ring Crimestoppers. I know what I'll be doing." He picked up one of the cards and levered a piece of apple from a tooth, then folded the card in half and dropped it in the bin.

"I think it's still tradition for this team to head to the Sanctuary for a de-brief when the going gets tough. I'm buying, whatever your decision is. But think carefully. There's evil in play here."

Bridie McGee entered the room. "Boy, it's windy out there." She ran her hand through her hair which had the first white highlight showing. She'd spotted it in the bathroom mirror a few days before. Actually, she didn't care, her hair would change soon and her hairdresser would say she was on-trend, whatever that meant. She considered herself to be a fine wine, improving with age.

"What did I miss?" She smiled, providing light to the room.

Francis outlined what had happened.

"He's a little too creepy for my liking," said McGee. "Did someone mention the pub?"

———

As he reached his office, Jenkinson stopped, looked around him and closed the door. He pulled his private cell phone from his jacket and dialled a number.

"I sowed a seed. Not sure if it will grow."

"Did you do your very best?"

"Absolutely."

"Then why worry?"

———

Across the city, a young and recently qualified analyst pressed save on an MPEG-4 file. He added it to a message and then hit send. His manager, in the same anonymous building, had the file seconds later and began to listen to it.

He frowned, then smiled.

"I'd be very worried."

———

Cade looked at O'Shea, watching the team file out, some heading to their own offices, others back out on the streets. Two of them stopped in the hallway.

"Looking for something, skipper?" asked Andy West.

"A haystack would be great," said Del Murphy.

"Don't you mean a needle?"

"No mate, the former. We have bugger-all clue of what we are looking for, let alone why. I'm praying for a sign, some sort of revelation." He was stopped on the stairs by a breathless constable.

"Hey sarge, you interested in bodies generally, or bodies unusually?"

Murphy replied "Come again?"

"Control is about to send us to a job, but I read on our digital signage boards that Orion were interested in unusual sudden deaths."

"Ah, I get it now, thank you. And what makes this one any more unusual than the other hundred or so we'll have this year?"

"Initial indications from the mortuary suggest this lad had overdosed. He was found in a car park just off the Tower Hamlets area. Not dumped as such, more laid out in the car park, between the white lines of a disabled bay."

"An overdose is hardly likely to get our team excited. I'd need more."

"How about the fact that he had about eight different drugs in his system and recent marks to indicate his wrists and ankles had been bound?"

"Where is he now?" asked Murphy, now animated.

"Poplar Public Mortuary skipper. Anything we can do to help?"

"No. Actually, yes, pop into the office and ask for Jack Cade, tell him where we are going and that you'd like to be seconded to Orion one day. We need people like you."

Before the constable, a year out of his probation, had the chance to reply, Murphy and West were gone.

———

An hour later and Murphy was calling Cade.

"Boss, Del here, I think we've got a live one."

"A live dead person, Del, now that's novel. Tell me all about it."

"Male, in his early twenties at most. No idea of nationality but the local mortician reckons she'd put her pension on him being Central or Eastern European and by the looks of the marks on his body he's had a rough life lately."

"Drug user?"

"Massively. But that's the thing, staff here have run some initial post-mortem toxicology tests and reckon there's poly drug use. In other words, many different types."

"What's the lead time for the full toxicology report?"

"Best case – four to six."

"Hours?"

"Weeks."

"OK. Not ideal. Well, let's push for that. What does the initial testing show?"

"Blood tests have shown up some standard controlled drugs, and a few prescribed ones too, you know, diazepam, but what concerned them were the levels of what they class as therapeutic concentrations, which they said were through the roof. They need to carry out quantitation, in other words, the concentration of drugs in his system at the time of his death. They are almost having a sweepstake here. They are talking about someone who had the intake of a regular addict who has been taken to the very edge of existence, almost held there, then his body gave up in dramatic fashion."

"Anything else?"

"They've taken blood from his femoral vein and from around the vitreous humour – the eyeball."

"Yes, mate, I know all about that, trust me, I've been down that path before..." Cade shook the image from his mind.

"Urine tests could be the quickest to come back for heroin or cocaine. Looks like he had both and a few other Class A in his system, too. But it's the strap marks on his limbs that suggest he was far from willing."

"Good work Del. Get some photos and grab whatever you can. Any ID?"

"What do you think?"

"CCTV?"

"Sweet Fanny Adams, boss. Not one camera so much as pointing his way, not a PTZ or static, not even some paranoid local with a dozen home systems all over their garden. Nothing. They're good..."

"Keep looking mate. We can but live in hope. Run him past local MISPERS and see what falls out when you wiggle the old oak tree."

"Will do, boss. I guess that all depends on whether anyone cared enough to report him missing."

———

Cade screwed up his notes and threw the balled-up paper towards the waste bin. It skimmed off the edge and landed at O'Shea's feet.

"Penny for them?"

"Cost you more than that."

"Coffee? Jamaican..."

"Deal. Come on let's walk and talk. I need you to cast a spell over this whole situation. It's giving me heartburn."

---

# CHAPTER TWENTY-FIVE

---

## THE OLD MUSIC HALL

"He's dead."

"OK. And how is our supply looking?"

"Quite healthy. A few more were picked up down near Waterloo Station overnight. A few homeless, one probably a runaway from a nice home in Surrey who now wishes he'd stayed there."

"Interesting. Start with him first tomorrow. The homeless ones can be resilient, some don't last and we need them to at least put up a fight."

"And the one that we took off the wheel earlier?"

"He's the dessert course, the chocolate cheesecake with extra double cream. Keep him fed and watered. I need him in peak condition, for the finale, where we make some serious money and better still, some important friends."

"Shall I send out the invite?"

"Of course. You don't need to ask my permission. I told you, as long as you do a good job and maintain a level of secrecy, you can do whatever you wish. Let me down, just once, and you'll find yourself spinning around on that wheel too. Have you replaced everything, cleaned up and prepared for tomorrow?"

"Yes, sir."

"Good. We have a new member joining us tomorrow. Usual rules Luca, meet and greet, and make them feel very special. They pay a lot for this privilege."

He pressed the red icon and slid the cell phone across the pure white marble island bench top. Across the water, the nocturnal city was coming to life once more. He watched as the lights shimmied as the river changed shape in the wind.

"A privilege indeed."

He dropped the white dressing gown from his shoulders and walked across the large apartment floor in full view of the world. His bath had been run by the young man who was the most willing of his house boys.

"Will there be anything else. Sir?"

Constantin smiled at him. He was what, twenty-three, twenty-five at the most? So much to learn, so strong for one so young. His hair was like that of a raven's: sleek yet colourful and tonight, tied into a topknot. His natural tan enhanced the muscular frame and the older man, the wiser man, could feel himself responding to the view, and the view that they provided to the people south of the river that were probably looking at them.

"No, Christian, I have no further need for you tonight. You may go."

Christian raised his eyebrows. "Sir, if you don't mind me saying, there is probably one thing I could do for you."

Constantin walked confidently towards him, took his hand and lifted it up to his own mouth, placing the index finger on his lips.

"No, there is not, not this evening. It has been a long day and a I have a very important day ahead tomorrow.

"But..."

The older man pushed the finger deep into Christian's lips, pressing them against his teeth, turning his usually red lips white.

"Shh... Learn a valuable lesson. When the master of the chemist says it is time to go, it is time to go. Now if you don't mind Christian, you need to *leave*, thank you for your service. It has meant a lot to me."

"Thank you, sir. I didn't mean to..."

"I told you to be quiet, didn't I? So be quiet, learn. And now go, and Christian, when a man like me provides an income to a boy from Craiova like you, never squander that chance. Did you enjoy sending those pictures of yourself to your friends? The one of you laying on my bed, the one in the bath, my bath? Well, did you?"

"Well, I..."

"I told you to be quiet. That I asked a question does not mean I require an answer. Swear you will never do it again."

Christian nodded, looking down at the white carpet.

The man of the house, the one with the blackened wave tattoo, naked and proud, picked up a white towel and draped it over his shoulder, turning his back on the boy.

"One last thing Christian, and yes, you can speak now."

"Sir?"

"Your phone please." He held out his hand.

As Christian fished in his pocket for the phone, a gift from his employer, Constantin swiftly wrapped the towel around the boys' neck, then twisted it, again and again, as if he were wringing out washing, stood by a stream. He watched as the veins on his young neck bulged, his eyes too. He had allowed him to speak, yet he only uttered a sound.

Now the master of the house was enjoying himself.

"Is that nice? Feels good to be taken so close to the edge, doesn't it?"

The young man tried to shake his head, tried to prize the towel from his throat.

Constantin walked him like a dog on a lead towards the bath. With one hand on the phone and the other on the towel he dropped the cell into the deep bath, then slowly allowed the towel to lessen its grip, allowing young Christian to breathe, to see straight and to thank the gods that he had lived.

"That's what happens to people that don't abide by the rules, Christian. Take that as the only warning you will ever get from me. Next time perhaps we can play a different game, how does that sound?"

He could only nod, swallowing hard, trying to look away from the master of the house, who was stepping into the deep blue bath water. He lowered himself down into the tub and fished out the phone.

"Yours, I believe."

The young man could have drowned him, fetched a kitchen knife and slashed his throat, punched him into submission and left him for dead. But something stopped him.

Fear.

He apologised profusely, turned and walked across the deep white carpet, put on his black slip-on leather shoes and left the apartment, double-checking the main door was closed.

Constantin flicked the remote control by the side of the bath and waited for the flat screen TV to come to life. He pressed AV3 and watched as the young man, barely a boy, left the corridor and headed to the main door of the apartment block in Chelsea Harbour.

He continued watching as Christian walked along the Thames Embankment, now nothing more than a rapidly moving shadow.

The Chemist picked up his own phone and dialled.

"Luca, I have a job for you, a slight change of plans, a late addition to the menu for tomorrow, call it a display of what true loyalty is all about. Send a few of your people to the location I am about to text you. When they get there, get them to look for the man in the photo, one of our own. Make sure he is in the right place tomorrow when the roulette ball enters the game. Goodnight."

———

In the hall, the two homeless young men and the runaway from Surrey were each cable tied to one of the red twisted poles, gagged but not blindfolded, their heads tied in place, looking straight ahead, aware of people either side of them.

The person they looked at across the room would soon share their fate.

DCI Jason Roberts, once the darling of the Operation Orion team and now suspended, charged with the murder of two people, one, the mother of his children, was slumped slightly, trying to suppress another tear.

He found himself in two camps. To the men and women of the Metropolitan Police, he had escaped custody and was now on the run, a wanted man, in many senses.

To Constantin Nicolescu, his captor, he was the star attraction, the one that would really make some serious money. It really would be a case of all bets were on.

———

The next day, the men would arrive once more. Entering a modern building some distance away, and navigating a course under the city into the bowels of the old music hall. Where, since its new benefactor had brought it back to life, there was entertainment of a different kind on the bill.

———

All Jack Cade and his diminishing team had to do was locate the hall, find their colleague, work out how to defend him and in the meantime, figure out a link between the not so random murders, the victims of which were slowly filling up Westminster Mortuary.

———

No pressure then.

# CHAPTER TWENTY-SIX

## CHELSEA HARBOUR, NEXT DAY

"Hello." He said nothing else, allowing the caller to talk first, discreetly running as many background checks on the call as possible. A call that ran over the internet via WhatsApp.

End-to-end encryption. Perfect.

"Sir, we have come up with a supply problem for tonight."

The voice was strong, but quiet. It said, I am capable, but fear the person I am calling too. You could just about slide a cigarette paper between confidence and recklessness.

"Remind me, isn't that what I pay you ten thousand US a month to do, to supply me with the goods I need?"

The caller knew how to answer and it only needed one word.

"Yes."

"Good. Now go and find some more stock and if you don't, I suggest you hide, or find yourself suffering the same fate as those you seek. I hear Waterloo train station has many willing volunteers."

"Then I shall send my team down there later."

"No, you will send your team down there *now*. What is it with the people I pay so handsomely that they are afraid to show their faces in public? Did not the glorious regime we came from teach us field skills, the best in the world, how to observe yet not be observed, how to become one with our environment?"

"Well, yes."

"Well, yes, what?"

"Well, yes, sir."

"No, you misunderstand me, make me out to be a tyrant. The answer, simply, was: well, yes, I agree, and I should be more confident – so confident that I can walk up to the people that are hunting for me and steal from their pockets."

"I am in awe, sir, has there been a time that you have done this?"

"Absolutely. Right here in this city in fact. I have an advantage though and I suggest you get one too."

"And, what is that?"

"That, as the British say, would be telling. Now go shopping. I need..." He counted on his left hand. "Three. I have one already but he is not ready. Usual rules, delivery to the office block. No questions, your money will be paid into your account in Bitcoin just like you asked."

"Only if that suits you."

"It does. In fact, anything that leaves only a slight trace or less is how I live my life these days. That, and surrounding myself with the right people."

———

He flicked the switch on his coffee machine and dropped an aluminium capsule into the aperture. Then dialled another number on his VOIP system.

"We have a show on tonight. Pass it on."

"I will. Usual audience?"

"Yes, but with one new member."

"I hope he knows the rules?"

"I can assure you that as the man who wrote the rules, I insist on instructing people myself. In this case it is a man who lives by them."

"No trace?"

"None, whatsoever." For the second time in minutes, he appreciated the upside of his own peculiar health challenges and advantages.

Constantin Nicolescu was a rare human being and being rare suited him. Why run with the herd when you could stand in the margins and marvel at the stupidity of the rest of society as it thundered toward the cliff top?

———

Born to parents who regretted his arrival into the world, he had battled with a few childhood ailments and some less common. What he 'suffered' from was in itself to be a blessing in disguise – for a criminal wanted by half of the law enforcement teams in Europe, and as far afield as New Zealand, it was the gift which kept on giving.

His father had it, so he blamed him and thanked him in equal measure. As a child, there wasn't a name for it. That there was now, made it no less difficult to pronounce.

Adermatoglyphia.

A rare condition indeed. In layman's terms, he had no ridges on the skin of his feet, hands, toes or fingers. Those almost microscopic and highly identifiable patterns, unique to everyone.

Some sufferers had the condition with no other obvious outward signs or symptoms. Nicolescu had the smallest abnormalities; slight blistering of the skin and white bumps on his face, signs that most of his associates had written off to his insatiable appetite for heroin some years earlier.

He also had no sweat glands in his feet or hands. This was a joy when it came to appearing supremely confident at the point of shaking the hand of a friend or an enemy.

The pads on Nicolescu's fingers were completely flat. Not a ridge or whorl to be seen or felt, nor a loop or an arch. They were as smooth as silk.

The uniqueness of fingerprints, those physical pressure ridges formed so early in the womb, fascinated him, but never enough that he craved their presence.

No two people have ever been found with the same 'prints, not even identical twins. More intriguing still, no one has ever been found to have the same 'prints on multiple fingers.

Criminally minded people, like Nicolescu, had been known to try to erase their prints in remarkable ways; super glue, physical abrasion, cuts and burns. The problem, for the criminal at least, was that they grow back, exactly the same, or new and equally identifiable marks are created during the attempts to disguise the original ones.

But for the Romanian, it was a win-win.

They called them latent prints and patent prints: invisible and visible. His were always invisible.

There was always DNA, of course. But this missed the point. He wanted to give his enemy a chance. Constantin didn't care if he got caught. Not with the friends he had, in the highest of places. He had proved that once and he could do it again.

He often wished he had fingerprints. The thought of being caught because a crime scene investigator had gone the extra mile almost excited him, whether they were using black granular, or magnetic powder, aluminium flake or latterly, cyanoacrylate – super glue to the uninitiated, it mattered not.

They had so much technology these days, even in the thirty years that he had been a criminal, things had changed. SOCOs used everything in their possession to find a mark, alternative light sources, ninhydrin – which causes the 'prints to turn purple – and others that made the images fluoresce. He was fascinated by it all.

His favourite part was the wider science behind fingerprinting, the chemistry. He enjoyed the statistics, too. He'd heard from a friend behind the wire that over seventy million sets of fingerprints were held within the Integrated Automated Fingerprint Identification System. His weren't one of them.

The system known as ACE-V was the icing on the cake. ACE-V stood for analysis, comparison, evaluation and verification. The last part is where another expert examines the marks to support or negate the opinion of the originating officer.

Constantin had his own ace and it wasn't up his sleeve, it was on the end of his hands. They would never find him, unless he wantonly spread his DNA over the city. That was what he intended to do over the impending days and weeks. You had to even up the odds a little or it was no fun. *Catch me if you dare, Jack.*

# CHAPTER TWENTY-SEVEN

## WILLIAM'S OF ST JAMES'S

As gentlemen's clubs went, William's of St James's was best described as traditional; stuffy, yet elegant, mahogany-laden, doused in brandy and gin from an early age, where cigar smoke-stained ceilings adorned public and private meeting rooms alike.

To become a member took years, and then, and only then, one had to be nominated and seconded by members who had themselves been present at the club for ten years.

Just one shake of the head was all that stood between acceptance and denial.

It weeded out the chaff. Things had to be done well, or not at all.

Hector Barrowby was a public-school boy – who wasn't in these elite circles? His mother had been a doctor, his father a surgeon, so it was never in doubt that young Hector would follow in their footsteps. The problem was, Hector hated blood. Pain, bones, sinew, were all fine. It was just blood he hated. A medical qualification seemed pointless. There was always the ecclesiastical world or the military. But neither appealed. What did appeal was a career based on the law.

He considered himself far too talented a person to join the police, and as he wanted to earn well and lead an almost hedonistic lifestyle. So becoming a lawyer was a way to meet those needs and appease his parents.

He'd risen rapidly. His work had created case law, or precedents which would guide future similar cases. He soon had a partnership, then his own practice, then at an incredibly young age he moved into the appeal courts. As he often joked, before they could say all rise, he had.

He'd studied law at St John's College, Oxford, where he read jurisprudence. Progressing rapidly and often with a trademark sense of good humour, humility and exquisite judgement, he had also become Chairman of the Sentencing Council, and Vice President of the Criminal Division.

His curriculum vitae was exceptional. Called to the bar at an early age, he had plans.

He ticked them off in a little black book, a height chart by any other name. Queen's Counsel was the next green tick, he considered a green pen to be more stylish than its black or blue cousin. He also adored the history and pomp of the English court system.

He much-preferred the feeling of the silk gown that came with the role. As such, he too had followed an elite group of men and women, known colloquially as silks.

Like many of his peers, he had been appointed on the basis of merit rather than experience. He had all of the prerequisites: he was well thought of, had classical education, impeccable breeding and sheer panache.

What he aimed for, more than anything else, more than a wife, more than offspring, was a role in the Court of Appeal and ultimately to become the youngest Lord Chief Justice at the age of fifty-five – allowing him upwards of ten years of judgements, power and a salary and pension that would allow him to engage in his other passions at the highest possible level.

There were currently only two problems with Barrowby's plans.

Firstly, he'd upset someone in the Royal Household – a throw away comment that was gathered up off the floor and dissected later. The second problem was the Right Honourable Sassy Lane, Prime Minister and all-round bitch in Barrowby's eyes.

Her day would come.

———

Hector was enjoying some rather ribald banter when his attention was drawn to a visitor at the club. A subtle nod from a member of staff in his direction was all that was required.

"Ah dear Phillip do come and join us." That was that.

He had joined the inner sanctum, one of the most respected and yet despised gentlemen's clubs in London, home to the elite.

As Barrowby had once suggested at the annual general meeting, "'Money doth not maketh the man", and as such there really is no place for riff-raff in this establishment.' This earned him a raucous cheer and back-slapping gestures that were followed up with copious amounts of his favoured malt – a thirty-year-old Islay.

Hector was cute with his money. Rumour had it he had lived a parsimonious life in order to fund the things he enjoyed most. He had his hair cut by the same barber as a member of the royal family: silver-grey; it was swept back off his forehead, in a style that was almost too young for his age.

He did many things, almost. Just like the times he almost once bought a round at William's of St James's.

"Can I get you a drink?" asked Phillip, knowing the answer. Hector had a habit and he had become so used to disguising it he never appeared drunk.

"Well, it would be rude not to! The barman knows what I enjoy when a celebration is called for."

"I am honoured that you see this as something to be celebrated."

"Dear Phillip, it isn't every day that a member of the police elite joins our club you know, they tend to gravitate towards the nearest lodge. No, this is indeed a damned fine day. Now, where's that scotch? Folk will tell you I like my women young and my scotch at least fifteen years older!" He laughed out loud, slapping the new member across the back.

It seemed like back slapping was a thing at William's of St James's.

"Yes, sir?" asked the barman.

He was called Nathan and had a discreet regional accent from somewhere near the border of Northern Ireland, he had teak-coloured hair tied in a ponytail and remarkably high cheekbones, which gave him the look of permanent surprise.

"I'll have two of whatever Mr Barrowby is having please."

"Judge Barrowby has his own bottle, sir. Are you sure he's approved this?"

"No, I'm not, but let's live a little on the dangerous side, shall we?"

"As you wish, sir. Shall I put this on your account or would you like to pay for this now?"

"I don't have an account yet."

"But you do, sir. Everyone here has one the moment they accept membership."

Phillip frowned. "Surely it's the other way around. When we are accepted by the club?"

"No, not at all, sir. Here you go. This is Bunnahabhain. It's an Islay of eighty-eight vintage. Thirty-year-old and from the rather excellent XOP or Xtra Old Particular series, bottled by none other than Douglas Laing. Deep and rather fruity wouldn't you say?"

"It's a malt."

"No, it's arguably one of *the* malts, sir. As it should be."

The term 'should be' came at a price. The test was whether Phillip Jenkinson, Metropolitan Police Directorate of Professional Standards and newest member of William's had the balls to ask how much it had cost him.

No one ever asked, and they settled their bar bills on time, every month, or risked censure.

"Just so I can look out for it how will it appear on my account?"

"It will just say two glasses of scotch, sir."

"That it? Hardly good for accounting purposes."

"The price will be there too, of course. As I have had to open a new bottle, this one is yours. We make no profit on it so it comes at the trade price of three hundred and fifty pounds a bottle. And you may like to know that Judge Barrowby collects the glass stoppers from these, highly prized they are too."

"Does he now? And how many has he got at that price?"

"I'd say in the ten years he has been a member, around a

hundred. They say they are lined up on his desk at home, ready to be made into a chandelier. Will that be all?"

Jenkinson squeezed his wallet, held deep in his jacket pocket, a signal that almost apologised to it for the beating it had just received.

"It will. Thank you."

He walked quietly back to Barrowby, who discreetly dismissed a young waitress who had appeared from the panelled wall with a plate of sandwiches.

"Ah, the drinks are here. Super. Did you have the same?"

"I did, sir, and here is a gift from me." He handed the glass stopper over.

"Marvellous. Only four more and I can make my chandelier. I like my scotch ten years older than my women you know."

"You said. Now, sir, can we talk about tonight?"

"Would be rude not to. I'll have another when this has gone. Have a sandwich – I put it on your account."

An hour later, Jenkinson had heard all he needed to hear.

"See you later, sir."

"Looking forward to it. And don't call me sir."

"What do you prefer?"

"Barrowby is just fine."

"Aren't you worried that would identify you?"

"Worried? My dear man, worried about what, or rather, whom?"

Jenkinson tried not to react. It was clear that Hector Barrowby QC considered himself bombproof. He shook hands with the judge and left.

As he started up his silver Golf he found himself challenging his own rules – integrity and professionalism. Had he really just had an over-priced salmon sandwich with a paedophile and been mugged by an Irishman? All in the name of belonging to something sophisticated.

"Men with ponytails. Not in my world."

He turned the key and drove back to the office, parked in his space and spent the next hour crafting a disciplinary file, one that saw its subject with less than one percent chance of having a career this time next month.

———

An hour later, he was sat on a bench at a railway station within walking distance of his office.

"This is extremely risky, you know. People might talk. You know, you being the head of the professional standards department and me being on most people's wanted lists."

"Well, they'll hardly recognise you dressed like that, will they?"

He was right.

"You should have been a detective, Phillip. Or were you not quite good enough?"

"More than good enough." He rose up to take the bait.

"I can only imagine. Anyway, enough of what you call banter and I call tedious drivel. You have a message for me that for some reason cannot be delivered by a simple encrypted phone call."

Jenkinson lifted his newspaper up again, covering his face, almost paranoid that someone was watching him and that to those people that were, the elderly woman sat next to him, shopping bag at her feet, was of course Constantin Nicolescu.

Jenkinson whispered from behind the broadsheet newspaper.

"I have received the fourth Osman Warning for you. You need to listen and pay attention."

"I listen to my inner thoughts only. And anyway, what is an Osman Warning?"

"We issue one of these." He held it up on the page of the *Daily Telegraph* so that Nicolescu could see it clearly.

It looked official. They were issued by police forces in England when they had viable intelligence of a threat to someone's life. Intelligence − not enough evidence to warrant an arrest. But they had saved lives and were named after businessman Ali Osman who was murdered in 1988.

His family argued in the European Court of Human Rights that the Metropolitan Police had breached Mr Osman's right to life, as they had withheld information that could have prevented his murder. Blank with pro-forma spaces, the document was as bland as anything Nicolescu had ever seen.

It had the scrawled signature of a detective inspector at the foot and was dated.

"You need to sign it."

"I don't *need* to do anything, Phillip. I have people watching out for me. You know that. After all, you are one of them, aren't you?"

"Of course," he replied, all too rapidly.

"Well then. Keep your little letter."

"I had my first visit to the club today." Jenkinson tried to change the subject, carefully secreting the letter in his pocket.

"And how was it? I have never been. Far too good for me. Funny how things will soon change in that regard."

"It was stuffy and expensive."

"But did you meet him?"

"I did."

"And did you record him as we discussed?"

"I did." His heart was starting to race a little.

"And...?"

"In a roundabout way, he told me everything you had. As if he felt that the chances of him ever being found out were less than zero."

"Welcome to the Old Boys Club Phillip. They take care of each other to the grave. Pass me the recorder."

Jenkinson let the black data recorder slide from his hand, shielded by the 'paper and into the shopping bag.

"It's all on there. It would finish him if it got out."

"And it would finish you if they found out how it had been obtained, wouldn't it?"

He paused. For the first time he felt like the hunter hunted.

"It could. But as you say we have friends in high places."

"You have done well. Last time I had his accounts checked, Judge Hector Barrowby had nearly two and three quarter-million pounds in his bank. I suspect that what we have recorded on that device is enough to convince him to forego at least half. We need to leave him with some money to play with. Quite how you managed to get that device into the stuffiest club in the city, with its legendary security is remarkable."

"It would appear that you have friends in very high places."

"Low places. Very low. Nathan has worked for me for five years now, he sees and hears everything. Doesn't miss a trick. I see to it that he is very well rewarded, both physically and financially."

Jenkinson snorted a laugh. "Is there anyone left I can turn my back on or trust in this city?"

"Me. And yourself. Possibly the Queen. Everyone else is a player, Phillip. And don't be so homophobic, it really doesn't suit you. Everyone has or once had a price. A wrap of heroin for a homeless boy near the back of Waterloo Station, or the betting shop debts of the elite. They all have a price. Even you have your mistresses. And I can provide whatever you or they need, whenever you or they need it. And at the same time, I entertain. Now go and stand over there."

Jenkinson wasn't used to being bullied or ordered around, but this was different. As the Romanian had said to him, 'Everyone has a price.' By the time he turned around Constantin had gone, blending with the crowd and by the time he left the train station, he had changed again, an inner-city chameleon.

———

At the old music hall, the running order had been updated and Christian had found himself on it, cable-tied to a red pole, gagged with his heart pounding into his mouth. There was a man opposite him. He looked too good to be there. The others belonged on the street.

# CHAPTER TWENTY-EIGHT

## THE OLD MUSIC HALL

He'd been working the cloth away from his lips for a while now. He had spent exactly twenty-one minutes doing it, according to the over-large station clock that sat at the entry way to the old building.

When they had wrapped the roughly torn cloth gag around his face and into his mouth, he had forced himself to stretch every tendon and sinew, tightened his lips and generally made his face larger than it normally was. This was far from normal. They were in different hemispheres.

He had waited for them to leave, the three men, well-dressed and well-disciplined. They had spoken in accented English, and he knew the accent so well it was beyond familiar. When the doors were closed and locked, he had started. First with his tongue, slowly wetting the cloth so it stretched just a little more each minute. Then he contorted his face.

All the while the handsome young man with the raven hair stared back it him, eyes wide and clearly frantic.

At twenty-two minutes he had got the cloth where he wanted it – on his top lip. He figured if he could move his jaw, he could at least fashion some words. Then before saying a word, he practised pulling the gag back onto his mouth, in case they arrived.

He knew there was another person to his right, his eyes ached from straining to see who it was. He needed to communicate with the man opposite.

"Hi." He swallowed hard; his throat was dry.

"Hi, my name is Jason. Do you speak English?"

The man tried to shake his head, but it was rigidly strapped to the pole. He grunted.

"OK, my friend. One grunt for yes, two for no. Understand?"

One grunt. Good.

"Do you know where we are?"

One grunt. Even better.

"Are we in London?"

A single guttural sound confirmed his best held belief that they had only travelled about twenty to thirty minutes from Wandsworth Prison. That could mean five miles, given the traffic.

He collected his thoughts. Right, next question.

"Do you know who brought you here?"

A single sound. Then the man tried to say the name. Three syllables. Three grunts, all the while looking at the main door, terrified that someone was listening, watching and waiting.

"Say again."

Three clear syllables. It was almost musical.

'Argh argh argh' but with the last syllable slightly higher.

"Do you know him?"

'Argh argh argh.' Then he started to cry.

"Mate, work with me."

Three noises, now getting frustrated.

Then another voice joined in. It was the male tied to the next pole to Roberts' right. The same, almost desperate chant.

"Con-stan-tin. Con-stan-tin..." They chanted in unison.

Roberts froze. So, he was right. He had lived by his instincts for years, most police officers did.

"Bastard." He stood still.

"Does he come here every day?"

A positive grunt.

"Is he with other people?"

Another.

"Do you know exactly where we are?"

Two groans. No.

They were still in his city. Hiding in plain sight had been one of Constantin's most favourite pastimes. He liked to get right under people's skin, and with the former leader of his criminal syndicate gone, he now had the chance to head it up – as was his right and his legacy.

The game he was playing in the old hall was not only making him money, it was also forging out a reputation as a man of power and influence. He had lived in the shadows for far too long. It was time to step out into the sun.

He liked it, rather a lot.

———

Roberts was thinking like a police commander again. There had to be a way of attracting attention. He knew that by now Her Majesty's Prison Wandsworth would have put up such a large red flag and that it would have been visible across the entire city. Senior police officers rarely got arrested for murder, let alone the murder of their own wife. Even rarer was for one to escape.

It just didn't happen, which made it all the more intriguing.

That is, unless you had helped to arrange it.

———

At the Orion offices, the team was also trying to work out where their friend and boss had gone. None of them believed the charge. Roberts was a good man, one of the best. What he needed, right now, was a better one to find him.

Cade was pacing, he found it helped him to concentrate, and it was something he'd done in his childhood. He didn't have children. He might, one day, if time and circumstances allowed, but he had a family of sorts, and they were sat in the office with him now, trying to come up with ideas. Brain-storming, they called it –

creating long lists on a whiteboard, then ticking them off one by one.

They continued to mind map and throw out suggestions – often the random ones were the best. Cade felt that if you dispensed with the crazy ideas first, they were less of a distraction, yet they often provided the best avenues to explore.

"Boss, for me, the most obvious first question is, 'Did Jason kill his missus?' And we all agree no. So, the next one is, Who did?" Dave Williams wasn't pacing as such, just stepping from foot to foot, it was how he concentrated.

"And why?" added O'Shea, sipping a caramel latte which was a new commodity for her.

"Well, look at agendas. You should all know them off the cuff. But we all know that people rarely kill for no reason: love, hate, money, revenge. And in this case, I'd go with the latter. A good old-fashioned case of hell hath no fury like a criminal scorned. Except in this case, the criminal is also a complete psychopath. If I were leading your mind map up there, I'd write the name Nicolescu in the cloud right at the centre and let everything else lead from that."

He looked at Cade, who was busy studying a text message.

"Boss?"

"I agree entirely, Dave. The problem is for us to simply kill Nicolescu is a crime larger than his against us. A pound to the first one to place that quote."

"*The Merchant of Venice?*" offered Dave Francis.

"Bingo. None other than our old friend Shylock Nicolescu, Dave. We need evidence to locate and lock him up or we need to put some iron into our velvet gloves. And as ninety percent of the staff in this room right now are fully fledged serving police officers, I can't expect you to go down that path." Cade exhaled.

"But wasn't it the PM herself who said take those gloves off, Jack?" asked Del Murphy, also drinking tea, from a stained mug with a long-forgotten message about Crimestoppers on the outside.

"It was. But you and I both know that the law is the law. Unless..." He pointed to Murphy's mug. "Someone was to ring that number and suggest, passionately, that the PM's life was in danger from our Romanian friend."

"Is it really that easy?" asked O'Shea.

"Well, unless anyone else has a better idea, I'm somewhat stumped Carrie. We've got potentially random bodies cropping up on all points of the compass, our friend sent to prison on some ludicrous, but difficult-to-argue charges and at the centre of our mind map, a man more squeaky clean than the Pope."

"Have you thought about ringing him?" asked Murphy.

"What, the Pope? No, and I suspect he'd be busy anyway." Cade replied, trying to smile.

"No! I mean Nicolescu. Why not ring him? Ask him outright. Get his call triangulated and let's start putting some pressure on him." It seemed a fair suggestion. In the absence of anything else.

"I did speak to him. He insisted that I needed to cut off all ties to the Orion team and so far, he has only sent me on a wild goose chase on a train ride to nowhere. Just for his amusement. The only piece of evidence I gained was that a man on that train wanted nothing to do with the whole thing. He was terrified. He delivered a message and that was it. Game over. He sent me on the journey to show he could. No other reason."

He took a second to mull over his own thoughts.

"He likes being in control. As for random bodies, come on guys, they are about as random as you knowing the lottery numbers for this week."

"How come?" Murphy again, putting his mug down onto an equally old placemat.

"How often do people die in a city, even as large as London, from toxins or an overdose of adrenalin? Poly drug overdose, I get, but there's a link here and if you can't see it, then either I need to go to the optician's or you all do."

He tapped into his keyboard and flicked the screen up onto the projector.

"This is the report from Dex Hodgkinson. Adrenalin overdose. On a man who didn't need an EpiPen. Nicolescu's former prison guard, killed, on video by a toxin so deadly it could knock out this entire building, he reckons a gram at the most would be enough. Then today, two young homeless men show up very dead from a multitude of pharmaceuticals and controlled drugs."

"Addicts, boss. They'll do anything for their next fix."

"No! They won't – they are creatures of habit, Dave; they tend to stick to one or two drugs. Look at the amount of stuff in Male A." He shook his head.

"Jesus, addict or not, that was enough to kill any number of large beasts. Male B – Ketamine, MDMA, heroin, cocaine, in amounts, delivered over time that most people in this room would not survive. Dex reckons he's never seen anyone with that amount in their system. Normal overdoses are just that – a few extra milligrams and they go just too far. He reckons these men were kept alive somehow. That takes a certain skill."

The sentence hung like an early morning fog on the Thames.

"And you really think he's having some sort of fun with these people, Jack?"

"Yes, and no. Yes, because he's not like us and this sort of thing turns him on, and no, I don't think he's doing it just for fun. He's greedy. He's unpleasant. He's cruel. But above all he's smart and for years he's lived in the shadow of others, and I'm convinced he's playing in the big league now; how else did he walk from a cast-iron court case?"

"He bribed the judge?"

"Worse. I think he blackmailed him."

"OK, what's the plan then, mate?" asked a tired O'Shea, staring up at the screen with the toxicology reports glaring back at her.

"I've got to do as he says. I can't put a foot wrong. If we are to find Jason, and prove that he's as innocent as we all know he is, I need to distance myself from the team and trust in you all to do what's right. Within these four walls I need you to start considering the connections between these people and what they are gaining by being associates."

He flipped the lid from a red marker pen and wrote four names on the board

A prison governor, a judge, a politician and a senior police officer.

"What's led you to that conclusion, Jack?" asked Williams.

"Gut instinct, mate. Nothing more. It's who I would be looking at, if I were in your shoes and your two most-trusted leaders had left the team. One gone, God knows where, and the other about to walk. As according to this text, I need to be at Charing Cross train station in less than half an hour. And if I am seen with anyone, if I have a phone, stop to talk to anyone or even talk to myself, as if I am wearing a covert set, then he's going to start rounding up more and more young men and delivering them to Dexter himself."

"He's got some balls, guv'nor, I'll give him that."

"Dave, he doesn't care about being caught, and that only happens for two reasons. One, he's got a death wish and two, he's got friends in high places. We've already established the latter."

He hugged O'Shea. "Look after this lot for me. I'll find a way of getting in touch. In fact, that's your biggest challenge yet. Do your analytical stuff and work out how I can stay in touch in one of the most connected cities on the planet – without doing anything obvious."

"Just carry a discreet phone, boss. Don't let him dictate the rules to us. We are the law. Not him." Murphy was getting more frustrated as the meeting went on.

"Need we remind each other who is running this bloody town?"

"Right now, Del, he is, OK? I'll take my phone. Contact me in thirty minutes. Carrie, you sorted it yet?"

She walked to the lifts with him and pulled him close to her.

"You don't have to do this. Please...I need to tell you something."

"We both know I do. This is all part of the game. I owe Jason this much." He whispered to her, "Trust only those people you would be prepared to die for, Carrie. Someone is talking. Someone close by. The other matter, can it wait?"

He checked the phone. Just the same text.

*Charing Cross. Thirty minutes. Male. Red jacket. Shopping trolley.*

"Well?"

"I guess so, Jack. See you later."

# CHAPTER TWENTY-NINE

## CHARING CROSS RAILWAY STATION

He got there with three minutes to spare. Two patrolling and overtly armed constables were doing the rounds, checking everything: scanning, watching, up and down and sideways, and again, and again. Anything that looked slightly wrong that tugged at their gut instincts, was checked.

It was part of their daily patrol, one which they tried to do at random times – all part of Project Servator, a City of London Police initiative to disrupt, deter and detect activities as wide-ranging as pick-pocketing to terrorism. The ultimate aim was to reassure the public.

If you watched your 'ground' for long enough, there were clues: things, people, acts – and they all stood out.

The two officers had ignored Cade, which was a good thing. Cops could spot each other just as easily as they could spot criminals. It was in their DNA. He hadn't dressed down, he was semi-casual, and as such, was just another passenger being dragged along on the battle rhythm of a city that never slept.

He'd walked through once, and once only. There was no point in giving the patrols the heads-up. It was things like that, even in a crowded public place, that stood out: signals that bled from humans who were planning or about to do something that wasn't 'normal'. Right now, the last thing that Jack Cade, who considered himself a life member of Operation Orion, needed was unnecessary attention.

'Just carry a discreet phone, boss.' This was what Murphy had said. Cade shook the thought from his mind. He trusted Murphy. He'd first met him years before as a younger detective constable who was a solid street copper. In fact, he trusted everyone on the Orion team. He did have his major doubts about one occupant of the building, but so far, he had nothing concrete. Certainly, they were not heavy enough to tie to his ankles and hurl him into the Thames with, anyway.

He walked into WH Smith's and browsed the magazines before moving through the building and outside to the street.

There he was: red jacket, Villiers Street, going towards Watergate Walk.

The man stepped up the pace. There was something about the way he carried himself that stood out. Then, as he was alongside Buckingham Street, he abandoned the trolley. He started to run.

'White male,' Cade said to himself. 'One eighty, thirty at most, short, shaved hair, slim build.'

As a hound chases a fox, Cade broke into a gentle run, then a sprint. They were both here for a reason.

They ran along the street with its black gloss doors and endless Range Rovers and men in suits, entering offices, with people to see.

Across John Adam Street, the male was now pulling away from Cade.

He pushed on, passing people, trying to remain as covert as possible. Ahead lay Buckingham Arcade, shopping centre.

Cade watched as the man ran. Red jacket hadn't taken the steps. He'd turned left into an alleyway: York Place. A hundred metres, with black wrought iron everywhere and old lamps on curved black iron brackets, faded hanging baskets, and at the end of the alleyway a street cleaner remonstrating with the male in red.

Cade looked up: no CCTV. This lad knew his ground. He knew just where to go to avoid anyone chasing him, the mark of a seasoned pro.

Reaching the end of the alleyway, Cade stopped. Breathing hard, he looked around for obvious signs of very recent chaos. Across a pedestrian walkway were a few more stalls selling London memorabilia. There were signs everywhere: a betting shop with a familiar name; the smell of McDonald's and a garishly signed shop that announced it could *fix any fone*. Cade had just enough time to hate the misspelling.

Red jacket had gone.

Cade checked his phone. As he did, the one pan-tilt-zoom camera opposite him swivelled in his direction. Then his phone vibrated.

"I told you. No phones. A shame. You were warned. Leave it in the beggar's hat."

The camera panned down, almost ceremoniously, pointing at a woman with multiple facial piercings, a teardrop tattoo, a dirty ponytail and a black-and-brown mixed-breed dog that looked in better condition than her.

Cade walked over to her and dropped the phone in her hat.

"And just what am I supposed to do with that fucking thing, eh? Just saying…"

"I have no idea, love. Sell it for all I care. In fact, can I have it back a second?"

The dog raised its lip.

"Only if you want to lose that hand, mate. Just saying…"

Her voice. It had a familiarity that he couldn't place, posh with a rough edge.

"Look, you can have the phone. All it will cost you is an answer. Did you see a man in a red jacket? He would have run along the alleyway. It's important."

She lowered her head but continued to talk.

Her face, what was it about her face?

Cade took the hint and leaned against the black wrought-iron railings, next to a sign that offered an open-top bus tour of the city.

"You a copper?"

"No," he answered, also looking down, out of the scope of the camera.

"Then why are you chasing him? You don't look like no drug dealer to me. Far too flash."

"I'm not a dealer either."

"Well, you're something. I can tell. Military Police?"

Cade frowned. It was a very specific thing to say.

"You're right, I am *something*. And I'm trying to save the kids' life."

"Too late, pal. They grabbed him and took him away in a black van." She now had a few real teardrops.

"Registration?"

"No idea. Had City of Westminster on the side. False plates, at a guess. Two blokes. Looked like you. You know, normal. I wasn't really paying attention. But I did when he managed to land a beauty on one of them, split his nose in two."

"Thank you. My name's Jack by the way."

"Is it really? Nice. I'm... MJ. See ya. Wouldn't wanna be..."

"Yeah, I know. Trust me, right now, you really wouldn't. Stay safe."

There was definitely something about her: short hair, shorter than his mind was willing to compute. She was familiar, so familiar.

He wrote it off to tiredness and a city where a vague lookalike in a city of doppelgängers was always possible.

She knew him. Of course she did. Her mind had been taxed somewhat, her body too. It had all gone wrong soon after that day, the one where she really shouldn't have survived. But she could pick out that voice in a crowd of thousands.

The kindly man that had looked down at her, and her dog, had saved her. He just couldn't remember, couldn't see through the fog of war and realise that the scruffy vagrant who sat on a piece of cardboard to lessen the cold was an old acquaintance.

She regretted not reaching out to him: split-second decisions. She had her reasons. After a few months on the streets and a daily habit had created a veil of paranoia, she had become cautious. She had gone so far in her former life, but on that particular day, she had fallen ever further. She'd changed her name, too. It was just easier than having to explain the back-story.

She should have done something to save Red Jacket.

———

"We have a new player, boss. He's on the way."

"So I saw. Tell him he did well. Not well enough, but well. He can go third tonight, I'm sure by then he'll be climbing the walls for some gear."

Constantin hung up and left the makeshift office at the back of the old hall, in his wake a dozen screens scanned and monitored, guardians in a city bursting at the seams with them.

It was about forty minutes later that Roberts heard the commotion as three men wheeled Red Jacket into the hall and cable tied him to one of the vacant red poles near to the main door. He was gagged and most unwilling to play by the rules. He kicked out at one of the men, catching him squarely and knocking the wind out of him. The guard straightened himself up and waited until his colleagues had the man firmly attached to the pole, then he rammed his knee into the man's groin.

Before he left, he tightened the cable ties and the gag. Then slapped him playfully on the face.

"Enjoy the game, little boy."

———

Roberts waited until they had left, then wriggled the gag down once more. He wasn't sure how much longer he could do this but he needed information.

"Mate, you OK?"

All Red Jacket could do was groan. But he was smart.

Roberts summed him up using his best profiling skills: a street kid, on the run and homeless from the age of thirteen, renting himself out to the highest bidder for drugs or food.

He couldn't have been further from the truth.

Red Jacket had adopted Roberts' technique and managed to get the gag into a position where he could reply. It felt like a victory for both of them.

"I am OK. I could take that bastard with one hand tied behind my back. I landed a beauty on one of them. Split his nose in two."

"I'm sure, pal. Good stuff. Listen, I need to know as much info as I can and quickly, OK? Where did they find you?"

"Charing Cross. Back of the station. It's my normal place to patrol these days. Where I earn and get food. I've been there eight months and three days."

"Sorry to hear that. How old are you now?"

"Nineteen."

Jesus, he looked forty.

"What happened today?"

"You Old Bill?"

Wilson was sleeping, which helped, or he would have undoubtedly yelled something anti-police.

"Do you think a copper would be in here?"

It was a fair point. A businessman then, one with a habit probably, the city was awash with them.

"I was minding my own, when some geezer that looked like Old Bill or a plain clothes MP started running after me. When some white bloke starts chasing you, especially if you are wanted, well you run, don't you? I lost him, was just about to get back to my girlfriend when three blokes dragged me into a black van. She begs near the entrance to the station. There's only one camera near there and where she sits, they can't see her. But today they saw me."

"Who was the bloke chasing you?"

"Look, I don't know, mate. Quite good-looking though, for an older bloke. Fit. Well-dressed, although he'd tried to dress down a bit. Looked like he could handle himself. I can pick them out. It was like he knew I was there. Can I ask you a question, mate?"

"Sure. Can't promise I'll know the answer."

"What's that under the dust sheet?"

There was a noise from the nearby office. Roberts paused.

"Trust me, you really don't want to know."

He thanked him and wriggled the gag back into place, then stood and wondered who the dressed-down pursuer was. He could only hope.

———

"I've changed my mind. Go and get the one you brought in. I need to send a message." He paused. "No, I've changed my mind again. Let's broadcast this live."

The three-man team entered the hall with a set of wire cutters and approached Red Jacket. One was filming on his cell phone. Whilst one held the man's head, the other took the gag off, then squeezed his nostrils together, held them in place until the man gasped for air.

A voice announced itself. From the phone. It was familiar, very familiar: a group chat from hell.

As the young man opened his lips, the third guard grabbed his tongue and pulled it outwards.

"Now, boss?"

The voice spoke very calmly.

"Wait, please. Hello, Jack. As it seems you are unable to play by the rules, this is what happens. Each and every time you cheat, I will play a game of truth or dare. As you can't reply, I'll just play a dare each time."

The camera moved in and out of focus for a second, then captured the scene perfectly.

"The young man you are looking at was due to play a game with my friends this evening. In only a few hours in fact. But I think he spoke to you and that is a breach of the rules. And in my world when someone speaks out of turn there is only one thing to do."

Red Jacket was frantic now, trying to resist. Unable to pull his head back, he fought desperately to retract his tongue, one of the strongest muscles in the body, and now his was severed in one clinical action. He heard the sound deep inside his head – a sort of crunching tone. He tried to scream.

The third male held about an inch of the bright red muscle up for the camera as blood poured from the man's mouth, down his throat, choking him. He was unable to slow the stream and now with the gag back in place, he was panicking.

The voice spoke again. "See, Jack? Another poor soul suffering, all down to your inability to listen to basic instructions. Now, if you promise to be a good boy, I may show you something else that will really excite you. I know it excites me."

He'd already briefed the three men and the one with the camera was poised.

"OK, let's go for a walk, shall we? It reminds me of an old English nursery rhyme. Jack and Jason... went up the hill to fetch a Romanian criminal, Jack fell down and broke his crown and Jason..."

The camera turned slowly.

A new male was staring back. He was tied to a pole, gagged, wide-eyed and helpless. Then, another. The camera slowly panned along the room, a room with no natural light.

Then it stopped.

"Hello, Jason. And how are you finding your new home? I do hope my staff have been kind to you, answering all your questions. Of course, how foolish of me, you cannot ask any! George, can you remove the chief inspector's gag for me?"

Roberts spat out at the camera, feigned trying to speak, as if he hadn't for hours.

"Now, Jason, I have been told that you are a true vegetarian. Correct? But you must be hungry by now, it's been so long since your prison breakfast, aren't they just so hideous, by the way? Team, you know what to do."

One of the males held Roberts' nostrils, pressed them really firmly until his lips whitened. He resisted for twenty long seconds. He counted them off, one by one. Then he opened his mouth, gasping for air.

"OK, time for dinner," said the disconnected voice.

The third man pushed the length of tongue into Roberts' mouth and pulled the gag up tight around his lips.

"I guess you have forgotten how good meat tastes, Jason? Swallow it... come on. It's good for you."

The camera kept recording and the voice spoke again.

"Jack was considering what my agenda was today, when he spoke in your team briefing, Jason. It's revenge. Nothing less. I hope you enjoyed your little amuse-bouche. Can't be easy eating someone else's words!"

He laughed. A cold, unpleasant laugh – a cooling headstone in a summer graveyard. It was where the Romanian wanted to end his days. Held by soft, brown earth, finally able to let go of his demons.

"And if you were wondering, it was Jason who came tumbling after..."

The recording ended.

———

There was that nursery rhyme again – childlike but no longer innocent.

———

In the near-derelict hall, Roberts was trying desperately to push the piece of tongue into his cheek and stop the bile from rising up his throat and flooding his mouth. Eventually, his mind took over and the vomit poured out of the gaps he made at the side of the gag.

He wanted to be anywhere but this place: playing with his children, even present at his wife's funeral, anywhere. He retched again, pushing the lump of flesh between his lips so that it sat on the outside now, slowly dropping until he was able to prize the gag away once more, allowing it to fall to the wooden floor without a sound.

For the first time in his life, he honestly wished he was dead.

---

# CHAPTER THIRTY

---

## THE OFFICE

O'Shea saw the large file appear in her email inbox. She didn't recognise the email address, but the system didn't detect a threat. So she opened it. She watched for a few seconds. Then, she ran to the ladies' toilets.

A few minutes later, dabbing her lips with a paper towel, she stood behind Francis at his workstation.

"Dave, we need to do everything possible to find the ISP for that email. I want to know where it came from, how it got into our system and where the author is right now. Tell me we can do it!" She stared at Francis; the guru of all things 'electronic'.

"Sorry, Carrie, it's bounced from all four corners of the globe. Someone knows their stuff. They've used the Onion Router. I have about as much chance of finding this as I do of winning the lottery."

"He's potentially in our city and we can't so much as reach out and throttle him?"

"He could be in this building. Look, I'm sorry. I want to find him as much as you do."

"Jack should be back soon." She walked around the office, running ideas through her mind. "He'll know what to do."

"Will he? He seems rather lost to me."

He was right. He did. For the first time ever, she had seen Cade almost give up. The once-confident leader now almost a frazzled shell.

The Onion Router offered those that needed it a chance to hide. It was so-named for its many layers. It enabled those that inhabited the darkest corners of the internet to carry out an act; there were hundreds of variants, and the user could disguise their footprint within a few simple steps, soon almost impossible to trace.

She re-ran the imagery of the video clip, making sure she hadn't missed something, felt the wave of nausea again, and raced back out to the toilets.

———

Cade reached the ground floor of New Scotland Yard, took the stairs, wished he hadn't, taking in huge breaths of air when O'Shea found him.

"You look knackered. You OK?"

"About as OK as you. You've been crying. Talk to me."

Cade leaned forward to kiss her.

"I wouldn't, I stink. It's tears of anger, Jack. We've lost this battle. He's running rings around us. We need to go live, tell the world, do something." Now she was angry.

"I agree. But for each transgression on my part, there's a body turning up somewhere. I lost my target. You heard him. He might say it's a game, but I'm not about to roll the dice on some hapless soul – or Jason's life for that matter. We sit it out and strike when the opportunity arises."

"And when will that be?" She stared at him. It had been a long time since he had seen that particular expression.

"I'm hoping you can tell me. I've had an idea. Keep talking and let's walk back to the office. My thighs are burning. I haven't run that fast since I last ran that fast." He smiled. Fading blue eyes with a subtle border of weary red.

He was drained, too.

"He's listening to us at home and in the office, Jack. It's like he's somehow got control of every piece of technology that is connected to us. We need to counter his next move. I'm over this game already. You need to come and watch a video I've received. It's disgusting. But Jason's alive. Or at least he was when the video was sent."

It was hope, delivered by a cruel man, but hope nonetheless.

"I believe he's alive too, Carrie." He ran the idea past her then borrowed her phone and ducked into the toilets to make a call.

"You're getting paranoid, you know."

"I am. And I feel that's the only place we might not be being watched." He winked at her but failed to raise her optimism. She worshipped the ground that Roberts walked on and vice versa. He'd looked after her, from the day of the accident onwards. There was nothing she wouldn't consider to get him back in the office, slagging everyone off for the wrong choice of biscuits and moaning about the many and varied criminals that were roaming freely about his city. It was the little things. The things she missed.

Cade came back and slipped the phone to O'Shea. "Come on, Carrie, show me your video."

He watched, slightly open mouthed.

"It's Jason, isn't it, Jack?"

"It is. And the kid that lost his tongue." He composed himself. "That's the one I chased earlier. Red Jacket. It's definitely him."

He punched the wall, leaving a couple of knuckle marks in the plaster. "Bastard. If I'd have been just five minutes sooner..."

He beckoned her toward him, held her close, then whispered, "Watch your back. I fear we have an intruder. He's got electronic eyes on us, but human ones too. I just know it."

"Jenkinson?"

"Probably. Just be cautious until we know. Now, what was it you wanted to tell me earlier?"

"It can wait."

"You sure?"

"No, but we have other things that are more important." She feigned a smile.

He knew her well enough to know something was troubling her, and that meant it troubled him, too. He made a note to ask her again later.

————

In less than an hour, the team was gathered. Some sitting, most standing, too excitable to sit.

Cade passed a dozen sheets of A4 around the room, face down.

"Right, team, you can turn them over. Have a read."

The group read, murmured and left the page facing up – as instructed.

A light knock at the door revealed John Daniel.

"Hello, team. I'm bored, anyone fancy a drink at the Sanctuary? My round."

"In that case, yes," said Murphy, first out of the door.

The team followed. They knew the drill.

————

"Can we have the door locked please Roger? Usual rules of engagement. We'll put an extra few quid behind the bar."

"You said that last time, Jack." Roger, typically ex-police and now running the much-loved Orion watering hole, knew they'd more than made up for it over the years.

"Go on. The place is all yours. I'm off upstairs to watch *The Chase*."

Cade waited a second.

"Right. Thanks for coming. Glad you were all able to read the sub-text in my briefing notes. Listen, someone is watching us, listening to us, following us. Day and night. They're good and well-funded. I'm adamant the man at the helm is Nicolescu. No ifs and a few buts. However, he's got irons in lots of fires and he's protected better than the crown jewels. But I'll buy the drinks all week if someone can disagree and explain why."

Silence.

"Thank you. Today I lost a foot chase with a young guy who ran away from me at Charing Cross. I was *sent* to find him. Not you,

Andy, or you, Dave, or you, Del. Me. The rules were clear. Find him, but don't talk to him. Rescue him, in fact. He was taken in broad daylight on a London street by three well-rehearsed men in a van that, according to a witness, was a council vehicle. I wasn't quick enough."

"That's bollocks," said Andy West. "Council workers don't run around snatching people off the street, boss."

"Correct. And that's where you younger members of the team come into our Plan B. I've risk assessed and re-assessed. Every time I try to take the lead, he holds me back. Someone is either pulling his strings or he's connected way above the level I am. And I count the PM as a favourite in my phone directory. Or at least I did when I had a phone."

"You're sounding paranoid, boss," offered West.

"I am, Andy. Everywhere I've gone lately either he's been there or someone who works for him has been waiting for me. That gives me a sense of huge unease. We are the guardians, for God's sake. We make the rules, don't we?"

"What's the plan?' asked Francis, a man who trusted Cade, and once with his life, from a time when much of what he knew was being washed down the drain or dropped empty into the recycling bin. He hadn't touched a single drop since. He knew how many hours sober he was, and that was down to a young copper called Constable John Cade, who had taken the time to knock on his door and ask if the kettle was on back in the day, in the week before Christmas. In doing so they had formed a friendship that had saved Cade's career and his own potential demise.

"Simple. We stop sacrificing homeless people and get them involved. In fact, we supplement their ranks a little..." The sentence wafted like an unpleasant smell.

"Hold on, boss, let me get this right. You want *us* to become Nicolescu's next victim, who knows where, doing who knows what? No way. It's unsafe."

Cade paused, long enough to think and gauge the room.

He sucked air through his teeth, then replied. "Team, I'd do it myself, but he knows me and after my escapade earlier I know that many of the city homeless are far younger than me. Addicts or not, they are always going to be quicker. The tortoise and the hare, except the hare, thinks it's a leopard and is not used to running for its life. Dave, I need you to find an avenue into another section of our society, too. I think they'd be up for a new mission. We offer a few quid, some basic kit and a few small luxuries, and food, and a decent bed for the night. I'll get the funding sorted."

"If I was to second guess you, Jack, I'd think you were talking about my old mob. Correct?"

"In one. Who better to run a disciplined street operation than military veterans?"

"It's risky, guv'nor," said Murphy, himself an ex-serviceman.

"Why?"

"Look, I'm on your side, but homeless people change, they have to, in order to survive. They are leopards who are made to change their spots. They won't be the men and women they were." Heads nodded around the room.

"They do change." Cade had to agree. No point in getting his team offside at this stage.

"And most homeless people in London are immigrants." A few more nods.

"Wrong, Del. Most are actually UK nationals. Most are white. Most are in their forties at best and most are male. Driven there by relationship breakdowns, redundancy, mental health, alcohol or drug abuse... shall I go on? It can happen to any of us. And in amongst that group is the one I want to harness the power of."

"Some of them are beyond help, boss. Some we just won't be able to trust."

"You are completely right. Drugs can do that to a person. But I have a little sweetener. Carrie?"

O'Shea stood.

"Guys, the boss asked me to do some digging into the areas where the homeless try to bed down, to beg or just get a warm bed for the night. There are three streams of people. As Jack said: white males, black males and immigrants and they make up far less of the population than urban myths would have you believe. We've all heard of the seven Ps?"

Everyone nodded. Prior Preparation and Planning Prevents Piss

Poor Performance. It was a much-loved military adage. The forces lived by their adages and acronyms.

"Well, there's a new one among their homeless veteran numbers and it's called the Eight Ds: Drink, Debt, Drugs, Divorce, Depression, Domestic Violence, Dependency Culture and 'Digs' – or somewhere to stay."

"So how many are we talking about, Carrie, roughly?"

"Four to six percent of the homeless population. Some say two to four. Either way it's a potentially large number, mainly blokes, out there now, looking for something to do and somewhere to rest their heads."

Cade took over once more.

"Thanks, Carrie. Team, we will launch Operation Dignity today. No point in putting out a social media campaign as ninety percent of our target audience doesn't have a phone, let alone internet access. Therefore, we do it the old way. Boots on the ground. Here's a bundle of ten-pound notes. Don't ask where I got them from, just take some and get amongst our veterans and ask them to help us. A few will run a mile, some will say no, but the core will help once they know that one of their own is involved."

"Boss?" asked Francis.

"The kid I chased. There was something about him. If he could have stopped, he would. It was as if he knew I was not the enemy. And a mate of his asked if I was an MP. He's a squaddie, on the run at a guess. I just wish I could have got to him before they did."

"And you mentioned us getting involved too – honey traps for want of a better word."

"I did, and I do. We have massive resources, far greater than them, whoever they are. We get level, they pull ahead. We play an ace; they play a royal flush. It's an inside job. Carrie, make sure everyone has that video. The face may come in handy."

———

Across the city, Constantin was preparing what he called his 'children'. He liked to refer to them as innocent things, lesser beings, better that way. His mistress, heroin, had nearly claimed him three times and he wasn't about to open that door again. He let his third in charge handle that.

"It looks very pure, sir."

"It does. It is, and the supplier knew better than to ever rip me off. Trust me, they will love it."

"We have a full house tonight. They are coming to watch the main attraction and I can't wait to see just how strong he really is."

# CHAPTER THIRTY-ONE

## THE STREET

THE ORION STAFF HIT THE GROUND RUNNING. THREE HAD dressed accordingly. Each had another colleague watching, a sort of triangular approach – one to watch the watcher.

Three more had split up and were walking the back streets around Waterloo and Charing Cross railway stations, trying not to bleed the word police. The homeless, especially those on the run, had a sixth sense that rarely let them down when it came to identifying authority figures.

Jock Brown was one such person. He was forty last Thursday. He'd suffered from five of the eight Ds: Drink, Debt, Drugs, Divorce and Depression. One more and he'd take a walk into the next life.

At a shade under six foot, he still had a triangular upper body. A physical training instructor in an infantry regiment he'd seen and heard most things: limbless bodies, lifeless bodies, disembodied heads, men who had given up hope and the ones who worked day and night in rehab centres to learn to walk on prosthetic legs.

He'd also had a stellar career, and had reached warrant officer when he learned that his schoolgirl sweetheart Jenny had cheated on him with at least three of his unit – all whilst his had been stuck in some 'boil on the arsehole of the world' and fighting for Queen and country.

He went so far off the rails it was a miracle they ever got him back on track. But he kept falling again, and again. Lately, he had been trying to help the youngest kids, mainly boys, with a few girls thrown in for good measure. It was his go-to place now – helping someone else rather than himself. But the Black Dog was always prowling.

He was leaning against a wall when one of the Orion team had startled him. His reaction was swift. He'd lost a lot of the bulk but he could still fight, and he was fast.

The triangular team swung into action.

One grabbed his right arm and tried to hold him, but Brown was quicker, and he was enjoying it now.

"Best you've got, wee man?" He danced and weaved and jabbed, catching Andy West square on the chin.

Mal Hackett drew his baton. He'd seen enough.

"Oh naughty!" laughed Brown, now in his element. "I'll bend that wee fucker over your heed!"

"Mate, please calm down. We are not here to cause you any grief."

"Oh, I get it, you just want a quiet word. Yeah, yeah. Heard it all before, buddy. Before you know it, I'll be down the custody suite with you lot exploring my backside with a Maglite."

West had recovered. "Pal, if you don't calm down, I'll shove my torch so far up there, when you open your trap, they'll think you are a lighthouse."

Brown laughed. "I like this kid."

He slowed. "Yous boys had enough yet, eh? I can go all night. Declare me the winner and I'll leave yous alone."

"OK, you're the winner. Now stop pissing about and listen."

It was as if someone had thrown a switch. He stood straight, arms at his side.

"Thank you." West cautiously approached him, very aware, as a city dweller would approach the back end of a horse.

"Mate, all I want to do is give you a few quid, offer you some razors and soap, a box of matches, a sort of modern-day survival kit, and a warm, dry bed for the night – and some scran in return for a bit of help."

"Why should I help you, bed and scran aside?"

"Because we've had some AI intelligence indicating that ex-servicemen are being taken off the streets by a syndicate of criminals and..."

"And what?"

"And honestly, mate, at this time, I don't know. But it doesn't end well." He beckoned him around a corner into a doorway and showed him a picture of Red Jacket.

"We call him Red Jacket. Do you know him?"

"Aye, the funny thing is I was actually in the Royal Green Jackets. I left them when they were disbanded back in 2006. We'd just finished our last tour in Basra." He shook his head rapidly from side to side and sniffed audibly. An affliction he'd had since he learned of Jenny's repeated transgressions.

"You were saying?"

"Aye sorry, kid. So where is Nick off to now?"

"Nick?"

"Red Jacket. He's called Nick. Good lad, he joined up as a boy soldier. Saw some real action then got injured, his girlfriend left him with their baby. I'm sure you've heard it all before."

"Not in this case, no. Look, mate, he's in real danger, if he's even still alive."

"OK, what do you want from me?"

"Your knowledge, your skills and above all your guile."

"How many razors?"

"Ten and some new clothes too; socks, underpants, that sort of thing."

"I'm in. Can I sell the razors?"

"Do what you like, pal. Shave for all I care. Right, listen to my boss."

Murphy spent the next half an hour briefing their first recruit.

"Happy? Any questions?"

"When do I get my kit?"

"Tomorrow. Here's twenty quid. Don't spend it all at once. Now, any chance you can introduce us to any more of your circle of friends?"

"Be my pleasure. But let me do the talking. They'll trust you as far as I could throw you."

Murphy was happy. Having a man like Jock onside, was worth its weight in precious metals. A grizzly bear with military training; as long as they kept him off two of the Ds they'd be just fine.

Within three hours, they had a dozen on board: eleven men and a woman with multiple facial piercings and a black-and-brown mixed-breed dog.

News travelled fast, but appeared to stop as quickly as it had begun. There was a reason for that and it lay deep underground.

———

Murphy stopped at a phone box, or as they called them in the police a 'TK'.

The humble telephone kiosk was almost obsolete. Some were used as pop-up stores, giving away free books to the needy. Some were used as public toilets. Most had that just-pissed-in fragrance.

This one was rare. It was undamaged and actually took the coin that Murphy pushed into the slot.

He spoke clearly and as per the plan. Walls have ears.

"It's me."

"Go ahead."

"All sorted. The side has been picked. We've even got some substitutes. And jumpers for goalposts."

"Roger that."

———

The last sentence that Murphy had uttered was critical. It meant his team had managed to select exactly the right mix of people.

It was getting cool. It would be a cold night on the streets. He hoped the few hundred pounds he had dished out would be spent on hot food, not cold beer or drugs.

For the selected few, it was a chance of a new beginning. An opportunity to regain some respect.

When he had left the group under the road bridge that spanned the Embankment, he felt he could trust them. The girl intrigued him, though. Scruffy as hell and painfully thin. But she moved like an assassin.

# CHAPTER THIRTY-TWO

**PLAYTIME**

"No more bets, gentlemen."

The Master of Ceremonies strutted into view – a beacon in the darkness. A single and powerful light shone down onto him and the large circular shape covered in a black sheet.

"You know the rules, and remember, there are no rules. Highest bidder wins and it all rests on how long our players last this evening. Sometimes you will be betting on how many hours, sometimes minutes."

He stepped forward and yanked the cover off in one practised move. It revealed two men, heavily strapped to the wheel by their ankles and wrists.

One was Red Jacket, or Nick, still covered in his own drying blood, stripped to the waist, revealing arms that were bruised and grey, not the veins but the muscle. Red Jacket wasn't a traditional heroin abuser. Since he had left the army, he had needed to control the pain of his injuries.

Day and night, day and night, when will it end?

He injected into his muscles, and it helped. His drug was medicinal, or what he considered, pure heroin – not adulterated by this or that, or poison or fillers.

As the Master explained all the rules, Nick lay and listened. He soon worked out what was happening, and that both he and the other person he knew on the wheel behind him were the centre of attention.

There were no winners. This contraption he was strapped to along with a Romanian man called Christian was best described as an oversized roulette wheel. It was a wheel that would decide their fate. There were indeed no winners and neither was ever going to walk the streets again. If one got lucky, he might end up back in the stable with the others, waiting until the next race, fed on very little and offered a cup of water a day.

"To reiterate, gentlemen, I spin the inner wheel. This decides on who our first player will be."

'Let it be me,' said Nick to himself. 'Let it be me and please, let it be heroin so I can rapidly exit this place.'

"Then we spin the outer wheel and that will tell us which commodity the player has chosen."

"I am not choosing anything, guys. OK? Just so you know." Nick was struggling to even speak, his tongue so swollen that he sounded heavily drunk.

"I can see you all up there in your pathetic suits with your drinks and smiles and garish lifestyles. I hope you all die a slow and painful death. And get syphilis!" He mumbled and pushed each word out as the taste of fresh blood filled his mouth once more.

Nick earned himself a jab from a device that resembled a cattle prod.

"That the best you've got, pal? I've been stung by worse bees than that."

He got another, this time on his neck.

"OK. I give in. Wankers." He spat more congealed blood up into the air.

Another zap. They would break him one way or another.

The Master looked up at Constantin, who was wearing a new suit, as he did each night. The old one was burned as soon as possible, shoes too. He left no trace. He could afford to indulge. He wondered why more didn't. All you needed was an apparently endless stream of cash.

Constantin nodded.

The wheel stopped on red. It seemed so pathetically convenient. "Red!"

He turned the outer wheel, which whipped around like a horse-less carousel. Then the ball was dropped. It danced as it always did: skipping, bouncing, pausing, into a slot, then out once more, rolling, bucking and then...

"Ah, now this offers a few options. We have an M."

He looked up at the gallery. Who would like to go first?

A bet arrived. Five hundred on MDMA.

They all knew it was a soft bid, but it would loosen the boy up somewhat. Make him more susceptible if nothing else.

One hundred and fifty milligrams were more than enough.

"This drug, which many users call Molly, is a drug that very much increases self-awareness and empathy. Whilst there are a number of ways of taking the drug, our player will snort it this evening."

He nodded to the two men in black. One stepped forward with the tray, like a magician's assistant, whilst the other scooped some of the crystal onto a spoon and held it over Nick's nostrils.

They piled it in. No point in holding back. There were plenty more Nicks out there.

Roberts stood and watched. Shook his head slightly, closed his eyes, tried to blot it all out. What had happened to him in such a short amount of time? He'd become a nobody, that's what.

'No, Jason, these people are all somebodies. You are, too. Buck your ideas up and work out a way of getting out of here. It's what you and the team do best.'

The team.

Were they even looking for him?

Of course they were.

He asked endless private questions. It was keeping him sane and warding off the paranoia.

But one of those men in black looked familiar. Roberts convinced himself he knew him. Probably a CRO, that would be it. Just one of the many criminals that he'd locked up in his time.

A CRO. Beneath the gag, he smiled an ironic smile. An acronym that was accompanied with irony that he now had a Criminal Records Office number himself didn't escape him.

———

Nick spun around, the table was almost silent, the ceiling became a tobacco tar and magnolia blur. What light there was, drilled into his eyes. To his left or right, were the red pillars, he remembered that much. He tried to slow down the imagery by blinking, but his over-stimulated mind was now reacting with the drug, his initial physical resistance crumbling.

Euphoria. It was starting to creep into his sub-conscious state. He was feeling warmer, not just physically; he even had empathy for the poor bastard who was also strapped to the wheel. He knew he was there, just couldn't really see him. He called out.

"Mate, don't let them grind you down. We've got this, buddy."

Then he laughed. "We've got this."

A single dose should have taken half an hour, but this dose was massive.

His blood pressure increased, quite markedly. He was very warm now, no longer a sense of mental comfort, more a physical heat. His skin was burning.

"Anyone else fucking hot?" he yelled out, as the wheel kept rotating.

"Just me then? Turn it down. Turn the heat down."

Constantin looked down at the two men in black. They shrugged their shoulders. 'We are not doctors; how would we know?'

The Master, sensing a climatic ending, strutted into the light. "Last bets... make this one count." He hated himself, he needed to leave this sordid place.

"All bets closed."

# CHAPTER THIRTY-THREE

THE WHEEL SLOWED. NICK'S MIND WAS STILL RUNNING TWO TO three times faster.

The Master whispered into a lapel microphone linked to Constantin's left ear.

"He doesn't look good. We should stop this now."

"What is wrong with you? I employed you to do a job and now you challenge me?"

"No, not a challenge as such. I'm just concerned that we will run out of players if we continue at this rate."

"I will be the judge of that." Nicolescu hissed. "And only me. Or should I have you introduced as the next player?"

"No. There will be no need for that."

Mallory St John was kinky, as kinky as the next man, as much as those men who had inhabited his very niche nightclub, built into the railway arches of an up-and-coming part of London, on South Lambeth Road.

St John – pronounced Sinjun – was a man who was both very well known and yet almost completely anonymous. It depended upon which circle you found yourself in. For a person to be in St John's world, you needed to be male, bi-curious and definitely on the rich side of well off.

The upper echelons of the city protected him. It was where

Constantin had met him, eager to fulfil his latest and rather unusual fantasy, all behind the enormous wooden fortress doors, guarded by two equally large security guards.

They would have laid down their lives to protect the man who had adopted the sobriquet Master Toby.

If your idea of a good time was to be spanked until raw, gagged until you were choking, stretched, wrapped in rubber, clingfilm or rope, dangled from a noose tied around the ankles, deprived of air and filled with liquid forms that normally belonged in a kitchen, or the minds of someone depraved, then The Rack was your first port of call, a club you were introduced to – and to its owner, Master Toby. Nobody just walked through the door. Unless you had a six-figure income and could prove it, you rarely made it beyond the portcullis.

Once inside, it was simple, you were the property of Mr St John. What he decided was best for you, happened. No one filmed anything, no one *ever* spoke of the goings on. Phones were locked away, forbidden. It was the most honourable of clubs and stitched together with one word: trust.

But lately the six-figure incomes had waned somewhat and with new online dominatrices appearing and cheap adverts in cheaper newspapers offering every possible pleasure, The Rack had struggled, and St John and his staff had struggled to come to terms with the loss of an underground celebrity status and the trappings of success. It was, St John had said, the worst year on record, his own *annus horribilis*.

When one of his team had broken down and sobbed at the thought of the club closing its doors, St John had slapped him and told him to go and stand in the corner of the cellar until they came to fetch him. He'd been there for three days when St John had remembered.

Now he found himself the ringmaster, in a circus full of rich lions with egos so large they had struggled to fit more than a dozen in the old music hall at once. None of them knew the other's names, none wanted to, and if they had betrayed the one written rule, the punishment was to find themselves strapped to the wheel.

Its constant presence was a reminder never to cross the line.

That Constantin had gathered evidence against each man in the hall was not unexpected, that each man had no idea, was the Romanian's ace card.

He had it all: video and audio evidence – the first-hand accounts of young boys and girls. He knew each of their police and intelligence records almost off by heart. He had what some of them had but in greater amounts: access to the darkest corners of their lives – one which they had foolishly considered kept in the dark at all times.

He had access to the deepest possible data; criminal, financial, personal, private and the sort of intelligence that normally sits inside a server, inside another, locked down, behind closed doors with swipe card access and countless multi-layered passwords or better still, locked down and only accessible via a secure pipeline between two buildings.

Take the judge who had seen fit to quash his serious charges. He enjoyed the company of both sexes, but as young as possible and rarely out of their teenage years, and ideally, homeless and unwashed. He enjoyed the smell of the street corners, the dirty phone boxes, the urine-soaked underpasses.

The dirtier the better.

There, in that hideous desire to spend quality time with the people he called urchins, was his Achilles' heel.

No wonder the convictions had been quashed. Brilliantly, eloquently, overturned with no route to the Court of Appeal.

There was the city gent, with this three-piece heavily pinstriped suit, handmade shoes and the gaudy gold Bentley Continental, the one with his name stitched into the headrests. He had a love of expensive odoriferous cigars, and cocaine, and girls from Albania – three at a time, in his office, overlooking the Shard, with its glorious glassy needle poking up into the sky like a phallic statement to the world.

It was always in his office, overlooking the Shard, with its cameras.

Silly boy.

Then there was the Chinese warlord – by day, a devout, family-oriented and very successful businessman. Married, four children, all at private school, almost enough talent to build an orchestra. He had a wife with manicured nails, so long, they could have shredded his back – if they'd ever had sex, which they hadn't in years because she despised his secret fetishes.

He paid her a sizeable income to stay loyal to him and the children and to never ask questions and importantly never tell. She told him she knew he had a dark side but assumed it was in people trafficking or drugs. It suited them both. Her nails were used to great effect on other men.

Her husband enjoyed the feeling of wearing his very best hand-made suits from the lightning-fast tailors of the Far East, whilst having his head wrapped in latex – it had to be red and shiny, no other colour would do. For him, red was a lucky colour, it signified wealth, but it had to be applied roughly, the rougher the better. He had learned to hold his breath whilst his woman for the evening entertained him in any way that she wished. Quickly, though.

No one except Constantin knew their names, and only he held the details of their bank accounts from which monies were taken and deposited. That part was above board – totally divorced from the taxman but otherwise legitimate, and no records for the anti-money laundering brigade to trawl through.

Tonight the warlord was up by twenty thousand. He had a keen eye for human suffering, knowing just when life was about to end. He had grown up in Singapore and had risen from the lower quarters, the area of the city where the workers lived, to become one of the richest and most feared men the small nation had ever seen.

He was known to the people that both feared and respected him, by another simpler name.

Now he hovered his right index finger poised over the button on the tablet. Standing above the old hall, poised, up on the gallery, staring down, devoid of compassion, he waited.

He held his breath, deciding that when he let go, he would hit the button.

Nick was slowing now, looking truly awful.

Any. Second. Now. He hit the button. Fifteen minutes exactly.

Nick was gone.

He who pays the ferryman...

Nick had left the world of the living and was en route to the world of the dead.

There would never be a post mortem. How could there be without a body? MDMA wouldn't have been the cause of death. Lifestyle would have been the cause. Now he was just another faceless former inhabitant of a pavement somewhere in the city, but Nick was different. Nick would be missed.

———

The Master announced that there was a winner, almost to the second. The closer they got, the richer they became. Although the house normally won, it didn't tonight.

St John had a feeling of unease. He had never enjoyed his part-time role; dressing up and performing was his thing, but not to this crowd of wealthy animals. He sought nor gained no pleasure from watching people die. The art was to take them very close, to the very edge in fact, from which he always brought them back, alive. In that regard, he was a sexual anaesthetist.

# CHAPTER THIRTY-FOUR

Roberts woke suddenly. He was still immobile. His gag was wet through, his throat was parched. His eyes were raw and heavy. His muscles burned and his back throbbed with a pain the likes of which he had never experienced before. His legs twitched, restless, dancing, in need of magnesium. The pain was deep inside his legs; a line of incessant ants marching up and down his femurs, gnawing at the bone.

'Just kill me.'

He had seen enough: losing his wife, losing his home, his children, his family, his job. He had lost all hope. There was nothing left to fight for.

"Just kill me!" he shouted.

But then, in that one moment, he saw it. The hint of recognition.

Internally, to an audience of one, he said it aloud.

'I know who you are.'

Then the Master looked back and nodded from behind the harlequin-coloured death mask.

Across the city, Cade jolted awake. He'd been burning both ends of the candle for days and it was catching up with him. But in that moment between sleep and a fully awakened state, he had had what he later told O'Shea had been an epiphany.

"What's this revelation, Jack?" she asked, stirring a mug of tea, five times anti-clockwise, and once the other way. She always considered herself to be compulsive, but never obsessively so.

"Would you believe me if I told you?"

"Do I have any choice?" she smiled.

"No. I saw Jason in a dream. That rapid eye movement state that we exist in just as we jolt ourselves back into existence."

"Jack, he's gone. He's either managed to escape and is too fearful to face the authorities or someone has him. Frankly, I hope it's not the latter."

"You've given up on him already?"

"No. Never. Just trying to create a safety net."

"Well, tomorrow if the plans come to fruition, we can start. We'll find him. Trust me?"

"Not as far as I could kick you."

"I should put you over my knee, but..."

"But what? Come on, Jack, what?"

"I'm worried I might put my back out." He knew as soon as he'd said it, it was the wrong thing to say.

She slapped him. Hard. She meant it.

"Bloody hell, I was only joking," he said favouring the left cheek.

"Well, don't, not ever, when it comes to a girl's appearance, two things are sacrosanct. One, their size and two, their weight."

"I apologise. I was trying to be funny." He meant it.

She paused for a second. "I'm sorry. I wanted to tell you something earlier. It's important." She was right, and he'd forgotten to ask.

"I'm sorry, too. Let's start again, talk to me, I know something is wrong."

She looked down at the ground, her lips moved but no words arrived. She fought back the tears.

"Carrie?"

"I was pregnant, Jack! OK? Back then, back there... back, in that place." She was visibly clenching her fists and biting her bottom lip until it started to bleed.

He moved towards her.

"Don't, please." She ran her hands across her face, then over her hair. "Just for now, just listen. In fact don't say anything, just let me be *alone*." She was somewhere between angry and devastated.

"Why didn't you tell me?'

"I asked you to leave me alone."

"And how long will that continue? I love you, Carrie, and this is huge, for both of us."

"Yeah, make it all about you."

"Bloody hell, Carrie, I wasn't, I was just trying to say or do the right thing, I'm not exactly well-versed in this either."

They both remained silent for a few minutes.

"I couldn't tell you. OK? I just couldn't. I was angry enough for both of us. I just wanted to go away and hide, for as long as it took, possibly forever."

She looked at Cade. His face was strained with emotion, not knowing whether to speak or remain silent, to stay or go.

"OK. Then when you are ready, we can try to find a way to..." He tried to hold her hand, but she pulled it away.

"A hug won't help, Jack. Nothing will. And before you dare ask, yes, it was yours, he, or she, was yours."

Cade stood, and chose to say nothing. He went to walk away, then turned back to her.

"I'm disappointed that you'd even think I would doubt you. I thought we were soul mates." He shouted, stopping himself. She didn't need it. He paused, pointlessly checked his watch, looked around. "Was it the night that you escaped from him?"

She laughed. It was the complete opposite of how she actually felt. She nodded, then began to cry. Her tears were pouring down her face, she was trying to breathe, trying to stay in control.

"Yes, it was that night."

Now he held her hand, and slowly she allowed him to hug her.

"I can't begin to understand how you feel. All I can do is..."

He stopped. What should he do right now? Go and find the man that did this to her? Kill him? Leave her here, more vulnerable than ever? Drink? Punch a wall so hard he'd break the bones in his hand?

"Carrie. These last months have been awful, and I owe you an apology, I've been so focused on the work that I almost forgot you. I'm so very sorry."

She half-smiled. "We are all guilty of that, mate." It's all she could say before the tears began again.

It was an hour later when he unwrapped his arms from around her. Now he wasn't sure what to say, Men were from Mars after all – what he thought might be appropriate, could potentially be the very worst thing he could say.

He found himself visualising what Constantin had done to her, out in the marshes of Kent, carving a cross into her stomach – the shock possibly depriving her of a child.

"Is that why you went away for a while, afterwards, you said there was something you needed to do?"

"Now you know. Don't ask, it's best that way. Why should you suffer too?"

He had tears now. "Because I give a damn. And because I never really considered us having a child."

"And now you do?"

"Yes, I guess I do."

She held onto him again. "Can we just leave all this chaos behind and head back to your place, take the boat and go out into the ocean and just drift until we come across a new life?"

"We could, if that's what you really want, but you could get sea sick, there are some big swells out there." He squeezed her and slowly let go.

"Come on, you, we're both tired, let's go and do something away from here. My mind is beginning to rot. I'll find us somewhere new to stay, bear with me, I will never let you down again."

It seemed like the right thing to say.

"You didn't, he did, and one day I will look him in the eyes and remind him what fear feels like. I'm OK." She wasn't, but this was Carrie O'Shea, as tough as they came, when it counted. "For now, that's the best I can be."

———

The two men in black dragged Nick from the wheel and across the wooden floor to a waiting van, then strapped the new player onto the device and the process started once more.

Roberts knew he was next.

He couldn't wait.

———

"Keep Roberts until we have no one else left. The waiting will probably kill him, which is suitable to me." Constantin took a sip of a drink he had managed to import from his homeland.

They called it Tuica – pronounced Tswee-ka. It was made from fermented and distilled plums and so popular that over seventy percent of the Romanian harvest was used to make the drink, a colourless liquid whose impact was not felt until it was swallowed.

It was now his only vice. Nothing else warmed his soul.

He raised a glass to Roberts.

"Noroc!"

———

They fed the remaining men, gave them a drink, then washed them down with buckets of warm, soapy water. It wasn't for them, but for the boss, who had told them the smell of filthy men reminded him of Pazardzhik prison. Getting them washed, or at least washing away the filth that surrounded them, had become a priority.

They knew better than to remind him of that place.

# CHAPTER THIRTY-FIVE

## THE EMBANKMENT

"You take me to all the nicest places, darling. I am *so* flattered."

She tipped her head to one side and grinned. Her face was illuminated by the sodium lighting, which cut through a hint of mist that rolled off the river. It was cold, Del Murphy was right.

She pulled her coat tighter, pushed her gloved hands into her coat pockets, deep, grabbing onto the material. She feared the shadows lately, had done since she had been taken to that old factory not so long ago. To her few close friends, she told the truth, and that was that she believed she would never leave there, that place, so close to the city, yet so isolated out in the marshes.

She had experienced true fear and extreme courage that night.

Now she was stood, waiting for Cade to reveal his so-called master plan as a sense of fear gripped her once more.

What was he thinking?

———

He was thinking that he needed to get a grip of the situation. The issue before him was that he had no real idea of what the true situation was. There was an enemy, at least one, with a group of loyal or misguided followers. Good leaders had them. Great leaders had them in droves. In Nicolescu's case, he was a leader who led with stories of the past and a healthy fear of the future.

He paid well.

What Cade needed to do was break down that wall, brick by bloody brick. The Romanian had done what he did best; hide and move, move and hide. All Cade had to do was find where he had hidden and anticipate his next move. He'd done it before and succeeded in putting his nemesis in prison for a very long time.

Except the plan didn't go quite as planned, when a senior, much-admired and criminally feared judge had intervened and released Constantin on appeal.

It still irked Cade. Irked was far from suitable as a word to sum up his feelings, but there were ladies present.

He smiled. What was he thinking? O'Shea could out-fish a fish wife when and if she needed to. She was his fiercest ally and sharpest critic. She was the fuel that drove him and he hated his target for damaging her so.

———

He'd achieve his aim, brick by individual brick.

———

They waited about two minutes, O'Shea shivering against the cold. Cade trying his best not to. Had Roberts been present, he would have cast doubt upon the ability of a brass monkey to retain his wedding tackle.

Cade rubbed O'Shea's back. Pulled her a little closer.

"You OK?"

"No, not really, you know that now, but I'll tell you how you are doing at the end of our romantic getaway to the hotspots of the Embankment on one of the coldest nights in living history! Come on, Jack, what *are* we doing here?"

———

The first person appeared from the darker corners of the buttressed bridge. Then another, looking around, up and down the street as if they mistrusted everyone. Because, of course they did.

Within twenty, thirty seconds at best, three people had appeared. There were no passers-by and only passing traffic.

They had an air of the undead, rising from the ground and it frightened O'Shea.

The largest of the group approach Cade.

"You Mr Cade?"

"I am. My friends call me Jack. I'd like you to."

"Where I come from friendship is a badge of honour, worn by the few and rarely celebrated."

"And where *do* you come from?'

He gestured with a thumb over his left shoulder. "Just there."

As answers went, it was articulate.

"I guess I asked for that. Try again. I'm guessing you are Jock. Is that your real name?" It was a mistake.

"I told the other copper that I would help. Let's leave it at that should we?"

"Let's. I apologise. I just like to know who I'm working with, call it paranoia."

"I get paranoia, Mr Cade, we all do, but you lot have no idea whatsoever, try sleeping on a roll of carpet under a layer or two of cardboard, waking up stinking of someone else's piss and you'll get it completely."

"Well, you smell OK to me right now, Jock." He held out his hand, left it there, stranded in the cold air, waiting.

Brown took it and squeezed, and Cade squeezed back, running his index finger up the inside of Brown's wrist. It helped reduce the pain, an old trick passed down from his police tutor, back in the days of roaming the streets of Nottingham.

"I can't imagine. The nearest I ever came to being homeless was when I walked away from my marital love nest."

"Did you have an affair?" He glanced at O'Shea.

"No, seeing as though you asked, I didn't. My ex-wife Penny did.

With half of the section I worked with. Sometimes at the same time."

"Ouch, that hurt," he laughed.

"It did, but the temporary love of a green-eyed Irish girl helped me to get over it."

O'Shea gave him a less-than-subtle nudge in the ribs. Too soon.

"Forgive me. Whilst we are exchanging names and pleasantries, this is Carrie O'Shea. One of the best criminal analysts in London, possibly in the country."

"And your girlfriend?" asked another man, who had slowly edged forward.

This group demanded honesty and Cade knew that if his plan had any chance of working, integrity would be key.

"Yes, seeing as though you asked, she is, more than that actually."

"Shame, I could, you know, if you weren't around..."

"I bet you could. And to be fair, if Jack wasn't so good to me, I might let you." O'Shea replied, smiling nervously.

Touché.

"Two to the body, one to the head." The ex-soldier grinned where once a row of white teeth had been. "Bullets that is..."

"I get it." She grinned back.

"I'm Jock. Jock's good friend and tactical advisor." He held out an ochre-stained hand.

She removed her glove and took it immediately, shaking it warmly. It was a test, and she had just passed.

"Good to meet you, Jock. Are you all called Jock? Can I take a guess at the names of your band of merry men?" She pointed to the others that had come out of the darkness, four in total and into the half-light, still protected from the now driving rain and the ever-present threat of cameras.

"Well, you're the analyst, miss. How about me, for starters?" A rough-looking man, in his thirties at most, stepped forward sharply, as if on the parade ground. He had a twice-broken nose and hooded dark brown eyes that were guarded by a forest of wiry black hairs.

"Hello..." He was actually darkly appealing, if you liked your men hidden under layers of charity shop sweaters and smelling of damp carpet and the last remnants of a discarded can of a famous brand anti-perspirant.

"I'm guessing your name is... Hugh?"

The group laughed. As a group of squaddies would, gathered at the back of a four-tonner waiting to head out on a route march, the last they needed to do before qualifying. That slight nervousness in their banter.

"Come on, mate, that was a surreal guess. You've got to give her that one," offered another of the group, who were warming to their visitors.

"I'd give her one alright." They all laughed, except one.

"McCann!" The surname was practically barked by a thin, greying man, once tanned, shorter than the rest, stepping forward, he parted the group.

"Allow me to apologise for Corporal McCann's overly vigorous view on the fairer sex, Miss O'Shea. Although I suspect he might have met his match in you."

The older man held out a thin hand, it was far warmer than she had anticipated. He then offered it to Cade, who had quickly scanned the new man, noting that he was very different to the rest, as chalk is different to cheese.

It was the accent, the way he carried himself.

"I'm Phillip Marriott and it is my absolute pleasure to welcome you to the best kept secret in town." He gestured towards the bridge.

"We affectionately call it *The Baguette*. Would you care to join us? The kettle is on."

# CHAPTER THIRTY-SIX

**GOING UNDERGROUND**

"After you, miss."

Hugh McCann was quick on his feet, up two stone steps and over a stone balustrade.

He held out his hand. "Take it, we haven't got all day."

She stepped up and in a second was over the balustrade, the Thames to her right and in the distance across on the South Bank, the iconic London Eye.

Cade was next. He took a moment to study his surroundings, on the bridge was a simple sign, it read, 'This is bridge 6XTD. Charing Cross. Victoria Embankment.'

On the stone wall that also acted as a flood barrier, a stonemason had carved *Victoria Embankment* and etched it in gold.

There was no doubting where they were.

Cade stepped up and over the balustrade and ducked down to join O'Shea and McCann. The others followed with the last man sweeping the terrain with his eyes, all that was missing was a rifle and the ghosts of a patrol on the streets of Londonderry.

McCann approached the red brick arch and slid open the wall, or at least that is how it looked to O'Shea. He stood and held the hoarding open. The last man watched every angle as the driving rain drove people off the streets, back to their warm hotels, flats and apartments.

O'Shea was wishing she was back in hers, only a sizeable stone's throw from here, but was also marvelling at the ingenuity of the doorway. Day or night, it had obviously fooled those that needed to be fooled.

Cade followed. It was a case of now or never. As he watched Marriott walk, he sensed a man he could trust, and the feeling must have been mutual or they wouldn't be heading down a flight of stone steps into a colder place.

"Follow my men, only a short journey. You have nothing to fear."

They walked along the candle-lined and partly lit corridor until they came to another doorway, guarded by a bear of a man who made Jock Brown look wholly inadequate and almost impotent.

"As you were, Terry."

Terry, the aforementioned bear stood aside and dragged a hefty sheet of marine ply to his left.

"After you, sir."

They carried on, Cade sensing they were heading deeper, but only marginally so. He felt inclined to walk with Marriott, leaving O'Shea two steps behind him, being chaperoned by the ever-attentive McCann.

Cade broke the ice first.

"I once chased our primary target along an underground network, not a million miles from here."

"Yes, we heard. Caused a bit of excitement back in the day. The old coffee shop from memory, just up the road from here at Blackfriars Bridge?"

"I'm impressed."

"Don't be. Standard operational procedures for us, Mr Cade. We pride ourselves on knowing everything that goes on below ground in this city and as much above ground as we possibly can."

"You genuinely remember that day?"

"Me? No hardly, I was somewhere else entirely, much warmer in fact, but urban legends like that don't just fade away from society like we all have. Tea or coffee?"

"Erm, tea. Thanks."

They were now in a much larger room; it was warmer too. A fire with deep red embers was doing an admirable job of taking away the chill and adding extra light. Where the smoke went, Cade had no idea.

"Apologies for the reception committee, but you can never be too careful around here. The Baguette is our home now."

"I have to ask…"

"Named, incorrectly as it happens by the brute of a doorman outside – he's called Warwick by the way, but prefers Terry. A Royal Engineer. Did his time, then found himself on the wrong side of the tracks. His kid sister was assaulted by a young guy from their village. Terry took exception and decided to have a little chat with the offender. He was in hospital recovering from the chat for nearly a year. Terry got out of prison, was discharged from the army and became a drifter in a city whose pavements are most certainly not paved in gold. In that respect, he's like everyone else down here in this rather magnificent display of Victorian engineering."

"And the name?"

"Ah yes, sorry, the cold outside has numbed my mind somewhat. Have you ever heard of Sir Joseph William Bazalgette?"

"Impressive name. No, should I have?"

"Not unless you have a penchant for drainage! You see Sir Joe, or as we call him Old Joe Bazz, was responsible for engineering the drainage systems in the metropolis of London. He created much of the embankment you have just walked on, his engineering skills saw to it that almost one hundred and twenty miles of modern sewage systems were built in London, cleaning up the Thames and eradicating cholera."

"Impressive man."

"That's nothing, Jack. He had a complete mental breakdown in his thirties and yet recovered to design much of what you see. He married and he and his wife went on to have ten children. That plaque outside is all there is to promote him and his work. He was a remarkable man. And men like him unwittingly helped us to find a new home some years ago."

"Sewers?" Cade clearly telegraphed his concerns, flashing back to the time at Blackfriars.

"Fear not, young Jack, no, we don't live in the sewers, as beautiful as they actually are. You know, Sir Joe actually helped remove what they called The Great Stink from this city. Given the reputation of the homeless, we like to celebrate his work, and in doing so provide for the poor and allow them to clean up their act."

"An underground Robin Hood..."

"If you like. Here comes Friar Tuck with the tea. Come on, I'll show you and Miss O'Shea around. Hope you enjoy a good walk?"

"Just how big is this place?"

"Large enough to send that tea cold by the time you return. I'd bring it with you."

Marriott walked, with a very slight limp, towards another door.

"We keep them closed to keep the heat in. This is the dorm block, across the way there is the mess, down there the latrines. All very Napoleonic, but that suits us."

"I note you have power down in this part."

"We do. The candles in the entrance way, and the abundance of what Corporal McCann calls old shite, is designed to create the appearance of a poor-quality squat, should anyone ever decide to try and examine the place."

"Has that never happened? Surely there must be maintenance work needed from time to time?"

"Of course. If the Chief of Works wasn't my old RSM."

"You have a regimental sergeant major on the council?"

"Indeed. Everyone needs an RSM. The difference is RSM Tim Hill found a path of gold when he left the mob. He has never forgotten his brothers in arms though and has skilfully altered plans to show this as capped, boxed in, beyond need of repair, best forgotten. A bit like a few of my people."

"I noticed the slight limp."

"Yep, quite literally a war wound. Bosnia. A lump of shrapnel. Only a small bit, but I ignored it and it went bloody nasty and I nearly lost my leg. Ironic really when you think I'd managed to lead teams in Kosovo, the Gulf, Afghanistan and even Sierra Bloody Leone. When I got back from Bosnia, I was accused of turning a blind eye to atrocities. It never happened, of course, like a few at the time, I was a scapegoat, a puppet of the government of the day, who were desperate to slash military budgets and in order to do so they needed some muck to spread."

"And you got in the way of the muck spreader?"

"If that's what we are calling him then, yes. One of the larger newspapers picked up my story – and before you know it my darling wife of fifteen years had picked up our little boy and hightailed it back to Arbroath where we met. I was investigated, of course. It took two years, Jack. In that time, I developed a dependency on opiates to numb the pain. They kicked me out because I refused to accept a formal warning. I was innocent. Before you could say homeless junkie, I was on those fentanyl patches, then stronger stuff until only the drugs I didn't need a prescription for would do the trick."

"Heroin?"

"Good Lord, no. I saw and destroyed far too much of that shit in Afghanistan. No, my downfall was ketamine. I mixed it with a few over-the-counter meds and life became bearable. Well, as bearable as it could be for a forty-something ex-soldier with a limp, five maxed-out credit cards and debts up to my eyeballs. And when my life was about to be washed downstream in the Thames, that bear of a man we call Terry, hooked me out of the water with one hand and dragged me inside this place."

"Impressive. And now you owe them your life."

"No, Jack. I owe them theirs. Anyway, turn left here."

"Good God above." Cade was genuinely impressed.

O'Shea stood, blinked a few times, and raised her mug.

"A toast to the Victorians and their building skills and to the new inhabitants of the Baguette. Unbelievable."

———

The maps that covered one wall were plotted. Beneath them, images of people, mostly unpleasant looking people. There were three desks and three chairs, and next to each, a filing cabinet.

There was a racking system with 'go bags' all ready to depart in a hurry, each filled with enough kit to enable its owner to survive a week somewhere else.

On the right wall a simple sign that slid in and out as the need arose stated the current situation.

BIKINI Black.

"You'll no doubt know all about that system? The MOD dropped it a few years ago, but we like to live in the past, when times were a little brighter."

"I do, but why Black?" Cade asked. "I thought we were much higher on the new UK threat matrix?"

"Oh no doubt we are, Jack. But this is for us and you are the threat. Or at least we thought you were until you met one of our team. We are rather hoping you know where Nick is and how we can get him back."

"Nick?"

"You called him Red Jacket. He was one of my new unit. His girlfriend is too. The only girl on the team. Between you and me none of us has the balls to kick her off! Come on, I'll introduce you both to Doc."

"Doc? Is she your medic?"

"And some. Like the rest of us, she chose a different path and lived to tell the tale. Doc!" He called across the room where in an alcove a young woman was working on a map. She stood up and turned around.

Cade was looking at a familiar face, she had multiple piercings, a teardrop tattoo, and a dirty ponytail.

"Hello. We meet again. I'm Jack, where's your dog?"

O'Shea gave him a look that said, 'Is there anyone you don't know?'

"He's under the table. Don't worry he's been fed. This must be Carrie_78?"

"OK – so you've managed to get some intel on me."

He smiled a genuine smile. Why fight it when the team he was talking to clearly had skills and were on his side.

"Never give your phone to an intelligence officer, Mr Cade, at least not with a password as appalling as yours." She turned, grabbed the phone, and tossed it to him.

"I think you'll find you can use it now. The password is now McKenzie*John*90." She flashed a brilliant smile.

"Don't mention it. The good news, by the way, is that your primary target doesn't stand a fat rat's chance of deciphering that. A little birdie told me you've moved underground to avoid prying eyes and listening ears?"

"We have." He looked over his shoulder to find the whole team had quietly entered what appeared to be the briefing room, for what Cade called the Operation Dignity team.

Realising they were all there, he decided to brief them.

It took ten minutes – no PowerPoint, no sexy slides or buzz-words, just straightforward talk.

"So, even within the walls of New Scotland Yard you are compro-mised, Mr Cade?." asked a Welshman with fiery red hair and a matching moustache. "That can only mean one thing in my book. They call me Taffy by the way."

"I would never have guessed. Which is what in your book, Taffy?"

"Well, you've got a trust issue. Line up the men and women on your team and tick them off one by one. Ask yourself, would you go to war with them? Do you trust them with your life? If so, and you really mean it, then throw the circle out wider, who does that encompass now? All the way, outwards until you're at the Commis-sioner's desk itself. Then come back, slowly checking and I guar-antee those with a hint of uncertainty will be on your new threat map."

"Would you put your hand in the fire for them?"

"I'm not sure."

"It was a phrase I heard recently, seems to fit now. Actually, Taffy, I don't need to do that. I suspect my net needs to be thrown over not only the police, but the wider system. The main player I'm hunt-ing, who coincidently got acquitted of some brutal crimes, just happens to be the ringleader of a group of men hellbent on causing me and my team utter misery and getting just a little richer in the process."

"Any signs that he means to carry this out Jack?" asked Marriott.

"My friend and colleague DCI Roberts lost his wife recently, blown to bits in a car wash with an apparently random passer-by. Then the former senior prison officer who had diligently managed my target turned up at his home as dead as dead can be — poisoned."

"And we've got a growing number of people, so far, all men, adding to that list and all dying in unconventional ways. I've had some news that one died of an overdose of adrenaline," added O'Shea.

"Easily done if you are acutely aware of anaphylaxis, miss."

"But if you are, you inject yourself only once. This guy looked like he'd been stood in front of a dartboard. Trust me, someone is having fun at our expense, their aim to piss us off, keep us off the trail and keep our noses out of their business." She paused to scan the room; they were all listening intently as she held her phone up for all to see.

"Jack is the key for us. Our target is this man. Romanian national Constantin Nicolescu and he's the driving force behind a resurgence of a criminal group we bagged not long ago and he, being a rather bitter man, wants revenge. And having experienced his hospitality, I know what he's capable of. And frankly, I'd rather spend the rest of my days down here in this palace with you lot than face him again."

"But what I don't get is why Mr Cade has to adopt some sort of radio silence. It makes no sense to me as an operator who's faced a few enemies in his time," said Taffy.

Cade responded. "Put simply, mate, every time I so much as veer off the music chart, play a bum note, Nicolescu is waiting to punish me. If I fail to listen to his explicit instructions, someone ends up dead, including your former teammate, for which I feel personally responsible." He waited a second for someone to lay into him, physically or verbally, but it never came. He nodded an acknowledgement.

"With luck on our side, we'll find a body, but not even that is guaranteed. This man is evil personified; well-trained, probably bank-rolled by someone wealthy and on a mission. I suspect this is his last, too. He's making hay at my expense. He knows damn well that I can't justify taking the lives of defenceless people." He paused again. "People like Nick."

Doc McKenzie spoke. "Then may I suggest we go and find him, Mr Cade? Before it's too late..."

"I suspect it already may be Doc." Marriott was very matter of fact. "If this group is as capable as Mr Cade suggests, then we need to be fully prepared to learn of Nick's demise. All we can do is equal the odds a little and with Jack's permission, that can start first light tomorrow."

He turned to Cade. "Do you have a moment? Forgive me, Carrie. I need to do this."

Cade looked at O'Shea. "You OK?"

She nodded, waved her hand, for now she was just that, OK.

The two men walked into another corridor. Old lights flickered to life.

"Fancy a walk back in time, Jack?"

# CHAPTER THIRTY-SEVEN

THEY HAD BEEN WALKING FOR ABOUT FIVE MINUTES WHEN Marriott had finished the summary of his life and was about to start on the back stories of some of his team when Cade stopped him.

"You've been abandoned by your families and the authorities? That hardly seems fair, Phil."

"You'll be telling me next that life isn't fair and I'd agree. In answer to your question, yes, we feel that society has abandoned us. They say we are like rats, never more than a metre away from one in this city. Where were those people in Kosovo, Iraq and Afghanistan, Jack? Don't bother answering that. Open that door, would you? The light switch is on the left."

Cade pushed open a heavy door and flicked the switch.

"Now that's both an impressive sight and a flashback. So, you are like sewer rats then?" He smiled in the low light as he ran his fingers over the glazed engineering bricks that lined the tunnel.

"They knew what they were doing back in those halcyon days of underground engineering, didn't they?"

"They most certainly did, and it's the subterranean element of this city that enables us to stay dry, and importantly, to move around undetected. With a few carefully positioned friends in high places, we've become the new version of the Desert Rats, who my grandfather so proudly fought with and as you so magnificently put it, we are the sewer rats."

"I didn't mean to offend."

He smiled. "Who said I was offended? It's a compliment. Fancy seeing a bit more? That map there, the one with the red and blue lines? That's the Victorian sewer map. They are in the process of starting a new super sewer to sort out the current issues, what with that and the new underground tunnels this whole city is awash with engineering masterpieces. We hear them often."

"And yet no one has bothered you?"

"Apart from the select few, no one even knows we are here. And that's how society likes it. They can commission a four-billion-pound sewerage system, but allow veterans to sleep in puddles and shop doorways."

"Is there any way I can help?"

"Not unless you can divert some serious money towards the situation."

"How many men and women are we talking about?"

"Hundreds? Thousands? Who knows? Nobody records the sort of data that doesn't look good on the balance sheets or becomes the subject of Prime Minister's question time. Anyway, enough of my idle whinging, I want to brief you on our plans. Forgive me for dragging you away from Miss O'Shea, but in our world, we trust very few people. Do you trust her?"

"With my life, and vice versa. And yes, we've been in that situation. I am what society might call a complete shit magnet."

"Well, then you are in the right place. See that cupboard?"

He looked. "Yep."

"It's full of Hazmat gear, the cupboard next to it is brim full of cleaning kit. We may lack weaponry, but we have bucket loads of experience, skill and guile. Consider us on side. We just need a signal – and that's where Doc comes in. She's a superb intelligence officer – fell under the spell of heroin whilst serving in Helmand, and soon found herself in Colchester with a raft of drug charges and a court martial. They missed just how ballsy she was, Jack. She tells me you were chasing Nick the day he was taken?"

"Sort of. Cops are like greyhounds, Phil. They see a hare running and their DNA tells them to chase it. Nick saw me and ran, and I needed to know why. I was so close to him when a three-man team took him off the street in broad daylight. No one even batted an eyelid. I knew Doc knew more than she was letting on. I also knew she was a sharp operator. What does her intel tell you about our common enemy?"

"That's a fine question. It tells us that homeless men are being snatched off the streets, some are lured, but mainly those that put up a fight are targeted. Nick was one of those. As you can imagine, we would normally debrief someone – where they'd been and what they had done, but so far..."

"None have ever returned?"

"In one, my friend. There are some power brokers behind this. For the life of me, I don't know the answer yet but you have my word that we will do all we can to support you. Come on, just you and me and a thousand miles of sewerage tunnels, what's the deal with your situation? Why no comms? Seems a little over the top for a well-funded police unit to be kowtowing to the likes of a mere criminal."

Cade watched a foreign body drift by in the pale green water that lined the very bottom of the old tunnel.

"It doesn't stink down here as much as I thought it would."

He sighed, which echoed along the brickwork pipe. "You see, the issue is that I received a message from one of Nicolescu's most ardent supporters and it was very clear. Back away, stop intervening, and no one will get hurt. Continue and we will pick off your team one by one, starting with Carrie."

"And you believe them?"

"One hundred percent."

"But your team is far bigger than theirs, surely?"

"Right again, but we've got a problem at the heart of that team, and he has a fearsome reputation and lofty connections. I can't prove it – yet. But I will and when or if I do, I'll happily slap the cuffs on him."

"Is that what you really intend to do, Jack? Can't some well-rehearsed accident befall him?"

"I tried to shoot him during the incident at Blackfriars – so close. An inch to the left and I would have ended all this misery."

"Could be arranged quite easily."

"Well, I'm not normally a violent man... sorry, what rank were you?"

"What *rank* I was is irrelevant. What matters is *who* I am now. I was in the finest fighting force on the planet – the old boys keep an eye on me, you know Christmas and birthdays, but ultimately I'm off grid these days and frankly that's how I like it."

"Then I'll do my utmost to keep you there."

"Sounds like a plan. First things first give your troublesome colleague to us, we'll take him out of the equation. Piece of cake, home in time for tea and medals and a binge fest of *Downton Abbey*."

"You watch *Downton*?"

"Love it, all the team do. That and *Coro*."

"You're winding me up, aren't you?"

"Am I? We've got all the mod cons down here; you just haven't seen the full set up yet. We'll save that for day two. Right, as we say down here, onwards and sideways."

"Thanks, Phil. And that chat we had about my team and their safety."

"Mother is the word of the day."

———

They returned to the main communal room to find O'Shea sat with McKenzie and being inducted into the world of the sewer rat.

"And you can pop up wherever you like? Jack, you should see this, it's incredible."

"I've just had a quick tour, have to agree, it looks impressive. Half of those tunnels have been forgotten about."

"Along with their inhabitants. It's disgusting."

"I agree completely. I aim to do something to help them when this is all over, but I'm not sure that isn't a little bit patronising."

"You think they like living down here?"

"Yes, actually, I do. Come on, we need to get some rest. Phil, can you escort us out and let us know what we need to do to communicate with you."

"Of course. Terry, Jock, if you'd be so kind to exfil our new team members. Thank you."

"Seriously, how do we communicate with you?"

"That's easy, just put your message into a little container and flush it down the toilet. We'll be waiting to catch it. Job done, so to speak."

Cade looked at a dead-pan Marriott. "You're kidding, right?"

Marriott beamed. "Of course I'm bloody kidding. Each bridge in this city has a number. Send a text message to us stating a location and a time and one of us will meet you. Carrie has the number in her right pocket."

"You've got cell phones?"

"Yes, what do you think we are, cavemen?"

———

When Cade and O'Shea reached the doorway, they immediately sensed they were somewhere different.

"Different door, Terry?"

"Absolutely, sir. We are a professional outfit. Have to keep the team on their toes. You never know who is watching. We might be homeless but we are far from useless."

"Look, mate, I wasn't trying to put you down…"

The bear held up his enormous paw and rested it on Cade's shoulder. He spoke in a broad West Midlands accent.

"Chill out, brother. I was winding you up. Look, you need to see things from our perspective. We live like this rather than under a cold and damp railway arch with a load of smack heads or glue sniffers. It's all most of us have. We earn enough between us to ensure we have everything we need, and for some of us this is all the famCily we have left. Isn't that right, Hugh?"

"On the nose, Terry," he replied in a scouse accent that was sharp enough to slice through granite.

"Can I ask what happened to you?" asked O'Shea cautiously.

"No. Because respectfully, miss, it's got fuck all to do with you."

"I'm sorry. I didn't mean to…"

"Don't worry. A kiss will clear your debts."

"Incorrigible. My dad was a Royal Marine, Hugh. Does that help?"

"Hardly. I used to despise them. I'm a para. Or was. Death from above and all that. And look where it got me, a knackered back from too many landings and a drug habit to clear the pain."

"You still using?"

"Nope. I've been clean now for seventeen months, four days and about eleven hours."

"Can I say I'm proud of you?"

"You can."

"Can I offer you some money? You know, for essentials. Would I offend you?"

"Hugely. How much?"

"Twenty quid do?"

"You were right, I am offended."

"OK, we'll go. But we'll hopefully see you again soon." She leant forward and kissed him on the cheek.

He laughed, almost blushing. "You know, miss, I'd have taken fifteen."

She smiled back as she walked away. "You know, Hugh, I'd have given you thirty."

"Bloody typical! Where you off to now, somewhere lovely and romantic, I bet?"

"Dinner, probably. We are both starving, it's been a long day and we have a lot to talk about."

"Enjoy and take care, yeah. I hear Covent Garden is smashing for a romantic dinner for two. You taking a cab or walking?"

"What do you recommend?"

McCann whistled down the street. "One of these. You can look like tourists, no one will even bother to look at you."

It seemed ideal. It was the first time in days that either had even considered relaxing.

# CHAPTER THIRTY-EIGHT

THE RICKSHAW PULLED UP ALONGSIDE THE PAVEMENT, IT'S REAR red lights flashing hypnotically. It had a bright red open cab and a frantically pedalling cyclist up front. The rider had been sat under the bridge waiting for a fare.

"Where to, chief?" The rider asked in a local accent with a splash of Warsaw.

"Upper St Martins Lane, please. I hear there's a great Mexican restaurant up there."

"Ah Covent Garden, yes, beautiful. Dinner with the pretty lady, is it?"

"Something like that."

Cade turned to look at McCann, but he had gone. With the skill of an aboriginal elder, he had blended into his environment and was nowhere to be seen. Camouflaged, it was as if he'd been wearing a brickwork suit.

As the rickshaw rider negotiated traffic, he deftly passed a phone back to Cade.

"It's for you, guv."

O'Shea looked quizzically at Cade, who held the phone to his ear.

"Yes?"

"Jack, it's Phil. Just wanted to say thanks for trusting us. Look there's been a slight development. One of our field team has witnessed something that may just play into your hands."

He passed the details. Cade noted the salient points, thanked Marriott, then hung up and passed the phone back to the rider.

O'Shea knew not to ask until they were alone later.

———

"Have you ever seen such a set up as that?" she asked, trying to change the subject but stay on course.

"No. And I don't think we saw it all either. What did you make of Phil? He was obviously the leader."

"Doc filled me in whilst you went walkabout. He was a captain in the Royal Marines. Two of his men were accused of war crimes, out in the Balkans, they made the media a while back. Marriott defended them to the hilt, said they were innocent. The board didn't believe him or his men and accused him of perverting the course of justice. He came back from the conflict zone an injured man and ended up a broken one. But according to Doc there is no finer leader and that is why the team follow him."

"I just hope they can help when the time is right."

"And when will that be?"

"When those planets align. I feel a break is imminent. Just a question of us being ready to act upon it."

———

Within seven minutes, they had arrived at the Cantina Laredo. It was an authentic Mexican restaurant that had once featured in some intelligence chatter about Nicolescu. Where better to eat than the lion's den itself?

Nicolescu and his then dinner companion had enjoyed Mexican food too, and the Cantina was considered the best in town, and that was the end of the connection. They both liked it hot it seemed - plenty of chilli peppers. The hotter the better.

For both Cade and O'Shea, it felt good to be doing something normal, for their lives had become anything but lately.

She leant forward and spoke, "It seems the Dignity team have an impressive network. They even have transport sorted."

"I can see it now, a pursuit in rickshaws! Jesus, Carrie, this is ludicrous. I feel I can't do anything without somebody watching. Even now, outside, look at that blue car, for instance, parked as if it was the most natural place in the world to park."

"Perhaps they are waiting for someone? Relax."

"It's a cycle lane. If I was on the beat, I'd give them two choices. A ticket or a tow truck. And look at the name of the building. Orion House. It doesn't get any weirder."

"Just because our team is called Orion you think that's a coincidence? Six degrees and all that. Come on, Jack, you need to let go a little."

He stared at the car through the tinted glass. He knew. He had that worrying feeling in his stomach. She wouldn't admit it, but she did too.

Cade walked as he talked. "You order for us, I'm just going to the gents."

"Yep." She stared at the menu, seeing nothing but blurred lines.

"I needed to talk to you, for God's sake."

———

Cade tucked in behind a party of five that were leaving, then exited the restaurant. A black cab pulled up and the group approached it. Cade added himself to the group until the cab pulled away, ducked in behind a delivery van and walked unseen to the large pillared entrance way to Orion House.

He positioned himself so that he couldn't be obviously observed, but could see the occupants of the dark red Vauxhall Insignia. He used the angled, glassy doorway as a periscope.

He watched for a few minutes. Cars passed by, pedestrians too. The two males inside didn't flinch. They never took their eyes off the restaurant. Some surveillance officers they were.

He'd picked them out in minutes. He saw them both as warts on the arse-end of the man who had all-but threatened him and the Orion team with prison if they so much as stepped one inch off of the line – the framework of values that was expected of an occupant of New Scotland Yard.

They were dressed down in a nice car, a nice car with very discreet blue strobes. For Cade, they were as discreet as a lighthouse in a darkroom. Amateurs.

He checked his watch, his favourite. The one with the large illuminated hands. Four minutes. Carrie would be getting suspicious by now. Time for those planets to align or collide.

He stepped out, onto the wide paved area, two steps down, four to the car. He banged the side of his fist on the driver's window.

The driver nearly leapt out of his seat and then composed himself quickly. He put the window down a few inches and spoke.

"What?"

"A man of few words. Perhaps I can ask you the same." He grabbed the ignition key and pulled his arm back through the gap.

"Give me those keys now or seriously I will…"

"Will, what? From where I'm standing, you two are a pair of badly drawn officers attempting to play the surveillance game. Well, let me tell you, you've failed. Now, unless you want me to drop these keys down this drain, I suggest you start getting chatty. Your call. And by the way, for two of Jenkinson's men you should be ashamed of yourselves, parking in a cycle lane, I mean what happened to integrity and honour?"

"Look, mate, I don't know what you are on about, we are here for someone else. Now do us both a favour, give me the keys back or I'll lock you up for obstructing a constable in the execution of his duty."

"Not until you tell me why you are here." Cade palmed his ID.

The driver looked, then shook his head slightly. "We were watching those two over there, who were watching you, as it happens, but you've put paid to that. Seems you *had* friends in high places. We are not on Jenkinson's team. Can't stand the man. But those two over there, they just might be. Keys, please. Now."

He dropped them into the driver's lap.

'Rookie mistake, Cade. Scan your environment. Don't add two to itself and end up with five.

His heart skipped; his stomach turned.

"Sorry, boys. I really am."

They started the car and drove away leaving Cade to look at the two scruffy men leaning against a shop doorway in the adjoining street – a hundred paces away and now as obvious as a nun in a friary.

He had two choices.

He chose the latter.

Running across the street, he caught O'Shea's eyes. She turned her head rapidly, dumped her drink and walked quickly towards the door.

'Not again, Jack.' She decided to ring it in. Sod the consequences.

"Dave, it's me, this will be very quick. Jack and I have a situation in Covent Garden. Can you get someone travelling that way now?"

"I'll do my best. Stay safe. Anything else I need to know?"

"No idea. Look for a red balloon. Or some other signal."

She cleared the line and headed out onto the street, with an inquisitive duty manager following her.

"Miss, is everything OK?"

She didn't look back.

The two men split up. One ran down Tower Street, the other, the slower of the two, along Monmouth Street. They were divided by a tall and narrow row of buildings, typical of the area and filled with upmarket retailers, cafes and perfumeries.

O'Shea chose to follow the faster of the two men, to see if she could pick up some intelligence, a car, maybe, or a better description. This was like the old days. A good old-fashioned foot chase with no idea where they would end up. She just wished she was as fast as she used to be.

Cade was gaining on the slower man. He was probably forty, with short mousy hair, jeans, desert boots – hardly the choice of an athlete. It was clear that whilst he was slower, he knew the area. He suddenly turned left, into Tower Court, a paved pedestrian walkway which jinked left and right, surrounded by a mixture of businesses and discreet homes with hedges and high fences.

Both Cade and his target were slowing, breathing heavily now. Adrenalin was working harder for one, more than the other, and

Cade needed something to go his way, divine inspiration would be fine.

The red rickshaw appeared alongside O'Shea.

"Miss, get in."

She grabbed the handle and leapt into the cab. Cade was right, a pursuit involving a rickshaw, this one would go down in her memoirs as one of, albeit not the most ludicrous chases of her career.

"We're gaining on him, miss." The rider was propelling them along Earlham Street towards Seven Dials, the famous landmark at the heart of Covent Garden, which from the air resembled the symbolic features of the Union Jack.

She was repeating the location in her head, just like she did all those years before – left here, right there, over a fence – he's dropped something; she missed it, the thrill of the chase, so much.

"He's going for that car!" she yelled to the rider who increased his pace. "What are you going to do?"

"I'm going to ram him, miss!"

"Dear God."

Foreign tourists pointed their cameras and smiled. Some tried to get selfie shots, convinced they were watching the making of yet another action film, deep in the heart of the city that never slept.

The faster man was approaching a white Peugeot, engine running and ready to go.

The rickshaw was metres behind now. O'Shea hung on, gripping the handles, wondering what she would do when or if they got there first.

"Hold on, miss!"

The rickshaw knocked the man, almost dragged him along, into the door of the Peugeot. The noise was awful. A sickening, flesh-crunching thud. He cried out, in genuine pain. Adrenalin takes you so far, after that you need painkillers or a doctor, or both.

He slumped to the ground as the rickshaw ran over his leg then veered off across Seven Dials and headed for the doorway to a theatre showing the latest musical.

The rider braked, then braked again, avoiding a calamitous skid and a sense of being completely out of control, he skilfully righted the machine and brought it to a halt.

O'Shea was running now. The red mist had lowered and her own adrenalin shunt had kicked in. She got to the injured male who was half in the passenger side of the white car, his damaged leg dragging along the road.

"Stop!" she yelled, but they were heading away, fast, faster than she could ever hope to match.

He was familiar. One of those faces that you could never quite place. Whoever they were, they were happy to abandon one half of the team. Cade was doing his best to keep up with him now.

———

He checked the street names as he ran. People either got out of his way or not. It was a city after all, and people ran, walked or jogged or sometimes just sat down. London was a smorgasbord of people, and to an extent anything went, whenever it wanted to and no one ever questioned why. Except one man.

----

# CHAPTER THIRTY-NINE

----

Best described as a shadow of his past self, he was driving his newly acquired panther black Audi RS4 along Shaftesbury Avenue, checking his reflection in the shop windows, looking for his newly acquired girlfriend, when he first saw the male running. He knew the city well nowadays and could read it like a thriller. He knew what belonged and what didn't and when something stood out to Geoffrey Pullen, then it normally proved to be interesting.

He liked to place his observations into police statement format, just in case he was ever needed to give evidence, again.

'When I first observed the male running at approximately...'

Pullen often told people he had been trained by the best – and few people believed him, citing it as a Walter Mitty trait. When, in actual fact, it was, in one small part, very true.

----

He blipped the powerful V8 motor, marvelling at the growl, driver's window down so he could hear it in surround sound. He liked the seats, heated and shaped to hug his new physique. He'd worked hard at it and he owed that to the man who had been more truthful about his size and shape than anyone he had ever met.

It was the man that fate saw fit to guide him towards that day at

East Midlands Airport, near Nottingham, in the centre of England. It was a Thursday from memory and it had been raining.

It was the man who had obviously worked hard to get to where he had, and who was a cathartic point in Geoffrey's life.

He'd said something, probably in the heat of the moment, along the lines of "Geoff, you stink and you're overweight – and to cap it all off, you're ginger. I mean, just how bad can one man's life get? And then, the God of vehicle allocation provides you with this mobile dung heap!"

He was referring to his beloved white Vauxhall, a car he had christened with the name Tracey.

He laughed now as he recalled just how bad his life had been, back then, in the days of clubs and pubs and the Ibiza rave scene. Back then, when he wore shiny red tracksuits and had his ears pierced and stank, actually, for the record, of Kouros, the seminal men's aftershave, which he considered to be the nearest thing ever to a commodity made to snap knicker elastic at fifty paces.

It was fair to say that on that rainy Thursday he had met his match – a man who was not only marginally better looking than him, who also smelled better than him and probably drove better than him. That he was holding a loaded Glock 17 when he jumped into his aging white Vauxhall, helped to settle the nerves and restore the balance of power.

He'd often wondered how he was that man who had led him on a riotous pursuit across the East Midlands of England.

The same man that was now running alongside him on Shaftesbury Avenue, London.

Surely not?

He gunned the engine and got alongside again, lowered the darkened glass and yelled.

"Jack! It's me!" He smiled a ridiculous smile, pointing to his own face.

Cade looked and kept on running, his target starting to pull away, a second wind kicking in and the knowledge that if he failed in his task, it could be his last.

"Jack! Get in. I've got this." Pullen yelled once more. He swerved into the edge of the kerb, ahead by fifty metres, then got out.

"Jack, it's Geoff Pullen. Get in!"

Cade was incredulous. He had vowed never to meet the forty-something DJ ever again, after what he would later describe as the pursuit from hell and cruelly one of the worst moments of his entire life.

But he opened the door and got in.

"Drive. We'll talk later."

"Your wish is my command."

Pullen pushed his foot into the machined-alloy pedal and the low-profile tyres dug deep into the road surface, before pushing them at warp speed along Shaftesbury Avenue.

Ahead, the target ran in front of a cream-coloured saloon. Its male driver slammed on the brakes, hit the horn and was about to remonstrate when he saw the handgun. Black metal, blued on the barrel, a plastic stock, he thought it was a 9mm pistol. He'd seen them before on active service in another land. He knew better than to argue. It was a rather nice Mercedes 500, and as lovely as it was to drive, it was hardly important, especially as it belonged to his employer.

He exited, hands raised.

"Take it." He almost ushered him into the driver's seat.

The Mercedes tore off along Shaftesbury Avenue towards Piccadilly Circus.

"Shall I follow him?" shouted Pullen.

"Is the Pope a Catholic?" Cade replied, fishing in his pockets for a phone that wasn't there.

"Don't worry, Jack, I've been on a driving course since we last met. What was it, ten years? Time flies, buddy. So how you been?"

"Geoff. Firstly, thanks for being there, but, secondly, what are you doing in London and in this car? And what happened to *you*?"

"Wow, a few questions there. We've got Jack on the line from London folks and he's talking about my new image. Jack and I met a few years ago now..."

"Geoff, what in the name of all that is holy are you doing?"

"I'm sort of introducing you, so you can get an idea of what I do these days, left here?"

"What?"

"Left here? The Merc has gone left."

"Yes, yes! Go left." He rubbed his eyes. This was a nightmare coming very true, a dream he had hoped never to repeat.

"Just keep it in sight, OK? Don't kill anyone, least of all us. You were saying?"

"I'm a DJ, Jack, right here in the big smoke, the city of London, the city that never sleeps and next up we've got the rather appropriate *Highway to Hell* by AC/DC."

The track came over the sound system as clear as it would in concert. It sounded superb, surreal but superb, as the Australian band belted one of their better-known rock anthems.

"Are you going to discuss everything as if it was a radio show?"

Pullen laughed. "It is a radio show, Jack."

He shook his head. Cade did too.

"Again? Run that by me again."

"You're live on Pulling Power FM. It's my station, see. A sort of play on words. I had a little win on the national lottery. Actually, quite a big win. Managed to buy my own apartment and a radio station. I've lost weight too, did you notice?"

"I did, you look amazing." He didn't know what else to say. Pullen had lost a huge amount of weight, he'd had his hair dyed too, lost the earrings and gained some style. So much so that Cade wasn't convinced he was the same person.

Was this really a bad dream that would end with him waking to find himself naked alongside the original Geoff Pullen?

"The lights are red, shall I stop?"

"No, just keep going, it's not as if anything I say is going to change your mind."

"Strap yourself in, kid!" He pushed the throttle deep into the footwell, rammed the gear lever into sport mode and gripped the wheel.

They went through the lights fast enough to attract the attention of a traffic warden, who had already tried to radio in the Mercedes, which had passed her at a speed she had described as ludicrous.

By the time she needed to recall the number of both vehicles, she was unable to remember one. It was a skill that not everyone was able to master.

"Regent Street towards Pall Mall," said Pullen enthusiastically.

"What are you doing?" Cade hissed, trying to keep his voice down; a combination of stage fright and genuine operational necessity.

"I'm giving a commentary. I learned it from you. You do remember that day we chased that car – that was a Merc too!"

"How could I ever forget?"

"Thanks, Jack, that means a lot. Anyway, it's 'Is the Pope an athlete?'"

"What?"

"The saying. Is the Pope an athlete?"

"Is the Pope a Catholic?"

"I've no idea what religion he is but they say he's an athlete. Left, or right? I'm thinking he's gone left. Yep, there he is. In standing traffic. I think we've got him, my friend."

"Go. Get behind him and I'll bail out."

"He's going down the inside, he's almost on the pavement folks, it's a genuine fail to stop right in the heart of your city and you're with your favourite host Geoff Pullen, brought to you by Man-Alive herbal products – when your man struggles to get up in the morning turn to Man-Alive."

"Right, shut this down, shut it down now," said Cade with a renewed sense of concern.

"I can't. I'm not controlling it."

"Shut it down," he whispered in a tone that said he would find the nearest heavy object and club him to death with it if he failed.

"But if we go down the bus lane, we can get in front of him."

Cade knew he was either in the presence of genius or a wildly eccentric man who he had genuinely hoped to never meet again.

"You're a genius. Yes, get ahead of him. Go!"

"Permission to ram him."

"Permission denied."

Cade began to think about O'Shea. She was miles away now and on her own.

"I need to use your phone, Geoff."

"Well, you can, but every one of my listeners might hear your call."

"And I'm guessing you've got, what, fifty, a hundred listeners?"

"Last count was over a hundred. Thousand that is. I'm big these days, mate, and I don't mean around the waist."

Cade dialled O'Shea and hoped she'd answer. She did.

Aware that her phone might be being monitored he spoke carefully. She had given up caring, having faced death once before, it no longer held any sense of mystery. She'd had enough of playing games.

Cade spoke quickly. "It's me. I'm fine. I'm with an old friend. We are south of your position. Are you OK?"

"Yes, I'm OK. A little shaken up and we owe for a new rickshaw. Truly. I'm a lot shaken up. The whole bloody thing was out of control. Have you ever been in an out-of-control rickshaw?"

He paused. "Erm…"

"Sod off. Look, where are you exactly?"

"I can't say. There he is!"

"Jack? Jack?" The line had cleared. She tried dialling back but got the answerphone of a radio DJ. She hung up.

The rickshaw rider was also on his phone, chatting in an animated manner. "Yes, that's right, a cream Merc 500. It had Lima Foxtrot and five four in the plate. Will do."

———

Cade and Pullen were thundering past the Canadian High Commission, maple leaf flags fluttering in the breeze.

The Mercedes continued at speed along Pall Mall before turning onto Trafalgar Square. The driver dropped the car into second, accelerated and held his hand on the horn.

As Pullen approached Trafalgar Square, the human traffic increased.

The unstoppable force was approaching the immovable object and their combined speed was horrendously high. It was getting late, but the whole place was buzzing, full of life.

There were people everywhere. Groups of two and five and one numbered fifty, at least. The latter all wearing the same bright blue tracksuits and carrying bright blue-and-yellow backpacks, with matching baseball caps. And they stood in the middle of the road taking photographs of each other and the landmarks behind them, all V signs, selfies and smiles and not a care in the world.

"Geoff, look out!"

———————
# CHAPTER FORTY
———————

THE MERCEDES EMERGED FROM THE SIDE ROAD STRAIGHT INTO their path.

"I see him!" He nodded, as if something deep in his psyche had given him permission to do what he was about to do.

The Audi hit the front right wing of the Mercedes, spinning it wildly out of control, towards the tourist group who parted in a balletic scene not out of place in an action film sequence.

The rear of the car grazed the leg of one man as he stood taking photos of it on his phone.

A few pigeons took to the sky, seeking refuge on nearby monuments or among the precarious window ledges and out of sight of the patrolling Harris Hawks that had cleaned up the iconic area.

The Mercedes came to a halt. The driver was visibly stunned. He checked around him, then accelerated again with Pullen directly behind him.

The pair were now travelling along Northumberland Avenue at speed: forty, fifty, sixty, braking, then back on the power. The Mercedes windscreen had a star-shaped dent in the centre where the driver had been hurled forward, striking his head and leaving a patch of bright red blood in the centre of the star.

It wasn't slowing him down, if anything he was speeding up, and Pullen, considering himself above the law, stayed with him.

———

O'Shea's phone rang.

"Carrie, it's Dave. We are picking up on some activity near Trafalgar Square. CCTV has gone a little crazy along with radio traffic, so I'm taking an educated guess that Jack may be at the centre of this."

"Thanks. I'll try to get there, but right now all I've got is a knackered rickshaw and I haven't got a hope in hell of getting to him."

"Copy that. I'll divert one of the team to pick you up. Will they spot you easily?"

"Absolutely, look for an angry, hungry ex-copper with a slapped arse face – someone who wants to be on a desert island, somewhere far away. Ideally, with you."

"State normal then."

The Audi was making a horrendous noise, a sort of primeval metallic sound from the front right. How the airbags hadn't deployed was a mystery to Cade, who was busily trying to figure out what he was going to do when or if they managed to get the Mercedes to stop.

"What's all this about then, Jack?" asked Pullen comfortably as the black saloon whipped along the tree-lined avenue, with its tall sandstone, multi-storeyed period buildings and rows of bicycles, mopeds and unattended upmarket cars, all on a meter and paying by the hour.

The Playhouse was advertising its new show, *An Inspector Calls* – it made Cade smile for a second. The irony that he could hardly call anyone without it jeopardising someone's life didn't escape him.

Pullen flicked the paddles on the flat bottom steering wheel, the double-clutch gearbox almost anticipating his every move.

Ahead, some hundred or so metres and to his right, was the familiar landmark, the London Eye. They had come full circle, back to the Embankment. You couldn't have written it.

The Mercedes was heading for the junction of Northumberland and the Embankment when it locked up, all four wheels dragging the deep tread of its Michelin's along the tarmac. The driver tried to swerve, but left it too late. It careered through the traffic lights, ripping up two pedestrian crossing control boxes and ploughed into the memorial to Sir Joseph Bazalgette.

Pullen brought the Audi to a spectacular stop in the middle of the junction, as all around him the drivers of black cabs, buses and commuter Jaguars sounded their horns and displayed their dismay. For them, it was just another accident on the busy streets of London. So much so that almost nobody noticed the activity nearby.

Then the rain came, as if someone had diverted the Thames itself; a deluge, hammering onto the pavements and road surface, filling the gutters in seconds.

Seconds later, and with the appearance of a well-rehearsed plan, the Mercedes driver was out of the vehicle and being dragged away.

Before he had chance to react or fight back, he had been cable tied and hooded, and was now hidden, waiting for the chaos to die down.

A well-meaning passer-by would tell the attending police units that the driver of the Mercedes had run away, over the Hungerford Bridge, towards the South Bank. They would say in all the confusion, with the heavy rain and traffic it was difficult to provide a positive description. That's what the public often did, wanting desperately to help, but when it counted, they often found themselves unable to.

With no driver nearby, it made sense to at least search the bridge. They could also send a unit from that side of the river to investigate.

Another witness said they had seen a black Audi – a sporty one – they weren't sure if it was involved, but it had stopped before driving away. There may have been some damage to the front. Perhaps the Mercedes had hit it? It seemed to be the offending vehicle.

Like everyone else, those witnesses were in a hurry. People to see, places to go.

———

The Audi stopped a few hundred metres along the Embankment, lights off, wipers sweeping an arc every few seconds, with Pullen calming down and Cade trying to decide on his next course of action. It was very much a case of stop, think, plan.

They were certainly stopped. The Audi would probably need a tow truck and a few weeks in a garage, at a hundred pounds an hour, minimum. It stank of superheated fluids and shredded rubber.

Cade was thinking, too. His mind was turbulent. His plan was simple: let the dust settle and find the driver. He had a feeling he knew where to start. But first, he needed to say something.

"Geoff, I'm not sure what to say other than thank you. And to your listeners I hope you all enjoyed the chaos."

"Jack," the DJ interrupted.

"It's fine, mate. I owe you an apology and my gratitude. You risked your life and whatever debt you think you owe me, is substantially paid off. I need to go and you need to let me. Perhaps one day our paths will cross again. Over a beer or three."

"But I need to tell you something before you go."

"Fire away."

"There weren't any listeners. I made it up. I'm sorry."

Cade could only shake his head and smile.

"The whole radio thing was bullshit? You are unbelievable Geoff."

"Oh no, that's all true. I did win the lottery and I did buy a radio station right here in the city. And until ten minutes ago I owned a pristine Audi. I got a bit carried away. You tend to do that to me, Jack."

"But, Geoff, we've only met twice."

"I know, but on both occasions, you led me on a merry dance towards Chaos City, Arizona."

He laughed. "Geoff, I think you'll find Chaos City is in Alabama. Look, I have to go. Have you got a card, so we can meet when this is all done and I can buy you that beer, you know, somewhere quiet, no vehicles, no guns, no chaos?"

"It's a date. Can I play you a record on my drivetime show in the morning? One for you and your lady. I take it you are still with that smashing girl we met in the cornfield that day?"

Cade shook his head. "I'm with a smashing girl, Geoff, but not the one you are talking about."

"I knew she was too good for you! Where is she now? Do I still have a chance?"

"Not unless you can find her grave – and I'm one of a few people who know where that is."

"Bloody hell, I'm so sorry." His look of sadness was genuine. He'd sat next to her on a plane and managed to find her attractive just by staring at her reflection in the aircraft window. "Look, is there anything I can do to help, you know, a sort of deputy?"

"If I think of anything, I'll give you a ring. For now, sorry about your car, and look after yourself, and yes, I deputise you as one of my finest sheriffs. Be good." He shook Pullen's hand, then left the car towards Bridge 6XTD.

# CHAPTER FORTY-ONE

## DIGNITY HQ

CADE WALKED ALONG THE EMBANKMENT FOR A WHILE, WATCHED the police units sweeping the crash debris off the street, with a couple of brooms that they always kept in the boot for just such an occasion. The recovery truck had been called and the Mercedes would soon find its way to a compound, where it might or might not get examined for fingerprints.

Those 'prints would certainly be on the national AFIS database – why wouldn't they be, as all police officers in the United Kingdom provided theirs when they joined?

Unless they, too, had the genetic quirk called adermatoglyphia.

———

He watched from a safe distance, stood beneath a tree, dodging the last of the showers. The two police constables in their high-vis were distracted enough, so he made his move. Walking quickly, he covered the ground and was over the wall and balustrade in a few swift movements. The doorway opened up, just enough for him to squeeze inside. It closed behind him and for a second, all was very dark.

The voice was familiar.

"Didn't expect you back so soon, boss. But you are always welcome here. Bit of chaos outside. We were listening through the air duct, sounds like a really reliable witness has done us all a favour. You know, with the driver apparently legging it across the bridge."

"Indeed. I doubt they'll ever find him though." Cade grinned in the dark, slowly becoming accustomed to the conditions, essential to avoid detection from prying eyes, especially those that belonged to two bored police officers stood in the middle of the busy junction, as they said in the job, waving at traffic.

They edged down the corridor and the lights came on.

"Hello, Terry. Good to see you again."

"Likewise. What can we do to help you?"

"Well, it's a long shot, but I suspect the driver never made it over that bridge, did he?"

"That's cynical, sir. True and absolutely accurate, but cynical nonetheless!" He smiled broadly.

"The job does that to you, Terry. Where is he? And importantly who is he?"

"Oh, I know *where* he is. Hugh and the Doc are planning to learn *who* he is. They've got some incredible techniques for extracting information. All totally illegal, I'm sure. Come on, this way, I'll go and introduce you."

They got to a side room in less than a minute and were met by Marriott.

"Welcome back to paradise, Jack. I'd normally keep this in-house, but when you left, we put a few of our field team to work and this looks like your handiwork. So be our guest if you want to ask any questions. I'll give you three – that way everything else after that can be deniable on your part."

"I'm guessing you run a rickshaw business as a sideline?"

"Is that your first official question?"

"It relates to Carrie's welfare, so yes."

"In that case, I'll let you have that one for free. She's fine, on her way back to your office with one of your team. Our rickshaw is knackered, but we'll find another one like we did that last time. So, to work."

"Thanks. What do you know about him?"

"He's got a rather sore head, so we are treading carefully. He's got a warrant card, too. Rookie mistake, but he doesn't strike me as being all too friendly, and certainly isn't pleading any right to silence. He's making a right old racket!"

———

Cade waited outside the door to the makeshift interview room. He could hear the woman they called Doc going through her script.

It was obvious she'd done it before.

"No one, and I mean no one, knows you are here, so I recommend that you start talking – and importantly, that little unsolicited chat had better explain where the love of my life has gone. You know, the day you and a few of your mates kidnapped him in plain view outside Charing Cross station recently."

She ran her hand over his face, almost stroked him, then grabbed him by the windpipe and slowly squeezed.

"Talk to me. Tell me your name and I will release my grip. Ignore me and I will squeeze until the noise you hear deep inside your head is your larynx cracking."

He ignored her, so she continued to add pressure. He wasn't going anywhere, tied to the old office chair and his head held in place by McCann.

"You see, my friend, they call me the Doc. There's a reason for this. I have served in some far away and dangerous places and saved many lives. No one will ever award me – you know, in the New Year's Honours List, but that's fine, I know I made a difference. Anything to say? Just a little name perhaps, go on, I dare you..."

He stared at her. He was doing well. But she knew he would break before his voice box cracked.

"You see, Craig – that's your name, right? Rookie error, by the way. If you want to get all moody and dark and try to portray some screen-like hardman, the first rule you need to obey is leave this at home."

She swiped the warrant card through his pursed lips.

"Transaction approved." She tossed the card onto the floor. It landed face side up, an image of a proud young officer stared back at its owner.

"You see, Craig, there are four stages to a broken larynx. We group them. Group one, mild symptoms of respiratory discomfort. Group two, moderate, the airway becomes compromised. If you were wondering, which I know you are, this is the stage you are at right now. Group three is where things get unpleasant." She added just a little more pressure.

"Group three is severe airway compromise. It's a hair's breadth from group four, which is really nasty, the voice box swells up, the cartilage tears, there are mucosal tears too and your vocal cords are often irreparably damaged. Your days as the station karaoke king will be a thing of the past. The difference between three and four is the nature and timing of the treatment. Or to put it in layman's terms, whether you can tell your girlfriend that you love her, ever again. Nice-looking girl too, isn't Facebook marvellous?"

She twisted her thumb and forefinger.

"OK, stop," he murmured, trying his hardest to swallow.

"What do you want to know? What's the base minimum I can tell you in order that you'll let me walk?"

She turned to Cade, raised her metal-studded eyebrows.

He entered the room.

"Hello, Craig. I won't introduce myself, as I suspect you know who I am. What I need to know is why you were observing me and why you just put an inordinate amount of people at risk – and carried out an aggravated taking without consent? Five years for that, last time I checked."

"Three if you get a decent solicitor."

"A man with a sense of humour, or was that not supposed to be funny? You see, Craig, I've got a great sense of humour too, I'm known for it, I can see the funny side of most things, but now, stood here, looking into your eyes, all I see is arrogance. Would you agree?"

"You don't intimidate me, Cade. I know you have to abide by the laws of this land too, so do your best, rough me up a little and kick me out of the back door of wherever it is I am right now... go on I dare you."

"Arrogance indeed. You are correct in almost all of your summary, right up to and including the part where you said I have to comply with the law. Technically, yes, morally, no. But you see I'm not going to harm a hair on your head. But these people..."

He looked around theatrically. "These people don't exist according to society that turned its back on them, so they have their own set of rules. When they are done with you, they can drop you face first into the nearest sewer for all I care, they say it's a terrible way to die."

He walked out of the room and stood with Marriott.

"Reckon he'll give in?" asked the ex-soldier.

"Two choices I guess."

"Most folk give up at the carrier bag stage. What do you want to know, the answers tend to come quite quickly, so if it helps, we could record them? It may assist you in the future."

"Carrier bag?"

"Yes, something that's logistically cheaper and easier than water-boarding, which is just inhumane."

"Care to expand?"

"How about you watch and decide? The good thing is these are bio-degradable, so no turtles or dolphins will ever be harmed down the line."

"Excellent. An eco-friendly interrogation."

He nodded to Doc, who produced the clear bag together with a large cable tie. It took one or two seconds only before the bag was over his head and the plastic tie had clicked into place.

Craig tried to remain calm. There was no way these people would kill him.

'Just remain calm. Count your family and friends. They'll give in before you do. Breathe. Stay calm. Breathe... calm. Stay calm, man. Close your eyes, conserve your energy, slow down your heart rate.'

He lasted thirty-two seconds. Cade timed it.

His eyes widened, his skin colour changed slightly, but it was the visible sense of panic that was most compelling. He thrashed like a rainbow trout on the end of a taut line.

Everything Craig told himself not to do, he did.

Now he was screaming, using up yet more of his most valuable resource.

"How far will you take this?" Cade asked, now slightly concerned that he might be witnessing a murder.

"Just a little longer. We've had people last a minute and a half."

"Beyond that?"

"Don't know. No one ever has."

Craig was beaten, his upper body slumped. He thought of his mother, his brother, his dog and his girlfriend, in that order.

"I'll tell you!" he yelled before fading into a state of semi-consciousness.

Doc didn't wait for any instructions. She just rammed a knife into the plastic, ripping a large hole and listening for the familiar whoosh of air into his lungs.

They waited a few minutes as he regained his composure and a normal breathing rhythm.

"How are we feeling about being honest now, Craig? This is genuinely your last chance. You can either leave via the sewer, in a body bag or via a door to the outside world, where you can see your loved ones, once again. All you have to do is answer Mr Cade's questions. Are you ready and willing and please know that these answers are full and final?"

"I'll talk."

"Thank you, Craig. My first question is hopefully very simple. Are you working for an active, operational Metropolitan Police unit?"

Craig thought about the question. He could answer it in one of two ways. Honestly, or what he thought was shrewd.

He chose the latter.

"Neither. Next question."

"You are not working for the Met Police?"

"I didn't say that, did I?" His arrogance was resurfacing.

Doc pulled a new bag from a box.

He looked down, exhaled, then took a deep lungful of fresh air.

"Hang on. Just bear with me. Yes, I do work for the Met, you know that, it's there on my warrant card."

Cade nodded to Doc. It said, 'Let him speak.'

"But what I'm doing in relation to you and your team, well, no, that isn't *exactly* operational – in the sense that we both understand."

"OK, thank you. Care to expand?"

"I can't."

"You are telling me you'd rather watch us drink tea through suffocating eyes, rather us be the last people on earth that you ever see?"

"You don't understand. And you wouldn't."

"I think I do, Craig. I think you've got yourself balls deep in something that you can't escape from. Well as it happens, I'm your get out of jail card. Which unit are you working for and who is your senior manager?"

"I think you know that already."

"I do. I just want you to tell me." Doc smiled at him.

He sighed. The words were teetering on the edge of his parched lips. "Can I have some water? Please?"

"Of course. Just keep talking whilst someone gets you that drink."

"My manager is Chief Superintendent Jenkinson. Now I've told you, what's the worst that can happen to me?"

Cade dug deeper. "Who else is assisting him?"

"In this – thing?"

"No, Craig, helping him wallpaper his bloody stairs and hallway. Yes, this thing as you so put it."

"All of us. Everyone. The whole unit. We are all knee-deep. Up to our bloody eyes in it. You have to understand, there's a rank structure..."

"I understand rank, Craig. And I get your concern, but the last part is utter bollocks and you and I both know that. If you are saying you are frightened to back away, then just say so."

"Yep. I'm terrified. I could go to prison."

"Like DCI Jason Roberts did. Talk to me about that."

"He's a good man."

"Fillers. All of these comments are unnecessary fillers, Craig. Bag please, Doc..."

"No, not again. I can't do that again. I had asthma as a kid, I can't do that again. Please, I..." He was finally being sincere.

"OK, back to DCI Roberts. What's the connection?"

"The boss hates him."

"That it? You'd help a boss that hates a colleague? Jesus, on that basis, half the force would be trying to outwit each other."

"No, you don't understand. He says Roberts humiliated him once and he finds it hard to forgive him. Then when he heard that Roberts had murdered his wife and an innocent bystander, he knew he had a chance to get him."

"Do you honestly buy that? That Jason Roberts killed the woman he adored. They were childhood sweethearts. Now I'm getting just a little angry here Craig my boy, so work with me. Where is Jason Roberts, right now?"

"I have no idea. Believe me." He stared at the bag in Cade's hand.

"No idea. Please. The boss keeps that side of the business from us. We get paid a bonus, but he keeps all of that in a separate file."

"He keeps a file?"

"You don't know him like I do. He keeps a file on everything, on every single one. He's got one on you and all of your team."

"Where is Jason Roberts?"

"I don't know."

"What does Jenkinson gain out of whatever it is he has done?"

"He's part of some elite men's club, OK? That's all I know."

"And what does this club do?"

"They meet, sometimes every night, in an undisclosed location. It's like the Freemasons."

"Listen, mate, the Freemasons are linked to policing, that's a known fact, but from my knowledge they haven't started murdering innocent people or getting hooked up with organised crime. Far from it, from what I've seen, they are decent people."

"I said like, not that it was."

"Then choose your next words carefully. Who do you think was observing you whilst you were observing me, you know, earlier today when I was trying to have a pleasant meal with my friend?"

"That I don't know, but I can guess. This got a lot bigger than me and my team and the boss's games, when we got involved with the judge." He almost retched, like he'd purged his soul, the word 'judge' almost fell from his lips, hanging there for a moment, on a cliff edge.

"Judge who?"

"Plural. There's a few of them involved. They help people."

"Help?"

"You know, they *help* them?"

"No, I don't know, Craig, that's why I asked."

"They overturn cases, make a cause for an appeal seem compelling, agree to make it all look above board."

"Anyone we know? Anyone recent?" He knew already.

"The guy you and Roberts put away for the Thames Barrier operation. I can't recall his name."

"Then let me refresh that memory. Surname Constantin. First is Nicolescu. Sound familiar?"

"Yes. That's him."

"Final question for today – there may be more. What is his connection to all of this?"

"He runs the game. He's the organiser. He coordinates the stock and the players and handles the finances."

"Game? Stock?"

Craig's head dropped. He knew now just how hideous this all sounded, strapped to a chair in an old Victorian building, figuratively miles from back-up, a million more from the moral high ground he had once inhabited.

"They bet on people's lives, Jack." He shed a tear; it was genuine.

"I'm pleased to see those tears, Craig. Trust me, if we don't find Jason soon, you will shed a few more in your cell. That's right, I'd rather keep you alive and watch you thrown to the wolf pack than stand at your graveside. It's every copper's nightmare, isn't it?"

He could only nod his head.

"Now imagine what it must be like to enter into one of those places when you have just lost the love of your life, and left your kids behind to grieve alone? Bad? Now imagine some organised lowlife like Nicolescu springs you from prison, to take you down an even darker path. You'd rather be dead, wouldn't you? I know I would."

"I'm sorry. I joined the police to make a difference. Things were going really well until I started living beyond my means. That's when Jenkinson stepped in. He found me at a low point and made me feel better. The rewards seemed to outweigh the risks."

Cade was exiting the room.

"Until now, eh?"

## CHAPTER FORTY-TWO

**THE OLD MUSIC HALL**

"ONE MORE PLAYER FOR TONIGHT, MY FRIENDS. WE WILL MEET again tomorrow. When the stakes are raised."

A message was typed into one of the tablets. The businessman from Singapore hit send.

'When will this improve? I pay good money to be entertained. When will the cop be playing?'

The Master of Ceremonies knew that Constantin had read the message. He waited for a response.

'So be it. Tonight it is! Thank you for your patience.'

The Master took the hint and asked the two men in black to bring Roberts forward. He was beyond fighting. He had thought about this moment for days. When they released him from the pole, he could strike out, take at least one down with him, possibly two. Then make a bolt for the door. If he could just get outside and raise the alarm.

But when they released him, he was spent. What energy he had left was being used to breathe and function at the lowest possible level. His legs buckled and he felt close to passing out. He needed food and water.

His clothes crackled with dried bodily fluids.

At that moment, any notion of a swift exit was as ludicrous as it sounded.

He was soon strapped to the device. The oversize roulette wheel that he had been staring at for days. The one which allowed rich men, he assumed they were all men, and rich, to bet on people's lives. They made people traffickers appear almost palatable.

The Master looked down at Roberts, who was strapped tightly to the platform and staring back up at him. All the Master could do was nod, slightly, so slight that it could be easily missed by anyone else watching.

"Spin the wheel, please," he asked of the two men.

Roberts' playing partner was another of the homeless men. For him, getting fed and watered and now supplied with a free drug was a genuine positive. It was only Roberts who still had the ability to realise that neither of them might actually make it out of this place alive.

Who was he kidding? *Nobody* left the old music hall alive, except the power brokers, businessmen and members of society who should know better.

The wheel turned, faster now. It was enough to make Roberts heave. He tried to control his thoughts, to think of Cathy, but all he saw was her shattered and bloodied body. He thought of his children, and saw them in care surrounded by well-meaning people, playing with them but never truly connecting.

He saw them in care, without their mother, their father gone for years.

Around and around and around.

'Focus, man, for God's sake. Focus. Remember those heroes who had emerged from captivity all those years prior? The fighter pilots and the church envoy, they survived worse than this. You can too, Jason. You have to, for those children, for your children.'

The first wheel slowly came to a halt.

The Master looked at Roberts. He whispered 'I'm so sorry.'

Roberts looked back up and spoke.

"Just get this over with, do me that honour?"

The wheel rotated again, ticking through the alphabet. He was hoping for C so that he could exit the world in a cocaine-fuelled frenzy, at least he could see what all the fuss had been about; better that than heroin, which he considered a dirty drug. Weren't they all?

He heard the ball ticking, skipping and jumping its way around the circumference. Then all was quiet.

"Gentlemen, we have an R this evening. Interesting."

The gallery viewers checked their own knowledge of drugs. Was there one beginning with an R?

Rohypnol. Roxicodone. Ritalin. None of them had the sassiness the men needed. They wanted effect – visual and audible.

Roberts no longer cared. "Give me the lot!" He shouted before being prodded by one of the black-clad helpers.

The next voice belonged not to the Master but the owner, and it sent a shiver across Roberts' body.

"Gentlemen, there are no suitable drugs beginning with R that I know of. However, I do have in my possession, in my magic bag of tricks, something beginning with the letter R that I would like to entertain you all with. Are there any objections?"

Nothing was said, which pleased Constantin enormously. This was a rarity – an occasion where he got to play God with a willing victim. As Roberts had clearly shouted, he was willing to do anything.

Constantin walked along the gallery, then down the staircase before slowly stepping across the floor of the main hall, until he reached the wheel.

He nodded to the Master, who nodded back and withdrew into the half-light, a scene almost court-like in its appearance.

"Thank you, Master, now, if you would all like to reconsider what your bet will be – and for this the minimum is raised somewhat. As always, gold, silver, or Bitcoin are all acceptable, as is a transfer as agreed in the terms. Is there anyone who wishes to withdraw?"

Those present knew that they were elite, if not imprisoned by their reputations and the knowledge that the Romanian had of each of them. He knew no one would remove themselves from the game. No man dared to leave.

"Thank you. Ten thousand it is then. Place your bets."

The businessman from Singapore asked a question. If anyone

had been in possession of a pin and had dropped it, it would have been heard outside of the city walls.

"Perhaps you might allow us to know what the commodity is first? Before we bet?"

The owner stopped. Looked up at the gallery to see the face of the man, also in the half-light, who had dared to doubt him. He would remember this day. They both would.

"Of course. I was just going to tell you. The letter R in this case belongs to a commodity called resiniferatoxin or RTX. Does that help? No, I thought not. Then allow me to educate you."

He produced a small glass vial from the black velvet bag that never left his side. He then dipped a cocktail stick into the vial and scraped the inside from a piece of green plant material.

"This cactus grows wild in Morocco. This particular sample is a little old now, as it was picked a while ago, especially for me. I like to experiment with chemicals, sometimes just to see what happens when one is mixed with another that we know really shouldn't be. Boom!" he laughed, but no one joined him.

"I have a real passion for toxins; those that occur naturally fascinate me. Their sheer power is so misunderstood by the human race, and in every jungle, there lies the cure for many of our ills. In fact, this tiny sample I have on the end of this cocktail stick is being researched right now across the world as a pain killer. That's right, it is so strong it can kill pain – dead!"

The audience remained silent.

"I once heard somebody say that opiates were like a five-hundred-pound bomb, in that they delivered pain relief in one huge dose. Whereas this little lady is the cruise missile. Laser-guided, straight to the spot. It is measured on the Scoville Scale. Some of you may know that the heat of substances is measured using this, chilli peppers of course being the obvious element."

Roberts had heard enough. "Come on, Stephen Hawking, let's just get on with this, shall we? I mean, do you really think that lot up there give two shits about all this? About your chemistry lecture?" He waited a moment, hoping his audience might take pity on him.

"No, they just want to know how long it's going to take for me to die. If I had ten thousand quid I'd bet on not very long, so cut the theatrics and inject it or smoke it and blow it up my nostrils, but please do something!”

Constantin held the tiny stick carefully, placed it across the top of the vial then clapped his hands together and laughed.

“You are still one of the funniest men I have ever met, Jason. I wish we could have been friends. No, really. How long have we known each other now? A year? Longer? Who keeps count? How’s the wrist, by the way, looks sore?” He leaned on the joint, causing Roberts to wince. “Still not fully healed, I see.”

He picked up the stick. “This substance is actually a capsaicin, but this one is ten thousand times hotter than the hottest chilli pepper known to man. Four and a half million times hotter than a jalapeño.”

“OK, we get it. It’s hot. The man from Romania has a chilli hotter than the sun...” Roberts was almost delirious.

“Good job I like spicy food, I mean, who doesn’t? The hotter the better. A bloody good Ruby Murray on a Friday night, perfect. A veggie chilli con carne with extra kick, delicious. Come on, get this done. Or are you too afraid?”

His blood sugar levels had dipped, way below where they should be, to be considered medically safe.

Then, just when he didn’t expect it, he felt the stick between his lips. He tried to bite it, to spit out the contents. It was tiny, the size of a matchhead, smaller probably. But the effect was instantaneous.

Constantin waited a second.

“I forgot to tell you; this delightful toxin is highly successful at destroying the neurons that are associated with inflammatory pain. Scientists think that RTX will soon be the go-to medicine for long-term pain management. However, it is normally fatal if consumed.”

The last sentence had all the charm of a death message delivered to someone’s door in the middle of the night.

“This little amount is enough to destroy the nerve endings in his mouth forever. You’ve heard the phrase ‘it felt like my mouth was on fire?’ that’s because your body is racing to deal with the pain as if your mouth actually was on fire.”

“Last bets, please!” shouted the Master, trying to seize the moment; and the figures rose, all except that of the judge who stood in the wings, trying to figure out a way of removing himself from what he now saw as a probable end to a glittering career, all for the sake of greed, and trying to isolate the shame that a set of images would bring if ever the owner chose to release them.

He was observing the murder of a senior police officer and one who he knew was innocent.

Roberts' reaction was immediate. His lips began to burn and swell. He was successful in removing the larger piece which ended up on the floor and would have easily burned the skin of anyone picking it up.

He licked his lips, tried to moisten them, desperately tried not to swallow. Things were happening beyond his control now, his body was taking over.

"You see what is happening to him? I read about this in a library once. Part of my medical studies, as I like to call them. This is called the Kratschmer Reflex. Basically, his nasal passages and throat are swelling and soon he may not be able to breathe. Now, we can either help him or see where this goes."

Roberts continued to thrash around in severe pain, praying for the next letter to be K for ketamine or F for fentanyl.

The Master spoke quietly. "Sir, may I suggest we keep the player alive for another night, after all he is very valuable to us?"

Constantin looked at Roberts. The Master was right. He nearly always was.

"Yes, yes, of course, we should keep this man alive for tomorrow. If he can withstand this toxin, then imagine what fun we can have with other drugs, we could combine some and take him to the very edge of existence."

He turned his back on the gallery.

"Do something Mallory, keep him alive or you will be on that wheel tomorrow."

He then walked back to the staircase.

"Tomorrow is another day. I shall consider this bet void. Your money is safe. Shall we have drinks now and then adjourn for the evening?"

He treated the whole thing – the whole sordid event, as a casino owner would treat his or her tables – a game of chance where some people won and the house invariably never lost.

"Tomorrow then!" The Master nodded for the lights to be extinguished.

Then he leant down to Roberts' side.

"Hang in there. I know who you are. I'll get you out of this bloody awful mess."

———

After drinks had been consumed and minor pleasantries exchanged, the group was ushered back to their transport. None of them liked it, most of them detested it in fact, but it was a moment of genius on the part of the event organiser to use it as a mode of transport. After all, who would even think to stop such a vehicle? Who would want to?

Constantin called out to them.

"I shall see you all tomorrow. Same time. I need to have a little talk with one of our volunteers. Catch up soon!" he waved a rather camp wave and cared not one bit what the other men thought of him. He despised them all equally and suspected it was mutual.

The Master was always the last to leave. He was responsible for checking the 'stock', turning the lights off and locking the door to the outside world, before making his way discreetly home, back to relative normality. As weird as society deemed it, he missed his day job.

Tonight, he waited, trying to clear his head. He sat up on the gallery with a glass of brandy, alone and in the dark.

The old hall had been cleaned up as it always was, the men in black had finished their tasks and were bedding down for the night in a side room that neither enjoyed, and both felt uneasy about. They had heard noises late at night that they could not attribute to the men that they kept there against their will.

There was only one man now – until tomorrow, when the new volunteers arrived.

There were dark noises, eery, unnerving almost. The venue helped to emphasise the sense of fear that none of them would ever admit to Constantin. But it was an old music hall in the heart of London's most vaunted area, as far as wrongdoing and murder were concerned. This was Whitechapel.

"They say Jack the Ripper's victims used to visit this place to watch their favourite theatrical shows."

"They say he used to wait for them afterwards, when they were slightly drunk and happy, walking home, down the darkest streets and alleyways."

"I heard that he killed some of his victims here, in this hall."

"Really? I heard that he was actually a woman, a surgeon, who carried her tools with her and sliced her victims apart with such exquisite skill."

———

Constantin knew about the conversations, in fact he supplemented them, stacked fuel on top of the fire and let it burn. Let them be afraid. That way, they will be all the more willing to do as they are told when the time for crisis arrived.

It always did – a few manufactured ethereal noises here and there wouldn't hurt either.

As he walked across the old wooden floor, he shone his torch, the small bright light from his phone. It lit up the red metal poles, one by one, until he reached the only survivor of the last few days.

The bright light caused Roberts to screw his eyes up.

Constantin lowered the gag, almost reverently.

"Hi. How are you, Jason?"

Roberts took a moment to compose his thoughts, his lips and mouth still burning and his words slightly numb.

"Delightful. Thank you for asking. Lovely evening. And you?"

"How kind, typically English, even at the worst of times you enquire as to my welfare. Fair to say since the first time we ever met I am doing better than ever. I inherited what was left of Alex's estate, an embarrassingly grotesque amount of money, what was left after Interpol plundered it and your friends at the Inland Revenue recovered goodness knows how much – can you believe they said it was the proceeds of crime?"

"No, that is just rude, isn't it?"

"Totally. I am fine. I have a lovely apartment too, right here in the city, down by the water. I spent some time in that water as you know, the victim of police brutality, then ended up in prison, again, what you might call a... travesty."

"Oh completely, an utter mockery of the British justice system Constantin, I mean, can you imagine what would have happened if you hadn't been pardoned by that judge? You know, the judge that stands up there on the gallery each evening like a Roman emperor, thumb in the permanently downward position?"

"Jason Roberts, are you suggesting that I somehow manipulated the system? I am horrified."

"You know damned well I am. But if I were in your shoes, I'd do the same."

"Would you? I feel you have changed since being here. Perhaps time to think has been good for you. What is the word? Cathy-artic?"

Roberts' breathing became laboured. He'd tried to lure his nemesis into a position of weakness, but then he had to mention her, his wife, his world. That he had used her name in vain, in an attempt at humour worsened it all.

His jaw muscles clenched and his fists balled, and the tears of anger began once more. "Never mention her name again!"

"Look at you, sobbing like a child. I have finally revealed the real you. A lonely bird's nest in the skeletal remains of an autumnal tree."

He was quiet for a few moments.

"Don't cry for the departed, Jason, they're not worth it. They are simply dust on the breeze. I know, I have aided in the departure of quite a few people in my time. And we both know you will be next. When the time comes, on that note, does the condemned man have any last requests?"

He ran his hand over Roberts' chest, then up across his neck. "A pity really, you are a quite beautiful man when you are angry. I could easily be tempted."

"Then how about a kiss? Just you and me. Alone, here in this lovely old building, wherever we are, wherever here is?" It shocked the Romanian, who tried not to show his feelings.

"Nice try."

"You can't blame me for trying."

"No, I meant the where we are part. I'm not going to tell you that, in case by chance you decide to try and escape. However, the kiss..."

He leant forward. Roberts reeked of bodily fluids and the remnants of death that had surrounded him for the last few days. It was enough to turn the stomach of any romantic fool. Yet strangely, it had an unexpected allure for the older man.

"You are a terrible tease, Mr Roberts. But just this once." He put his face up to Roberts' and began to kiss his cheek, the stubble was rough, days of growth creating a beard, a once-in-a-lifetime situation for the career police officer, whose breath was stale and whose body was sapped of all its strength.

"I wish we had met at a different time," he pushed, slightly, hoping.

"Me too," he lied.

"Is that nice?" Constantin asked. Alone in the hall, in the dark, with just their night vision for company and guidance.

Roberts swallowed hard. His throat was so dry it hurt. His breathing laboured.

"Very." His voice crackled on each word.

"How about this?" He ran his hand down towards his waist.

Then with beautiful timing, Roberts struck. His teeth bit onto Constantin's left cheek and ripped the flesh apart, like a young jackal tearing into a wounded zebra's hind.

He shook his head as much as he could, tearing the chunk of skin from his face before spitting it across the floor. He spat the blood out too, heaving at its strong metallic taste.

He screamed through clenched teeth. "Does that hurt? Good! That makes us equal for feeding that bloody piece of tongue to me. You're sick. I'm a bloody vegetarian, for God's sake. I hope that really hurts, you psychopathic bastard. Every microscopic sinew should be stinging now. Every time you look in the mirror, from this day on, you'll think of our romantic time alone. Just you and me, Connie. Wasn't that what Lucy used to call you?"

Constantin slapped him hard, with the back of his hand, then grabbed him in the groin and twisted. Roberts could barely move, tied rigidly to the post. The pain was excruciating, but he started to laugh. It actually felt good to strike back, and his laughter appeared to be an endorphin of sorts.

The older man strutted around the room. He lifted his cell phone up to his face to look at the damage on the camera.

The men in black burst into the hall and saw the blood.

"Go away. Go on. Please... I am OK."

He looked at the gaping hole in his face, bright red blood oozing down his neck. The bite was nearly all the way through his cheek and into his mouth, he could have almost pushed the tip of his tongue through the wound.

He knew he could and should physically punish him for hours, but that wouldn't really hurt him. He knew what would.

"Stay there, you. That's right, I forgot, you have no choice..." He was shaking, livid, about to embark on a destructive path. Strutting like a livid catwalk model.

"Stay and think about what it is you really miss. A clue, you were married to it."

He returned with a leather bag, inside which was a small rack of bottles, each contained a powder, crystalline substance or some plant material.

"I have enough raw material in here to euthanise a blue whale, Jason. What does that tell you?"

"It tells me you need a bigger hall." He smiled, still trying to clear Constantin's blood from his own lips, spitting it onto the old wooden floor.

"Such a funny man. You should have been on the stage or on television. Perhaps in the next life?"

"And you? What do you hope to come back as? A nun? A virgin schoolboy? A serial killer? I know, a human being perhaps? And never ever refer to my wife as it."

Another slap.

"I can kill you in a second with what's in this jar. You should have seen the look on my old prison guard's face when I injected a tiny amount into his throat. Panic isn't the word, Jason. He went so far beyond panic as the toxin's rapidly shut down his defences, one by one."

"Well, at least I got one of my last confessions from a suspect."

"You want a confession? I've killed many men in this city that you police – or used to. I killed a complete stranger on a golf course, too. He was in the wrong place at the wrong time, a guinea pig for an idea I had. He was rude to me so I showed him how to be more respectful."

He ignored Roberts' comment about his confessions and continued.

"All that power from a tiny little frog. Isn't nature beautiful?"

"I beg to differ. I mean, it created you and you are seriously ugly, have you looked at yourself in the mirror lately? A little too soon, perhaps?"

"And you didn't caution me, so my confession doesn't count."

Constantin ran his hand over his face. It was damp, sticky almost, already beginning to congeal.

"This scar will heal along with all of the others. Those from my childhood, those mental ones from my teenage years and the many physical ones from the long nights in a prison, a long way from the comparative hotels that you sent me to."

He placed his index finger on Roberts' forehead. It had a nail that was slightly longer than all of the rest. Just a little longer, but it sufficed.

He began to run it slowly down Roberts' forehead, resistant at first the skin started to pull away under the nail until the uppermost layer has been scraped away. Then the blood started to trickle down into his eyebrow. He'd carved an N. For next.

"Finished?" Roberts asked his captor.

"Yes, thank you."

"What was the point of that? Haven't you harmed me enough, Constantin?"

The Romanian looked into the British man's eyes until his own vision blurred. He could smell Roberts' fetid breath.

"No."

He produced another small brown bottle.

"This jar? This has a pure Class A drug in it. They say one hit is enough to make you an addict and with someone as gentle as you, it would probably kill you. Tempting. But I need you alive for tomorrow. You're going to make me some serious money, then, just when everyone is trying to figure out what or who hit them, and their precious accounts, I will be gone. And so will you."

"State normal, then? A common thief, after all. But you know we always find you. You seem to crave attention so much. I'm guessing you've replaced Alex as number one most wanted by Europol? Something for your elderly parents to be very proud of in their Bucha-rest home. See what I did there, right at the end of my sentence?"

"No. I didn't. Now we play a little game. Scissors, paper, drug."

He shook his fist three times. The first shape was scissors, then paper, then an awkward D shape.

"I'm thinking that the D shape will appear every time?"

"No, that would be so unfair. At least let me try."

He shook his fist three times – paper.

But instead of a sheet of paper, he placed his palm over Roberts' face, covering his mouth and nose and held it there feeling his breath on the skin of his right hand.

"Had enough?" He smiled manically. "Yes?"

On the second go, he produced a pair of fingers. He clapped his hands. "Perfect. Now, where are my scissors?" He rooted around in the bag until he produced a set of surgical scissors, still wrapped. He pulled on a pair of purple powder-free nitrile gloves.

"I prefer this type. Such delicate hands."

Then he grasped a small piece of Roberts' cheek with his left thumb and forefinger and neatly snipped through it with the scissors. The nerve endings screamed at Roberts ,who fought desperately not to show pain.

"Instead of an eye for an eye, we'll call it cheek to cheek."

"Bastard!" He gritted his teeth and squeezed his fingernails into the palms, trying to divert the pain. He took a moment for it to ease. "Why do that?" He swore for a full minute, having read somewhere that to do so reduced the pain.

"What is wrong with you? Did your parents hate you or something?"

"Yes, they did. Particularly my mother. Next question."

"Do you hurt people for fun?"

"Yes. Any more questions?"

"No." He grimaced at the sense of pain. He looked down and saw the little lump of flesh. It was a lot smaller than the piece he had removed from Constantin's face, which he considered a victory of sorts. The problem was, the older man had the upper hand in almost everything.

"Right, I'm thinking that you need a painkiller for that little wound, Jason? How about some cocaine? Have you tried it? It's your sort of thing; middle class, socially acceptable etcetera..."

"Can't say I have, but if it rids me of the pain, and of you, then let's snort away, shall we? Go on, Connie, give it your very best shot."

# CHAPTER FORTY-THREE

Constantin had chosen the easiest method of ingestion, straight up Roberts' nose.

The problem was, he wasn't a particularly willing participant. Each time the man from Craiova pushed some of the substance into his nostrils, Roberts snorted it out, rather than in. There was only one solution.

"You asked for this. I offered you the easy way, but no, DCI Roberts, the man in charge, even when it comes to taking a bloody drug." He feigned a British accent which only succeeded in making him sound like an affected Londoner.

"Just relax, would you?"

"No, I won't. Because stood here, stinking of my own piss and in desperate need of a shit, the very last thing I feel like doing is relaxing. Allow me to drop a superintendent off at the pool, then I might play your games."

"What? There is no superintendent here."

"It's a phrase among coppers, you halfwit. I didn't expect you to get it. I'll try again. Let me go for a shit in peace and then I'm all yours."

"And then you will try to run away and my people will have to kill you, and that, as they say, is the end of that. No, you can stay there and we'll hose you down if we have to. I trust you about as much as I trust your boyfriend, Cade."

Before he could reply, he produced a strip of aluminium duct tape and sealed it across Roberts' lips, forcing him to breathe through his nose. Once the natural rhythm had returned, he placed a line of the pure white powder onto a plastic bank card, about sixty milligrams, which he thought was a reasonable amount, then held it under his nose, and waited.

Roberts resisted, trying to blow away the powder. Constantin pushed his stomach, forcing his diaphragm to work, and causing the Englishman to inhale, just slightly, then again.

The hit was far from instant. But Constantin knew this. He'd spent long enough around heroin addicts in Europe and inside prison to understand the effects of other drugs.

It took just over five minutes for Roberts to notice a change.

It was a change that he could not have predicted. It started with the physical effects; his heart rate elevated, his temperature increased, a heightened sense of stimulus, his skin felt alive, he swore he could feel and count every hair on his body. There was no nausea, thank goodness, but he felt suddenly confident, more so than his normal confident self.

"Fancy that fuck now?" he smiled. "Go on, you know you want to. Let's do it here and now."

Constantin was initially quite shocked. He knew cocaine reduced inhibitions and raised confidence, but this was the head of a major police team, actually propositioning him for sex.

"Yeah, come on. Let's do it. Now. Come on. Don't tell me you haven't thought about it. Me and you."

"Not right now, no."

"You've changed! Are you shy? Come on, Connie, join me, have some Charlie, this is incredible. For the first time... in my entire life, I feel great. I need to tell Cathy about this. Imagine it, me and her and you watching us having sex. Me and her and you and the men in this room. Ha! Imagine that. Go on."

He was manic. Talkative, but verging on the ridiculous as far as Constantin was concerned.

"It's hot in here. And colours. Lots and lots of colour." Roberts continued. "So bloody hot. I have no idea. None at all. Did you want something? No problem. Who? Ah, forget it. Why don't you... forget it?"

He was rambling now.

"Jesus, a unicorn in my head, that's all I need. And now it's riding on a pogo stick. And the winner is..."

He paused. "Dark thoughts. Darker still, and yet, so many colours."

———

The Master was motionless. He needed to do something, but knew if he intervened, the result would be unpleasant at best. He'd tried cocaine, tried a few drugs in fact, but what worried him was that he knew the dealer in the old hall wasn't going to stop with just cocaine. He was getting a thrill from this. He could see it clearly.

———

"Jason, how do you feel? Do you want some more? Or something else?" asked Constantin.

"Everything, give me everything. I want it all. This is different, I mean, so very different, so very, very different. Different is as different does, as my brother used to say."

He laughed. "I haven't even got a brother. But if I did, he'd be younger and uglier than me. Taller perhaps, but smaller, and my manhood would be twice the size of his. Twice, Connie. I mean if I could show you with my hands right now I would, but you see I can't because some rather nasty men have tied me up!" He laughed and couldn't stop.

"Here we go. And they are... off! And as they come to the home straight, it's Constantin from Constantin with Constantin coming up in third place, but making a move on the second place it's..."

Roberts' central nervous system was in a haywire state. His body had never experienced this before. Adrenalin, from the job, yes, but this, never.

His dopamine levels were also erratic, his brain's pleasure centre losing control.

"Something about dopamine. I can't recall. It interferes with my brain. I can't turn the dopamine signal off. Yep, I'm fairly screwed up now, Connie. Do you know where my switch is?"

Constantin began to wonder if he had given too much. He was The Chemist. He should know. He'd experimented with so many drugs, but when you were already taking them, in a bedsit or cell or in the back of a car, you forgot to care about weights and risks and sharing blood-soaked paraphernalia.

At least he was here to care for Roberts, which was a dichotomy at best.

"Dry mouth, are you OK? I am. Actually, I'm not. But thank you for asking. So hot. Wow, look at me, Cathy. You should see this. Just me and no one else. Dry mouth. You should see this. Come on, Cathy." He was sounding robotic.

Constantin looked inside his bag. Perhaps another drug might slightly reduce the effects, which were far more pronounced than he had imagined. It was clear that Roberts had never taken anything like this before. He knew that cocaine was potentially addictive, not as much as heroin, but bad enough to be rated in the top five, one above nicotine and two above alcohol.

"I need a drink, man. Get me a drink. Anything. Gin would be nice, with some tonic and a slice of fresh lime. None of that plum shit you lot drink. Or a nice cold lager." He over-emphasised the 'a's.

"With a hint of lemonade. Ask Roger down at the Sanctuary. Go on. Gin and lager and lemonade and a smoke. I don't smoke, but I would like one please. One of those that the cowboy smokes."

Ten minutes later, the effects were wearing off, but the lasting sensation would continue.

"You know I miss her so much. She was here, then she was gone. We were away somewhere the other day. We did it in the shower. She liked it in the shower. Then she was dead, Connie. Bye-bye. Gone. Never coming back. Ever."

He snorted a laugh. "Ever, Connie. And *you* killed her."

"Do you want something to make you feel a bit happier?"

Constantin asked his captive with almost a sense of a reversal of Stockholm Syndrome.

"How about some ketamine, might help to take the pain of losing her away."

"Who? Who are we taking away now? No idea. Did you get that lager?"

"I cannot give you a drink, Jason. The two stimulants bind together. Not good for you. Cocaethylene is formed and that's really bad for you. It's what kills many users."

"Do you mean being strapped to a red shiny metal pole, for days on end, and being fed dog food and a sip of water, knowing that you and your circus is in town and is going to spin my life away is better than this? Oh, yes, give the man a biscuit. But not a ginger nut. I cannot stand them. Evil bastards. Do you know they are somewhere between a proper biscuit and... a nut?"

"I can get you some food."

"Look who's being Mr Niceperson all of a sudden. Well, no thank you Mr Nicepersonalescu." He laughed again. He was coming down now. "I may have said some nice things about you. For which I royally apologise."

"Ketamine? It might help."

"Do your worst, my furry friend. Gentlemen, we shall rise at dawn and march... where are we marching to again, Connie? Seriously, I really have no idea."

"Drugs are like quicksand, Jason, the harder you try to get away from it the harder it becomes. Why should I be the only person to have suffered the night sweats and chills, the hallucinations, the depression, the self-doubt, alone in a darkened room talking to myself and constantly broke?"

"Are you better now? Not that I actually care!" He giggled to himself. "This is really weird. Can I call you Connie? Is that OK?"

"Do you know what K-holing is?" he asked.

"No, but it sounds painful. Does it involve you shoving anything tubular up one of my orifices, because if so, frankly, Connie, I think I will pass on this occasion. No way, José."

"We should try you on some Kit Kat. It will help. I have read about this. It will help you disassociate from your problems. You have some real problems right now, Jason, yes?"

"Two fingers or four?"

"Sorry?"

"OK, it's fine, it was about the Kit Kat, the moment has passed. So, you are a qualified doctor now? You can help?"

"Not exactly."

"Then I don't want to not exactly try one of your cake holes. Thanks."

He grinned. "Not today. I'm closing the front door on you, please remove your foot from my door."

———

The amount was the problem. He'd never tried it. He'd heard about it, read about it too. Surely the same dose would be fine?

He tipped some of the ketamine onto the bank card and repeated the earlier process. This time, the effects were likely to be more rapid.

He stepped out of the room and returned quickly, carrying a black canvas bag in which was a metal cylindrical object. He lifted the cylinder up behind the red pole and pressed Roberts' palms and fingers onto it, rolling them slightly, as a police officer does when taking 'prints, highlighting every whorl and ridge and loop.

———

The Master sneaked along the gallery, trying not to make a sound. Using Roberts' groans to shield the creaking floorboards he edged his way slowly to the fire escape.

# CHAPTER FORTY-FOUR

"Breathe in, Jason. I'm here with you. I promise I won't leave you." Constantin's words were sensitive, caring almost.

"What am I doing now? I need to know. Yes. Or possibly why not?" Roberts was rambling again now, incoherent.

"You are making no sense, Jason. You need to trust me, my perfect little guinea pig."

"Pig is an offensive word where I come from, you know."

"Then how about piglet?"

"Piglet is fine. Only if I can call you Pooh?" He laughed like a little boy.

The ketamine was taking effect. Constantin had administered about a quarter of a gram. For regular users, that was a lot, not huge, but a lot. Already it was proving to be more than enough for the career detective.

"You know those things, those men?"

"Which men?"

"The ones that wave their arms around? You see them at car dealers and vacuum cleaner shops. They are like semi-inflated clowns. Their bodies blow in the wind and they wave like this." He wiggled his body, restrained as he was.

"I have no idea what you are talking about but it sounds like fun." He knew the ketamine was taking him to what they called the K-hole. Soon, he wouldn't care about his current woes.

"You know my body weighs eleven tonnes, Mr Constantin – I don't think I could walk anywhere right now. Not even on the moon. Heavy arms. Heavy legs. Heavy heart. Heavy, heavy. Very heavy. Your little head is made of plasticine. I could roll it up and make a tractor out of it. No, really. I could."

Constantin knew the dangers of the two drugs mixing. So far so good. This was an ideal chance to trial the drugs, singularly, or as poly drug cocktails. Why not try it out on his most esteemed enemy? The man that was tied to the pole and smiling inanely?

"That man up there has those funny arms. He's waving. We should wave back. Hello, how are you? I'm fine. Thank you. My body is amazing. It's tingling everywhere. It feels like I may be on fire. Am I on fire, Connie? You would tell me, wouldn't you? He's gone, by the way. He waved. Nice man. I can see myself now. This is very, very odd. Should I wave to myself? I will. Shall we get naked?"

"No, not this time. Perhaps another night, when you are really relaxed."

"Mate, I couldn't be more relaxed if you tried."

Constantin checked his leather bag. He had more commodities. He considered pushing the boundaries, flexing the very thin ice he was walking on and decided that for tonight, enough was enough.

"I think we will leave it tonight. You have done well. Would you like a drink?"

"Do you know, I would really like a banana daiquiri. Coconut milk, spiced rum, lime and something else. Come on, man, something is missing, what is it?"

He slumped slightly and was almost asleep.

"A banana! I must admit, it sounds good. Perhaps when I get to where I am going, I'll have one. We all can. Thanks to you, you raised the ante somewhat."

"Ooh, are you going on a big ship? To an island?" Roberts asked, caring not an iota what the answer was.

"What was it the pirates said? 'Dead men tell no tales'..."

"They wouldn't be able to then, would they, you daft prick, I mean you'd be dead, wouldn't you?"

"Or gone without a trace." The Romanian wiggled his fingers in front of his captive's eyes. "Without a trace."

"Whatever. So which island is it? Go on, tell me, it's not like I'm ever going to leave here, is it? Is it Barbuda?"

He whispered in Roberts' ear. "That's for me to know, my dear. For me to know. Have you had fun?" Constantin checked his watch. An hour had passed.

"I have no idea. I feel a bit sick. My chest hurts. I may have had a little heart attack. I'm fine. Goodnight, you both take care. And I've changed my mind. I think it was Antigua."

Constantin looked around. The hall was empty. He could hear the men in their room, probably playing cards and drinking. He stopped at their door and asked them to check on Roberts every twenty minutes.

"Any problems you ring me. Not an ambulance. Not a doctor. You ring *me*. I know what to do. I will leave you to lock up. Tomorrow is a big day for us all."

"We'll soon be on the *Guardian* and heading to our new life."

He was about to walk away when he stopped and spun on the spot, leaned over and grabbed him on the face, squeezing his cheeks into his teeth until he could almost feel them crack.

"You *ever* mention that name again and you will be placed into the sea chest for the crabs to feed on. Ever. Understand?"

The guard rubbed his face and nodded. It was better to say nothing at all.

———

The Master waited silently in the wings. He could hear his heart beating and Roberts talking to himself. He edged around the wall of the large hall, behind the red poles, until he reached Roberts.

"Jason. It is a friend. I am going to try to get you out of here. Do you understand?"

All Roberts could do was giggle and try to form some words.

"Whatever you say. Are you the vacuum man? Who is Guardian?"

"I don't know. But I'm your friend. OK? I'm going to get help."

Roberts' breathing was slowing now, his heart rate too. He felt agitated.

"Well, best you go to do whatever it is you are going to do, because my legs aren't working and neither is your face."

"It's OK, Jason. You've had some powerful drugs. Remember the night I saved your friend? Your friend Carrie? I want to save you now."

"Carrie?" Roberts shook his head. "Nope. Can't say I do."

He slumped once more and began to sob. What a place, what a desperately lonely place to be in. The feeling that he had lost everything he had worked for; his family, his friends, his job, his home, but most of all her. Gone. Never coming back.

His tears dropped to the wooden floor and began to dilute the pool of drying blood at his feet. He'd had enough now. Was ready to die.

————

Fifteen to twenty minutes later, the hall was locked. The outer doors too. The van was stored elsewhere and the men in black had already failed to check on Roberts.

He was awake now, and thinking deeply.

"Carrie. Now there's a name from the past. I wonder where she is right now? Importantly, I hope she knows where I am."

His body was exhausted. He slept standing up. Clinging to life as he had for days. He imagined himself being one of those people, buried alive by an earthquake, or natural disaster and gripping onto the very edge of life for a week – up to the point where the rescuers were about to give up, until they heard a very faint noise.

He was there, at the point in his life, and he knew the clock was ticking loudly.

'Help. I'm over here.'

## CHAPTER FORTY-FIVE



"But Sassy, it's not that easy. We've been watching around the clock. Their comms has almost dried up completely. It's as if they know someone is watching them."

"Well then, you had better sort your people out and soon."

The British Prime Minister Sassy Lane didn't suffer fools gladly. Things had improved since a thorough cleansing of her team had taken place, the legacy members of parliament, left over from a former dynasty now all but one gone, put out to pasture, forgotten.

"I think you and I both know this is as difficult as we allow it to be. The Operation Orion team are in substantial credit as far as I am concerned, so when our 'people down the road' stumbled across, or found a chance to save their hides, then they came to me, via you and this is where we are right now."

"Yes, but with respect... I cannot be watching, as you so perfectly put it, our 'people down the road' every minute of the day."

"Oh, do shut up with your 'with respect', we both know you don't mean it. We are in a situation where we know the lives of one or even all of the Orion team are at risk, possibly imminently. We know this because we have been watching them ever since the situation with the previous Home Secretary and his merry band of brothers raised its ugly bloody head. And I hate myself for sanctioning it, but thank God we did or we would have missed this entirely."

"I don't think we would have missed it all..."

"Yes, we would. This latest incident from Covent Garden is an example, Cade identifies two of the so-called elite surveillance officers who bail out rather than helping him and in half an hour there's carnage on the streets of London."

"But our people need to maintain an air of anonymity Prime Minister, you know this as well as anyone..."

"Sod off, Robert. If they needed such a veil then they should have done their damned job properly in the first place, not stuck out like a baboon's arse in a snowstorm."

Lane's Home Secretary, Robert Cartwright, a man who was occasionally right and rarely honourable, was a candidate she had chosen by virtue of the fact that no one else had his experience, or the ability to stand in front of a camera and either lie, or bluff his way out of a searching question on police numbers, or budgets or some form of developing scandal – or all three.

The fact that Cartwright even had a job with the current government was a matter of huge debate in the quieter meeting places of the Houses of Parliament. Lane had tried to convince him to resign. He had once, sort of, but sadly for Lane, she was unable to rescue the letter from the fire.

Yet he still remained, doing a job, treading water until the bitch finally walked out of her office one day.

She kept him there, at arm's length, doing a job, until equally one day the bastard finally realised he'd never make PM and resign.

Yin meet yang – a shame you'll never combine. Legend had it, Yin was the cold, wet, dark and negative side of the equation – the feminine part. Whereas Yang was the warmer, male side.

Typical of her luck that not even a Chinese symbol from the third century, which epitomised two halves making a whole, could actually work out to be productive. As far as things looked, it was more Yin Yin.

"Robert, you are responsible for both the police *and* the security services. You are supposed to have oversight of both organisations, so may *I* respectfully suggest *you* open your bloody eyes and look? I will not have a free for all in my country, let alone the capital. My last briefing indicated that we have some well-connected people, working in unison to allow known criminals to walk around town with their middle finger firmly pointed in our direction."

"Partially true, Sassy, yes."

"Which part?"

"The middle finger." He grinned like an errant schoolboy.

"I'll snap it off and insert it. You know I will. You know damned well I will, Rob. I suggest you burn some midnight oil and get me an answer, before the tabloids start sniffing around. I do not want my arse in a bun for breakfast."

"Hardly a very ladylike expression, Prime Minister."

"It belongs to a police contact of mine who is certainly no lady."

"And who might that be?" He knew.

"DCI Jason Roberts." She knew he knew and was a little fed up with dancing around the issue. It was about time to shoot the elephant in the room, or at the very least let it out to roam freely.

"Ah yes, messy business with his wife and the poor man who tried to help her. Still, it goes to prove you never know what is going on behind closed doors. No doubt he'll eventually serve time."

She turned towards him and locked eyes. "He's innocent. I'll wager my reputation on it. He's gone missing as you know, where and why, we have no idea, but *your* people *down the road* might be able to resurrect some pride. Get to the bottom of this information. Do what you are paid to do, make it into intelligence, find out why the Orion team is being targeted and sort it out. Play by the rules at all times and do not deliver a headless bird to my doorstep. I either want the whole body or nothing at all. Understood?"

"As clear as an alpine stream Prime Minister." He answered as if he was swallowing his own bile.

He stood and left the room, pulling the door shut just a little too firmly. He dialled and spoke quickly.

———

"I fear we are being watched. Our timeline may be somewhat reduced."

"I expected better of you, Robert, much better."

"It seems my money is acceptable to you, perhaps I should withdraw that, too?"

"Oh, come now, we both know it was you who provided the opportunity to raise the stakes significantly. Freeing Mr Roberts as you did was a master stroke. And to then provide the next rank up, sheer genius. Shall we see you tomorrow evening?"

He thought for a moment. How much deeper could he allow himself to go, before the pack of salivating dogs from Fleet Street stepped out from the shadows to corner him?

"Yes. I will try to be there. I also have the information I need to get you the next link in the chain."

"And how did you come across it?"

"Let's just say a little birdie told me and leave it at that, shall we? I have to go."

# CHAPTER FORTY-SIX



"Good morning, National Crime Agency, how may I help?"

The smartly dressed thirty-something with ash blonde hair was multi-tasking; speaking to yet another caller and pointing to the visitor's log, whilst producing a computer printed identification badge and checking ID.

John Daniel smiled nicely and gestured that he would wait by the seating area. It had taken him ten minutes to get this far.

The agency was housed in a modern brick building, surrounded by an impressive two-metre-high black fence, which was topped with ornate spikes most humans wouldn't have even considered climbing over, let alone try.

He sat and checked his phone. One message, from the man he considered to be his protégé. They had been there, done that, but lately had become somewhat distant.

*Hi mate. How's things? Longing for the beach and a cold one? JC.*

Daniel replied.

*Hello. I'm just visiting some old friends in town. Agree one of those Coromandel beaches does have its appeal right now. You buying?*

Cade replied.

*Aren't I always?*

Daniel was head down, composing a witty reply when he heard his name.

"Mr Daniel?"

"Yes."

"Come with me please, sir."

He followed the young man, twenty-five at the most, wearing a sharp, almost shiny grey suit with narrow legs which struggled to contain his substantial thigh muscles. His thin blue tie looked tight too. Daniel couldn't help but want to take him to his favourite London tailor for a makeover, but knew the kid probably felt great.

"There you go, sir." He opened the door of a middle-aged woman, fifty-something at the most, she had conker brown hair cut in a bobbed style, which rested just onto her shoulders. She wore make up, not much, a hint of blue to emphasise her blue eyes and a fine layer of pink lipstick.

It was her enigmatic smile that was the most captivating thing – and one Daniel hadn't seen for a few years.

He waited for the door to close and allowed her to stand.

"My god, Leslie, you look amazing!"

"You don't look too shabby yourself, JD." Her Scottish accent was immediately obvious. Her father, a devout Scotsman, had insisted her name was spelled the Scottish way.

"Nice tan and you've lost a bit of weight there I see."

"It's worry, Leslie."

"Then I should be five stone wet through!"

Daniel had worked with Leslie Whittaker for a few years, back in the day when they were both trainee detective constables, serving in the Metropolitan Police. She was younger than him. She'd learned the hard way in some of the toughest areas, before leaving the Met and spending some significant time in a few adjoining forces, then re-joining the Met Police as a senior commander at the rank of assistant commissioner, one of the youngest women to hold the rank in the history of the force.

"Tea? Coffee?"

"Only if you have time."

"Always time for tea with an old friend, JD. What do you think of the office?"

"Rather impressive. Lovely view of the river. You've done well. How's it going?"

"Like drinking from a fire hose so far, JD, but taking this role has been so exciting, we get to play in the largest sandpits with the naughtiest boys and girls."

"So far so good, then? And I hear you are opening up a new anti-corruption centre?"

"Your sources are still valuable." She smiled at him as the tea entered the room together with a plate of biscuits that both wanted but neither would eat.

"We'll also look to host what is likely to be called the International Anti-Corruption Coordination Centre, here at the NCA. So far, it's looking likely the key members of the Five Eyes community will join us. Some of the cases we will look to take on would make an old DCI's eyes bleed, JD."

"Sounds right up my street. What will the key goals be?"

She counted them off. "Bribery of public officials, embezzlement, abuse of function and the laundering of proceeds of crime."

"Juicy stuff."

"Absolutely, ever the detective, I must ask why you chose today to come and renew old acquaintances, lovely though it is, and I mean it genuinely."

"I was busy yesterday and tomorrow's looking like rain." He locked eyes with her. "Leslie, you know I'm supporting a team called Orion."

"The Scotland Yard squad who locked up the Eastern Euro team a while back?"

"The same."

"And?"

"And as you probably know, their role is forever expanding, with a mandate to rid the city of the mid-to-upper echelon criminals that are targeting the place."

"A bit of deconfliction might be needed moving forward, do you not think?"

"Agreed, however, there are very few risks of mutual interference from our side, more a case of supplying you with intelligence and leaving you to it."

"Who bankrolls Orion?"

"Do you know, I have no idea. I suspect the Met, with a little help from Downing Street after the incident on the Thames."

"Heard about that, too. OK, so long as we are clear, I don't want the Orion staff getting involved in our world. They can piss in anyone's pool but ours. First sign of anything that fits those criteria, you, or a nominated person comes to my team. I'll give you some points of contact."

"Fair enough too. The last thing we want is to be falling over each other. You know, out on the ground..."

"What are you getting at, JD?"

"Leslie, we've known each other a long time. Let's not play games. One of our team was being surveilled by two people I suspect were from yours. When he confronted them, they bailed – par for the course – but the subsequent pursuit through the city caused mayhem, and I'd like to know if it was your team and why?"

"And if I confirm this?"

"I'll let you into a little secret that two of our best analysts have uncovered. I'd bet my growing pension and my restaurant in New Zealand your team are listening to ours, watching us and waiting for a mistake to be made. There won't be one Leslie."

"And the secret?"

"You first."

"You haven't changed."

"Neither have you, still as gorgeous as you were in our younger days, when if memory serves me right, I cleaned your shoes at training school each night."

"You're still a smooth bastard. Those were the days. My memory of them is sometimes disproportionately important, JD. I sometimes wish I could turn back the clock." She locked eyes with him. There was still chemistry after all those rapidly vanishing years.

"This information is for you, your team, and their supervisors only. It has *not* come from this office. Are you telling me you are gainfully employed by the Met again?"

"Something like that, yes."

"Right, if anyone asks, your man Cade put two and two together and came up with four."

"Deal. And you have *my* word, Leslie. If it helps, some of our targets are involved in bribery of public officials, embezzlement, abuse of function and the laundering of proceeds of crime."

"It's like you just read directly from my coffee coaster."

"I did. But it fits."

"Targets?"

"A high-ranking Met Police officer and his entire team."

"Unit?"

"Directorate of..."

She stood up and walked around her large office. "Jesus, you sure? Prof Standards? If this unravels, you know what it could lead to? The pack of wolves on Fleet Street would rip them to bits."

"Did I ever strike you as naïve, Leslie?"

"Many things; charming, caring, supportive with a sense of restraint that I admired, but never naïve. Go on."

"And there are some very well-connected business people."

"Brits? Or foreign?"

"Both."

"That it?"

"You know me, always save the best course for last. An Orion operation from the past called Breaker has been re-opened. It seems one of the senior players from that op has found his way to the very top of the food chain with this one. He's got hold of intel on those officers, the businessmen too, and here's the crème de la crème."

Whittaker sat again, placed her coffee cup carefully onto the coaster, lining it up with the existing mark. She leaned forward slightly, as if reducing the distance between them would help Daniel divulge.

"How does the most senior Court of Appeal judge in the land grab you?"

She shook her head. "Christ. By the very short and very curliest." She rubbed her face, sub-consciously trying to rid the words.

"Right. You have a deal. Yes, we have been watching you. Orders from on high."

"First name Robert, by any chance?"

She smiled a stubborn smile. "You are and always were the better detective, JD."

"I'll take that as a yes then." He stood.

"Be careful, John."

"You too. Remember what they taught us about trust and choices."

"I can only remember the analogy about a pilot. They can choose whether or not to take off, but landing is always mandatory."

"Something like that. Take care."

They shook hands, then hugged for a few seconds too long and he left her office before getting into a black cab bound for New Scotland Yard.

## CHAPTER FORTY-SEVEN

"Del, I need your team to take some downtime, we're all running on empty. Go home and let's regroup tomorrow. Dave can run the team and Carrie can press the cyber flesh, see what favours we can cash in."

Murphy had a lot of time for Cade. He remembered the first time they met and he didn't strike him as just another new boss, there was something special about him. He trusted him and it counted for a great deal.

But he seemed unsettled. Cade had spotted it over the last few days.

"Boss, forgive me, but we have no idea where Jason is, and until we do, I'm not inclined to go home, order or not. I cannot see us go back to last year and the madness that ensued. Not sure about you, but I am fed up to my back teeth with groups of people causing chaos in my town. All they ever want to do is corrupt, cheat or cajole their way through life, and I'm sick of it. I'm sure we all are."

Cade was about to respond when he was interrupted.

"Hello, looking for Jack Cade?" It was an Indian male with a mane of thick black hair, without a grey in sight and eyes like pools of freshly extracted double shot espresso.

"You've found him. If you can ID yourself, you are welcome to come on in."

The man held up an ID. "That do you, sir?"

"Looks fine to me. But you are hopelessly lost with that badge. What can I do for you?"

Murphy sat down; the boss would ask him to leave if it was secret.

"Can I talk freely in here?" He asked, closing the door.

"One hundred and ten percent. My staff are all cleared to TS level – unless this is strictly need to know?"

"Let's kick it off and perhaps we'll decide between us whether it is?"

"Good call. I'm all ears."

"Right, my name is Nigel Malik, I'm a senior investigator with the National Crime Agency. My team currently works for the government itself. We normally look at insider threat and corruption, amongst other sexier police-type work. But right now, we are somewhat occupied with a group of men who are now considered wanted for..."

He physically counted the crimes on his left and right hands.

"About a dozen offences in total, among which are murder, attempted murder, robbery, aiding and abetting the above and quite a bit of traffic offending."

"And these people are?"

"Members of our own professional standards team, Jack," said John Daniel, who had been waiting outside the door and had entered when he'd picked up the thread of the conversation.

"And you know one very well indeed."

Cade smiled, then returned to his more serious face, inhaling slightly, allowing his diaphragm to control his breathing, then letting the air out slowly, giving himself chance to think.

"Let's get this right, you are investigating the Met Police professional standards team for unprofessional conduct?"

"I'm afraid so."

"Any brighter sparks of news?"

"There's also a few businessmen too, from 'interesting' quarters of the world."

"Hong Kong? Singapore?"

"Spot on. I'm impressed."

"Well, don't be, I've spent some time in these places. I know it's likely to be there or somewhere else like the Balkans or Eastern Europe, but I'm desperately trying to find my team something different to work on. You know how it is, all work and no play makes Ivan a dull boy."

Malik smiled, then ran his unmarried hand through his mop of well-cut coal-black hair. He wore prescription glasses too, with a bright blue tint. He looked for all the world like a Bollywood star, but sounded as if he'd been born and bred in the southern half of London.

"I like it as much as you do, sir. We got involved when an informant briefed our director, turns out the group just about fits all the criteria we work on, why we come to work each day in fact. The issue, as I'm sure you can imagine, is we are dealing with some serious players, including one known to you, so we need to get all of our ducks in a row before we go kicking in doors to upmarket apartments in upmarket streets."

"And locking up people with upmarket lawyers. Of course you do. How can I help? Rather, how can we help? We've got a vested interest if the known person of interest is this man." Cade slid a photo across the table.

"What do you know about him?" asked Malik.

"More a case of what don't we know, Nigel," said O'Shea, beating Bridie McGee to it.

"He's the final piece in the jigsaw of an op we ran last year. We lost some great people as a result and all he lost was a few months' liberty. Now it's almost certain he has our boss held captive and we'd very much like him back."

"You think he's involved and your boss didn't kill his wife then?"

"No way!" The answer came from about six people in unison.

"Good enough for me. In exchange, what do you know about this person?" He slid his iPhone across to Cade.

Staring back at him was one of the most well-known faces in the United Kingdom.

"You serious?" asked Cade. "A kid in their third year would know him."

"Deadly. This room only. There's some so-called intelligence flying around that he's involved in the group we are now both hunting. You can imagine what this would do to the government."

"Especially after the last debacle with the Thames and Alex Stefanescu. I suspect the PM is still taking tranquillisers now."

"Absolutely, three times a day. Rumours abound that he's setting his sights on the top job, but the lady of the house is not in any mood to leave just yet, to quote a famous female occupant of Number Ten – 'this lady is not for turning'. She maintains he's a potential threat but more of a nuisance. Keep your enemies close and all that."

"And you, the agency, what do you maintain?"

"To be honest, we think he's up to his balls in something."

"What is it with that position and deceitful behaviour?"

"Not with you, are you saying the previous Home Secretary was bad news too?"

Cade looked at Malik sceptically. "You obviously didn't get to read that report, Nigel. Just about as bad as you can get without going full circle."

"But he was shot."

"He was..." replied Cade. "Rather accurately too." A wry smile.

"Foreign shooter?"

"No, right here in London, from about three hundred metres."

"I meant..."

"I'm playing with you, Nigel. Yes, a foreign sniper, but as off the record as it can ever be, working for the British government."

"Crikey. I thought our intel was the best there is."

"Don't we all?"

"For us, then, it's wheels up later today. We've got informants on the ground and we are running the electronics. They're good, mind you. Hardly any online chatter, not even the obvious channels."

"Sounds familiar. At first Nicolescu insisted I play the game, Nigel, his little game. He locked me and the team down, no comms at all if we wanted to see Jason Roberts alive again. He had me running around like a right prat. Then, after a few drinks at our off-duty briefing room, we all decided, to a man and woman, Jason would probably have some choice words to say about that, and to never concede. Therefore, we've decided to play ball on the surface…"

"I sense an and…" Malik asked.

"And not so nice underground. Look I'll let you into a secret, Nigel, we've stumbled across an entire network of homeless people who want to help us."

"Sounds incredibly dodgy, dangerous, in fact, I'm sure I speak on behalf of my managers when I say…"

Daniel held his hand up. "Nigel. Let him finish, please."

Cade nodded and continued. "What if I told you this group was well-trained, well-organised, drug-free and willing to do their bit for society?"

"I'd say they sound like my old mob."

"Military?"

"Yep. There's plenty of homeless veterans in this city, sir."

"You would be right. And you can call me Jack, you know, everyone does. Are you happy to run your side and we'll run ours?"

"One hundred percent, Jack."

"Good. I suggest you embed someone in this room and if you'll allow, we'll do the same on your side."

"Done."

"And you have been, I hear your facilities are far more upmarket."

"In that case, boss, I'll volunteer to be the liaison officer for our team, if that's all good with you and Mr Malik?" said McGee.

"Nigel?"

"More than happy." He smiled at McGee, who gave him her text book smile in reply and said "Here's my card. Ring me day or night."

Cade wrapped up the meeting.

"Alright, seems we've moved on a fair distance since yesterday, team. Let's not get slack though. Remember, the SOPs for this remain the same. No media. No routine discussion with the front-line staff and that includes the senior officers. We target Jenkinson's team later today, pick them off, one by one, see who is willing to break first."

"I'd like to run that if I may, Jack?" asked Dave Williams, seeing it as an opportunity to add weight to his upcoming promotion board.

Cade looked around. No objections.

"Granted. Team One. Acting DI Williams takes the professional standards team members. Leave the boss for us though, we suspect he's the key to this. His involvement in the syndicate or boy scout group he has got involved in needs handling with kid gloves – gloves with barbed wire inserts."

"Team Two, boss?" asked Murphy, now ready to roll again, promising his team would stay away overnight and get some rest.

"Team Two DS Murphy. You work with the Dignity team, seeing as though you were instrumental in getting them on board. Exploit their knowledge, make sure we buddy up so there is always someone on hand to actually dish out the caution and make the arrest. We get this right first time, team. These are serious players and will go legal on us before we can say, 'New Year's Honours'."

"And who's going after the men at the top?" asked Daniel.

"I'm assuming that's your team, Nigel?" asked Cade.

"Assumed correctly. We'll deploy a number of teams along with a specialised firearms unit and a CSI team plus some forensic accountants. Rumour is we are talking in the higher millions. Therefore, we will be looking to implement the Proceeds of Crime Act. They play with someone else's money, all for fun."

"I heard they play with people's lives, also for fun."

"We heard that, too. Let's hope we find your man before it's too late."

"Yep. Couldn't agree more. See you here tomorrow, or shall we come to your place?"

"Seeing as though you have serious refreshment envy, why don't you come to us. But bring some biscuits or cake."

"Roger that and no gingernuts?"

"Not with you."

"Private joke, Nigel."

# CHAPTER FORTY-EIGHT

## THE INDUSTRIAL UNIT, SOUTH LONDON

HE HAD RENTED THE INDUSTRIAL UNIT MONTHS BEFORE FROM HIS prison cell. It suited his needs perfectly. He knew he'd paid well over the odds, and had done for a few months, leaving it empty but securing it in the name of Alex Stefanescu – he'd kept one of his old friend's bank accounts active and so far, no one had even noticed.

Alex certainly hadn't.

What was the phrase the British used? If the cap fits...

In this case, the cap fitted, perfectly.

The unit was a year-old and had almost been purpose-built for him. It had excellent insulation, so it retained the heat and kept out the cold; it had a bathroom with shower, somewhere to park a few vehicles, and above all, it had a ventilation system that was state-of-the-art and had been used previously for storage of medical equipment – this aspect was the most important.

They, the people of his homeland, had given him a number of names over the years: The Surgeon, The Doctor, and latterly the one he enjoyed the most. He adored reading about scientific matters and had read everything in the prison library and had asked for more, which the staff gladly agreed to. He was trying to rehabilitate at last, why not support him? It was one of the visions of the modern prison system.

Using common sense, guile and sprinkling in some spoonsful of luck, he had managed to concoct a few things whilst inside the prison walls; compounds made from easily obtained materials, if you knew what was required. Dry runs, without a trace.

He knew exactly what he needed. The music hall could continue without him if necessary, although he was adamant his presence guaranteed at least a fifty percent increase in numbers.

He'd be there tomorrow, for Roberts' swansong, then he would leave for two days – he'd call it rest and relaxation or something similar.

Whilst restful, it would be hardly relaxing. His plan was to head to the unit; bed down, eat there, sleep there, wake there all until the job was completed.

He wanted to finally put his chemistry skills to the test. The little ugly boy from Craiova, the one despised by his parents and who had for so long lived in the shadow of his apprentice Alex.

Cometh the hour.

------

He was alone in the unit and reading the world news on a small HP laptop. He did this whenever he could, as well as pages from the public elements of the Interpol website.

If nothing else, he got to look at a picture of himself from a few years ago. He felt he looked so much better these days, and with his teeth due to be capped and straightened, he would also finally be much more appealing to his fellow man.

As he scrolled through the pages of the French news media, he stopped to check on a story from the previous year. He spoke out loud, as he often did when he was alone. He found it provided the finest answers.

"I see the French military just allowed someone to walk in to one of their bases, the one in Miramas, and walk out with forty grenades, nearly two hundred detonators and enough explosive to sink three battleships. I wonder where those things ended up?"

He laughed. He knew exactly where. The grenades had been sold quickly on the darknet for a healthy profit. He didn't want to know who to, or where, in case they were used for nefarious reasons.

"What else would you use a bloody grenade for, Constantin?" He asked himself mockingly. "Let alone thirty-nine more!"

He turned on the car stereo and selected a playlist: Rachmaninoff.

He was suddenly alert, sensing his visitor had arrived. He didn't turn around, instead focusing on the job in hand. A small pistol was nearby if the need arose and as he trusted the individual enough to carefully tap the PIN code into the external door system, he continued. They were the only two people who knew it. It was Cade's birth year.

His visitor was wearing the same clothing, down to the very last detail. He had dressed in the reception area prior to entering the larger, almost empty room, which had once been used to store specialist supplies.

"Rachmaninoff's *Piano Concerto No. 2: II. Adagio sostenuto…* isn't it just exquisitely beautiful? One of his more soulful works, written during a time of great personal trouble and depression. It is what the younger people might call my go-to track. Not that Sergei would have appreciated the term."

"Sounds like *All by myself* by Eric Carmen to me."

"Philistine. Mr Carmen cleverly used the score. So much of so-called modern music is pure plagiarism. This piece was said to have lifted Rachmaninoff from a dark period in his life, when he suffered from writer's block and deep anxiety. I too have been in this place, all by myself, where there is no light, let alone the end of a tunnel."

"What can I do to help?"

"First you can shut up and let me finish!" He yelled, spitting his words onto the painted floor.

"OK, calm down."

"I will calm down when this is done, when my purpose has been fulfilled, until then I suggest you keep those open and that shut." He pointed angrily to the visitor's head.

"If you want to be of use, go to the box and bring the contents over here, in numerical order. I have done that so if they find me first you can complete the job."

The visitor walked the short distance across the industrial unit to a large black plastic case, the sort specialised work units carried their kit in, they were almost indestructible and looked the part.

"The pelican case?"

"Yes, and hurry up."

"Alright, I'm going as fast as I can, this marvellous fancy dress gear is hardly conducive to leaping around, is it? And besides, if it wasn't for me, you wouldn't have half of this stuff."

"Three things. That fancy dress, as you call it, is the difference between you living a pleasant life in retirement on the Spanish Costas, or not. Two, there are hundreds of people just like you I could call upon and three, please don't forget who I am and what I know. One call and your life as you know it, ends. Understood?"

He nodded. "Where do you want this and exactly what is it?"

"What it is, is probably beyond your comprehension, just as English as a language was many years ago to me, but I studied, I taught myself during the lonely torch-lit reading sessions in those cess pits they laughingly call places of rehabilitation, and now I can converse with the best."

He took the item and carefully packed it into the container.

"And the greatest difference between us, is that whilst you managed to *obtain* this 'stuff' as you so call it, I know what to *do* with it. And trust me, it will create the sense of chaos we are trying to achieve. They don't call me The Chemist for nothing, dear boy."

He held his hand out for more of the same, the surgeon to his houseman, methodically building the container to his exact specifications. As yet, it was untested, and wouldn't be, it just wasn't safe to do so. He trusted his judgement and skill. Not only would it work, it would allow them all the time and space they needed.

"Make sure the case is secure and sealed."

The visitor lowered the pelican case into another and then snapped shut the locks.

His role was important and Constantin knew this – he was right, without him, much of what they now worked with in the unit would have remained just out of reach. He had been skilful too, gaining access to places that contained exactly the right ingredients – those on the shopping list his new boss had drilled into him – as children play the shopping list game he too had to memorise. There were no paper lists or texts or emails. Not even their phone calls existed.

From the moment they met, it was all set down in a calendar full of falsehood.

Constantin had tasked him to gather a small amount of what he needed most, from differing sites across the region, thus spreading the footprint far and wide, disconnecting the dots and creating only a vague picture for whoever might want to start re-joining those dots.

Medical facilities, engineering sites, construction works and scrapyards. They all had what he wanted and it would take a certain type of person, with the right credentials to gain access, find what they needed and leave; leaving only the smallest of legitimate foot-prints in their wake.

The scrapyards were often the best source. He chose the ones with the poorest record keeping, then, whilst suggesting ways to improve their administration or face prosecution, they had turned a blind eye to him taking some car parts for an old classic car project. It seemed like a reasonable deal for both parties. It was the same deal at a few sites until he had found what he needed.

Classic cars indeed.

———

Then there were the more advanced burglaries. The ones over the weekends where the alarms were bypassed and entry made with the merest hint of a forced entry. It took a real expert, one of the best in Europe. This was no place for a boy, or a drug-riddled thief trying to make a quick deal for heroin money.

These burglaries required finesse and cunning. They needed someone trained, and for the price, there was simply no one better.

Constantin had made the call to an old acquaintance – all via the phone system, in Romanian – brief, clear and with a hint of ambi-guity – that would throw even the best investigator off the path.

He needed the same man to enter a few more buildings, more

secure than a scrapyard. He said he could do it and Constantin didn't need proof.

He had ordered some portable density gauges; they were locked away in the secure room of a well-known construction company and they contained the common element he needed, at a strength he needed. They would be missed, reported quickly for insurance purposes, the victims believing wrongly that the thieves were pure opportunist's and had taken the goods because they looked expensive. They were, very. But their potential marketplace was so narrow it would probably be a matter of hours before the trade picked up on them being offered for sale.

A pity the majority of the high-value equipment was now already back among a pile of scrap at one of the yards visited.

"Watch closely. I will show you twice and you can have a go. It is completely safe."

He hit the block of explosive, with a spanner causing the visitor to leap backwards.

"Are you actually barking mad?"

"I thought you were an expert in these things? I'm disappointed you are so easily scared. This is French military grade plastic explosive. You can shoot it, stamp on it, throw it off a cliff. Generally, it's fine. It needs a blasting cap and something to initiate that blast. I have it all in hand."

"I'm not scared, but if you are not careful, you'll have no bloody hand left. In my defence, I don't tend to hang around people like you very often."

"And what does that mean exactly?"

"You know damned well what it means. Just show me what to do and let's get out of here, shall we?"

"Once we leave here, we won't be coming back, you do realise that, don't you? Everything stays here, or as you like to say, what goes on tour, stays on tour. There is no going back..."

"Whatever you say, I'm just getting nervous."

"No need. I have got this all under control. Are you ready to try now? Remember, this is safe. Trust me."

"Yeah, I've heard that before. When a bloody great mushroom

cloud appears over North London, I'll remind you of this conversation."

"Right stop! Put it down." He waited.

"This is not a nuclear bomb. Are you really so stupid? Have I not told you twice now? What more do you want me to do to prove it is safe, lick the container?"

The visitor was tempted to say yes.

"No. I just want to get this done and go back to normal."

"I told you, there is no going back to normal now, my friend. This is what you wanted. You needed a way to repay your debts and normal financial channels were not appropriate, and let's face it, you can hardly walk into a bank with a shotgun and demand they fill up your pillow case with cash, can you?"

"Alright, I get it. Does this go here?" He pointed to the flask, which was about the size of a shoe box, cylindrical, matte finish steel with a sealed, screw down top.

"It does and now you just add this and boom!" He grinned as Rachmaninoff's piano concerto came to an end.

"Stop panicking." He shook the canister. "*Boom!*"

The visitor edged backwards once more.

"It's safe. You are missing the whole point."

He shook it again.

"If this were to explode, which is only possible if I make it happen, then the resultant explosion will be far more damaging than any radiation. That's the whole point of such a device. In here we have just enough radioactive material to get the authorities excited."

The visitor looked puzzled. His host continued.

"You know, close down an entire area, evacuate homes and offices, call in the bomb squad, who will call in their scientists and after a while someone with enough knowledge will allow it to be opened, and they will find just enough explosive to perhaps shatter windows for a hundred metres."

"So why the ridiculous suits?"

"My friend, they are only ridiculous if you want to allow yourself to be caught. I don't know about you, but I don't want my name attached to any of this. A dirty bomb in one of the busiest cities in the world, can you imagine the media coverage? The UK government wouldn't rest until they found the source and I would be banned from Twitter and probably Facebook.

He smiled sardonically at his apprentice. "And as they have both of our fingerprints on file, I suggest we take the greatest care in that area before anything else." He was suddenly serious again.

"Look, mate, I trust you, I'm just on edge. I'm out on a limb here."

"I'm not your mate. I'm a criminal associate. They are as different as a nuclear bomb, a dirty bomb and a device designed to disperse nothing more than fear among the naïve and vulnerable. And for the record you are way beyond any limb, you are clinging onto the smallest piece of slippery driftwood as the rescue boats from the SS *Carpathia* search for you in the frigid waters of the Atlantic."

"It was the RMS *Carpathia*."

"Well, hark at the expert all of a sudden. If I am ever on the show where I need to phone a friend, I shall be sure to ring you first."

"*Who Wants to Be a Millionaire?*"

"We all do, don't we?"

"No, that's the name of the pro... Ah, yep, I get it. You know, you are brighter than you look."

Constantin gripped the visitor's wrist. Then twisted, daring to reveal his bare flesh to the radioactive material that the visitor was sure they had worked with.

"Remember who is in charge here. Never forget. Now carefully clean up and gradually make your way backwards to the door, go into the reception area, clean down again, place your clothes into the bag provided, then wait. When the area is clear, which you will see from the cameras, you leave, on foot, back along the street to your car, just as we discussed."

"And then what?"

"You will know. I can promise you that much. Now go."

"Before I go, what is that smell?"

"Petrol and as much fuel as I need to watch this place burn. Leave no trace. There are people out there who get a kick out of sending people like me, and especially you, to places like Belmarsh, and trust me I am never going back.”

“When will I get what I am owed?”

“You will get it, as we arranged, all in cash, usual rules, all perfectly clean and above board. And I thought I was the paranoid one.”

“Will I see you again?”

“Only if you want to for personal reasons, you know, for fun?”

“No, I didn’t mean... I meant, will I need to see you again, physically?”

“Probably not.”

“Then it’s been nice doing business with you.”

“The pleasure has been all mine. Disappear before I change my mind.”

The visitor left, walking in a staccato fashion, back to the reception area, where he carried out the instructions to the nth degree. He had checked, then double-checked and checked again, wishing he didn’t have fingerprints. They were a curse, but he knew their ’prints were buried in the AFIS system along with millions of others and accessible in seconds.

He turned the light off as instructed, then kicked the door shut with his heel, being careful not to leave a footwear mark.

———

Constantin spent a full fifteen minutes carrying out the next-to-last phase of his planned operation. He had only ever been in two rooms. The reception area and the main open space. He had ensured they had operated in a very small area, so small he had marked it on the ground in electrician’s tape.

He was working in what he mentally viewed as akin to a Russian doll; gradually decreasing the footprint until he was gone. The unit had been hired using a cryptocurrency via about seven degrees of separation. The owner, an already corrupt businessman looking to recoup some losses, was more than happy with the amount paid, more than twice what he would have received for a few months’ rent.

All that remained was to start the fire, one of the parts he enjoyed the most. He had always been fascinated by fire. He had never considered himself an arsonist, more an artist with flames. He loved to watch the colours change as the inert became the living and consumed everything around it. He stopped for a moment and recalled a time from his past when he had killed an old man with a single match. He had no regrets. Life was too short for those.

The flames were ripping across the concrete now, gorging on the fuel, melting the yellow tape as they raced towards the back of the building. The sprinklers hadn't worked for a year, the owner, to be fair, had warned of such in a brief exchange.

He opened the boot, lowered the box containing the cylinder into the void and closed the lid, before methodically undressing, placing each item into a large paper bag which was stained with fuel residue.

He undressed quickly and placed the bag in the path of the fire. He knew his accomplice's bag was in the reception area – where there was no additional fuel and where the fire brigade would probably search first.

Silly boy, he had failed to follow his own instincts. He'd also been blissfully unaware forensically, leaving just one fingerprint behind – missing to all but the trained eye, it was there waiting to be discovered. Less haste, more speed. He had indeed left one little biologically unique mark behind.

Whereas Constantin, who had none, hadn't.


He sat in the Mercedes, engine running, waiting for Rachmaninoff's *Prelude in D major* to begin. The music loaded and began to drift through the cabin from the front and rear speakers. He sat back in the heated leather seat and let the music soothe him. He could sense the flames getting closer now. He put the windows up and drove towards the large electric shutter. The door clattered open, the chain pulling the door up and back on itself.

He waited, watching the fire in his mirrors. He was tempted to reverse back in and close the shutter once more. Perhaps he'd had enough of this life? It was tempting. It always was and had been for longer than he cared to remember. One day soon, he knew he'd give in.

The music stirred him, telling him a story of how the composer felt, a story told by the young Chinese pianist whose hands floated softly across the keys, urging the music to tell its tale.

He edged forwards and pressed the button to the shutter, waiting until it was about a metre from the bottom before tossing the remote under the door.

There was no one around. The same eager businessman owned the other four units and they were also empty. It guaranteed no prying eyes, and it was worth the rent on those, too.

They could all burn for all he cared.

The Chemist selected drive, indicated, turned left and listening to Classic FM headed to Chelsea Harbour, where if everything had gone to plan a new employee would be waiting, to cook him a fine meal and scrub his back, in his white bathtub, in the white bathroom of his pristine white apartment.

———

The burglar hired by Constantin was called Valentin Iliescu, he had learned his craft working for the Romanian Intelligence Service, the SRI. He was an almost legendary figure, able to work at short notice to an internationally recognised and expected high standard – going by the nickname Copilul – The Child – a pet name given to him by his old team – simply because he made the most complex operations look like child's play.

He was both feared and revered, depending upon which side you voted for.

These days, he was on the side of the righteous. Working for the wrong people. But always for the right reasons.

If the good people wished to work with him, to bring him out of an early retirement, they only had to raise his name on the Interpol website, perhaps resurrect an old news article about him. It was his simple but effective cue to make a call.

This was his second.

"Jack, it's me. The bait has been swallowed along with the hook –

and now you just need to sit back and watch the line start to unravel from your reel."

"Both fish?"

"Yes, both."

"Who are our targets?"

Copilul named both men, one Cade already knew, the other came as a shock, a genuine one.

"And their plan?"

Again, he summarised brilliantly.

"I owe you once more my friend."

"Perhaps we can go fishing sometime?" Meaning he expected no fee.

"We shall. My treat. Stay safe." Acknowledging, he understood.

"You too." He meant it.

The ever-present risk of working with a double agent was their ability to take it one step further, but it was a risk worth taking, for Cade, who valued the Romanian's knowledge and intuition.

As he did so well, Copilul soon drifted back into the ether of mainland Europe, back to his home, the one with the minuscule footprint, under his new name, and a whole new way of life, provided by and protected by the British government.

He would always have an alert against his name, tucked away in the Interpol database in Lyon, France. His latest notice was blue. He'd had red and green and orange and purple. He considered it his criminal spectrum.

The blue one was simple: to locate, identify or obtain information on a person of interest in a criminal investigation.

He could breathe again these days, knowing even if he was to be stopped at a border, he would eventually walk away unimpeded. An expert for hire with friends in the highest of places.

# CHAPTER FORTY-NINE



THE RIVER THAMES IS FAR LONGER THAN PEOPLE IMAGINE, OR expect. Rising and flowing entirely in England, it is the country's longest river. The Embankment, however, is shorter by some one hundred and eighty miles, but it is the jewel in the river's crown.

It provided exactly what Constantin needed: a place to garner attention and cause less than subtle chaos, but limited loss of life. He needed to drive people away from one of his primary targets and towards another.

It was simple, really, if it worked.

He was cruising along the beautifully lit roadway with the famous river to his left, scanning for the perfect location. A bridge seemed to be ideal. It was what the police commanders would consider a strategic point, a point of failure. Take out a train bridge and you sever an artery into the city, hint at another bridge being equally vulnerable and you shut the place down and instil fear. Terror by another name.

But Constantin had never considered himself a terrorist, he abhorred them. His was to be an act of mischief – gross mischief probably, grievous perhaps.

He just needed to create a diversion and he trusted nobody else to do it. He couldn't quite believe he had been out of prison for so long and not been observed, surveilled, or stopped. He longed for the day he could stop looking over his shoulder.

This was his one and only, his last chance to stop staring in the rear-view mirror or the reflection of a shop window, waiting for the hand of fate to land on his shoulder and lead to that hideous moment, stripped naked in the receiving office of a prison, squatting to prove all you had about you were your wits and a bag of basic clothes and provisions.

Then there was the BOSS chair. The Body Orifice Security Scanner, introduced by the prisons to locate SIM cards or phones, secreted in places not ordinarily accessible.

He shuddered. He'd spent far too long in prison. Much of his adult life had been interspersed with the endless and confined days and nights where he traded tobacco for drugs and vice versa. Trading his body for drugs and learning to forget the shame. You did what you needed to do to survive, and only the fittest did. He wasn't a powerfully built man, but he came with a reputation. His tattoo saw to that, and invariably, unless he instigated it, he was left alone.

———

He turned the music down and lowered the green tinted glass. Driving slowly, he listened. A siren pulsed and echoed somewhere in the distance. He heard the low-level throb of a diesel engine somewhere out on the Thames. Nearby, a gull screeched as it flew along the river, announcing its presence to anyone who cared.

There were more sirens, back in the built-up area from where he had come. He smiled at himself in the mirror. "Make pumps five."

He knew by now the entire industrial complex of half a dozen or so single-story units was well ablaze, along with all the damning evidence. He hoped the fire brigade had got there before the flames had engulfed the reception area, especially the front door.

He slowed, checked all around him, then pulled into the side of the road: no obvious cameras, no homeless witnesses tucked up under a cardboard bed. All was quiet. He pressed the hazard lights and lifted the bonnet on his car.

He opened the boot of the Mercedes and removed the cylinder. Then he walked at an average pace along the footpath, for about seven minutes, alongside the trees and the cycle lanes. He felt alone until a solitary cyclist whirred by, tyres on tarmac, two sets of red lights flickering wildly, announcing her presence.

Then he was there, alongside the Battle of Britain monument, a tribute to The Few. It was beautifully carved, at its heart it featured two Royal Air Force pilots, running, perpetually, towards a mythical fighter plane, frozen in bronze.

Constantin looked at the names of the dead. There were nearly three thousand of them. He wondered if they were looking down at him now. He despised ghosts, shook himself back into the current moment and swept his environs with the eyes of a professional. Across the road, the home of the Metropolitan Police itself, New Scotland Yard. Soon to be spick and span and currently occupied by a limited number of staff, who were just months away from being a permanent police presence on the Embankment once more.

The memorial was hardly a bridge, but tactically, so much better.

As far as Constantin could see, this all meant relatively limited damage. There would almost certainly be some, what he called collateral damage, a few windows perhaps, some blast damage to the memorial, which seemed a great shame. After all, those men and women of the Royal Air Force were heroes.

He decided to move the cylinder fifty paces upstream, better to annoy the few government staff hunting for him than an entire nation. It meant the security team behind the heavy black gates had a reduced line of sight, too. He was amazed how easy it seemed.

He stopped at a bench next to which was a black-and-gold litter bin. That would do.

He calculated quickly that the blast would be minimised by the Embankment wall, and the steps and the trees and the monument itself. The initial explosion was the klaxon, the wake-up call. Once the specialists had arrived and checked it for every possible outcome, they would have detected the radiation reading, and that would be the start of Phase Two.

He took a second to line up the cylinder before walking away, quietly praying no one picked it up. Half way along the path, back towards his car, he stopped. What was he doing?

Did it need to end like this? Did there need to be a Phase Two?

Of course there did.

# CHAPTER FIFTY

## THE OLD MUSIC HALL

"Jason, you need to work with me here, darling, we haven't got long. They are asleep. This is our only chance."

Roberts grunted. He was flirting with unconsciousness; deep within a dream, so real he couldn't extract himself. He didn't want to.

He was back in the lodge with Cathy. She smelled of lemon groves and her skin was as soft and smooth as the tip of a Labrador's ear; just perfect. Her eyes smiled. She didn't speak, but somehow she communicated with him.

'I'm OK, my love. You need to go now, for the children. For the children, Jason. Please... *Go.*'

The Master shook him gently, trying to decide what might shift him from his torpor. He knew he was married; all the best ones were. He guessed he had children. So he whispered as loudly into his ear as he could.

"We need to go, Jason. Now, for your wife, for your children."

*For the children,* was all he could recall as he jolted awake, his heart racing like a jackhammer, his breathing uncontrolled.

"My kids!"

The Master held his palm over Roberts' mouth and held his

index finger up to his lips. "Please, you need to be quiet. Do you remember me, Jason? I am your friend, from the club."

Roberts screwed his eyes up, shook his head. He had a familiar look and through the fog of war, he actually recognised him.

"Lucy. Yeah, Lucy sent us to you. She's gone now. Good sort. Never quite sure if she was a girl or a boy, but it doesn't matter, does it? Seriously, where the hell am I?"

"Wait there."

"Sounds like a plan." He was still partly under the influence of the drugs, his blood sugar levels had plummeted, he was dehydrated and dangerously close to shutting down.

The Master returned from a kitchenette with an apple and a small serrated knife.

"Great, you're going to kill me."

"I will if you don't shut up. Stay quiet whilst I cut these straps."

He sawed through the first one holding Roberts' head in place, causing it to flop downwards, cracking a long-immobile joint back into place which sounded like gunfire in the silent hall.

Then he cut through the straps around his ankles. His clothing stank, the ammonia was overpowering, but he held his nerve. "Not long. Are you ready to go when I say?"

"I'm in your hands."

The Master began cutting the wrist straps, sawing away through the thick black plastic until they snapped free.

Roberts dropped noisily to the floor.

The Master waited. There was movement in the side room. Footsteps.

He left Roberts in place and stepped quickly towards the main door, alongside which was a fire extinguisher. He had no idea how old it was and had never used one. He figured he had one chance.

He said to himself the acronym: PASS. But what did it stand for? He'd been shown it once by a handsome firefighter.

He had seconds. PASS.

Pull the pin. Aim towards the fire. Squeeze the lever. Sweep from side to side.

He was saying it to himself again when the door opened and the first of the two men in black walked in. They had always looked capable – two men who had been there and done that. They had a presence. Military, possibly?

But what they didn't expect to meet was a man wearing a diamond ring, a jacket of deep red velvet, a red bow tie, black guardsman trousers, studded ears, high heels and a hidden tattoo of a rainbow on his right buttock, and all finished off with a harlequin-coloured death mask.

Yet, they didn't see him at all.

He pulled the pin, aimed and squeezed all in one fluid motion; the explosion of white potassium bicarbonate powder went everywhere he directed it, mainly into their faces.

Then the high-heel wearing Master found his darker side. He knew he had the advantage for a short time only, so he swung the extinguisher into the face of the first man, who reeled, then lunged forward, earning him a strike to the chin from the heavy base of the cylinder.

The second man wasn't quite as lucky. The Master drove the extinguisher into the top of his head as he tried to right himself and stand up. He didn't manage to stand, rather dropping to his knees and falling onto his back, knocked out and needing stitches.

His skull shattered like an egg against a mixing bowl.

For good measure, he hit the first man again. Then once more for luck. He dropped the extinguisher and ran to Roberts.

"Come on, Jason, we are out of here."

"But they'll know it was you." Roberts offered, trying his best to make sense.

"They never saw me. I'm fine. We need to get you away from here and quickly."

He held Roberts' hand as they walked as fast as the former detective's legs would carry him.

"This way, come on, left here." They opened a door which led to a longer corridor, at the end of which was a black door.

"Not long now. Keep up. Think of the kids."

They reached the door, opened it, and found themselves in the foyer of a modern office block. Roberts struggled with the brighter lights for a second, then appeared to come around from his state of stupor.

"So that's how they do it." He breathed deeply. "Cunning bastards."

"They use this as a front. It's actually an old office building but has tunnels from the war. How Constantin found it, I'll never know. I suspect only the locals would have known about it. They use the prison truck to arrive in the other street and leave via this one, then picked up in taxis or by their employees, body guards or whatever they have."

"Who are *they*?"

"No time to explain, come on, you stink and I look like the interval act from Cirque de Soleil. We need to be less conspicuous." He took his high heels off and carried them, trying to look less obvious, as the bedraggled Roberts shuffled behind him.

"You do look less conspicuous without the heels."

The Master ignored him. "Around the next corner is a phone box. We make it there and you are safe."

He handed the apple to Roberts. "Here, eat this quickly, it will help restore your blood sugar."

———

"Hello operator. Which service please?"

"Police. But listen, I need you to put me through to a very particular member of the police."

"I'm sorry that's not how it works, sir."

"Well, it is tonight. Check the records for Jack Cade. Ring him. I'll hold."

"And what exactly shall I tell this Jack Cade when or if I get through?"

"Please, just get us through to police, now!"

The call taker answered quickly.

"This is Detective Chief Inspector Roberts from Operation Orion. I need urgent back-up. I've been kidnapped and now freed. I'm on..." He looked around, searching for a street name, then remembered the old phones had their location written on the wall.

"...Fletcher Street. We are on Fletcher Street. Please hurry."

"*Jason?*" the call taker asked.

"Yes."

"Jas, it's Betty Day."

"Oh God, Bet, so good to hear a kind voice. Get a team down here. Let Jack Cade know." He started sobbing.

"Jason, it's OK. Keep talking to me, my love. Do you need an ambulance?"

Betty was his first ever sergeant. She was a legendary woman, from the days when woman police constables didn't work nights and were paid less. She had fought her way to the rank of sergeant and was always the defender of the weak, a seeker of equality. She was loved by all and sundry, except the command staff. Now a civilian operator, she was the voice of reason Roberts needed.

"They killed Cathy, Betty. They killed my beautiful Cathy."

"I know, my darling, I saw. Listen, we all believe you are innocent. Just breathe with me; and one and two, and one and two. Help is coming."

———

The sirens were approaching in the longest five minutes of Roberts' life.

Long enough for Phil Jenkinson to sit in his car and observe.

He needed to make a call.

"It's me. We have a slight problem."

Constantin laid back in the bath and shooed his helper away as if he were wafting a bluebottle from his steak.

"Can you still see them?"

"Yes."

"Are they alone?"

"Yes."

"Then take control, it's what you are paid to do, both by me and the Metropolitan Police."

"But I can't just drive up there and start attacking them, what do you think I am?"

"I know what you are, I also know who you are and where you live, and above all, Phil, I know your darkest secret. Is your car insured?"

"Yes, what a ludicrous question. I'm the head of the Professional Standards Unit. Of course I'm insured."

"Then perhaps you need to have a little accident. What is it you policemen call them? A bump? Perhaps a timely bump is in order."

"I'm not with you?"

"My bath water is going cold, Phillip. Do I need to explain everything? Drive up the street and have an accident, hit the phone box, kill them. It's not like you haven't done it before. I expect results. Goodbye."

He hung up, made another call. The men in black were replaceable. Jenkinson had found the previous two, he would find the next four from his own cohort. The call made, with assurances his instructions would be carried out to the letter, he sunk beneath the blue bubbles as his house boy ran more hot water and offered a cold drink. Before he left, he turned on the local drivetime talk back show.

Constantin enjoyed listening to the irate callers.

Life didn't get any better than this.

———

For Phil Jenkinson, life had been treading water. Constantin was right, the chief superintendent did have a dark secret. Almost too dark to bear.

Not so long ago, he had attended a work function, someone had done their thirty-year dash and was leaving. Jenkinson didn't like him, but the food and drink were free, so why not?

He'd picked up his new car that day, a beautiful German hatchback – he favoured them. Driving to see his sister, he marvelled at the quality of the switches and bathed in the sound coming from the upmarket sound system. He particularly liked the soft glow of the blue lights on the dash board.

Approaching his sister's place, he slowed, glanced down at the GPS map system, which always seemed to be one step ahead of him. Fishing around in the door bin, he found a surviving toffee among a bag of wrappers. His favourite. One of life's little pleasures. He unwrapped it carefully, then at the optimum moment, he dropped it into the floor well.

What was it they called it? The two-second rule?

He stooped down and found the caramel, grabbed it with his fingertips, then swung himself back upright.

There, frozen in time, captured by the blue-white piercing lighting, was his nephew, his favourite nephew.

"Tim! Move for God's sake, Tim, move."

But Tim stayed put. Frozen to the surface.

His uncle didn't even brake.

In fifty metres, he had decelerated fiercely, but it wasn't enough. Tim lifted off his feet, onto the bonnet and landed on the windscreen, denting it with his head.

Jenkinson saw him land on the road, scanning his rear-view mirror for signs of life, he waited.

The off-duty officer had travelled a few hundred metres, slowing now, still no sign of life. He began to speed up.

Tim had promised he would be waiting at the floodlit local park, football under his right foot, just as Uncle Phil had told him to. He said he'd be waiting to show him his latest skills.

He had been, and now he was lying on his back, legs immobile, as his favourite blue-and-white leather football rolled along the gutter.

Jenkinson began to panic. He drove faster, across town, heading south, over the river to a quieter area, distancing himself from it all.

'What would you do if *you* were looking for *me?*'

He stopped at the side of an industrial complex. There would be cameras. He moved on, then located an even quieter spot. He opened the hatch and saw the red petrol can.

That's what *he* would do.

But what if someone had seen him? A twitching curtain, a Neighbourhood Watch busybody. Crimestoppers. There was always Crimestoppers. Someone would ring in, or message them.

Calm down, Phillip. Get this under control.

He retraced his steps. Figured out where he might have been seen. He knew where there was no surveillance, a rare moment of privacy in a city which never slept.

That is where he fabricated his first ever lie, under oath.

A carjacking. A taxing. Call it what you like. He was extremely convincing. The two constables, one young, the other not so, listened, offered sympathy and plasters and a genuine promise they would find his car and the offenders.

They found it a few days later. A paintless wreck that would soon rust over. A shadow of its past and glorious self, its exterior stripped of all reference points, the interior molten and ruined, only the rear number plate and the chassis number confirmed it was Jenkinson's.

That was it. His car would be replaced by the insurance company and he would become a statistic in an elite club of millions.

His nephew Tim ended up in a wheelchair wondering who or what had hit him.

———

A dark secret indeed, Phillip.

———

Now he was sat, in a side road near the old music hall watching them in the phone box. It was lit up, the one seam of light in the otherwise darkened corridor of shade. He checked his seat belt, turned the radio up, he didn't want to hear the cacophony about to start. He looked in both door mirrors, then scanned ahead.

Now!

The Volkswagen surged forward, covering ground quickly. Lights off, it was only partially visible due to its silver colouring and the fact it was covering ground faster than anything else.

The human eye reacts to movement in milliseconds. They called it a saccade, those who knew. The simultaneous response of both eyes, in this case had reacted to a threat.

It was the Master – or as he wished to be known from this day forth – Mallory St John who saw it first. He pushed against the door, dragging Roberts with him.

"Jason, come *on*."

"*Jason?*" asked Betty Day. She could hear the car, then the door opening and the engine screaming in the background.

Roberts stared down the street. He'd had enough. He stood, sentinel.

'Give it your best shot, after all, I haven't got much to lose.'

"Jason, we have to go." St John was yelling, trying to pull the shattered wreck of a man with him, but he was resolute. The phone receiver swung from left to right, slowing quickly, the handset upside down, pointing at the damp concrete floor below, the only link between the authorities and the authoritarian leader of the most stringent police team in the city.

Good cop, dreadful cop.

Roberts held the door slightly open.

"No, let's see who is driving this, shall we, Betty?" He knew she was listening and had never felt more sober. "I'm ready to die. And you will hear my dying declaration." He'd salvaged some strength from somewhere.

Jenkinson lowered the driver's visor, then put the lights on full beam, hoping any witnesses would be dazzled.

Quite what he'd do when he had demolished the phone box he didn't really know. But he'd gone too far now. He hadn't just crossed the line, he'd vaulted it.

To his right, a flicker of blue strobes caught his eye. Approaching fast. Then another. It was enough to jar him back into reality.

He rammed his left foot onto the brake, mounted the kerb, damaging a tyre, then veered back across the road as Roberts remained steadfast.

The senior man looked at the colleague he despised, a long cold stare, colder than hell. Then there was Roberts' look, colder than hell and then some.

"Betty, if you can hear me – it's Jenkinson!" he said rapidly.

She typed furiously into the CAD system.

"Jesus, he's aiming for us." Roberts threw himself as far to the right as he could. Jenkinson's VW missed by a metre and jinked along the road, trying to regain its composure. The first patrol car passed by so quickly that the driver didn't register the VW was even there. He had his eye on the prize, getting to a kidnapped DCI first.

The second car did see it and called it in. Then carried on.

Another operator in the CAD room ran the plate through the PNC 2 system and saw the silent alert. She put two and two together and came up with three. It was a vehicle registered to a Met Police address, so must have been a friendly.

———

It was an agonising forty-seven minutes later when Cade took the call from the CAD room.

"Carrie. Grab your kit, they've found Jason. You're not going to believe who's involved!"

The team mobilised quickly, people grabbing kitbags and radios and phones, throwing on body armour and trying to be the first one to the car keys.

"Where do you want us, governor?" asked DS Bridie McGee.

It was a good question.

"Find out where he's been held, Bridie. Get there, take some back-up. Seal the place off, no one in or out unless you'd trust them with your life."

"And us?" asked the next pair of Orion staff.

"Get Phil Jenkinson's address off the system and get there as soon as you can."

"And do what? Do we need a warrant?"

Cade explained in short sentences what he wanted them to look for.

"And the warrant, guv?"

"I'll sort it later. Put my name to anything you need to. Let no one stop you. Clear?"

"Clear, boss. What are we looking for exactly?"

"Ideally him, seize any phones, laptops and the clothes he's stood up in. And ring the duty professional standards officer from one of the adjoining forces, ironically they need to be involved."

"I'll do that." offered Del Murphy, leaving the office.

His call went straight to Jenkinson's answerphone, as expected.

"Sir, can you ring DS Del Murphy please, soon as possible. It's extremely important." He spoke clearly, leaving his number.

Dave Francis was sipping on a stone-cold lemon tea when he spotted the registration on the event log. It just got better. The team had left the building, but he made a call.

"Jack, Dave here. You got a second, free to talk?" It was the standard question in law enforcement.

Cade switched to hands-free.

"OK, Carrie and Andy are with me, what have you found?"

"I'm not sure you're going to like this. Remember the case I helped you with a few years ago, back in Nottingham?"

"How could I forget? Inside job, conspiracy and integrity issues all rolled into one. The very reason you and I are now talking to each other about the latest shit show in hell."

"Exactly. Well, I have a theory about Jason's case."

"We're ahead of you, mate. He named Phil Jenkinson as the driver of the car that was aiming for them. He reckons if the local units hadn't got there in time, he would have driven into the phone box and killed them. He said they had managed to escape via some office building connected via a series of tunnels, when they saw him approaching."

"I understand," said Francis, quietly opening a chocolate bar, his latest addiction.

"So why the call? I haven't got time to go around in circles, mate. I've got a potentially corrupt police manager pissing in my pond at the moment and he's probably the link we've been looking for."

"Yes, you have..."

Cade knew the tone. He'd rescued Francis from a date with death once, a red-labelled-bottle too many, and he knew when things got a little edgy, operationally, Francis calmed down even more. Two tours of Northern Ireland had seen to that.

"Go on."

"Jenkinson is more than just a bad apple. Not sure what his connection is, but I've run his plate through the system, carried out a HOLMES 2 type enquiry and started spotting links. He's tried to put up firewalls everywhere. But he's rotten to the core."

The Home Office Large Major Enquiry System was the computerised data building block for Senior Investigating Officers, and had led to the arrests of countless people who would have previously escaped prosecution.

"I've gone back a year or so and it makes for rather interesting reading. I've got him, or rather his vehicle, pinged at countless places across the city."

"Nothing unusual. If I want to nail this dishonest thug's coffin lid down, I need extra strong nails, Dave."

"How about welded shut?"

Cade turned to O'Shea and smiled.

"His car activated ANPR in Whitechapel every night recently."

"His family were from there, Dave," said O'Shea.

"All dead. No, you see, he's been in *that* particular area. And when I scanned all available CCTV, I found him. A bit shadowy but we can clean it up. He pings the camera, then parks up down a side street, walks for a while, then goes into an office building. A building, which according to our records hasn't housed a company in over six months."

"The one Jason says he escaped from?"

"Eyes down, full house, we have a winner."

"OK, so we can link Jenkinson to the scene. That's good but he's like an eel. I need more."

"Eels can be trapped if you know how, Jack. You just need the right bait. Dialling back a while and opening the search parameters, I found an old job related to Jenkinson's previous car and a carjacking, the same car that ran down a young boy and crippled him."

"You're losing your audience a little, Dave."

"Not at all. The little boy is Jenkinson's nephew. The car turned up burnt out across the river. No forensic evidence and a lightly grazed superintendent. However, an elderly witness in the street spotted his car and made a note of it, even timed and dated it. Ex-copper. Witnesses don't come any better."

"Let me guess."

"You guess correctly, the information was buried deeper than the *Titanic*, never to surface again. Seems like our man is as bent as the proverbial nine bob note."

"Right, so what if he is? I need more."

"For starters, how about the two blokes Bridie and the team

have just found in the venue known as the old music hall down on Wellclose Square?"

"Tell me more..."

"There's a whole lot more. Not sure you are ready for it. Jason reckoned they were putting on foreign accents. They are two of Jenkinson's team, Bridie recognised one, even with the abnormally large wound on his face. Listen, JD's just joined me, I've got him cashing in a few favours with his old command colleagues. This will go all viral and front page unless we keep a lid on it."

"And can we?" Cade asked, knowing Daniel was nearby.

"One hundred percent, Jack. You know me, I'm a whore when it comes to cashing in favours."

"I've heard you called worse, JD."

He laughed; he was always calm in a crisis too.

"Listen, Jack, what Dave was getting around to telling you is that when he ran the ANPR and CCTV searches, he found something a little unpalatable."

"If you tell me Alex Stefanescu has come back from the dead, I'll eat both of our hats. Please put me out of my misery."

"Your hat is safe, mate. But we've got an issue closer to home. Standby." He walked over to the office door and locked it.

———

Just over an hour was all they needed. Constantin had made the call to one of his most trusted allies. He'd offered a hundred thousand pounds to enter the old hall and remove all traces of their existence. The clock started and the minute hand began to sweep around the face. Time, waiting for no man.

That is, all except the two men in black. That was a message that needed to be sent.

The small recovery team had done everything required, stripping down the large wheel system in sequence so it could be reassembled elsewhere, then systematically removing obvious traces of human activity.

At two minutes past the hour, the white prison truck had gone, loaded with the wheel assembly and black bin bags filled with anything vaguely evidential. The gallery had been checked, the toilets flushed and cleaned, the hallway doused in bleach, the red poles sprayed and wiped down, the rags bagged and cable tied into the black rubbish sacks ready for burning.

He could have easily burned the place to the ground, but this was no modern faceless building, some architects wet dream, this was a building, built by craftsmen for actors and singers and entertainers from a bygone era – and he admired them. He wasn't actually worried about being caught.

Leaving little or no forensic evidence wherever he roamed, he was becoming impatient at the lack of attention he was receiving. Time to ramp things up just a little.

The red velvet curtains were drawn and the old music hall became just that once more; a past splendour, a relic of Victorian entertainment in the haunt of Jack the Ripper. The haunt of young and old.

It had taken fifty-eight minutes.

Stop the clock.

———

Francis continued. "Just before JD breaks your heart, I need you to know Bridie's team got in via the old office reception. She said it smelled musty, as if it had been unused for ages. It certainly looks that way, according to the records I could find it was rented long-term by a company from Singapore – Orchard Assets. Never heard of them until I started digging. Interesting connections, but nothing recent."

"Keep going." Cade navigated the busy traffic, lane changing to save time, resisting the need to initiate the blue strobes and wake-the-dead siren.

"I think you should ring Bridie. She's keen to talk. Do you need anything else from me?"

"Only an answer from either you or JD. Put us out of our misery."

"Jason and his guardian angel are with a local unit and a paramedic. He wants to stay down there until you can get to him, and it seems we have a mole."

"Is that so? We are close now. Thanks, Dave. Nice work. I owe you once more."

"I think this makes us almost even."

## CHAPTER FIFTY-ONE

Cade rang McGee. She felt the phone tremble in her black business trousers, the ones she'd had tailored to fit. For her sake, not the various lecherous men who worked in the same building.

"Jack, you have to see this place. It's an old Victorian music hall. It's beautiful. I so wish I could have seen it in its heyday."

"Bridie, as keen as I am to take you to the theatre one evening, I really need to know what you have found down there. I'm trying to be in five places at once."

"I get it, boss. You see, that was my point. This place looks just like I imagine an old Victorian music hall to look. Except it stinks of bleach. There are some exquisite red velvet curtains..."

Cade knew to let her continue. He admired her as a person as well as a detective. She did things her way and got results.

"...with fresh hand prints on, as if they've been dragged back into their old place today. And underneath one of the chairs stacked to the side of the hall was a solitary cable tie. It's got a piece of skin on it. I've bagged it."

"Is that it? All we have to go on is a pair of red silk curtains and a cable tie? As evidence goes B it's a bit thin. Even for a time-served DS like you."

"Not sure what you are suggesting, boss? I've never set anyone up, not once, never will either."

"Not suggesting that at all. I'm saying I need more than what you have, to prove a kidnapping."

"Well, correct me if I'm wrong, but we have a DCI's word he was kidnapped, don't we? And another witness who looks like he's just escaped from the set of *The Greatest Showman*."

She laughed an exhausted laugh. "What is it with you, boss, that brings out the worst in me and everything you touch? Honestly, you are indeed a complete bedlam magnet."

O'Shea gave him a look, it said, 'I'm not sure I like the under-lying flirtation.' It was just a quick look, but it spoke volumes.

Cade could only laugh back. "Had enough of working with me?"

"Never. Now, do you want the other two bits of evidence I've found?"

"I'm all ears."

"When we entered the building and had come down off the natural high that only a few hundred gallons of bleach can induce, we found two bodies. They were in the hall. No signs of any weapons, but it looks as though someone had decided to introduce them to a blunt and heavy object. Now, given they were also covered in fine white powder, I'd say that object was a fire extinguisher. Sprayed in the face, then belted with it. Whoever did it, did a good job of one, the other, however, is sat up against a wall having his wounds tended to."

"Do we know who they are?"

"Not exactly..."

"Which means?"

"Which means we know who they worked for and this might put a spring in your step. The deceased isn't known to me but the survivor is, and despite concussion he's talking like his life and career depends on it."

"One of ours?"

"Sadly, yes. In fact, he's one of Jenkinson's."

"Marvellous. This just gets better all the time. We'll be with you in ten. Keep him there, patch him up, no ambulance unless he takes a turn for the worst – and if he does get your notebook out and grab a signature."

———

Cade pulled into Wellclose Square to find another three marked patrol cars had arrived. A young sergeant had sealed off the street and was in no mood to argue with motorists who said they needed to access the place – their businesses and homes could wait.

He spotted Cade's car and waved him through.

"CID?"

"Technically, not. Where's DCI Roberts and the member of the public?"

"Back of the ambulance. He's a real DCI? I wasn't sure – you know, with the outfit and everything. We were told not to talk to them, other than immediate welfare stuff."

Cade laughed. "I've just got to tell DCI Roberts you thought he was the one in the costume." It was probably the high point of the day, of the week, in fact.

"Listen sergeant, can you keep this street locked down for me until you hear from one of my team?"

"Consider it done. Is there a story attached to this lot?'

"Longer than a Hollywood thank you speech."

He walked with O'Shea, leaving West to gather what he could from anyone who had emerged from the nearby small block of apartments. Somebody must have seen something.

"You like Bridie, don't you, Jack?" O'Shea asked frostily.

"Random question, but yes, I think she's a first-rate copper and a really nice person – captivating smile and sense of humour – that aside, why?"

"There's more, she fancies you. Just be careful."

"Says the seductress of Scotland Yard!"

She pushed him sideways into the road.

"I could have you for assault!"

"You and whose army? Come on, let's go and give Jason a hug."

Cade tapped on the back door of the ambulance. A battle-hardened grey-haired paramedic with a growing pot belly opened the door and stepped out, closing it behind him.

"We're getting ready to take them to the nearest hospital for a check-up. One is fine, just here for moral support, the other one is a tad dishevelled, stinks to high heaven bless him and has had some recent controlled drugs – not ours, you understand."

"But he'll be OK?"

"Says he's a senior copper. Told me he's lost his wife recently, said she was killed, then started rambling about a man who was hunting down his team and killing them off one by one. Between you and me, I think the LSD has got to him."

"Everything he's just told you is probably very accurate. I can't comment on what he has taken, but he was far from a willing volunteer. Don't be surprised if he discharges himself."

"Well, if he does, you need to keep a very close eye on him. I can give you some advice on the proviso you get him to his doctor at the slightest hint of trouble."

"On that basis, we'd be at his surgery every twenty minutes. You have my word. Can we have a minute with him?"

"Sure. Not sure what he looks like normally, but right now, he looks awful. Don't say I didn't warn you."

Cade stepped up and into the ambulance. Sat on the left was a distinguished-looking man in red and black, holding a pair of high heels.

"Nice, you got those in a size ten?"

"You simply couldn't afford them, darling. Educated guess says you must be Jack – and this lovely lady, well she could easily be the woman I saved a while ago – in my other life. Please don't hug me, I am feeling a tad vulnerable."

O'Shea looked at him quizzically – sat there, holding his treasured shoes, in his red shirt with matching hand-knotted bow tie.

"Have we met?"

"Not exactly, but Jason and I did once. It was on your darkest night, as I recall. If your name is Carrie?"

Cade looked at her. "Far too long a story for here. Over a stiff drink later."

He held out his hand and shook Mallory's when he offered it back. The grip was stronger than he imagined. And the look said 'Your friend is a lucky man.'

Then he turned to Roberts who was laid on his side, staring at the sterile panelling. He put a hand on his shoulder and waited.

———

Jenkinson slowed in traffic, tried to regain a normal heart rate. He slowed his breathing right down, in through the nose, held it for a few seconds, then exhaled. He rang Constantin.

"It's me. Things are unravelling. I've had a missed call from our man on the inside and I was unable to deal with Roberts as I had hoped to. I'm trying to get back to work, but I'm hearing there's some chaos down there too. I want out. Right now. I don't want to hear from you again and you won't hear from me. Agreed?"

"No, not at all, Phillip. That is *not* how this works. Not at all. We go to Plan D."

"What happened to B and C?"

"You screwed them up. I've dropped a little something off near your work, should keep the dear old wolf from the door for a while. A man with your credentials will get in, though. Do what I showed you, run the anti-money laundering software over the company when you've done, and make sure we don't even raise an eyebrow. You remember how to do it? How to delete the links?"

"Of course, I'm not a bloody idiot?"

"But you see you are, a wise man wouldn't have let this happen. You know where to be and when?"

"Yes."

"Good, well try not to be late and all being well, you and I can share in some of life's little luxuries. All courtesy of a few business-men, a corrupt judge and a very shady senior bank director or three. Money laundering is so beautifully simple. You put your money in, you take your money out, like the song of yours, the *Hokey Cokey*..."

"It's not my song. It's infantile."

"But that is what it is all about, my friend. Money. Money. Money."

Jenkinson said nothing. Then, when he felt he had regained control, he spoke.

"You want to live in a world full of riches, whereas I am happy to be better off and away from all of this. Before you go, what exactly have you done at my workplace?"

"Me? I just left a package next to a bin opposite Scotland Yard.

It's not fully occupied yet so the damage will be minimal, I'm not an animal, just needed a bit of a diversion. Just a little dirty device."

"What *have* you done Nicolescu?"

"Don't ever use that name on here again."

He hung up immediately.

———

Phil Marriott was watching it all unfold. He knew a drama when he saw one. He'd been involved in a few in his time. This one looked fascinating. He'd asked one of the crew to take a closer look.

Terry the bear walked down the street, minding his own business and collecting information as he walked; listening, looking and taking it all in. Despite his size, he was used to being ignored.

———

Stuck in traffic on the other side was the latest radio sensation in town, Geoff Pullen. He didn't see why he needed to wait a moment longer, but as always, he was keen to find out the reason for the delay. There was nothing on the radio about it, just traffic delays. He knew just who to ring.

The problem was three other people were ringing him at the same time.

Cade answered JD first and made a note to listen to the voice-mails as soon as he had a second.

"Jack, my boy, we've got a bit of an issue at work. Turns out some dear soul has left a cylindrical device directly opposite the Yard, next to a waste bin. Just like the old days, before they removed half of the bins from our cities."

"Back then we always got a warning."

"We did. And we sort of did this time too."

"How come?"

"Our old Romanian friend."

"The one we like?"

"None other. Turns out he's been doing a bit of overtime. You know how he operates – straddling the void between good and evil. He's sending through some intelligence as we speak."

"Intelligence or information?" There was a difference to those who knew.

"Intelligence, Jack – I'd score it further up the scale too. B2."

Put simply, it meant the source was generally trusted and the information was likely to be true.

"If it's the same friend, then I'd score it as an A."

Trusted. They'd risk their lives on the strength of the information.

"OK, talk to me, John."

"Our man reckons he's been tracking an associate of Nicolescu's. Not good news. Worst is yet to come."

"Right, go with the first."

"Nicolescu's right-hand man is definitely one of our own. He's close to home too." He paused, letting it sink in. The reaction was unexpected.

"Murphy?"

"Yes, how did you know?"

"Let's just say a little mole told me. And the second piece of intel?"

"It seems we have a potential dirty bomb outside the Yard."

"Holy bloody hell. Have you evacuated?"

"No. Seems we are safer inside than out. EOD are already here, they got diverted from something else. Looks like the Royal Engineers. Usual SOPs, they'll work behind the cordon and establish just how much damage it might cause. Been a while since we had anything like this to deal with."

"What makes you think it's dirty?"

"The CAD room has just taken a call to that effect. A foreign voice advising we put some distance between us and it."

"You thinking what I am?"

"Jack, I'm not sure we ever think exactly the same, but if you think our other Romanian friend is behind this, then yes. I'll feedback to you as soon as I know anything worthwhile. Before you go, Murphy…"

"I'm listening."

"Our man V for Victor has been tracking him. Not sure who tasked him, but he's done a first-rate job."

"I may have suggested it, you know, in passing."

"You should be more suggestive, more often mate."

"What has he found?"

"His movements are interesting. I'm not sure what the ethical thoughts on attaching a lump to one of our cars is, but it's managed to provide enough rope to hang Del Murphy."

"I didn't suggest he should add a tracker, JD."

"And I didn't suggest you did for a second. He's a free agent, getting his salary from somewhere, if the rumour is to be believed he's set for life. Anyway, Murphy has been to an industrial unit which almost burnt down, leaving just a hint of forensic evidence. From there he's been to the vicinity of the old music hall, far too often, in his own vehicle too. His comms is limited, but he's left a footprint bigger than a yeti."

"Silly boy. I'm gutted. I liked Del. Are we bringing him in?"

"No, our old friend Nigel Malik will. Easier that way. Turns out they've been tuning into Radio Orion more than we realised."

"Ah, it's starting to make sense now. Can we assume Nigel has recruited Victor?"

"Assume away. I'm pleased he's on our side again. Listen, we could be stuck in here for hours. I have a feeling this is ramping up, so far though I haven't got the slightest clue where this is heading."

"Me neither. Stay in touch. I need to support Jason and stay on the ground, you know how Nicolescu works, John, once he lights the blue touch paper the fireworks soon commence – and he only buys the very best."

"Indeed. Let's hope this time they are cheap imports that go with a fizzle rather than a bang. Speak soon."

# CHAPTER FIFTY-TWO

THE ARMY TEAM FROM 33 EOD ROYAL ENGINEERS HAD BEEN ON site for a while. The senior police officer had handed over control to them and was now waiting in the wings to pick the investigative side up once the bedlam had diminished, once the city had returned to its comparative state of order and civility.

The team carried out almost the same standard operating procedures as their colleagues the world over.

Preservation of life came first, always. Then, property. Then forensic evidence preservation and recovery – this was how the teams learned, from experience, as contrary to popular belief, many bomb makers died building their devices and those that didn't rarely discussed their art.

Finally, there was the restorative state, what society considered to be normality.

They had carried out all their post arrival drills – the most senior police officer at the scene, an inspector with only seven years' service had handed over and had offered as much information as possible, gleaned from the first person who had called it in.

In this case, an apparently homeless ex-serviceman, who had been nearby when he had spotted the device next to the bin. He had used experience and muscle memory to call it in, flagging down a passing patrol, who almost ignored him.

He was able to describe the size, and his knowledge of the area, he explained how he considered its placement near to the Royal Air Force memorial as relevant, and last but by no means least, he'd offered some context, based upon his own experience of time in a number of conflict zones.

He was what the police staff considered a reliable witness.

He had carefully described his route along the footpath. This was critical; he'd survived the short journey; therefore, it was reasonable to assume that pathway was the safest.

Suddenly, the apparently homeless man with the scruffy beard and faraway eyes had a value. If anyone could find him again.

He'd vanished, gone underground.

———

Screening the device from afar, the EOD operator was a walking encyclopaedia of knowledge, who liked to let his students know he'd forgotten more than they would ever know. To his credit, he was probably right. Where possible, the goal was always to use technology rather than expose a human operator to danger.

Following suit, Terry the bear had tucked himself into the side of a large tree, partly for cover and partly to make himself less visible. He watched as the EOD operator steered the small Dragon Runner 20 down the footpath.

He nodded, it was great to watch the boys in action, never throwing caution to the wind, but wanting to get the streets open once more. Less hasty, more safety.

Philosophies, Principles and Mandatory Actions.

These ideologies were the bible for EOD teams, as was what they colloquially called 'soak' – the safe waiting periods that were instilled from day one. Better to watch and learn, gather information and formulate an action plan, than to wade in with both feet and lose them.

———

The Dragon tracked vehicle was so portable it could be carried in a backpack, thrown into the theatre of risk, and even driven into a sewer. It was the ultimate army rat for the terrorist drainpipe.

This one had a much bigger brother, the Talon, waiting in the wings. The DR20 had also been fitted with an attachment that could detect biological, chemical or nuclear traces, and right now it was earning its keep, its operator secured at a safe distance, scanning, listening, watching, waiting, all from the device which resembled an oversized, well-engineered gaming handset.

"Small radioactive trace, boss. The X-rays are indicating some plastic, a detonator and the means to get it all singing from the same hymn sheet – rudimentary really, basic stuff, but well thought through. If this was designed to cause chaos, it did it very well."

The sergeant who had many years' experience in Northern Ireland, the Balkans and Afghanistan nodded, ticking off his own mental check sheet.

"Options?" He knew, but his lance corporal was the newest member of the unit, and days like this didn't come along very often, so it was a great training opportunity.

"Manually, disrupt by moving the device. Disrupt by removing the power supply. Disrupt by removing the payload."

"You forgot something, we adopt the single operator policy, minimise loss at all opportunity. Don't *ever* forget it. Don't ever forget to say it out loud. Less is always more in our world. Good. Next?"

"If we decide to use the robot, then it's standard stuff. Get a good view, X-ray, film, listen, leave disruption device, reverse cameras, remote detonate then return using the same route and carry out post disruption SOPs viewing the device and components. Confirm safe disruption. Cordon and contain for the next team to do their thing."

It was rigid, and he'd learnt it rote fashion. He'd passed.

"As I see it, option one is not an option, is it? So..."

"But what about the radioactive trace?"

It was a very fair question and potentially far more important than any conventional explosion. London had seen its fair share of those and had survived them all in one way or another. It was what the city did best; raise two Churchillian fingers to the world, keeping calm and carrying on.

"Initially, we were right to check it. Having made the call back to the office, I'm content the amount whilst above normal is no higher than it would be if we were about to pack a medical machine with explosives and blow it to bits. It was designed to scare people. Frankly, I wouldn't emit a squeaky fart for such stats. Let me know when the figures go off the scale and I need to call in the geeks. Until then, we crack on."

"We detonate – in situ?"

"You asking me, or telling me?"

"Telling you."

"Good man. We do. Right, let's get this sorted then, there's a city waiting to start up again, every minute we are stood here with our fingers up our collective arses it's costing a fortune."

"Is that the course of action you are following, sergeant?" asked the police commander, partly curious, partly covering his backside.

"What about the intel that it's a dirty bomb?" He appeared to be genuinely more concerned about this than the army team.

"Sir, the bomb may have some mediocre traces of a radioactive nature, but I've certainly seen a whole lot worse. Yes, there is a trace, but then there's a trace in my wristwatch and in all hospitals, some building sites, you name it, go hunting for it and it's there. As for dirty, honestly my estranged wife was far dirtier, and that, let me tell you, is saying something."

The onlookers looked, the motorists tutted or put their seats back and grabbed a chance to relax, windows up, downwind, the black cabs diverted, meters running and in one upmarket car, DJ Pullen had a gem of an idea.

———

In the Audi loan car, Pullen was fiddling with some tech kit. He'd been stationary for a while now, couldn't see anything and had been told, forcibly, to stay in his car.

In a few minutes, he had rigged up a microphone, his laptop and some other wizardry and had created a mobile studio. He rang his operations centre on a spare phone.

"It's me. I've got a chance here to get some first-hand news; we could entertain whilst we wait, you know, get all the folk down here singing along to the same tune."

His technicians were soon running what Pullen needed and as the clock headed toward the half hour he started speaking.

"Hello London." He paused. He looked around himself, then continued. "This is your old friend Geoff Pullen with a live update on what is happening down here on the Embankment. I am here, on the spot, surrounded by the emergency services." He lowered the window slightly to allow the pulsing doppler effect of the sirens to wash over the listeners, adding a heightened sense of drama.

"We've got every man and his dog down here; a helicopter standing off across on the South Bank, police everywhere, Scotland Yard practically shut down before it opens, and the army is in town too. I can clearly see our brave soldiers, kitting up and ready to approach what I'm told is a bomb. Right here in the city, within a stone's throw of some of our most iconic landmarks."

He paused for effect once more.

"Right here among us. Is this a new wave of terrorism or an individual with a grudge I ask myself? I'd dearly love to spend five minutes with whoever has chosen to cause chaos, to frustrate commuters and potentially harm the good people of my adopted city... If you are out there and are brave enough, why not give me a ring?"

His tech's teed up *London's Calling* by The Clash. It seemed fitting, if a little clichéd.

___

# CHAPTER FIFTY-THREE

___

THE BANG WAS JUST THAT — LOUD, NOT STRONG ENOUGH TO shatter windows, but more than sufficient to scatter every bird for a mile and knock one unaware cyclist from his lightweight racing bike a few hundred metres away.

It was a bright crack, like an immense whiplash which echoed for minutes from one side of the river to the other. By the following day, all that would remain would be a reasonable hole in the pavement, incident tape and two constables who looked as if they'd drawn the shortest straw.

The long-lost souls, those that extended outwards from the bronze air force statue nearby, continued their journey, not startled in the slightest. It took more than a simple explosion to do that.

They were, after all, The Few.

___

Pullen had recorded the explosion perfectly. He knew the station ratings were rocketing and he also knew he could sell the rights to anyone in the world who wanted a piece of his action. Worst case, it was great publicity and that attracted advertisers — who ultimately paid for the station to run. *Quid pro quo.*

The problem was the drama itself had ended. There was still

traffic chaos and sirens and men and women pointing, scratching their chins, taking photographs and making notes.

But as the sergeant had said, the city never slept and he'd allowed it to stay awake.

As Pullen was beginning to wrap up his show, his other phone buzzed with a text message.

*Caller Line 1*. He only had one line, but he knew what it meant.

It was a risk. There was no delay on this broadcast and there was always a risk of abuse or foul language, or better still, for the ratings at least, a terrorist making a claim. He'd take the chance.

"Hello, this is Geoff Pullen, welcome to the show. I understand you know something about the terrorist event earlier. Who am I talking to and what can you tell us?"

There was a pause. Pullen was a pro; he allowed a moment for the caller to compose themselves, people were often nervous.

"Nothing to be afraid of my friend. I'm guessing you are a first-time caller. I'm here to help you through this. Must have been bad for you?"

"Hello." A male voice. It was difficult to gauge whether it was calm or terrified.

"Hello, who am I talking to?"

"My name is Nicolescu."

"Hello Nick, lovely to be talking to you. What did you see?"

"No, my name is Nic-o-lescu. That is my surname. My first is Constantin."

"I'm so sorry, Constantin. I'm picking up an accent. Russian?" He was proud of his skills in identifying people. Something he'd been inspired to do, having spent only one frantic afternoon with Cade many years before.

"I'm mildly impressed, but no, I am from Romania." He ran his hand over his cheek, the hole Roberts had caused was weeping.

"And you are very welcome to be here, my friend."

"But I'm not your friend, Geoffrey, so stop saying that. Anyway, I was just having a wonderful bath when I accidentally tuned into your station. I prefer something more classy, more classical. However, you were talking about my work, down on the Embankment, so I thought I would ask, how was it?"

Pullen scratched his groin, then his head. Looked at himself in the rear-view mirror. Shook his head, then spoke.

"If you have a classic request I can oblige later, how about a bit of ELO or something mellow by The Carpenters, or more upbeat, how about..."

"Shut. Up. And. Listen."

"I've not heard of those, are they new?" Pullen was trying his best to keep the caller on the line. It's what they did in all the best films, except in this case, it made absolutely no difference.

"Two ears and one mouth, Geoffrey. Call yourself a professional journalist? God gave them to you in this order for a reason. I said you were talking about my work, that should have been a red flag. You know from that statement I'm either a firefighter or a paramedic, or even a bomb disposal officer, or perhaps the man running the Operation Orion team. Do you know him Geoff?"

"No, I don't." He was rapidly texting the station.

*Do something quickly.*
*Try to alert the police.*
*I think I've got the actual bomber on the line.*

"Ok, well his name is Jack Cade."

"Well, then I do. Jack's an old mate of mine." He wasn't sure whether this was the right way to handle the situation. "We met years ago when he worked at East Midland's Airport. I've got a story to tell about that day that would amaze you."

"I can hardly wait for your version. Perhaps when I've finished mine?"

He sounded so cold, a land shark; eyes of black and little empathy for his fellow man.

Pullen got a reply that the station had alerted the police, and to keep him talking. Not that they had the ability to trace him, they just thought it might help.

"Now, don't interrupt. I placed the device next to the litter bin. It was packed with explosives, from the batch stolen from the Portuguese military some time ago. It also had radioactive material in it. Ask yourself this, if the army has detonated it, do you really want to be sitting in a traffic jam right now?"

Pullen looked in his mirror. Cars were beginning to turn, to do three-point turns. They were trying to mount the pavement, to be anywhere other than here. If it took ten points to turn around, it didn't matter to them as long as they were heading the other way.

"Well, I'm sure the army knew what they were doing."

"Absolutely. But you see, they just like to… what is the term… blow shit up. Then they can go home for tea and medals. And tomorrow in the House they will all try to point the finger of blame at each other – and one party will say the other shouldn't have reduced the police numbers, and the other will say they did, and the others should do more to support them blah blah blah. Now, Geoffrey, I have a favour to ask."

"Fire away." Pullen was running with what he had – very little, but this could lead to something significant and really put him on the map.

"I have a list of names. I would like to read them out, if that's alright with you, perhaps in between *Don't Bring Me Down* by ELO or *We've Only Just Begun* by The Carpenters?"

"But I think if you carry on harming our city, it could be the *Last Train To London*…"

"Geoffrey. You are only paid to listen and play inane popular music, not offer what your infantile listeners might consider to be intelligent debate. Can you even do both at the same time? I'll start, so I recommend you all listen. This is a list of people, some very famous, some not so. People who foolishly got into bed with me some time ago and now find themselves hung out to dry."

He inhaled loudly.

"Their greed and stupidity led to this, but mainly their greed. You see in life we can be greedy or grateful. I was grateful, I have a lot of money, a grotesque amount actually, but I was looking for new friends to play games with, and along with the fun the rewards were excellent."

He then sighed loudly, squeezed some water onto his back from his natural sponge – speculating for a second where it had last swum. Then he questioned himself. Could they actually swim? He decided wherever they lived would be a finer place, a warm place, and one he'd rather be in.

"Those rewards for the twelve people I am about to discuss were monetary, and for some just pure evil, manifested by way of a game of Russian Roulette – or in my case, Romanian Roulette!" He laughed at his own joke.

Pullen tried Cade again, via text.

*Jack, tune into my station NOW! Constantin is speaking live. You need to hear this. GP.*

# CHAPTER FIFTY-FOUR

CADE GAVE THE PHONE TO O'SHEA. SHE TUNED. THEY LISTENED.

"Jack, it's him. It's actually him on the radio. Can we trace this?"

"I don't think he cares, Carrie. I think he wants us to catch him. Death by cop by another name."

"But why? He's got plenty of money if our intel gathering is anything to go by. He's got protection in Eastern Europe and within this city, someone likes him enough to allow him to operate with impunity. Why not just up and leave, go and live on the coast, the Black Sea, or Spain, anywhere, live out your days?"

———

She was right. But no one really understood Constantin's motives.

He just wanted people to like him. Not hard, surely?

From his pitiful days as a boy living in the shadow of his malodorous and malevolent parents. Then there was his school – or rather the brief time he spent there, abused by his fellow pupils and very much abused by his male teachers. In later life he had abused himself, pumping his veins and nostrils full of drugs until he stumbled across a relative of sorts in Alex – a man he truly loved for many reasons. Alex and his brothers were his family.

Constantin continued.

"You see I just want people to like me, Geoff."

"I like you…"

"*NO!* You don't." He shouted so loud that he spat onto the phone handset.

"You say it to make me feel like we are somehow friends. You don't even know me. We've never met and never will. We came close once, but you don't have the brains to realise."

"East Midlands Airport, England, 2004, a Thursday, to be precise. You were in a white Mercedes Benz trying to escape with a young woman." He hoped he was right. Cade listened and didn't know whether to scream at the radio or hug Pullen when he next saw him – it was a very fine line indeed. Dental floss in the mouth of a tiger.

"What?" asked the Romanian.

"Constantin, I *was* there." Pullen pinched himself. This just might be the pinnacle of his radio career.

"You see, people think I'm just some daft northerner who plays house music to acid-tripped teens in Ibiza. I was, once, but I have a brain too and I study people for a living. To run a talk back show you need to understand callers of all shapes and sizes, and yes, on that day I was there in the old white Vauxhall. It was me. Jack and I were pursuing you. We rescued the girl. So, now we are on a level playing field, perhaps we can start again? Why do you want to read out these names?"

"You're spirited, Geoff, and far brighter than I gave you credit for. I'm sorry, and for the record you, were very brave that day too. And yes, you did rescue dear Nikolina." He didn't mean a single word about Pullen's gallantry, but he felt he could now play him like a desperate sailfish.

"Apology accepted. Look, the people of London are listening, so make it count, I'll hold off the news and the ad breaks, why do you want to name these people? Are they really so bad? Can you not go to the police?"

Pullen cleared his throat, holding his hand over the phone, he hadn't smoked since 2004 and his lungs had almost healed. He'd stopped using cheap anti-perspirant too, he could afford the finer things now. But they weren't helping the two large damp stains under his arms, and he was desperate for a cigarette.

"No, you see a few of them *are* the police, Geoff. And there's a judge! To be fair, he's a lovely man. I owed him a lot because he managed to get me out of jail free – you could say he has the monopoly on such things in London." He waited.

"It was a joke, Geoff. What is wrong with you people? Lord Chief Justice Carlton was a very senior judge indeed – at the highest possible level, but like every one of the twelve good men, and true, he has a secret; gambling, sex addiction, criminal offending, debt, shall I continue?"

"Please do." This was award-winning material.

"Then there is the Lord Justice of Appeal, a man called Hector Barrowby. I can tell you and your listeners are rapidly searching the internet to see if this is true, well, the names anyway. I have nothing to lose by naming these people, everything to gain, in fact. Judge Carlton likes a flutter on the horses and the whores. Whereas Judge Barrowby likes his whores to be of the same sex. Likes to dress them up in his wigs and court clothing. Weird, don't you think?"

Pullen couldn't believe what he was hearing.

"Can you prove this?"

"Prove it? Why, of course, do you really think I would come onto some mediocre radio station and start throwing these names around without proof?" He yelled the last word.

"No, of course not. And for the record, it's rated as the fifth best radio station in the city. Please go on..."

"Then there's my new member. A clever man who has been feeding me secrets, like the sweetest grapes, dropping them into my willing mouth as I lay on my pure white chaise lounge and look out across the city. He won't admit it, but he does enjoy the feeling of being dominated. That's his downfall. Actually, he's not much of a willing party to it. But he has a secret, and I know it. Isn't that right Chief Superintendent Phillip Jenkinson, Metropolitan Police?"

Cade slowed and pulled to the side of the road. He held the back of his head, then stared up at the roof lining.

"Record this. Are you recording this? I should have thought sooner. Pullen may have it on tape, may not. What the hell is he playing at, Carrie? Andy, you're a bright young detective, any thoughts?"

West sat up slightly, stared out of the window at the endless traffic jams.

"Revenge? Honestly, I can't think of any other reason, boss. If he's mixing with big names like that, why would he throw them under the train? Makes no sense. Unless it's simpler?"

"You heard what he said, Jack. He just wants to be *liked*." O'Shea left the sentence to dwell like a bad smell in a lift.

———

Police units across the city were scrambling to listen into the programme and at the National Crime Agency, DS Nigel Malik was no exception.

"So far all he's mentioned are public servants. Do we think we should be briefing the PM's office?" he asked his manager.

"Not yet... the way he's going with this list he's likely to name one of her staff."

"The way he's going he's likely to mention her!"

———

Pullen turned the aircon on. It was cold outside but he was sweating. This could be the making of him. One man, profiting from another's expense. In that regard he was no different to his caller on line one.

"Please carry on, Mr Nicolescu."

"Ah, it's Mister now, is it? How the mighty have risen. How are those listening figures looking, Geoff? On the up, I suspect. I want nothing in return."

"Thank you. Please go on." He was shaking now. He was on board a roller coaster, a pleasure ride with a dead end, a long drop, no brakes, and the screams were only getting louder.

"Where were we? Three down. Add three of the city's most eminent bankers, two from foreign banks, one from a household name here in the UK who loves to entertain Albanian teenagers, in his office overlooking the Shard — a truly iconic symbol of testosterone if ever I've seen one."

He slowly named all three. Their names. Their banks. Even in the case of the man who used to overlook the Shard, his wife who was busy emptying their joint account and her walk-in wardrobes.

He totted them up on his spare hand. "Six, then there are the four international players — Nigeria, China, Taiwan and Singapore."

Now the phones were lighting up in all of those places. Day or night, it mattered not. People needed to be informed.

"The man from Singapore is *very* interesting. Not that his cousins from Taiwan and China aren't, but whilst he likes to play my game of roulette, he also has his own, but what that involves is his business entirely."

Pullen rubbed his eyes. This was unbelievable.

It was obvious Constantin had drawn an imaginary line between the British players and their international contemporaries.

"I will be naming the foreign players before the end of the day. To be impartial, they are more loyal than the British ones, and for me, loyalty and kindness are the most important values anyone can have."

O'Shea was nearly sick. "Kindness, you..." She stopped herself, reflecting back to a time when he had meted out such cruel punishment upon her and her friend.

"I need to speak to him, live," said Cade, driving once more, now not sure whether to head to the bomb scene, the office or just stay out — as they called it in the police — floating around, waiting for something to happen. He chose the latter.

Constantin continued, enjoying the exposé now.

"The judges and the bankers, they made a lot of cash, borrowing their gambling money from the state, then the international players laundered all they needed to, simple. And why do I tell you this? Well, as I mentioned, it comes down to loyalty. You see, everything was going really well until people became greedy. There was no need. We were all making money."

He paused. He ran the scenario through his mind for a brief second, knowing what he was doing wasn't without risk. But he simply didn't care anymore.

"The Nigerian player was ripping off the judges, they in turn were trying to steal from the bankers, the Chinese were stealing all of their crypto currencies and data, the Taiwanese from the Chinese – all like the beautiful big wheel on the river, a sort of rotating wheel of corruption, with each pod containing someone more corrupt than the next."

"This sounds like the stuff of films, Constantin. How do we know it's actually true? I understand you feel you have been betrayed, but where's the proof?" He was pushing it now and enjoying it.

"The proof? Piccadilly Circus in exactly one hour. For all to see. Be there, or not, the choice is yours. If your media partners are listening, I would be making my way there right now, grab a space on the front row. While you still can. It's safe. No bombs there. None *I* have planted anyway."

He let out a little laugh, almost child-like, which made it so much more disturbing.

West spoke first. "Boss, the lights at Piccadilly are all off. They are doing a massive make-over, bringing it all up to date with new technology. He's bluffing. Hundred percent."

On the radio, the Romanian continued.

"And before your listeners phone in saying the advertising system at Piccadilly is off for repairs, they are right."

"No point in my media partners racing there, then?" asked Pullen, smugly.

"Of course. Geoff, who do you think shut them down? They are installing facial recognition systems like no other. If they see a man like me strolling along the street, it will flash up adverts for male grooming, or a car it thinks I might like. It will respond to the weather. It's really very clever. And guess who is the financier?" He took a theatrical pause.

"That's right, our CEO, who adores young Albanian girls. I know because I bought shares for it. Shares that don't exist. They said the system will be offline until 2017. Except they had no idea I was way ahead of our banking friends and their fictitious shares. Revenge. A dish best served cold and in full view of the public. Be there. One hour."

"Believe him?" asked West.

"One hundred percent. He isn't the type to bluff, Andy. Get someone from the team there. Be in the vicinity, I want live feeds of what is happening. And get hold of Nigel Malik's squad, see what they know – and, Andy..."

"Guv?"

"Good work. Thanks."

———

In the city, people were shutting down, deleting, shredding, burning if they could, then shredding the ashes. The city financiers were unlinking links and distancing themselves from any involvement, first, second or third hand.

The Metropolitan Police Directorate of Professional Standards needed a new leader, that much was clear. New staff too. The job temporarily fell to an Assistant Commissioner, who raced around Scotland Yard and the internal phone directory gathering her best possible people. This was going to hurt, best find people who knew how to apply a nice tight bandage.

In Abuja, Nigeria, a passport had just been cancelled. Hang him out to dry.

In Taiwan they gathered as much data as they could, seeing it as an opportunity.

In Beijing, they waited and watched.

In Singapore, the government listened and also waited. They knew exactly who the man was, and they knew better than to upset him. He was well-connected, with familial roots spreading across the city and all the way back to China.

They all feared the man they called, The Moth.

# CHAPTER FIFTY-FIVE

In Chelsea Harbour, Constantin stood naked, looking at his reflection in the tinted glass, back-lit, he could see out across the city. All the way along the river and into the next county. He could have easily lived a quiet life in this apartment block, acquired a handsome yacht in which to cruise up and down the river, parking it almost outside, like the other foreigners did, if he had chosen to.

Could. It was such a negative word. Past tense, the opposite of can. He wanted to surround himself in positivity from this day forth. The problem, the issue for the man from Craiova, was now he had the wealth, the cars and the apartment on the river, he had also surrounded himself with enemies – both on the side of the virtuous and the nefarious.

One would seek to lock him up and throw away the key, and there was no way he could go back to that life now. The other would seek to bury him in a forest or feed him to the pigs. He let out a long sigh. He genuinely didn't know which side he wanted to fall down onto anymore.

The time for playing games was over. He needed to make his next move, and with the city's media rampaging across town, fighting for a prime spot in one of the busiest hubs for cars and people, he knew there was no time like the present.

The Embankment was crawling, cars still trying to recoup some ground from the earlier chaos. It would take hours.

He dressed – a suit seemed appropriate. It might be the last time he got to wear one. He chose grey, with a pink shirt, no tie but expensive shoes. Only the very best from English artisans.

He was ready.

He said goodbye to his housekeeper, and as it was possibly the last time, told him to help himself to anything from the pantry and wine cellar – just not the more expensive new world wine he had developed a taste for.

Everything else was fair game.

The housekeeper took nothing, cleaned the bathroom and left for his much smaller flat, south of the river.

Constantin's driver exited the plush apartment complex, remotely shutting the roller doors. The black Mercedes oozed quality and with performance on tap, it was ideal. It was one of thousands in the city – luxuriously anonymous, on cloned plates too – lavish *and* anonymous.

Constantin started answering the many text messages he had been receiving from the men he had publicly shamed.

He replied to the first, then copied and pasted and repeated the action until he'd covered the British – leaving Jenkinson until last.

His message was clear.

*You knew the risks. You knew the rules.*

To Jenkinson he added:

*And you left a young boy to die in the street. And for a man who preaches integrity that is inexcusable.*

———

The Mercedes arrived at a faceless office block fifteen minutes later. The car waited, engine running, the driver was given strict instructions: if anyone asks you to move on, point them to the number plates and smile.

Diplomatic plates, they were worth their weight in gold. Or in this case, cryptocurrency and electronic accounts. No diamonds, they were hard to dispose of, as he'd found out once before, gold was too heavy and silver was for the smart people who stored it and waited for when it would one day explode back onto the market — but a kilo of silver was still a kilo and he needed to travel light.

He was met at the main door and escorted down into a secure room. He felt confident, not like the past when he was forever looking over his shoulder.

"Are we still on track?"

"Absolutely. You did what we discussed?"

"I did, what do you take me for?"

"A thief."

"It takes one to know one."

Constantin smiled and shook the hand that was being held out.

The hand was lightly tanned, had a few white scars on the knuckles from adventures past, and belonged to a striking male who also wore a tailored suit, a dark red shirt, no watch, but a ring on the second finger of his right hand, it contained a single diamond which was very visible, with a simple animal pattern, chasing itself across the white shiny metal band.

Born in 1970, he was always happy to have been associated with the Year of the Dog. Chinese people regard the dog as a genuinely auspicious animal. When one appears at their homes, the Chinese see it as a symbol of pending good fortune.

The God Erlang had a loyal canine partner who helped him to capture the many monsters they encountered.

Monsters, loyalty, prosperity: Constantin had seen his fair share of all three.

He wasn't entirely sure which character he was — a snake probably, or a rat.

"This way." The Chinese male gestured for Constantin to enter the room. As he approached the open door, he had a sense of unease. He looked at the Chinese face. It was smiling. Smiling like a dog with a bone.

"We played your game, Constantin, and now you play mine. Enter your account details and transfer what you owe me, plus your other deposits from the other players you have stolen from. I read you like a very bad book, each chapter unfolded and this was the worst book I have ever read." He gestured around the room, placing his metaphorical chess piece in line with the king.

"You need a new mentor if you are going to take on people like me. Right now, you are better to have upset me than the other men. One call and they will know where you are. Just one call."

There were no guns on display, no weapons at all. The Chinese man was supremely confident. With two larger men in the room already, he knew he held the high ground.

Constantin could only hope his driver was listening to the one call he had made to him before leaving the car. The one that was live, broadcasting from his pocket.

———

Jenkinson was stuck in traffic. He needed to get back to his office. He needed to remain calm.

Stay calm and no one would suspect anything. He was the epitome of sure-footedness. The man people looked to in a crisis, the one who remained aloof at all times, watching for others to fail.

He was muttering to himself as he tried to weave amongst the stationary vehicles. There was nowhere to go. The pavements were more secure these days, cars were unable to get onto them, better that than allow a terrorist hell-bent on running people down, as they went about their lives.

He could see Scotland Yard ahead – the new icon on the Embankment, almost ready to allow itself to become the face of the Metropolitan Police once more. The headquarters had moved from the riverside to Broadway and now back to the river.

He could see his office – the one overlooking the river, the London Eye and the old County Hall building.

He needed to be sat behind his desk, discreetly destroying electronic and physical documents. Why hadn't he done this before today?

Why? Because he couldn't, that's why. There was always the risk of someone watching the watchers. He no longer trusted anyone.

He reckoned he was minutes away: five or six if he ran. He stopped, let the car drift into the kerb, opened the door and started to run through the traffic. His phone was vibrating. His mind racing. People stared at him. They knew. He convinced himself they all knew.

———

Cade's phone rang. He swiped the icon, pressed it to his ear.

"Boss, he's not at his apartment. We've found some interesting exhibits and we've seized his laptop and an old phone. Shall we leave a business card or something? Seems the right thing to do."

"No. He doesn't deserve to be treated decently. Make sure the lights are off and lock the door on the way out. No, stand by a moment..."

He ran a few options through his mind. What would Jenkinson do?

He'd either leave the country. Destroy as much evidence as possible, or end it all. He was too selfish to end it all, too much of a coward. Option one or two then.

"Check for travel documents, anything which might indicate he's looking to leave."

"Guv?"

"You heard, just go and look."

It took only two minutes.

"You've struck gold, boss. There was a packed suitcase in the walk-in wardrobe. In an envelope was a ticket to Bali. Singapore Airlines to Denpasar. Strange destination."

"Not at all. Very nice part of the world, lots of entertainment, cheap accommodation and above all, no extradition treaty with the United Kingdom. Smart move."

"Not so smart sir, he's left his passport here."

"Superb! Right, bag it up and stay put for a while. We'll ring you when you can stand down. And get a border alert entered. I do not want to lose him."

He hung up when he saw a red-and-green icon on the screen. Another call.

"Cade."

"Marriott here, Jack. Listen, old mate, there's a lot going on down here and it's a little close to home. We are keeping our heads down, but anything we need to know? Anything we can help with?"

A team of ex-servicemen without a mission. It seemed unfair. Then he nodded.

"Can I send you a photo? Someone we are keen to locate."

"Urgently?"

"Very."

"Any chance he's linked to the device the Royal Engineers have just blown to bits down here?"

"Indirectly, directly, possibly, probably."

"Both good enough and vague enough for me, we'll shift our alert status up a peg or two. Send the image. And, Jack, if we see the target, what should we do? You know, given we have no power, above ground anyway!"

"Sit on him. Make a citizen's arrest if you have to."

"Are we OK with that? What's the offence?"

Cade ran through all the options.

"PACE – Section 24A, use that and arrest him for..." He looked at O'Shea and West, screwed his face up tightly. "Arrest him for perverting the course of justice."

"Bit deep, can't we just lock him up for murder?"

"If only. I think we can find evidence to support that later, but right now I can't prove it, but I reckon we can prove the former, and its indictable so you are covered. He's got himself involved in something bloody, and we are only just scraping the scab off. When we do, I suspect it will bleed profusely. And if anyone in uniform or otherwise asks, you are preventing him from destroying property."

"Namely?"

"Namely everything he's connected to. Imagine someone balls deep in anarchy and trouble and you've got Jenkinson wrapped up tightly with a bow on him. Bottom line Phil, I want him in custody today if I can. Stand by for the picture."

"Standing by. Good to be back in the mix again. Glad we met, Jack." He looked at the screen held out in front of him. "OK, I've got it, I'll deploy a few on foot, all I can see outside is a wall of cars and people holding cell phones. Speak soon."

Marriott hung up and gave a rapid briefing to his team. He liked Cade and if he was honest; it was good to be respected once more. Cade and his team had given the men and women new purpose, which was an added windfall. That the man they were looking for was running towards the rail tunnel, right now, was just the break Cade was hoping for, the beginning of a rainbow on a darkening day.

"Go! Get him. If anyone asks, we are the security service. They'll soon back away after the mayhem that's been occurring outside today."

The bear was first. He was a huge man, but remarkably nimble when he needed to be. Over the balustrades and onto the pavement. Followed by Terry as Hugh joined them from across the road, having entered the street from another door. It paid to be flexible.

Using just nods of the head and the discreet military hand signals they had developed since being homeless, they moved quickly through the building crowds, hoping to get through the blockade.

Jenkinson was sprinting now. He knew he only had a minute or two of oxygen and stamina left, he also knew he needed to calm down somehow, before he entered the building.

Bear stepped up now, breaking into a stride. He'd seen him first. With a point of the hand Hugh was off and running, Terry, too. The Marine versus the Para. If ever there was a display of competitiveness, it was right there on the crowded embankment.

Terry edged ahead; lighter, he was marginally faster. Jenkinson looked over his shoulder, stumbled slightly, righted himself and dug deeper. He hadn't run this fast since his first foot chase as a probationary constable hunting down a bag snatcher.

Who was the man chasing him, and why? To his left, he saw another man breaking out from the parked cars, heading towards him.

Ahead an ambulance, lights flashing hypnotically, sirens screaming, ricocheting off the buildings and trees, enough to wake the dying.

The sound rattled around his brain. The street began to close in on him as the brightly lit vehicle headed towards him.

A police officer waved it through the cordon. It was building up speed rapidly, into second, then third, sirens getting louder, the driver focused fully on getting their status one patient to the nearest trauma centre, as her passenger, a time-served paramedic, fought to keep the patient alive.

Time versus luck. They had an hour at best – the golden hour.

Terry was within reach, he pushed harder, Jenkinson found some extra energy and pushed ahead. To his right, Hugh was piling in towards him, as fast as he could possibly run.

Jenkinson changed tack, side stepping twice, a rugby player surging towards the try. He turned slightly, looking back at his pursuers, and then life stopped.

He was propelled forwards, airborne for a few seconds. Life didn't slow down like they said it did, those observers who had never actually experienced extreme trauma. Everything happened rapidly. In the time it took for the ambulance to stop, for the paramedic to right herself and check on her patient, for the driver to call for help on the radio, then run from the ambulance, in that time Phillip Jenkinson's life had changed permanently.

He looked up at the clear sky; the sirens were still yelping and wailing. He turned his head slightly to his left, then his right. He could see trees and buildings. He could see his office: the window, the one with the Newton's Cradle, with its stainless-steel balls that clicked and clacked and gave him time to think.

He swore he heard the song of a blackbird. Then he heard the crackling of leaves in the wind and people talking.

Then he saw the faces of two men. They just stared at him, looked at each other as if they knew something Jenkinson didn't.

He wiggled his fingers. They worked. Then he rocked himself slightly from side to side on his shoulders. Again, no issues.

His head hurt. But he could feel it – a positive sign.

The medic told him to stay still. Hugh also told him to stay still. Terry was backing away, blending into the traffic and the increasing mayhem of a post-bomb, post-crash, inner-city event.

Hugh needed to go too and soon, before people started capturing him on film, and uploading both it and him to the world. For far too many people Hugh was missing, presumed dead, and for now he needed it to stay that way. He nodded to Jenkinson, knowing he was in good hands, then walked away, mingling, merging, disappearing.

Jenkinson tightened his stomach muscles. He could feel the resistance. He was breathing. So far, so very good.

He could taste blood in his mouth, he knew he'd knocked his head on the ground as he had landed an ambulance length from where he was hit.

The medic talked to him, told him to stay very, very still.

Then the chief superintendent, from the office across the road, with the view and the clicking, clacking silver cradle, realised something awful, something terribly dreadful.

He could not move his toes, or his lower legs, his knees were immobile. Physically and grotesquely twisted as he was, he offered a view the medic has seen only once before. They both knew from that moment on Phillip Edward Jenkinson, only son of Albert and Doris, two working-class people who had survived the Blitz and had raised their son in Whitechapel, in the East End of London, would never walk again.

# CHAPTER FIFTY-SIX

Phil Marriott climbed down from the railway bridge that gave him a superior view, walked anonymously with the crowds, then timed his entry into the subterranean void he called home. He'd seen enough.

"Jack, it's me. Something untoward happened with your person of interest."

"Did your team have to resort to PACE and reasonable force?"

"Not entirely... and the force was far from reasonable."

He outlined what he had seen, summing it up eloquently.

"A case of one down, no idea how many more to go. Next task, Jack, we're ready to deploy as soon as you give us the nod."

"Thanks, Phil. Listen, mate, what you can do is get the ears to the ground. Our secondary target is on the move."

"I thought you'd be looking for your primary target? Wasn't the guy who just got shunted down the street by an ambulance your secondary?"

"Yep. He was. But he isn't now. Once he's left hospital, if indeed he ever does, I will get the correct team to interview him. I suspect his career choices have been limited by another emergency service. No, our new secondary target is closer to home. And he's leading us up the garden path to Goldilocks."

———

Derek Murphy could hear it all. The tone was neither friendly nor threatening. But he knew from years of policing how things could change in less than the blink of an eye. He pressed the hazard lights and placed a false card on the dashboard.

Romanian Embassy. The correct address and an incorrect phone number.

Then he left the car.

What was he thinking? He was walking away from a career and a cast-iron pension, for what?

A quick fix for a long-term debt.

He opened the entrance door and quietly walked along the corridor, listening to the conversation with the phone pressed tightly to his left ear.

"I knew from the beginning you were a thief, Constantin."

"So why did you not walk away?" he answered, genuinely interested in the response.

"Because I love a challenge. And you were the most interesting challenge I had seen in years, and besides, I enjoyed playing human roulette."

"Which part did you enjoy the most?" He was stalling now, praying Murphy had detected a change in the tone.

"The way different drugs affected different people. You know I had a plan for you? My friends from China and Taiwan had agreed that if we ran out of players, we were going to strap you and the strange man who called himself the Master to the wheel and pump you so full of drugs, you would never survive."

"But at least I would die deliriously happy?" He smiled at the Singaporean, who wasn't smiling back.

"At least you would die and we would *all* be happy; the best part was we would use the money you stole from us to bet on your life. Instead, I have to stand here demanding you give me back my own money, or these two will tear you in half. And before you ask, yes, they can, and yes, they have."

"So, you plan to give the other players their money back? Very honourable."

The Singaporean man grinned. "No, absolutely not. I am going to keep every last penny. I am honourable; I'm not stupid. But I will be blaming you entirely. Now start typing."

Constantin thought about entering the wrong log-in data but knew it was futile. He needed two minutes if Murphy was going to arrive and bail him out. The irony that he was hoping to be bailed by a police officer made him laugh.

"What's so funny?" asked the Singaporean.

"A private joke. I'm in. Now what?" The screen displayed a figure in the low millions. More than the man from Singapore needed, and much less than he thought.

"Is that it?"

"What were you expecting? It's still a lot of money. Do you want the few hundred from my current account, too?"

"Yes, actually I do, I want every cent you own."

"I was joking. People like me and you do not have current accounts. Everything of mine is hidden away. Crypto currencies like those on the screen and cash in accounts shielded by layers of security. I also have some precious metal buried in my homeland for a rainy day."

"I was joking too. I'll just take that amount and your accounts in the two foreign locations. Now, please. I haven't got all day and as yet it hasn't started to rain."

"And if I don't?"

"They will tear you apart. I thought I'd told you?"

The Romanian saw it in the Singaporean's eyes – rapid movement. He was here.

"Armed Police! Down, down on the ground now. Do as I say and you will not be harmed."

The two protection officers moved forward, hoping to challenge the white male who had appeared in the doorway, leaning into the room with what looked like the square profile of a Glock.

There was simply no way that the male with the pistol was a police officer, which meant he was fair game. The chances were high that the weapon wasn't even loaded.

The larger of the two reached into his jacket pocket. Murphy waited a split second, staring at the target over the barrel.

What was he thinking? For that matter, what were they both thinking?

The weapon the protection officer withdrew was nothing more than a phone. It probably had a stun gun element installed. It was enough for Murphy to focus on and he fired once, scanned and covered the room.

The round left the pistol and caused the phone to explode, before driving onwards through his hand and into the wall behind him. He yelped like a puppy, a much higher pitch than everyone in the room expected.

Murphy stood resolute. Holding the Glock at the low ready. Any movement would result in him punching the weapon up and into the aim. He felt he had little to lose now. He had finally crossed the line. He had paid the ferryman in whatever currency he deemed fit.

The Singaporean nodded almost imperceptibly to his remaining protection officer and they both rushed at Constantin, hoping to drag him into their custody and bargain with him. It was clearly something they had done before.

Before they reached him, two more rounds had left the short barrel of the Austrian weapon. Two quick rounds, grouped perfectly. Murphy allowed the trigger to reset, scanned once more.

The first hit the largest male in the chest – a small puncture wound, dark red and bleeding. It left a hole the size of the bullet, slightly raised, with a pure white circumference just below one of his ribs.

Inside the man's body, the copper round was creating havoc. It ripped through his abdominal aorta. If the round had stopped at that point, it would have caused sufficient bleeding to kill him without imminent medical attention. That it diverted, fragmenting and hurling pieces of metal around his vital organs, meant his chances of survival were best counted in extremely low percentage terms.

His boss, the man they referred to as The Moth stood his ground. He knew when he was outgunned and outsmarted. For now, at least he would live to fight another day.

The greatest mistake both Constantin and Murphy made was not finishing the task.

"Come on, we need to move." Murphy yelled at him – torn between a rock and an even harder place. His old life left behind and his friends now all rapidly fading. He had waved goodbye to them all the moment he had squeezed the gentle trigger on the pistol – a shot so good he never felt it coming.

'What have you done, Derek? What *have* you done?'

Constantin pressed the backspace key, then deleted his account details.

He walked towards Murphy and safety.

He faced The Moth.

"This was never about the money. But now, it is. And I've taken your share. If you had been reasonable, who knows, perhaps I would have refunded you. But not now. Let's go."

They reached the corridor and out into the foyer. Murphy opened the door and stepped to the side allowing his new boss to get out first. He turned slightly to his left and saw the Chinese man running toward him. He was holding something, a metal bar? A baton? Whatever it was, it was no match for fourteen more 9mm rounds.

But this man was on a mission. He was moving quickly, using as much cover as he could, and when he was within five metres, he knew he had a chance. The Englishman was just staring at him. A rabbit in the headlights.

But the rabbit was armed, and it had teeth. Murphy knew killing this businessman was an option, but would his people come after them? They would anyway, so why not deal with him here and now?

He fired once, hitting him in the leg, then raised the pistol slightly and fired again, missing with that shot and the third that ripped out of the weapon, Murphy hardly allowing time for the trigger to reset.

The man born in the Year of the Dog was remarkably quick.

Murphy raised the weapon but his target wasn't slowing.

"Shoot him!" Constantin yelled from the car.

There was always Plan B: run and escape.

He fired again and moved towards cover. His instructor would have been livid – missing with four rounds, what a waste.

With Constantin in the car, Murphy was caught in no-man's land.

"Stop! Please. I will shoot you. Just back away..." The police officer once more, calmer, trying to reason, never wanting actually to pull the trigger.

But he did. His target stopped.

The Moth was a wise man. Far from old, but very wise.

"You shot me in the leg." He grimaced as the pain hit home.

"You could have shot me anywhere and for that I thank you." He was drawing air through gritted teeth and into his lungs, trying not to show weakness.

"You would be better working for me than him, he will bring you nothing but bad luck and luck is very difficult to come by. You have one chance. What will your choice be?"

He favoured the leg which was bleeding and seeping into the material of his hand-made suit. He could always order another. It was all he needed to do; email his colour and style preference through to his tailor and in two days it would be en route to him.

"Tempted. But I need to sort this pile of excrement out first. I'll get an ambulance on the way."

"Good of you. The last person who shot me didn't offer such a fine post-trauma service." He smiled. He actually smiled.

"But then I had him located and sent away. You, on the other hand, may just live to fight another day."

"Thank you. You know, for not sending me away."

"May. I said may. Now go whilst I'm feeling charitable. And tell your boss this – tell him I will never rest until I find him. I have a big family with a reach way beyond what a man of your connections could ever begin to imagine. And you, if you get in my way, you will suffer too. You have been warned." He leant back against the wall and hoped a medic arrived soon. He ripped open the suit material, the wound was a lucky one, having passed through the outer edge of his thigh. It hurt, but it wouldn't kill him. He'd had worse.

———

Murphy backed out of the building, jumped into the Mercedes, and quickly joined the traffic. Nothing was said for a mile. Then he looked in the rear-view mirror and spoke.

"What exactly just happened?"

"You shot one of the most feared criminals in South East Asia, but failed to kill him. A naïve thing to do. But we have his money and more besides. The remaining players will either make their way to the pick-up point or begin hunting for me – and you, once they find out we are a couple."

"Listen, mate, we are *not* a couple. Far from it in fact. I'm married, or rather was, and I've always held my head high, until now."

"I meant a team, not a couple. And they say the ones who protest the loudest are the most intrigued." He caught Murphy's eye in the mirror and winked.

"Seriously, you try any of that funny business and I will do a far better job of shooting you, Constantin."

"I think you are mildly curious and anyway you would miss, even though you have thirteen bullets left. Just drive if you want your wife's drug debts clearing before midnight. I take it she's still in hiding?"

"She is. I suspect my marriage is over though after this."

"She hardly holds the moral high ground."

He laughed. "You're right. It's caused me endless sleepless nights, even when we were hunting you last year, she was still scoring from her dealer; thirty, fifty and a hundred a day at one point. I was doing overtime to fund a habit. Now look at me. I'd be a professional standards' wet dream."

"I have no idea what that means. Right, onto the task at hand. You know where to go? You know what to do when we get there? You are sure you can drive the truck?"

"Yes, to all those."

"Good, then once we get the loyal players to safety and heading toward their new futures, we can transfer the money across to your account. You should have enough to pay off your debts and live comfortably forever and ever, amen."

# CHAPTER FIFTY-SEVEN

## THE BEGINNING OF THE END

CONSTANTIN HAD SENT THE BURST TRANSMISSION – A CODED message which decoded read quite simply:

*We leave exactly on time. Anyone who misses the bus knows the cost.*

In other words, be there or lose everything you have ever worked for. Judges and jury. The judges had decided – badly as it happened, allowing themselves to be manipulated into freeing him, against all legal and logical opinion.

The Mercedes arrived at the new industrial complex within twenty-five minutes. Murphy checked the obvious places and declared the warehouse safe. He felt anything but, even considered running out of the door, dialling 999 and pleading for clemency.

"Start her up please, Derek."

Constantin stood like a proud father before the great white hope – the DAF prison van, which gleamed with freshly polished paint-work and told a lie via aged but expertly cloned number plates.

"She looks amazing. Cloned plates are a simply perfect addition, any number plate recognition hits will just refer back to an identical truck owned by the Prison Service." He checked his wrist, no watch, he'd put it in a place of safety, it was a habit formed since he had sold his favourite timepiece to buy heroin, something he did when the pressure built. Now, he no longer feared his mistress, he was finally, completely and honestly, clean.

"Fifteen minutes and they should be here. They know the rules. No cars. No phones either. Dump them in the acid vat and walk in. No cameras on the route in."

"You did well."

"Why thank you, Derek. I feel you are warming to me."

"Seriously, debt or not, I will shoot you."

Constantin's phone vibrated.

"The first one is five away. Punctual. He must be British."

Murphy met the merchant bank CEO, checked him for weapons. He had complied. Not even a wallet.

He dropped his phone in the plastic oil drum. A modern-day version of going off radar – for good.

He had never been in trouble, so his fingerprints were not on record. If the police needed to identify him, it would be just that little bit harder. His teeth would be a good start, fortuitously, the central registry of dental work was in a town not a million miles away.

It was the same for all the British players. Well, except the judges. Their 'prints were on file. Naturally.

In half an hour, the British members of the syndicate were sat in their cubicles, prisoners of a different kind, in their upmarket clothing and with a general lack of criminal convictions.

In another thirty minutes, the Nigerian, the Chinese and the Taiwanese were on board. They were seated on the left of the van, the British on the right.

"Where is Henry Tan? Where is he?" asked the Chinese industrialist who had made and naively just lost a large part of his fortune.

"Don't worry, he'll meet us there," offered Murphy. "Now please, get in. You need to go into that cubicle. The one on the right."

The doors were closed and once more the prison van became just that, the white elephant in the room. The heavy diesel engine rumbled into life and Murphy engaged first. He hadn't driven anything bigger than a Transit van since he left the army. It felt good to back behind the wheel of something significant again.

He merged, checked the blind spots, indicated and began to head south.

Constantin sat alongside him. The passengers couldn't hear a word.

"Have you enjoyed stepping over the line, Derek?"

"Not really. But what choice did I have?"

"You understand, half the people in this truck will hunt you down and try to kill you, whilst the other half will seek to prosecute you and send you to prison, you realise that, don't you?"

"And the rest will ensure I never get another mortgage approved. Yes, I get it. Same applies to you. More so. You are the leader of this operation."

"Ah but you see, dear Derek, I really no longer care. I don't have a care in the world in fact. And I've never had a mortgage. But you on the other hand, do. It's what makes people like you easy to deal with. You are weak. Yet you have morals. I haven't met a truly bent British cop yet. You all have a never-ending sense of right that shackles you and prevents you from ever becoming truly free."

"Do you think *you* are free? You seem to spend a lot of time looking over your shoulder."

"That's paranoia, borne out of a lifetime addiction to heroin. There is a difference. This operation, as you call it, will pay off the debts, clear my obligations to my mistress and finally allow me to live for as long as I have left. Twenty-four little hours is all we need, Del. I can call you Del, can't I?"

"No."

———

The van continued south, being captured on countless cameras. No one flinched. The public never looked up from their newspapers or phones. Why would they? It was a prison van, full of prisoners, heading to somewhere other than their towns, good, hopefully they didn't leave for a very long time.

If they had known that on board were the most senior judges, supercilious bankers and devious heads of organised criminal groups, they might have taken a second look. All sat in musty prisoner cubicles, tapping their feet and fingers, where countless, faceless prisoners had done so before them, anxious they too had made the right decision.

The situation reeked as much as the remnants of those prisoners' past; a heady cocktail of dirty feet, sweaty armpits and a lack of general hygiene. A fruity, dirty almost earthy smell, mixed with the total and utter sense of vulnerability.

It was a miserable place to be, with its blue floors and grey faceless plastic seats, grey walls, machined metal panels and darkly tinted glass. The only colourful highlight was a bright yellow seat belt. Murphy had told them to wear them and they complied without a single question.

They joined the A100 and crossed Tower Bridge. On any given day it was a spectacle of British engineering worth standing on and looking up at in awe. Now the occupants faced forward, silently, waiting, hoping, some even quietly praying that they would make it.

To where? To the future Constantin Nicolescu had promised them on day one, many months before when they had all signed up to a gambling syndicate, that promised them the world, or threatened their lives and their livelihoods. Gamblers did that, every day. It was what made the addiction so exciting – the sheer thrill of winning and the sheer intoxication of losing, but then winning it all back and some.

Just one more throw of the dice, a turn of the card, the futile trajectory of the little white ivory ball, the meteor of their lives, on a trajectory to God alone knew where.

They all had that in common. They were prepared to let the ball go on a journey, all except Murphy, who was new to gambling, and he now was banking on everything coming up black. Or should he have bet it all on red? One was luckier than the other, right?

The men inside the van knew Nicolescu had arranged their departure from Britain to a tax haven, where they could live out their days, debt free, and where they could be so wealthy, they could gamble with impunity. They didn't know how, and most didn't care. A few days or weeks of suffering would be worth it in the end.

Each of them was there because they had first won the ultimate spin of the oversized roulette wheel, the one which had started this whole sickening rollercoaster ride.

They had each been placed on the wheel – with their full blessing – the same one that was now dismantled, hidden away ready for the next time. It now resembled a fair ground relic from a bygone era, washed down, stripped of the DNA of so many young men; homeless men, stateless people, ex-soldiers, rent boys and city gents with impossible class A habits.

They had all died on the wheel and were now dismembered, chemically erased, burnt, washed away, gone.

Some had actually volunteered for the experience – upon the promise of a bed for the night, food and whatever unforgiving commodity they wanted to pump into their veins.

"Can I have heroin *and* ecstasy?"

"Of course. It's your life..."

Others had been pure victims – pounced on by the voracious leopard, the one who promised he would change his spots, the man from Craiova. The man who had racked up at least a dozen lives, individual notches carved on his conscience. By the time the subsequent enquiry had begun, and ended, the numbers would have risen. He didn't care, just like nobody cared about him.

He'd had so much fun with them – and the special ones that he had found out, in the wilds of London were the most enjoyable, those made his heart beat so fast, his mouth drying out in seconds, so dry you could hear him swallow. It was often the last thing his victims had heard.

There was the man who was expecting to fulfil his wildest open-air fantasies with a stranger, executed by an adrenalin rush.

The prison officer, bound and forced to wear a ridiculous mask, there was no need, he could have just stupefied him and injected it into him. But he wanted him to suffer and sense true humiliation, wanted to watch his eyes darting about in their sockets as his mind tried to figure out just what the hell was going on, realising he would never speak to his girlfriend again, or his parents, or his brother in his last moments.

The brief eclipse when time stood still yet raced ahead. He knew he was going to die and there was nothing he could do about it.

You should have been nicer, Rick.

*Here lies Richard Chamberlain.* That summed it up for Constantin: his prisoner, his slave, his killer, the liar.

He would never forget those eyes, the way they pleaded was quite beautifully pathetic. They said, 'I will do *anything*.'

There were more bodies, too. The police had been so incompetent they had yet to put two together with itself and come up with four. Surely a series of poisonings, of random toxic deaths, weird departures, wonderful exits and, quite frankly, bizarre sudden deaths should have been one enormous red flag. But the Met was a huge force, surrounded by others, and often, they just didn't communicate, didn't look for those flags.

Well, now they might.

He'd injected them, scratched them with dirty blades, forced them to inject, even syringed one noxious substance into a young boy's eyeballs, because he'd read in prison how the human body absorbed things faster that way. They were wrong. The poor little bastard with his month-old clothes, greasy hair, jaundiced skin and equally yellowed fingertips wasn't gone in seconds, it took many minutes.

It was hardly what Constantin called a spectator sport, though. The next ones took longer still. He read and re-read; studied book after book, managed to dig deep into the vaults of the internet and find coronial and post mortem reports. They were his *Playboy* and he loved them.

The problem, or in the Romanian's case, advantage, was that London was such a huge city, that half a dozen murders south of the river might not be linked to a similar amount north.

Until today. Until the call.

# CHAPTER FIFTY-EIGHT

## TWO PLUS TWO

DEXTER HODGKINSON HAD BEEN SAT AT HIS DESK FOR HOURS, scratching his developing beard, favouring one whisker, staring at the screen, page after bloody page of it. *Sclerosis of the liver, heart failure, influenza, multiple trauma injuries, old age but suspected of being poisoned, stepping out in front of a train.* All apparently sudden and some unexplained, and that was where he arrived into the mix.

Not even the last one attracted more than a raised eyebrow. He'd lost count of the number of shattered bodies he'd examined. He'd been in the game as long as he could remember, longer in fact than any of his peers in the city. He'd seen bodies in almost every form, perfectly complete, yet somehow dead, mauled, burned, decapitated and even in pieces, bagged and put back together like a jigsaw.

When he had started as a forensic pathologist, Deoxyribonucleic acid or DNA was an acronym hardly anyone had heard of, let alone used to help gain a conviction.

Then, two young girls, Lynda Mann and Dawn Ashworth, had both been brutally murdered in the county of Leicestershire, in two separate events that shocked the entire nation.

Their seemingly unconnected murders were solved five years

later when their killer was found and convicted using DNA samples and subsequently given a life sentence – to serve at least thirty years.

Hodgkinson knew his professional life had changed then, forever, for the better. He was genuinely excited that the darkest inhabitants of society were going to be dragged kicking and screaming into the light.

Since that day, he had devoted his life to the cause, or as he called it, the calling, one which meant he would sacrifice countless hours of his own personal life and almost his marriage. But now, he felt defeated by the monotony of death. Perhaps it was time to drop the latex gloves into the bin for the last time?

———

He pulled the whisker until it was so taut, he could have played a note on it. Then, he realised that his assistant was watching him.

"What?"

"Tea, boss?"

"Only if it's Yorkshire. None of the local rubbish, my dear mother used to say, it's like the scrapings off the floor, brown dust in a cheap paper sack."

"Is that a yes?"

He smiled at her.

"My dear Kitty, where would I be without you? At least you've hung around long enough, not like my last one, look what happened to her! Yes, tea, strong, no sugar, and Kitty, would you take a look at this screen for me and tell me what you see? I need a fresh set of eyes over it. Youthful eyes like yours, not crimson cesspits like mine."

"I could look now, postpone the tea?"

"Woman, have you gone mad?" He grinned at her, dropping the errant whisker into the wastebin.

"Tea first, then screen."

It was about four minutes later when she wheeled a chair over to his desk, sipped on a mug of tea, made exactly the same as her mentor's. Then she looked and looked again and juggled the words, altered the stats in her mind.

"Well?" he said, blowing the steam from his prized Yoda mug.

"Seek and you shall find you will," she said in her version of the voice that she knew Dex adored.

"Go on master, do tell." He leaned back in his chair, almost too far, correcting it in style by flailing his arms around and grabbing the edge of the desk. "Bloody bollocks, this place will be the death of me!"

"There," she said confidently. "Look." She filtered the cells within the Excel spreadsheet and created a new list.

"Toxin. Poison. Deadly toxin. Deadly poison. Very deadly toxin and poison. Shall I go on?"

"No. I'd spotted it too. And if we get the map and plot these we end up with an almost perfect circle around the city."

"We do. I hadn't noticed that part."

"Thank you, you've made an old pathologist very happy. I needed confirmation I wasn't just making it work. And how many of these were referred to police, do you think?"

"Can I guess?"

"No. Because you already know. Get Jack Cade or one of his team on the phone right now, I've got some calls to make."

———

Hanson phoned the Orion office. Dave Francis answered. She outlined what they had discovered.

"Where are those bodies right now?" he asked.

"Here, there and everywhere. Some probably aren't physically with us anymore."

"Bugger. Is there enough evidence on file to prosecute?"

"Possibly. We should have samples. Cases like that are rare. Or at least they were until we started plotting them ten minutes ago, and now it looks like someone has been rampaging around the city with what might be a bucket of Allopumiliotoxin 267A and injecting it into the less fortunate."

"You lost me at 'Allo... You get off on this sort of thing, don't you?" he asked, forgetting his place for a second.

She laughed. "I guess you could say so. It's my life now. You find locking people up pleasing, I find toxicology reports fascinating."

"So, how does this stuff work?" Francis asked, genuinely interested. He'd killed a few people in his time, two or three intentionally and one by accident.

"Simply? The poison prevents nerves from transmitting impulses – and the lack of impulses leads to the heart stopping. Death occurs, if the victim is lucky, in around ten minutes."

"And the cure?"

"There isn't one."

"Nasty."

"Or beautiful. Depends which side of the argument you sit."

"If we can collate the bodies and get as many to you as possible, have we got any chance of linking to one particular person?"

"Possibly. We can request those samples. If they were taken, really depends on what the team observed, but toxicology should confirm it. But I doubt most people would be even looking for it. Can you provide us with a name of a possible offender? We could do some work on the individual when they are arrested – you know, match them to the scene – you'll have staff that can do that, too, but we may as well combine our strengths. As far as public interest cases go this would be front page of every newspaper in the country – probably global."

"Jack and the team are planning to provide you with more than a name, if he has his way, given what has happened to the Orion team, he'll provide you with another body."

"Well, if they do, can you make sure it reaches us before five. We've had a long day and we really don't need any more overtime. Before you go, there's something else you should know."

# CHAPTER FIFTY-NINE

"Jack, it's me. I've got some good news and some great news," said Francis, tucking the phone into his neck as he navigated around the screen with his right hand.

"Go with the great news first, that way I can't lose." Cade was walking and talking, trying to get a gauge on the current situation, watching the twenty or so pristine bone china plates he had spinning at the same time, desperate not to let one crash to the floor.

"If I told you Dex Hodgkinson is ninety-eight percent positive he's identified a dozen more bodies, that he is willing to stand up in court and say are almost certainly linked to our golf course and our gimp mask murders, what would you say?"

"I'd say I owe you a foaming pint of... ginger beer. When did this happen?"

"About three minutes ago."

"Brilliant. They are different as chalk and cheese though."

"Apparently so, but the mere fact they are all unusual means they fall into a special category, the one Dex calls 'interesting'. The guy on the golf course was jabbed repeatedly with an EpiPen. Way too much, apparently. The prison officer stood no chance whatsoever."

"But does it link them one hundred percent?"

"No, but it's the best we've got. And once we get our man in custody and take samples from him, Dex reckons he'll bleed evidence. Ask me about poison dart frogs."

"Another time Dave. Get one of the ACs on the phone. Tell them, from me, we need some serious CID back-up. Let's go live on this, I'm sick of dancing to that bastard's tune. What more can he do that he hasn't already done? I want this investigating as if our lives depended on it, Dave. Get JD to exert his significant influence if we have to."

"But before you go, Jack, and in the true spirit of TV retailing, wait, there's more!"

"I forgot. Go on. I need this. My day is improving after the shit show from hell down here. Utter chaos."

"I saw on the cameras. He's running us ragged, mate. He's having fun at our expense. I think it's a distraction for something else."

"His lot tried the Tower of London once before, they hit Hatton Garden, even tried to piss off HRH. I think he's just a good old-fashioned criminal on the run and somewhere, hanging onto his coat tails is our very own traitor, Mr Murphy."

"Well to cheer you up, if I told you that what was left of the body from the car wash, not only had tiny traces of explosive on it, as you would expect, but also a rather rare toxin, found in only a few rare animals on the planet…"

"The same rare toxin used to kill Chamberlain?" Cade actually crossed his fingers.

"The very same."

"Dave, I may make it a double ginger beer."

"I'll hold you to that. Perhaps a cherry and an umbrella too?"

Cade cleared the call.

———

"Sounds like we've finally got a break. All we need now is another one."

O'Shea felt the subtle movement in her pocket. Another call. She was exhausted. Spending time with Cade meant life seemed to accelerate, and when you decelerated rapidly, it was normally because you had crashed. She really couldn't be bothered to answer, but twisted awkwardly in her seat, until she extracted the phone and looked at the screen.

"It's Jason!"

Cade looked across at the phone. "Don't answer it, Carrie, he needs to rest. He *has* to rest."

It continued to ring.

"Ignore it. You know as well as I do, Jason cannot be considered a viable member of our team. We can't risk exposing him to more harm. He needs time out, with his kids. He needs space to grieve."

"I guess you're right. I guess we all do. Does he want that space though? You know it's been utter hell since I met you?"

West coughed awkwardly.

"Sorry, Andy, you don't need to hear our domestics. Still ringing, I see," said Cade, nodding towards the screen.

"I need to answer this. He needs me. I've known him longer than you, Jack. Please."

"OK. But hands-free. I need to protect him."

"Deal."

She answered. "Boss. My God, are you OK?"

There was a moment of silence. Then he exhaled and spoke.

"I'm fine, Carrie. I've spent a few days chasing unicorns and golden ponies riding whales, huge glittery whales. Whatever that stuff was, part of me can see why people take it and the other half thinks they must be bloody mad."

"Male or female, mate?" asked Cade, breaking the ice.

"Jack, brother, how are you? The unicorn or the whale?"

"The unicorn obviously."

"Do you know what mate I never really found out. We were riding across a massive rainbow at one point; golden, shiny, anyway I think they are unisex. I never once asked it what it was."

"It spoke?"

"Christ, mate, where have you been lately? Yes, it bloody spoke." He laughed, a moment of pathetically light relief. He needed it.

"Seriously, Jack, I'm OK mate. The kids are with Cathy's folks and as fine as they can be. I can't go to the house for fear of being stared at by the old dear across the road, or locked up by some passing patrol car. I need help. My life is screwed."

"For now, yes." Cade knew to be honest with someone like Roberts who had seen enough chaos to write a trilogy. "But not forever."

"If you tell me time is a great healer, I will literally piss on your grave, Jack."

"And I would let you. Actually, I was going to say life just gets less shitty. Chapter by chapter. Now and then a really shitty chapter catches you off guard and you just have to deal with it."

"But how? When I was strapped to that pole, then on the wheel, I saw a different me, a different ending to it all. Everything I had taken for granted was there, watching down on me, waiting for me to fight or fail, to live or die."

"Mate, it must have been terrible."

"Darkest days of my life. The thing is, I've got more to come. I've got a funeral to plan that I can't attend. Do you have any idea how that might feel?"

"Honestly mate, yes, I do."

"You would, wouldn't you?"

"On this occasion, yes."

"Pub?" It sounded ludicrous when all things were considered. But he needed normality.

"Sounds good, pal, but we're a little busy."

"Chasing shadows mucker, chasing shadows."

"What do you mean? We've got people everywhere now, searching and scanning. In places you wouldn't believe and even an old radio host surfaced from God alone knows where."

"Constantin is playing you like a fiddle, Jack."

"He's been taking the piss for weeks; we now need to turn the tables somehow."

"He just doesn't care what you do. He *wants* to get caught. I think he gets off on it, the whole chase thing. Think about it. When we first met, what were we doing?"

"Chasing him." He was right.

"Yep. And we still are. But let me let you into a little secret."

"Whales are hermaphrodites?"

"You know, for a bright man you can be a complete tool."

"You know the drill then."

"Fuck off, Jack. I no longer find you funny."

West coughed awkwardly again.

"Andy, mate! How are you? What are you doing there?" asked Roberts, struggling to string a sentence together, his limbs twitching with tiredness and a lack of nourishment.

"Hello, boss. How did you know it was me?"

"I recognise that awkward cough anywhere. Look, I'll tell you my little secret, shall I, seeing as though Captain Cade is too busy trying to sex a humpback."

"Go ahead, boss. I've missed you by the way."

"No time for romance, Andrew, listen, I was off my face for much of the time I was in that place. I have little recollection of some of the long hours I was there, but I reckon those drugs gave me a sense of heightened awareness. No, really. Forget all that unicorn bullshit. Listen, I could hear Nicolescu talking to two of his people. Just before a tall thin man in high heels belted them around the face with a fire extinguisher."

"We are all listening," encouraged Carrie.

"Thanks. I remember pages of the book, but it feels like most of it is back on the shelf at the library. Make sense? Listen, the thing is I think he's sick."

"He's sick alright boss," said West.

"No, really sick. I think his past is catching up with him. He looked rough. His eyes were yellow. Like he had a liver problem. I saw it in my Auntie Dot once. Anyway, if he's ill, it would explain why he doesn't give a flying fig what happens to him. But the tall bloke in the heels, he was telling me millions were going through the tills at that freak show I was a part of."

"Which suggests he's not physically sick, Jason. Just mentally."

"Or he's planning a big farewell party. Somewhere away from here, and I reckon he's taking the players with him. At least they think they are going."

"Jason, what are you talking about?" asked Cade, trying not to sound frustrated.

"Mate. I was strapped to that pole for hours. I feigned being asleep or unconscious, but I was listening. When you don't expect to live, and your life is in tatters, you tend to focus on the minutiae.

They reckon it's the last sense to leave us. Up on the players gallery there were some powerful people."

"Names?"

"No idea, Africans, Chinese. A few other races too and British men. They were all men. That much was clear. Some upper-class voices and some typical city dwellers. I reckon I knew one of the British voices, Jack."

"Celebrity?"

"Only if you are into very senior judges."

"Judges?"

"Yep. You heard. Like the one that freed Nicolescu."

"Appeal court? Jason, be careful here. Mate, this is damning at the highest level."

"You can be the judge of that." He was tired and laughed at his own pathetic joke.

"Another thing. If Constantin was involved in a shed load of murders, which I believe is entirely possible, then why is there bugger all evidence at the scenes. He even filmed one murder. We are adamant it was him, but when the CSI team attended the address, not a mark anywhere."

"And I think I know why." He reeled off a few reasons. All feasible, but one was ridiculous.

"No fingerprints? Come on, Jason, between me, you, Carrie and Andy, we've got about fifty years' police experience. I've never heard such nonsense before."

"Well, believe it now. The bastard has no fingerprints. What evidence he leaves behind he does so because he wants to. It's one big game. Listen buddy, where are you? Come and pick me up."

"No."

"Please."

"No."

"Pretty please?"

"No!"

"What if I ordered you to come and pick me up?"

"I'd remind you that technically you are a fugitive, on the run with no police powers and you're like a grenade with the pin missing."

"Nice. I like it. Tonight, on Sky Movies Jason Roberts plays Ralph Cook in *Grenade* 2."

"How could there be a sequel?"

"Because Jack Cade arrived in time to put the bloody pin back in. As he always does. And if he's any kind of a mate he'll do it again now. Pick me up. Please. I need this."

Cade looked at O'Shea, who shrugged her shoulders. Why deprive a man of what he loved best, when much of what he loved had been taken away?

"Where are you?"

"The Royal London Hospital about to discharge myself."

"We'll divert. Just one important question."

"Fire away."

"Ralph Cook?"

"Great, isn't it. He's been an action hero of mine since I was a kid. Lantern jaw and a shock of straw-coloured hair. Green eyes and biceps like melons."

"Can he ride a unicorn across a rainbow?" Cade laughed as he drove back to the north east side of the city at speed – happier again.

"Mate, Ralph can just about ride anything. See you in ten. Don't be late. Out."

———

Roberts leant against the wall in the public area of the major hospital. He was exhausted, but driven, weak but could feel the surge of adrenalin. He had places to go and people to see. Putting the jigsaw pieces of his life back together would hopefully wait. The two most important ones were his kids.

He needed twenty-four hours at most, then after that, who knew what might happen?

He dropped to the floor and closed his eyes and waited.

People walked around him. They had no time to look down, to pity him. He was in their way. The bedraggled man who stank, unshaven, with encrusted blood on his forehead and abrasions on his wrists.

Someone should have asked if he was OK. Somebody should have taken one minute, lowered themselves down and spoken to him. He was in a hospital, for goodness' sake.

But this was life and life had a tendency to pass people by when they needed charity, compassion and a kind-hearted hand on the shoulder.

He closed his eyes.

The images came immediately.

# CHAPTER SIXTY



THE PRISON VAN ARRIVED AT A CONTAINER YARD IN SOUTH London. Once through the barrier system, it turned left as instructed, followed the roadway for three hundred metres, then slowed before entering a large purpose-built storage facility.

Murphy turned the van around and backed it into the building, which was the size of a small football pitch. Well-lit, with clean machine-shop facilities it looked exactly like it was – a modern facility south of the river, hardly anyone took any notice of. The company paid their people well, paid their taxes on time, and openly invited inspections.

This new task was one of many that month and it would be completed ahead of time, as they all were. Better to allow flexibility than struggle against the clock. It was typical of the quiet efficiency of a company owned by a successful family from South East Asia, who had bought it when it was being sold for far less than it was worth. Business was business, after all. You won some, and in the case of this company, you really won some.

Murphy and Nicolescu stepped out of the cab and waited at the side of the building as politely instructed, before a team of up to ten men, all wearing navy blue overalls, started work.

It took three hours. In that time the occupants had done as instructed and sat as still as possible, no point in adding suspicion to the situation. They had been fully briefed. Precisely half an hour after the vehicle stopped, there would be noise, organised commotion Nicolescu had called it, all part of the overall strategic goal. No need to worry. Sit tight. Or leave now.

The team stripped the white panels from the van. They came away relatively easily and in an hour were all stacked up at the side of the building, labelled and bar coded. It was obvious they would live to fight another day.

An hour later, the cab had changed from arctic white to fire engine red, with simple magnetic labels affixed to the doors.

Sixty minutes later, exactly, the major work had been finished.

Constantin wanted to applaud the team. It was quite remarkable what they had achieved. But then it was always going to be achieved – the van was only ever going to be a hybrid, a Trojan Horse, left to roam the streets of London, unfettered and ignored.

"Impressive," said Murphy, almost forgetting who he was, what he was, and why.

"It is, Derek. I don't mess around. I only deal with professionals. I have learned in life you get what you pay for. Look at it. I am so pleased. And those passengers on board have stuck to their side of the deal too. Not a word. Are you ready?"

"As I'll ever be." He looked at the cab, now scarlet with white logos and the rear passenger compartment now a rusty red corrugated shipping container, sitting perfectly over the old interior, complete with regulation markings and corner castings, lock rods, lock boxes and the important CSC plate – the small identification label showing the container was safe and approved.

"Do you think we should check on them? You know, make sure they are still alive?"

"No need. They will be fine. They have water, food and toilet facilities. They don't need anything else."

It had vents too, lots of them, to the highly trained eye, perhaps one too many. To the man in the street, it was just another container, those corroded, unappreciated patrons of the high seas that crossed the oceans and circumnavigated the globe, time and time again.

"All done, sir?" The Romanian asked his countryman.

"Yes. Exactly as you ordered. I won't be asking you to sign for anything. We don't work like that." He grinned.

They didn't shake hands, and he just pointed to the door.

"After you."

———

The van was now a truck. It had a new identity, in appearance and legally. Another cloned plate meant it was exactly what it looked like to an ANPR camera or a passing, inquisitive patrol officer. A DAF flatbed carrying a container and en route to a container port. As a cover story, as a blatant lie, it just didn't get any better.

Whilst it felt no different to drive, Murphy found himself driving it slightly differently, as if that would somehow subconsciously create the air of a driver who was slightly less worried about his cargo.

Another container truck flashed to let him into the lane and he flicked the hazards on and off for a second. They had blended perfectly.

———

It was nearly an hour later when they had arrived at the impressive container port known as DP World London Gateway. One of the newest container ports in the world it had expanded into the Thames, creating a new coastline on its northern shores from millions of tonnes of dredged sand.

Constantin leant across the cab and handed an ID to Murphy.

"You'll need this. Each time you come to a yellow pod, just scan the card. It will work. Trust me."

He didn't. Not one bit, but he had little choice. He hadn't just crossed the line; he'd pole vaulted over it.

As far as logistics and freight forwarding were concerned, DP were considered among the elite. It was the United Kingdom's fastest growing deep-sea container port, handling some of the largest ships in the world.

With the best tidal access, local and national road and rail links and international connectivity with a global reach of companies in forty countries across six continents, they had moved nearly one hundred and seventy thousand containers that year.

A highly ethical company, they employed the best, from all walks of life but with a common goal; excellence.

To allow a container through its security gates and onto the state-of-the-art facility meant pre-checks, checks and counter-checks.

It lived by three by-words: safe, reliable and efficient.

Murphy rolled up to the Optical Character Recognition House. A large grey building which housed cameras and scanners, each container being filmed from two hundred and seventy degrees, ensuring there was no obvious damage and, importantly, that it had a valid container number.

It did. Why would anyone wishing to smuggle such valuable cargo out of the country play at such a professional game?

Murphy started the vehicle again and entered the six-lane pre-gate security system. A row of automated checks commenced: number plate recognition systems and cameras, all were dovetailed into the broader DP system, checked and verified in seconds.

If the vehicle passed the first checks, it was ushered forward via a traffic light system, towards the main gate, which looked for all intents and purposes like a border crossing.

At the main gate, it was the turn of the driver to be checked. If he provided sufficient evidence to show he had an ID and was trained to drive a vehicle on site, and importantly, operate the auto-mated stacking cranes, some of the highest in the world, he could proceed to a pre-defined module.

So far, so incredibly easy.

But it would be, wouldn't it? A company such as DP were far beyond bribery and corruption. They had carved a reputation that was deservedly second-to-none. There was always a risk of them becoming unwitting victims, of an insider threat, and any organisa-tion needed to mindful of such a risk – even an organisation like the police, as Murphy was about to reinforce. He'd now crossed into no-man's land.

The system identified him as both trained and capable. He engaged first gear, took the ticket and moved forward into a paved holding area where they would wait until their ticket number appeared on a large screen. When it appeared, they were through to the next stage.

Murphy was anxious. Nicolescu just sat and marvelled at the sheer scope of the operation. In the distance, standing like vast skeletal robots were the quay cranes, highly automated but still requiring the final bastion of safety, the deft human touch of the operator who sat on high watching the mechanical and human ants below.

The large screen displayed the registration number of their vehicle – in oversized amber electronic figures. Then a phone number appeared on the screen. It was there for a few seconds. Then again.

It was the signal Constantin had been warned about. He dialled the number which connected after one of those long singular tones that often denote a call to a distant international location.

Constantin listened, nodded, made low sounds, all of which were in agreeance with the caller. It was going well.

They were called to Module 6. Murphy's lucky number. His police collar number was 666. He was offered the chance to turn it down, but he loved it and its veiled association with the devil. Perhaps luck was on his side after all?

It was seamless. He backed the container in and allowed the system to take over. All he had to do was make sure he was parked between the lines and stay the hell out of the way of the cranes. The last thing he needed was an accident. A dozen systems ensured this could never happen and the main and most effective was him standing with his finger on the start button. If he let go, everything stopped. Simple.

The container engaged with the spreader and the crane started to lift the red box up into the sky before it reached the shuttle area. The shuttles picked up the container and moved it quickly across the complex in a carefully choreographed series of movements until it was set down at the quayside.

Now it was the turn of the goliaths, the large cranes that dominated the skyline of the Kent and Essex countryside, just twenty-five miles from the centre of London.

The cranes, built by the Shanghai Zhenhua Heavy Industries Company, were soon powering the container into the sky, high, higher still until they were at the same height as the London Eye.

Now wasn't an ideal time for anyone on board to try and open a door and look down. In the container, a single torch provided light, just enough to show total fear in the high-flying bankers' face. What in the name of the God he hadn't visited for a very long time was he thinking?

What had started out for Mark Hills had been fun, he was reckless, but with other people's money, and to be honest he'd been doing it for a decade and had a lifestyle to match. What they didn't know wouldn't hurt them. He considered ninety percent of his clients to be naïve – the remainder crooks.

He'd bet ten thousand on the first turn of the wheel, watching that poor young boy spinning around and turning towards his destiny, which was guaranteed to be miserable. The drugs and the meagre food offering he received in return were luxury items compared to a life of living beneath damp, old cardboard.

Hills had no idea what his name was. Didn't care.

On the second person, and already ten thousand up, he raised the ante.

Fifty says he won't last three minutes.

He'd studied the effects, knew the game back to front. The man from Guangzhou did too and they ended up in a bidding war which saw them reach two hundred thousand. On one spin of a bloody wheel, in an old music hall in the East End of London. He had won and banked the money. In the Bank of Nicolescu.

With high interest rates and little chance of keeping it, the house always won.

Hills knew the rules, thought he'd make a few million with borrowed funds, slide the amount borrowed back into the system and cream off the profits. Nice work if you can get it.

The last thing, or rather the very last place he expected to end up, was a hundred and fifty feet up in a dimly lit container near the Thames, with him and the cut throat bastard from Guangzhou, who was now staring at him as if he wanted to open the door and dangle him outside.

Maybe he was afraid too? Everyone had their demons.

In the control room, DP employees worked twenty-four hours a day to ensure a continuous and smooth transition of containers from landside to the ship, which once loaded, navigated the short distance downstream to the widening Thames estuary before entering the North Sea, next stop USA, Europe, Asia or the Pacific.

The container was to be one of the last to settle down on the rear starboard side of the colossal container ship the MV *Guardian Orient*.

The *Guardian*, as she was affectionately known by her mixed international crew, was far from an accidental host to the rusty red container. She had been chosen.

Constantin Nicolescu had fallen foul of the Romanian government once upon a time, and other European countries too, all had once tried to erase his identity and condemn him to a life inside prison. But he refused to kneel before them and was still fiercely Romanian, still proud to sing the uplifting national anthem.

Now he was the victor, and he was about to take the spoils. The *Guardian* was one of the largest ships ever to be built in Romania by the Daewoo Magnalia shipbuilders. His homeland. Wherever possible, he liked to buy local. Apart from the cars that were made in his mother country: he despised them and always bought upmarket European, mainly German. Because he could.

————

The *Guardian*'s captain was an equally proud Romanian, a man with a stellar maritime career. Less than eight months from retirement, he had it all planned out. He would return home and build a house on the coast, where he could watch the new wave of merchant seamen sail to faraway lands, as he strolled on the beach and returned home to her.

Except he had lost everything on an investment, in the course of one day. Everything. Now he worked every hour they gave him just to try to put some money into the bank. At the very least, he wanted to buy a small caravan near the coast. The plans he had made were just that now, plans, a large sheet of paper with an architect's signature he had yet to pay for.

All he needed was a lucky break, a new investment, a throw of the dice, and he'd be home and dry. It didn't matter once upon a time when he was young and sailing from country to continent. But now, he was hoping to return home to marry his childhood sweetheart and she had expensive tastes. He had so few paydays left.

Captain Ciobana stood on the bridge and surveyed the decks, scrutinising the containers being loaded. He would never tire of watching the almost balletic movement of the cranes. His name meant shepherd in Romanian. It seemed appropriate.

He was proud to captain the sixty-five-thousand tonne ship. At nearly three-hundred metres long, she was considered on the medium side of large. Compared to the largest, the *CSCL Globe* she was relatively small, a whole hundred metres shorter in fact.

But the *Guardian* was *his* ship, his last ship, and he adored her. He'd sailed her into atrocious weather and across mill-pond seas. Since she was his, it meant he could do almost anything he wanted or needed to do within the laws of the land or sea.

That included supervising the loading of the ten decks of containers at the port facility so close to London. Close enough to see easily from his lofty position on the bridge. Close enough to watch Constantin's truck approach the various stages of entry and more than close enough to see him through powerful binoculars, as he stood, slightly anxiously at the side of the truck as the container entered the system.

Close enough to remember just how bloody ugly he was, too.

Close enough to know how much he had hated accepting the largest and only bribe of his illustrious career. The one that gained the ID and the entry to Module 6.

But it would put him back on track, the architect could fulfil his promise of a glassy property overlooking Lake Techirghiol, famed for its therapeutic waters that would sooth the weary bones of a man who had worked at sea since he was sixteen.

Fully laden, the *Guardian* would sail to Rotterdam, where she would discharge some of her cargo in the midships section, only to replace it with more.

There they would reload her, send her on her way across the globe to Singapore, where a new shipping company would take over, using similar systems and similar cranes. This time the company was called the Henry Tan Shipping Company Pte Ltd.

The owner was the only player from the old music hall who wasn't sitting in the red container. Henry Tan was a man of his word. Even though Nicolescu's bodyguard had shot him in the leg, he would maintain his side of the bargain. It was business after all. He needed to remember that the other seven containers that Captain Ciobanu had shepherded onto his beloved ship were full of a commodity Henry Tan desperately needed. You scratch my back sir, and I will arrange to have yours scratched by two of my finest girls.

He liked dealing with the British suppliers too, they knew how to load a container, knew how to pack them, down to the pipes that formed the hinges, all full, packed with white and crystalline brown powders that would soon sell for many times more than he had bought it for. Business was business.

He'd also arranged for the last container on the *Guardian* to be placed just where Ciobanu could see it.

Hands had been virtually shaken and the deals set in stone. Tan paid Nicolescu a handsome amount to bribe the captain and the captain had accepted the princely sum to watch the eight containers lowered onto his decks, into the framework that held them in place.

He wouldn't be the first skipper of a large ship used to carry illegal goods. Some of the modern vessels were so large that covert underwater activity in a port meant drugs could be loaded into a few areas of the ship, below the water line and out of sight, to be collected at the next port, using the same method to remove them, often at night, often without the ship's crew being even slightly aware.

If he was challenged by the authorities, he would claim a

complete lack of guilty knowledge and hope they never excavated deeper into his electronics – phone, laptop and bank accounts.

All the captain had to do was navigate her away from the United Kingdom, down into the Bay of Biscay and onward, east and her final port for this voyage. That, and be ready to adapt and respond to any new instructions from the owner: a man who dangled his retirement plans like a beachside carrot on a string; and the men in the red container achieved their dreams.

Exactly.

Now, they waited.

It would take four weeks to reach Singapore and by then the men would be missing, presumed dead. Constantin had allowed for this. He'd allowed for *everything* in his calculations – the food and water and even fresh clothing. They had to disappear completely. There would be no audacious attempts to cross borders. Theirs were Interpol Notices of many colours: wanted for this, sought for that.

All they had to do was trust him to reduce their global footprint, allow them to disappear. It was what they had signed up for after all. They were now trying to escape their varied pasts, he who is without sin and all that.

The bankers and their avaricious leeching of baby boomer retirement funds. The judges, with their countless get-out-of-jail-free cards, issued to criminals who knew better. The Nigerian, for his part in a five-year long scam designed to suck the life out of innocent but naïve men, online, out of reach. The Chinese businessman from Guangzhou and his Taiwanese counterpart, expunged of their kinky lifestyles and the majority of their ill-gained profits.

———

Money, for the men, was what Constantin called the 'route of all evil'. Now, as he stood on the quayside in London, he held the compass.

———

As he watched them both, Henry Tan smiled, shifted his weight slightly in his seat, favouring his good leg. There were different degrees of trust in his world. He trusted his father at the very top, call it ten out of ten; his brothers Wilson and Charles at eight; his business partners, the good ones who had been a part of the wider Tan family for years, a seven.

The Romanian had earned himself a dubious three. He should think himself lucky he was so far up the scale. He'd had people killed at more than that, but he needed to dangle another carrot in front of him for just a little longer, needed to settle his nerves, like a fisherman tickles a trout, lulls it into a false sense of security, then when it is almost asleep, strike!

When he had struck, he could clear all the lies and filth from the files Constantin held on him, the exposed truths about his seedier side, the ultimate game of truth or dare each of the music hall syndicate had agreed to admit to.

Then, when that had been tidied up, he could start all over again, just as his ancestors had, creating trade routes from the Far East into Europe. This whole episode had been one untidy mess, and he liked order and discipline – a bit like the English police officer, the one his sources told him was responsible for taking down his most ardent barrier to what he considered free trade in Europe, one Alex Stefanescu.

He liked Cade very much – by reputation, if nothing else. They had never crossed swords, and it always paid to have a few government people in your back pocket. But Cade and his team were different, exceptions to the countless bloody rules and beyond apparent corruption.

All except the cop stood next to Constantin, on the quayside.

Tan picked up his phone and dialled.

"Yes, I would like you to put me through to Jack Cade, please. Yes, of course I will hold."

# CHAPTER SIXTY-ONE

Murphy watched for a while. He stood, trying to shield himself from a developing breeze and the reality that he had sold his soul to the devil. He had paid the ferryman and had got no change whatsoever, just the promise of a sum of money that might make it all worthwhile.

The *Guardian* would sail on the next high tide and with it the syndicate of bankers, bullies and businessmen, and then what?

Could he head back? Could he go back to work and pretend he had somehow been the victim of an elaborate sting? He spent the next ten minutes trying to convince himself whilst Constantin made a number of calls, from the cab, away from him.

———

Half an hour away, Cade had also spent time on the phone, wishing he could have recorded it, turning up the volume so West, O'Shea and now Roberts could hear. All four sat in Cade's car listening to a man they'd never met but whom Roberts knew by voice alone.

"And why would you ring me with this info, Mr?"

"My name is of no relevance at the moment, when I'm ready to tell you my name, I will, but be assured the information is what you people might call A1."

"A1 in my world means I know the source, trust it and consider the information to be completely true."

"Well, then call it B2 if it helps."

"Not really. Look, at the very least, can you explain why you want me to know this? It's not a lot to ask."

"Actually, it's a huge amount. But let's start with your teammate. He shot me. End of. I don't blame him, but you don't shoot someone like me and completely walk away, how you would say scot-free, whatever that means?"

"I have no idea, go on."

"His new boss, the Romanian, is a different, how you might say, kettle of fish…"

"Again, I have no idea about that phrase either, would you get to the point?"

"I was about to. You seem to have the patience of a sinner Mr Cade, so I'll just tell you. Head to the port facility called DP. You'll find your targets there if you leave now. Hurry though they are due to leave the UK tonight."

"And how exactly do you know this?"

"I got into bed with Mr Nicolescu. Let's say I needed his influence to further a business transaction. Things were going very well until greed took over, possessed him and spoiled what could have been a most beautiful relationship."

"Sounds like him, typically romantic. Any chance you might kiss and make up after I've ridden into town and cleared up your mess?"

"Consider me the female praying mantis, Jack. We'd make love and then I would eat him. A simple enough analogy for you?"

"Perfect. And how will I find our former colleague and your dinner companion?"

"Get to the holding facility at the port. They are waiting to swap the truck with someone, a chance to throw the authorities off the scent. It's all I know." He knew so much more. "I'm sure you will recognise your colleague. I'll try to detain him for you. The least I can do seeing as though he shot me."

"Ex-colleague."

"Whatever. Adopt the praying mantis method… where I come

from, people consider seeing one a symbol of good luck... it works for me."

The call ended.

————

The four Orion staff sat for a minute. Roberts spoke first.

"Well, I may have been as high as two kites on ketamine recently, but it strikes me that the caller was pissed off with our main target. I suggest we head off to Essex right now. Anyone disagree?"

Cade replied, "You know you are technically no longer in charge, don't you, Jason? You realise you'll probably need a ministerial pardon or sectioning under the Mental Health Act?"

"Section 136, mate, you never forget. I've lost far too much to actually care about work right now. What I'm looking for is complete and utter revenge."

O'Shea looked at Cade. He knew she wanted the same thing. As far as retribution was concerned, it seemed that there might be a pecking order, with Roberts first, then O'Shea, then Cade, after which they could open up the floor to anyone else who fancied enjoying a dish best served cold.

Roberts continued. "The pardon would be nice and I'm sure the rather perceptive Ms Lane would only be too willing to make it so. For now, can we just crack on and get this sorted?"

Cade looked at his colleague. They'd known each other for some time, and each in turn had bailed the other from the grasp of defeat, more than once. Right now, Roberts looked truly awful, and it was the empty look in his eyes that spurred Cade on.

Roberts checked his appearance in the mirror.

"Look at me, Jack, my forehead resembles Harry bloody Potter's and my lips are like some bird's from a reality TV programme."

"Let's get to Essex. Covert or full noise, Jason?"

"Is there any other type of noise? Mind if I press the switches?"

————

Cade took the fastest route on the satnav, through Limehouse, Blackwall and Canning Town, sirens screaming, forcing a way through the traffic, with Roberts remonstrating at times and at others staying silent, deep in thought. Cade had no idea where his friend's mind was, let alone what he was intending to do with his thoughts.

He had two people to worry about now: an old friend and the victim of the man they were hunting, who'd put his partner through physical hell. She was strong, but even steel bends.

That retribution list was becoming more complex by the hour.

"Listen, when we get there, Andy and I will deal with Constantin, you and Carrie can convince Del to come quietly. Deal?"

"He's armed, Jack," said O'Shea, stating the obvious but needing to remind them all.

"Fair call. Should we get a Trojan en route or an Essex ARV?" asked West.

"We should," said Cade. Having carried a gun on and off for years, he knew a trained firearms unit would make sense.

"Why spoil all the fun, Jack? Trust me, having survived the wheel of death, I feel somewhat invincible. We can ring Essex later, you know, let them come and clear up the mess and do all the paperwork. Isn't that what you coppers do?"

"Jason, you'll be re-instated. Let's just get through the roadworks, shall we?"

"Nothing on the satnav?"

"It was a metaphor."

"I know." He smiled warmly for the first time in weeks. "I've missed you lot, more than you could ever know." He fought back the tears and resisted the constant urge to scratch his skin, which itched incessantly from the opiate overload.

Cade recalled the first time they had ever met; it seemed a long time ago now.

"Fair to say we haven't missed you, you pain in the arse. You've caused chaos."

"Says the single largest excrement magnet I have ever had the pleasure of meeting."

"Touché."

"Go left here, it's quicker and let's change the soundtrack, this one is boring."

He flicked from yelp to wail as they stormed down the A13. The navigation system said thirty-eight minutes with traffic and forty without. It made no sense to anyone. He needed to halve that time, and at the pace they were travelling, it was achievable.

To their right the impressive Queen Elizabeth II Bridge dipped its toes into the Thames carrying the M25 north to south. They were deep into the County of Essex now.

"Ten minutes. Fifteen, tops!" shouted Cade over the sirens.

The town of Stanford-le-Hope announced its presence as Roberts shut the sirens down, leaving the strobes to flash hypnotically, now was the time to make progress but not wake the dead. Or alert the living.

"Anyone know how we get through this lot?" Cade pointed to the rows of containerised freight and security systems.

"Straight through the grey shed. Looks empty." He was right.

"Lane Three – it's clear, mount the kerb to the left, nice and easy, we are bound to attract attention soon anyway, leave the strobes on. Ram the bloody barrier if we need to." It was good to be back.

As they sped towards the main gate, the barrier on lane four opened. An observant operator had seen them coming and knew it would be cheaper to raise the barrier than explain why he hadn't and watched them demolish it.

They were now into the call forward zone and lost. There were trucks everywhere in the vehicular maze. With no idea what to look for, a decision was made. Leave the car, split into pairs and search, and if anyone from the company arrived, as they would, tell them to go forth and summon assistance.

O'Shea felt more vulnerable than she had for a while. West sensed it.

"We'll be fine. Come on, let's go find a traitor. It'll look good on our CVs."

"Speak for yourself. I'm done with all this. I just want to get on a plane and head to New Zealand. Deserted beaches, great wine, good coffee, breath-taking mountains and lakes."

"Any good-looking women?"

"More than you could shake a stick at. Everywhere you look there's a nice-looking girl running, skiing, cycling or surfing."

"Sounds exhausting... wait. There..."

It was Murphy, and he was running, followed closely by a man O'Shea recognised immediately. She'd know that bastard anywhere. Instinctively, she started running with West, who was already pulling away. The hound and the hare.

Murphy was quick. He had more to lose, he turned left behind a row of containers, then ducked underneath a truck, missing a beam by inches, then right, left and right, zig-zagging across the zoned park, desperate to throw them off his trail. He had no idea where he was going either. For now, the river looked good; he contemplated swimming to freedom, but knew he'd end up like the last fool, washed up, downstream, days or weeks later.

He kept running until he reached a higher stack of containers. Then he paused. He had a pistol. Why was he running? Time to even things out. Time to attract attention to himself.

West appeared at the far end of a stack of containers and froze.

Murphy, his teammate, was stood in a solid A-frame pointing the pistol at him. They were both breathing heavily.

West spoke first. "Del. Let's not do this, brother." He held his left hand out in a partial gesture of peace and control.

"Back off, Andy. I seriously don't want to shoot you. Believe me." He could feel his own breathing changing. It changed from athletic to anxious. He could shoot West but felt like he had more to lose. He was what they called emotionally charged.

"Then, don't. We can sort this out. Drop the weapon and I'll say you were acting under duress. You have to trust me."

"It's good of you, mate, but we both know I've gone way too far." He raised the weapon to his chin.

"No! Del, don't do it – think of your family."

"I am, Andy. I am. That's why I need to do this." He pushed the pistol deeper into his throat. It was now or never.

It was also the time O'Shea chose to take control. Having quietly crept around the back of the stack she was within feet of Murphy.

She took a deep quiet breath, then lifted her right arm and drove it down onto Murphy's head. What she hadn't worked out was the presence of the pistol, which fired, sending a round sky high, scuffing his left cheek, the heat instantly cauterising the small wound.

Murphy sank to his knees; the blow had almost knocked him out.

West approached him quickly, gathering up the pistol.

"Nice work, Carrie. He didn't see that coming." He propped Murphy up against a container as he put one loop of his speed cuffs onto his left wrist.

"Necessary?" she asked, knowing the answer.

"Come on, mate. Walk this way." West hoisted his one-time colleague up onto his feet. They headed away from the stack and towards a single container, which had a large metal hoop on one end. He clipped the spare loop onto the metal bar, content Murphy was secure, he dialled Cade.

No answer. Voicemail. Out of touch and mobile, somewhere in the vast facility. Not good.

Cade had already answered another call.

"Yes."

"Jack. It's Henry." It was the type of call a friend would make.

"Henry who?" He knew the voice and now, possibly the name.

"We spoke earlier. The chat about a mantis? You remember. They have strong spiritual relevance to many people. Did you know the bushmen of the Kalahari worship them? Isn't knowledge a wonderful thing?"

"Oh, it's marvellous. Now, any chance you can actually help me?"

"I suggest you turn right, walk about two hundred metres. Make sure your friend can keep up with you, he looks lively, but he's had enough drugs to kill two horses recently. Watch he doesn't crash. And for the record, tell him I never placed a bet on him. Not once. It didn't sit quite right with me. In my world we cherish our relationships with law officials."

"You mean you bribe them to stay on side?"

"Cynical, Jack. Keep walking. The man you are looking for is hiding among the containers."

"Right now, I count a few thousand. How do you know which one he is hiding near?"

"The mantis can fly. It can reach great heights. Not my absolute favourite creature, you understand, but fascinating enough. Keep going, quiet now, he's very much on edge." He was almost whispering.

"Where are you?" Cade was looking around, trying to find a camera. The problem was they were everywhere and Cade was using instinct to back a decision based on a detached voice on a phone, belonging to someone who may or may not be an ally.

"In a position of great advantage. Twenty metres now."

———

Constantin hadn't been as paranoid since his days of heroin addiction. He was so close now. The players were in the container, ready to go, he had plans for Murphy too, and then all he needed to do was get to the pre-arranged location and head by boat to Europe where its borderless states were a free passage back to Romania. He had some unfinished business there first, then, the world was his oyster. Albeit he detested the things.

He ticked off the list in his head.

Transfer the money into a number of accounts, convert some to cryptocurrency, more to precious metal and some to cash, he could bury both on the family plot of land outside of the town he grew up in. He was indeed very close.

He checked left and right, up, down and under as he walked slowly, trying to look for a number of escape routes. His heart was beating rapidly and he was sweating. An hour was all he needed. On the floor beneath a container, a bright yellow tabard blew in the breeze. He grabbed it and slipped it on. Better to blend than stand out like the sorest of thumbs.

He had no idea where Murphy had run to and honestly didn't care if he ever saw him again. He had served his purpose. Goodbye.

He was walking with more confidence when he saw Roberts. He froze. Fight or flight?

Flight seemed the logical option and this was reinforced when he realised Cade was with him. One of them hated him the other wanted to kill him – and frankly you could reverse that sentence all day long and come up with the right answer.

He timed his run perfectly, dodging behind one of the monstrous shuttles that glided around the complex. Now he was running alongside it, trying to use it as cover. For around seventy metres, it worked. The driver couldn't see him as he was focusing on what was ahead – more shuttles, in the port that never slept.

As they approached another row of red-and-white and blue containers, he ducked down a new corridor and kept running. How long he could keep this up, he wasn't sure. Adrenalin gave him the chemical surge, but it was a short-lived drug.

It was footsteps that gave him away – a rapid, staccato noise against the deep, industrial tones that surrounded them.

Cade was first, sprinting, with Roberts pushing his own personal limits, a shattered body trying to summon up the energy, knowing when he reached his target, he would need more reserves, if nothing else to wrestle him to the ground and keep him there.

He knew from years of street fights that pinning someone to the floor was far more troublesome than it looked on the small screen. It took boundless energy, guile and reserves of strength.

He'd once battled with an eighty-year-old man for ten minutes – punching, scratching and biting his way through the event until he eventually gave in, his transparent skin blued and blackened, and adding real depth to his then young constable's pocket book notes about why his prisoner was quite so badly damaged.

Constantin had been running for minutes, it felt like days, his bright yellow tabard was flapping in the onshore breeze and slowing him down, he discarded it, allowing it to twist and turn in the wind like a gull in a storm.

He jumped, mid-stride, onto a container and tried to climb up it, made it half way, momentum slowing rapidly until he collapsed onto the floor.

"OK, I give up!" He held his hands aloft, hoping for witnesses, but they never appeared. Except one – in his eyrie, aloft, looking down on the skirmish.

Roberts edged forward now: the dog and the rabbit. It was as if

Cade had slowed slightly, deliberately, a sense of 'after you my friend, he's all yours.'

Roberts hit him hard, full-on, his left shoulder dropping and landing square on its target in a powerful tackle; a rugby union of sorts.

The Romanian flew backwards, hitting the corrugated metal of a Maersk container, packed with who knew what and heading to who knew where. He slumped to the floor, winded and in genuine pain.

Roberts got the upper hand quickly, kneeling on top of him, pinning his arms to his side with his own knees. It left his hands free and the temptation was too great. The first punch was weak, entirely due to the fact Roberts was spent, the short run, the last few days and the expulsion of energy had emptied the tanks.

The second followed a sneer from Constantin. "You are pathetic, Jason. My mother could slap harder!"

Roberts hit him again, this time using raw anger. The older man's right eyebrow split, bleeding heavily.

"That's the best I've got. The first was from my kids, for what you did to their mother. The second was from me, for the same reason." He drew in a deep lungful of air then grabbing his head with both hands slammed it into the concrete.

"That, is for what you did to me back in the freak show you dared to call a casino." He went to do it again, but Cade stopped him.

"Enough, Jason. Enough now." He was right, he was already suspended, an escaped prisoner and a double murder suspect – if the judge was to be believed. Look at him, the forty-seven-year-old man at the top of the judicial ladder, as Roberts had once said, three rungs short of a half century and now hiding from his own authorities, a non-royal scandal the likes of which the British tabloids had never encountered.

"*You* sent me to prison. *You* killed the mother of my children. *You* killed an innocent man just to make me look even bloody worse. And don't even start me on what happened before, I lost good people from my team because of you. And what about Del Murphy? What tales of evil did you tell about me to make him jump ship?"

"Your man was malleable. He needed the money. The end. He's not really a bad man. You two are worse in comparison."

"Does your head want another meeting with the floor?" He gripped the greasy hair, almost ripping it out.

"Why not? Go on. I have nothing left to lose." He was lying.

"You'll wait. You know what they say about revenge and how it's best served slightly chilled?"

"No, I hadn't heard that one."

"Come on, get up."

Cade handed his Speedcuffs to Roberts. "I brought these just in case. Seems appropriate you get the arrest."

"Not sure if I still have the powers of a constable, Jack," Roberts replied as he heard the ratchet sound of the Speedcuff teeth locking into place on his prisoner's left wrist. He ensured they were tight, then double-locked them to stop them from cutting off his circulation. Smiling, he thought the last thing he needed was a complaint.

"Consider yourself re-instated," said Cade. "I'm sure the PM herself will sign off on it. Once she's finished editing numerous reports on how the highest echelons of her judiciary appeared to implode. I think you'll be just fine. You might want to caution him first."

"Bit late for that, but you're right." He cautioned Nicolescu in the time-honoured fashion. "Do you have any comment?"

"You have absolutely no proof that I killed your wife, or anyone else for that matter. Evidentially, I think you are on very thin ice, Jason. Just saying."

"All white noise to me, mate, but I'll be sure to write it down verbatim. And as far as I'm concerned, even thin ice is ice, and if it's enough to keep our case from sinking, so be it. And by the time the Orion team has finished delving into your past, present and future plans, we'll find what we need. We always do. Just saying."

They stood him up, with Roberts applying some pressure to the rigid cuffs.

"You're hurting me!" said the prisoner.

"Good," said his captor.

As they walked back towards Murphy, Cade's phone chirped into life.

A message from O'Shea.

*We've secured Del.*

Another from an unknown source.

*You did well. Tell him he owes me nothing, as I now have everything anyway. He'll understand. Tell him so I can watch his face.*

Cade delivered the message. "That was from a well-wisher. Hope it makes sense?"

"Total sense. I'll deal with that when I'm free."

"Free? I doubt you have many allies left in the courts of this country."

"Then you doubt wrong, Cade, not everyone is as squeaky clean as you."

"Trust me, I have enough bones in my closet to create a graveyard. But I'm pleased you think so highly of me. And I know how precious you are about your appearance. So let me just remove that stray hair from your face."

He gripped the hair in his thumb and forefinger and pulled sharply. The newly created scab ripped away from his face causing it to bleed once more. Constantin, a man already in pain shrieked, tried to say something but was lost for words. He composed himself and looked at Cade.

"You knew damned well what you were doing. Why did you feel the need to hurt me?"

"I think that's classed as a rhetorical question, but if it helps, I really enjoyed it. And when you find yourself back in a custody unit and the young officer asks how you got your scar, you can tell them that two of their colleagues inflicted it. I'm sure it will brighten their day. It did mine. Now, stay, and try not to get into any more trouble."

# CHAPTER SIXTY-TWO

Roberts and Cade reached West and O'Shea.

"OK?" asked Cade, dragging his prisoner along behind him.

"Never better," replied O'Shea, meaning it but not reinforcing it.

"Good. As for you Del, what can I say?"

"Sorry. Guv..." He looked at Roberts. Then lowered his head down. The boy admonished by his father.

"I have one excuse. I did it for money. My wife, you see, she has a ferocious drug habit, I tried to keep it under control. She was a professional woman once, heading towards an executive position, we didn't need my salary, then she found drugs and quickly everything went pear-shaped." He spoke quickly, then sighed a genuinely emotional sigh.

"I borrowed money – money to pay her dealer. I used to have to meet him off-duty. They filmed me for Christ's sake, Jason. Once I started down that road I couldn't get away. It was like I had the addiction, too. That's why I volunteered for all the overtime, even came up with ideas how we could get more. I was done for, until *he* bought the debt and employed me." He pointed at Nicolescu with total disdain. "I'm done, aren't I?"

Roberts glared at Nicolescu, then looked at Cade.

"It's looking that way, Del. I trusted you, and as we know, it's the one commodity you don't trade or cash in. But as far as I'm aware you only broke a few laws."

Murphy looked at him, trying to shuffle on his feet, awkwardly cuffed to the container.

"I shot someone."

"You did? Was it one of our weapons?"

"Well, no."

"Well, that's good then. Secondly, you bought cocaine off a dealer."

"I did. I can't deny it."

"How often?"

"A lot."

"Did you ever go there in a job car, in work time, or use police funds?"

"Never. Well, actually I drove there once but bottled it and drove away."

"Good. To recap, you didn't shoot anyone important, never bought drugs on duty and had nothing to do with the murder of my wife?"

"Boss, I can't believe you even asked that. I *adored* your Cathy. You know that. You need to look closer for the man responsible for that."

"The answer I expected, and for the record, old son, Cathy adored you too. The thing is, Del, you still broke the rules."

"I did."

"But according to some schools of thought, so did I. Here's the thing. Apparently, I'm still your boss and I can put you on paper – write you up and make you look like a traitor, a common criminal, or I can leave you here for a while and let you come up with the case for your defence."

"You'd do that for me?"

"I would. For one reason, life's too short, I've decided to do just that. You've got all night to stand here and contemplate your future." He paced for a second.

He glanced at Cade for approval.

He nodded, not entirely sure what Roberts had planned.

Roberts continued. "And to make you realise how decent you

actually were, still are, I'm going to attach you to this piece of human waste and he can spend all night thinking about which prison he'd like to visit. I'm thinking Belmarsh would be nice, down by the river, with Mr Chamberlain's old colleagues, I bet they'd love to welcome you home. What was the music you loved, Burt Bacharach?"

"It was Rachmaninoff," announced Constantin passionately.

"Classic answer."

He pulled him along the concrete roadway and snapped the free loop of the handcuffs onto Murphy's right wrist.

"Andy. If you wouldn't mind?"

West took the hint and fished out another set of cuffs from his jacket, quickly cracked the steel loop over Constantin's right wrist hitting the radius bone with just enough force to make him wince, then edged him closer and finished the job by sealing the loop over the locking handle of the white and well-travelled Hapag-Lloyd container.

Murphy considered arguing, standing his ground, but he knew tomorrow was another day and Roberts might just let him walk out of the complex and into the sunset. He fixed his gaze onto Roberts.

"Sir. I can never repay you."

"No, you're right, you can't, but I'm sure you'll have a good try. We'll see you tomorrow. I'm sure there's someone we should ring, or some paperwork we should be filling out. But I'm contemplating heading to the Sanctuary where Jack is going to buy me a pint of malt whisky which I'm going to scull, then I will find a shower and a razor and a bed so I can try to rest long enough to rid my mind of the hideous day dreams that taunt me, then..."

He turned away from Murphy, crying, struggling to stay on his feet.

"Then I'll go and see my children and hug them until I'm ready to tell them the truth about their mummy. That's what I'm going to do."

He started walking away, back towards the unmarked car. Towards a new chapter in his life, one that may or may not include the police. He paused.

"Del, I've made up my mind."

Murphy looked back. "Thanks, guv. I appreciate it."

"You might not. I'm going to recommend you get charged with purchasing a Class A drug – I could do much more, could say it was for supply, but let's call it a favour for all your devotion and prior loyalty."

"I'll get sent down for that, guv."

"Yes, Del, yes you will."

Cade and West followed. Cade had nothing to say to either Murphy or his new Romanian neighbour. He'd learned over the last few years that sometimes you were better to say nothing at all.

He considered making a call to Essex Police control room, identifying himself and asking that they send a unit or two to secure the scene, do it by the book. So far there was little point, as other than placing two men into custody, there wasn't much more to do and Cade wasn't watching the clock as far as the custodial procedures were concerned. That would have to wait. What was it Sassy Lane had said to him the year before? *Take the gloves off, Mr Cade.*

In the court of public opinion, he felt that her statement still remained, so he had, as she had instructed: iron fist in a velvet glove.

O'Shea leaned into Murphy and whispered something, then kissed him on the cheek. "The difference between you two is like fresh and salt water, Del. You can drink both but one will make you sick after a while. You'll be OK. Just do everything by the book from now on, yeah?"

Murphy nodded, a solitary tear trying to burst over the top of his left eyelid.

"I'm finished, Carrie. You know I'm a good man, but this will finish me. I did it for my wife. You understand that?"

"Possibly. It's what you do from this moment on that counts."

Then she stepped towards Constantin.

"And you, how are you doing?" She wore a look of compassion, of weakness.

"I'm surprised you care. Go on, get it over with." He smirked at her.

"By the way, nice to see your hair is finally growing back. I preferred it short."

She laughed. "Funny because Jack loves it short, too. Enough small talk. I just wanted to clear the air between us, you know, after the way we finished last time, I never really had chance to say goodbye."

"Goodbye?" he said coldly.

She began to walk away. Stopped. Counted to ten then her inner voice agreed that an opportunity like this might not come around again soon. She turned back, approached him and jabbed him swiftly under his jaw, driving the bottom set of teeth into the top. Heroin had weakened them badly, so the blow cracked two and shattered a third.

"Is that it?" He hissed, his mouth slowly filling with blood. He tried to spit it at her, but she was quicker, stepping to his right side, then spinning back on her left foot and driving her knee into his groin, then once more for luck. She hit him so hard she swore she felt one of his testicles rupture.

The single scream confirmed it.

The pain barrier had been broken in style. He was feeling nauseous and could feel a wet patch in his underpants. She'd actually made him bleed.

Then she did it again, this time causing him irreparable damage.

"The first was from me, the second from Lucy, the third for my friend Cynthia. And yes, that is it. I'm done."

She stood and looked at the two men, one broken, one repairable. Then she realised she wasn't quite finished with the Romanian.

She stepped in as close as she could. "My dear old mum once knocked a bloke out in a pub after he'd tried to touch me up. I was so proud of her, shocked, but proud. I was only little. She said that no-one would ever harm her kids... I didn't really understand back then."

She stopped speaking, looking down at the ground, the raw energy of emotion building, then she pulled her arm back and drove a single punch into his face, hitting him in the eye.

"I guess it runs in the family."

She walked away, nursing a sore hand and enjoying the sensation of pain on her knee. She had waited a very long time for that moment. The fact that being cuffed to Murphy and the container meant he couldn't sink into the foetal position made her so very happy. Her mum would have been proud of her, too.

————

Back at the car, the four regrouped, discussed what had happened and decided Cade should deal with the DP vehicle that had arrived with two suited and hi-vis staff on board. His explanation was simple. The two men were wanted by police but had escaped, probably crossing the railway line and into open country.

It was ludicrous, but his demeanour meant they were likely to believe him.

He agreed that yes, a helicopter or a dog would have been appropriate and assured them that he would do his best to keep asking for one. For now, he promised them that there was no risk to their operation or reputation and that they would be back soon with other units.

In a massive parking lot of containers, he hoped they wouldn't find either man until the next day. It was feasible. If it worked, then it was meant to be.

Job done. Cade started the car, and they followed the signs for the exit.

"Do you think we should have left them there all night, Jack?" asked O'Shea.

"No intention of doing that, Carrie. Jason and I had a little chat earlier. He's hoping Del can get some intel out of his cellmate. He wants to return in a few hours with the troops and sweep up the mess, tell a few white lies to the company, then piss off. Standard SOPs for our unit these days."

"But it's not funny, Jack, people could have died."

"I wasn't laughing and yes they could and the way you rammed your knee into Nicolescu's bollocks he could have become a eunuch."

"You play with the big boys expect to have your balls stolen now and then..." added West, desperate to join in the banter which was seen by some as relentless. It was. At times it had to be, a shield, a cloak wrapped around the horrors of policing.

"You lot are horrible at times."

"Says the woman who once stabbed a DCI with a pencil. Come on, let's find somewhere to grab some food nearby. Give it an hour, I reckon Murphy will be ready to do anything it takes and Nicolescu will be sky high with pain."

Roberts smiled at Cade, but it was shallow. Cade knew he was close to shutting down. He was surprised he'd lasted so long.

———

In the eighth crane, the mechanical megalith, the grey and yellow sky-high structure, and one of the twelve apostles that stood guard over the river, the Singaporean sat, with his back to the chair, one hand on the joystick controls, the other on his phone.

He sent another text.

*Our paths might not cross again. We owed each other. You had what I needed. I had what you wanted. The debt is clear. We are now free to make our choices. I have a business empire to run. Good luck.*

Henry Tan took another look around him, from around three hundred and fifty feet he had a jaw-dropping view, to his left the river, to the point where it met the sea, straight ahead the county of Kent, behind him Essex and to his right the city of London.

He could see the landmarks clearly. A cloudless sky with a dipping sun emphasised the glassy towers, tall structures and the sense of a financial oasis rising up out of the horizon.

Aircraft took off and landed, overhead a leviathan of the skies, the A380 in Singapore Airlines colours cruised quietly overhead, reducing height and speed as it approached London Heathrow.

It was a sign, time to leave. His work was almost complete.

He hoped to be on that very plane later the same day – first class all the way home.

Having been involved in the business of moving goods across the world since he was a teenager, Henry knew how to operate just about every device to be found on a quayside. He knew the pitfalls and the thrills of operating huge equipment. Knew as much about shipping and the mighty vessels that plied the trade routes as almost anyone. He enjoyed being around the docks, but it was the ships that fascinated him.

The one below him was very familiar. It should have been. He owned it.

# CHAPTER SIXTY-THREE

Tan sat for quarter of an hour. He scanned the port below him, then the horizon. Time to move.

Below were the rows of containers ready to join the *Guardian*. Filled with every commodity possible, en route to the huge South East Asian transport hub, for onward transit, replenishment and within weeks they would be somewhere else, nomadic, almost featureless global travellers.

He adjusted the crane, which normally picked up the containers and transferred them to the lashing stations, twenty metres above the ground, before a team of two set up the twist lock systems that ensured the containers remained locked into place on board the ship.

He lowered the assembly downwards on eight immensely strong cables where it met the first of two containers. He had a clear view of the ground and could see what was about to happen.

The system locked into place and the Hapag-Lloyd container began to slowly lift off the ground.

Constantin resisted. Tried to stand his ground, then realised the container was moving a little faster than he expected. He looked at Murphy.

"We need to work together." He looked genuinely afraid. Because for possibly the first time in years, he was.

"Work with me."

"How? How exactly can I work with you? We are finished." He looked around.

"Help!" He shouted as loud as he could. "Help us!"

He felt as if he was at the bottom of a canyon pleading for help – and with no one at the top to listen.

Above him, the grey lashing platform was rising rapidly. In the container, one of the men started to shout. The bank chief, no longer a willing party, wanted to leave, right now. He screamed. But no one heard him either.

Constantin was also shouting, a distressed sound like no other as his right arm started to stretch, pulling at the tendons and sinews, his wrist and forearm were intensely sore, then his shoulder socket began to pound with pain, the rotator ready to burst.

He looked to his left. Murphy was still partially on the ground.

"Do something," Constantin pleaded.

"It's too late. It's just too late." Murphy knew his decision to work with the older man was flawed beyond belief. Then he felt the pain in his right wrist: hot, like barbecue tongs onto skin, but a slower, more deliberate, far more painful experience, as if someone was holding the tongs in place, allowing the heat to penetrate the layers of skin, burning away the nerves.

He stood, steadfast, gritting his jaw muscles, trying not to shout or scream, trying to focus his entire energies into staying on the ground, on surviving. On getting home to his wife and finding her the help she needed. He had the money now after all, but at what cost?

The Speedcuffs ripped at Murphy's wrist as Constantin edged higher.

Henry Tan allowed the crane to do the work, looking down at the scene and wondering what, or perhaps who was going to break first.

He had enjoyed the recent hours spent at the old music hall, betting on the lives of young men. All was fair in love and war was how he saw it. They knew what they were getting into. Well, some of them. They were fed and watered and their addictions were supported. Yet he felt no remorse.

But this was different. The Romanian's arm was at breaking point. This was worth betting on.

Ironically, the one attached to the container was standing firm, refusing to give in to the forces of nature. It was as if it had a mind of its own.

The left arm, however, was dislocated and now the tight network of ligaments and tendons that held the shoulder joint together were strained, obscenely taut, their resistance was impressive but it was just a matter of time before something gave way deep inside.

The shoulder is a notoriously unstable joint, but this force was beyond the comprehension of all but a surgeon.

The Surgeon. There was a time when he was known as that. Now, as he found himself being stretched by vast machines, he would have settled for just plain Nicolescu, the man from Craiova.

He needed to survive long enough to enjoy what he had earned. Selfish? Of course.

Murphy was yelling now. Surely someone would come? The noise of the port complex was louder, so loud that no one heard him.

He kept his arm bent, creating a fulcrum, hoping somehow it would allow him a few more seconds to work out what to do.

Above him, the crane began to winch, the cables rolling upwards and back into the main assembly.

Constantin was airborne, with Murphy following. Now the pressure on the Englishman's left arm was obvious. They were being hung and drawn and possibly quartered. This was medieval.

Henry Tan increased the speed.

The cables retracted.

The bank chief shouted louder, hammering his fist on the wall of the container. His city colleagues joined him. They could hear the screams outside. Something had happened. Something had gone horribly wrong. Enough now, they needed this to end.

———

With a hideous crack, Constantin's left arm detached. The tendons snapped, the ligaments, once rigid, gave way and the head of the humerus left the shoulder socket. The weight of the arm surprised

Murphy, who was still shouting when it sprung back towards him, then landed heavily on the concrete. The hand still firmly attached to the cuffs. It was a grotesque sight for someone who had spent years picking up the pieces.

Murphy stopped and just watched. By virtue of strength, or luck, or both, he had been left behind on the ground.

He was exhausted. He slumped against the container. He knew it contained something other than people. He knew he'd been left behind. For now, at least. If the crane came back for his container, could he survive by hanging on by his left arm alone?

The crane was the height of the London Eye. It was impossible. Impossible to escape, impossible to survive. He would die trying though.

He pulled at the left cuff. Trying to narrow his fingers to slide the loop over the wrist, like countless prisoners of his had tried over the years, behind their backs in a patrol car, in the back of a PSU van, in the custody waiting area.

He twisted his hand, pulling at what was left of the skin, happy to deglove the hand if it came to it, but as much as he tried to escape, he was stuck fast.

His right arm was now cuffed to someone else's and its owner was gone. It was surreal, almost ridiculous – a limb, just dangling from his own. Large drops of blood pooled below the stump.

He looked up. Constantin had vanished. The container was swinging inwards, towards the ship, a step closer to the Far East.

Tan moved the box with dexterity, edging it along the assembly until it was over the ship. He'd bypassed the lashing station process for a reason.

Below him, seven more containers were arriving on shuttles. Avoiding the stationary one and seemingly ignoring Murphy, who was now close to a nauseating state of insentience. No one came, no one at all. They knew. Somebody, somewhere, had been paid to ignore this. It seemed Tan's reach was further than his homeland.

The businessman lowered the Hapag-Lloyd container onto the *Guardian Orient*. In less than two hours she would be met at the mouth of the Thames and escorted out to sea by the pilot before sailing east.

On board the ship, Constantin tried to calm himself down, tried to think of how he could survive this. He was bleeding heavily. It was just a matter of time. The ship was huge. A hundred feet wide at a guess. But where were the crew?

He tried to bang onto the container with his right hand but failed, the hand locked in place by the rigid bar of the handcuffs. Instinctively, he attempted to lift his left arm but realised once more that it was gone. The whole arm was missing. All that was left was a darkening hole that he stared at. The shock was setting in rapidly. He knew shock killed and found himself wondering why it was taking quite so long.

He banged his head against the metal work. Then heard someone shouting back.

"It's me. It's Constantin. I need help. Please."

"We need help too. What have you done to us? This isn't what we discussed," came the anxious reply.

"I need help now. I am very badly injured. Do something. Ring someone."

"You took our phones away. *You* did this to us." The bank official was frantic. He'd had enough. Singapore was weeks away. The nearest port the ship was scheduled to arrive at was Rotterdam. It was too risky. They needed to disappear, and this foolish plan was not going to work. The judge picked up on the anxious state of his fellow prisoners. Maybe they could create a combined noise when they arrived at the next port – surely that was only hours away?

"Let us out, Constantin. I will pay you double what I have already," said the city gent.

Constantin was hyperventilating. "There is nothing you can pay me that will help me or you now. I am done. I am dying."

He sobbed, facing away from the container. Trying to focus on the coming minutes, which he knew would be his last.

He wanted to experience the high of heroin again, to slip towards death like those young men on that wheel. He counted upwards of eight, maybe nine. Then there were the ones out in the city, the ones who'd never made it because his experiments had gone woefully wrong. He'd keep them to himself: an album of shame.

Was it right that he couldn't remember how many men he had killed? That he had no genuine remorse?

He looked at the container below. It was soaked in a puddle of sticky, bright red, blood. He was becoming light-headed, he stumbled. Not long now.

He knew from his other sinister experiments, the human body could lose just twenty percent of its total blood supply and be in serious trouble.

At thirty, or forty percent, real trauma started to set in. He was a long way past this point now. He had to be. Hypovolemic shock, they called it – he recalled reading about it in a prison book. The library at Belmarsh was excellent. His mind was drifting. He longed to be there, sat in the library, reading about hypovolemic shock and how to treat it.

His skin was clammy and pale.

There was blood on the quayside, on the crane, on the lashing platform, and now down below him.

Minutes. He had minutes.

He was dying.

His heart rate increased, whilst his blood pressure dropped. He didn't notice, but his breathing had become shallow, short, pathetic gasps.

Was this how it ended?

Tan picked up container after container, winched them up onto the ship, stacking them perfectly, one, on top of the other, getting heavier as the stack increased. Then he selected the Hapag-Lloyd container and placed it on top of the stack. The ultimate game of Jenga.

The weight of the tower was impressive, matched in turn by the one next to it and the one alongside that, row after row, supported by iron-red frames, eighteen in total.

There were containers everywhere. Every single possible space was taken. They were ready to sail soon.

On the bridge, Captain Ciobana watched. He'd told his crew a lie and they trusted him with their lives. He had decided to retire even earlier and said that when he reached his final port there would be drinks and a bonus for them all. It was the least he could do. He shook his head. All those years of safe passage, his very reputation dangling by a thread.

Constantin Nicolescu was slumped now, trying to stand but hanging by his right arm, a pitiful puppet.

He'd lost everything and would have lost it all again for one more chance of life. He had no end-of-life remorse, no insurance policy, no pity for his fellow men, the ones he had sentenced to death, he actually consoled himself, for the loss of all he had strived for.

So much money. Yet with money came power and with power, respect. He'd been living under so many shadows for so long and now he was in another; the lengthening one that loomed like a childhood summer memory, the end of a wonderful day, of play and laughter and joy. A childhood he never had, and if he did, one he struggled to recall.

———

An hour had passed. The ship was preparing to get underway, the crew carrying out their well-rehearsed departure checks and processes. It was a seamless event, having been done a thousand times before in a hundred ports.

Ciobana was on the bridge; watching, listening, checking in with his key crew members. This was to be a departure unlike any other. He scanned the decks, the stacks, the various colours and the uniform way the many hundreds of containers appeared.

Fifty-two minutes later, ahead of time, they were away, sailing slowly east from the facility towards the sea.

The *Guardian Orient* called up the port, said goodbye, and communicated with the pilot and the local coastguard. Just as they did every time they arrived and departed, in English, the language of the sea.

On the highest stack, starboard side, at the stern, was the container that interested Captain Ciobana the most.

Hanging on the outside like a lifeless ragdoll was the rule maker, the casino owner, the one-time henchman of one of Europe's most feared and deadly criminal leaders. Dead.

The Chemist was gone.

He had been dead for nearly two hours. Drained of blood and suffering a heart attack at the end of his tawdry life, he had died in pain and complete misery – alone.

It made a lot of people rather happy.

All except the men encased in the rear, starboard container. Captain Ciobana knew it was part of the broader operation for which he had been handsomely rewarded. He also had his instructions and they were clear. Unless he was advised differently, he assured Constantin Nicolescu that yes, he would follow through with his orders to the letter.

Business was business. It was just a container – drugs probably, and honestly, he didn't need to know any more than that.

# CHAPTER SIXTY-FOUR

CADE APPROACHED THE COMPANY GATEHOUSE. HE'D DECIDED they should do it by the book this time. He told them a story of how the escapee had disappeared without a trace, that it was a training exercise and that limiting it to the fewest people possible meant for a realistic experience. He had assumed his Essex police colleague had cleared the entry and use of the facilities, and vice versa. It happened, the police were far from perfect, he said, convincingly.

He explained how one of their team had been identified as badly injured and was still on site, suffering from injuries that required an ambulance. That part was not in the exercise and was very true.

On cue, the sirens announced the presence of an Essex paramedic on a motorcycle. His other colleagues would be there soon.

It did indeed look like a well-run exercise.

Essex Police also sent three units, including an inspector who immediately challenged Cade on the situation.

"I have full control and oversight of this place. There has never been an issue here, not one. And I'm not about to let their reputation for excellence suffer due to some cocksure training operation by your city cowboys. Never an issue, do you hear me?"

"And when I have finished writing up our reports, there still won't be one, OK? Consider the paperwork complete," Cade replied, brushing away the inspector like an unwanted cobweb.

Cade had an in-depth discussion with the commander and assured him he was most welcome to take over the case, that all they would find was an undercover officer strapped to a container with a man who was wanted in three or four countries.

"Typical Met Police, is all I can say. I've been in the job a few years and this is yet another fly-by-the-seat-of-your-pants operation..." He had a ruddy face, worryingly red, as if he needed to lower his cholesterol urgently. Obviously overweight, the top two buttons of his white shirt were straining, he had thinning mousy hair and a pale complexion that belied his actual age.

"Inspector, know your audience. This was no cowboy operation. I appreciate you have a job to do, and I won't stand in your way, when the time comes for you to do it. But right now, I am asking you politely to stand down and wait for further instructions."

"You have no right to tell me what to do. What are you anyway?" He picked his nose, subconsciously trying to rid himself of something unsavoury.

"Who, not what. Look, mate, we can stand here and see who can piss further up the wall until we run out of ammunition. We both have a job to do. And now, here, on your patch, my need is greater than yours. Accept this, and show me some respect, please?"

"Respect is earned."

Cade looked at Roberts who nodded. 'You've got this, I'm far too tired.'

Cade put a hand on the inspector's black uniform jacket, brushing the two silver pips reverently.

"I have those too. That dishevelled-looking man there, he's got three. And you see that river over there?"

"One can hardly miss it," he replied haughtily.

"Good, well when one was tucked up in one's bed last year, this rag-tag motley crew, and the other members of the Operation Orion team were preventing it from destroying your home. But you never heard about it, just like you've never heard of Orion, which is fine. It's kind of a need-to-know outfit. And trust me when I tell you, half the stuff we deal with, you really wouldn't want to know, let alone need."

"You've got an hour."

He sniffed and began to walk to a sergeant and a group of constables, giving them each a job to do.

"No, we have as long as it takes. This is not for discussion. What has happened here is way beyond your jurisdiction. Accept that and rescue some pride before it's too late."

"My patch. My people. My place. My need to know. Get it?"

It wasn't going well and Cade's patience had already worn thin at the 'what are you?' comment.

"OK. Folks come over here, would you?" He beckoned to the inspector's team, who found themselves somewhat uneasily gathering around Cade.

"Thanks, team. Listen, I know you all think I'm some city cop with a huge ego, but actually I came from a force just like yours. I've been there, I've done that, I've got the T-shirts and the tea towels. But I'll say this to you. Please allow us some room to breathe here. You have no idea what the team has been through, a few in particular." He looked at their leader, his friend Jason.

Cade spoke quietly. "One chance left, inspector. Do as I say or I make a phone call which will well and truly piss on your parade."

The group, including a time-served sergeant, looked as if they understood. Sometimes in policing, you just didn't *need* to know.

"I told you. My place, my..."

"Yep, I heard you. Stand by. I'm making the call and it will be on hands-free. Then you can tell me when to end it with a simple hand gesture."

The sergeant grimaced. He clearly wasn't a fan of his boss, a man who had risen through the ranks faster than his reputation had. There was an unwritten rule in policing. You often got rid of the problem children by promoting them into positions where they could do the least damage. It was almost as if the older man knew what was coming.

Cade dialled. The dial tone was interrupted by a male voice.

"This is the Cabinet Office; how may I help you?"

"Hello. Thank you. Could you put me through to the Prime Minister's office, please?"

He waited. The inspector shuffled from foot to foot, smiling confidently, but as every second elapsed, his smile faded.

"May I ask who is calling, please?"

"My name is Jack Cade; I am the acting officer in charge of Operation Orion."

"Thank you, are you happy to hold, sir?"

"Absolutely."

He looked at the rotund inspector, who was trying to avoid eye contact. Cade raised his eyebrows, a sort of invitation for him to hang up, to allow the inspector the chance to retain some dignity.

After a minute the line connected.

"Hello, I understand you wish to speak to the Prime Minister?"

"Correct, in person, if possible, please. It is a matter that she is aware of, or rather was and one which has escalated a little."

"And to confirm, your name is Cade from the Orion team?"

"Confirmed. I appreciate she is busy, but this is important."

It was obvious he was on hands-free. He could hear activity in the background.

The phone hissed, a key was pressed, causing a short tone and then a female voice could be heard.

"Jack. Long time, no speak. Can we assume the city is in one piece?"

"You can, ma'am. Look, I know you are busy, but I need a quick decision from you. It's about the matter we briefed you on a while ago."

"Oh, yes." She recalled it well. She had the memory of a London cabbie. "And how is that going?"

"The key offender is eluding us, ma'am, and we've got a group of well-placed men trying to evade us too."

"Any particular well-placed men?" She knew when Cade's team pursued people, they were normally the senior players in the game.

"The main person of interest is a leftover from the operation we conducted last year in which your Home Secretary chose to take the path less righteous. Then there are senior bank officials, a few foreign visitors and best of all, the upper echelons of your justice department."

She sighed. "How upper is this echelon, Jack?"

"The very top. Chief Justice level. I'm sorry."

"Bring them in if you can. You know the rules. I need to go. Anything else?"

"Long story, ma'am, but we are at the largest container port facility in the region and we seem to have unwittingly stepped on Essex Police's toes, I wonder if you could sort out the politics for me?"

"The DP site?"

"The same."

"Incredible operation. I met the CEO a while ago. Lovely chap."

"It certainly is. There is not one shred of evidence to connect the company to the current event. Not one. Sadly, we have a few people who have got into the complex and caused some havoc. Our aim is to clear them out and allow the firm to get on with what they do best. Do I have your approval?"

"One hundred percent. Do you want me to ring Essex's Chief Constable? I will..."

He looked at the inspector, who looked a little ruddier than normal. He shook his head at Cade.

"Not required, ma'am, but thank you."

"Good. Look, I've got an appointment on one of these awful phone conferences. Before I dash off, I heard on the grapevine about DCI Roberts and the terrible business with his wife. If you see him, please do tell him he has my backing and that I send my best wishes."

"Consider it done, Prime Minister, as it happens, he's stood next to me. I'll let you go."

"Stay well and I expect a follow up on this, Jack. No excuses."

"Done. And thank you."

He cleared the line and waited for the inspector to talk. All he could do was look out across the river and instruct his sergeant to respond on his behalf.

The sergeant indicated they should take a short walk.

"Sorry, sir, we'll leave you to it, perhaps let us know when or if we need to return. I'm here to help." He held out a business card and shook Cade's hand. "And try not to hate him. It took us a year not to. Albeit we are not entirely sure where sometimes, his heart is probably in the right place."

"So, as an octopuses, Sergeant Newton? But apology accepted. Follow us, would you? I may have something for your team to do."

————

O'Shea suggested they find their old colleague, and Constantin.

Cade drove the short distance to the quayside with the Essex commander following, still watching and waiting for a chance to pounce on what he saw as the adjoining force's inadequacies – especially as the well-dressed one with the salt-and-pepper hair had humiliated him so.

"I think he's a little bit pissed off with yours truly. Ah well, it will be a day to remember, a chance to regale his career with his grand-kids when the time comes." He winked at O'Shea via the rear-view mirror.

She was on a hands-free conference call with JD, McGee, Francis and Williams. She explained how what Murphy had done was for valid reasons and that at some point he might even return to the team. That decision would fall to DCI Roberts and no one else, but it was looking unlikely he'd escape without punishment.

West was clearing some calls on his cell when he looked at Roberts.

"Boss, are you OK?"

"No, Andrew, I'm not. I think I need to hand in my ticket. I'm physically and mentally tired, my body hurts, my eyes are raw from crying and my optimistic nature has been pulverised. I may never be happy again. And for all I know, I may have a hundred-a-day crack habit."

Cade looked at the man he considered to be his partner.

"You'll be fine, Jason, I doubt you've developed a habit just yet and if you have, we'll get you the best help you need or want. Del, too. It will be up to you whether you ever have him back. Ironically, he was honest in the end. I think you need some serious downtime. How about I arrange for you and the kids to go away somewhere nice?"

"I've always fancied the Cook Islands."

"Hop and a skip away from my place in New Zealand. Come and

stay a while – stay longer, my casa is your casa. Seriously, bring the kids and I'll do the rest. Carrie and I can foxtrot oscar and leave *Spindrift* to you and the kids. They'd love it. Then, if you still feel up to it, I can get you to the airport and your Cook Island dream is but a few hours away. Open invitation, and you know I'll be offended if you turn down my hospitality. I'd even pay for your flights."

"Why did you call your place *Spindrift*?"

"Good question. It's the name given to the spray from cresting waves during a gale. Normally defines a Force Eight."

"I learn something each and every day."

"There's a good-looking boat in the harbour too, Jason. She's called the *Black Marlin*," said O'Shea.

"Thanks, Carrie, but I don't trust myself to ride a bike at the moment, let alone drive a boat."

"You skipper a boat like the *Marlin*," offered Cade.

"See?" asked Roberts, holding his hands aloft.

They arrived at the quayside, Roberts was too tired to joust with Cade anymore and leant on the wing of the car and just nodded a few times.

"Thanks for the offer. I just need some serious space, Jack. Time to think. I may come back. I may not. We were OK financially, but now the mortgage will be cleared, once the insurance pays out." He stopped himself.

"Once the insurance pays out. What's become of me, Jack? That all I think about when I think of Cathy is how much she was worth. What a complete bastard."

"No mate, the complete bastard is the person who killed her, killed those young boys and tried to kill a few of our team, too. Time will heal you all. And you need to go away and try to think of something else other than now. But this will invade your quietest moments no matter how hard you try to put it in a box and tie a bow on top."

"Think of some*one* you mean?"

"Way too soon, Jason. It will happen, trust me, but for now concentrate on the important things."

"Like, where did Nicolescu go?"

They rounded the corner and Cade stopped quickly.

"Bloody hell. Look at the state of him. Christ, look at his arm."

The others just gawped. There was Murphy, still strapped to the container, but holding another complete arm, or rather letting it dangle onto the floor.

"I didn't even get his watch," said Murphy wearily. It was awful, not even funny, but for Murphy a moment that allowed him to breathe again. How he had survived Constantin's fate was beyond him.

Cade got to him first. Murphy was partly slumped, stood next to a pool of vomit.

"You need an ambulance mate, there's one here, let's get you seen."

"I'm fine boss. Just... fine." He began to shake, the tears flowed and he tried to gulp air into his lungs, trying to avoid a panic attack. He looked at his arms. Both were damaged, one might never recover. Deep, dark bruising was appearing now and the skin on the left forearm and wrist had peeled back to reveal tendons and muscles, how he'd missed severing his artery he would never know. "My arm is killing me, I have no idea how I..."

"Let's separate you from that for starters."

Cade extracted the cuff key from his pocket and carefully undid the link that connected Murphy to the arm.

"Thank you," Murphy replied before retching.

"Steady on there, mate, you'll be OK."

"Can we get him in our car?" asked O'Shea.

"At a push, yes. Isn't he better to go to hospital?"

"Once a team player always, Jack. Let's have him checked out, then take him ourselves, keep the locals employed," said Roberts.

"Your call, you're the boss."

"You're right and I will be again one day."

Cade looked across to Sergeant Newton.

"Sergeant, can you cordon this mess off, start a log, and get some imagery? You might want to get your CSI team down here too, and photograph that. I'm guessing its owner will be around somewhere." He gestured down to the restrained, detached arm.

"He's gone," said Murphy, wiping his mouth on his shirt sleeve.

"Dead? Where Del?" asked Roberts, starting to regain some composure and wanting to see the body.

"No, guv, just gone. He went up on the crane. I watched him go. The other arm stayed attached. He just went up in the air, hundreds of feet, like some freak fairground ride. There's no way he should have been able to hang on."

"Then where?" pressed Cade, needing to find the man who had caused him serious issues for years. Quietly wanting to find him alive so he could ask a few last questions of the condemned man.

"Up onto the ship. The bloody great red ship." He paused. "*Guardian* something. She's gone." He was starting to drift now, the pain overcoming the adrenaline.

A new voice joined in.

"If I may offer some help, folks?"

"You may, and you are?" asked Cade, introducing himself.

"I run this place. Mike Evans, ex-HM Revenue and Customs and now operations manager here. This is far from ideal, you know." He looked around, tutting and shaking his head.

"I do. And rest assured there are no fingers pointing towards you, your company or anything connected to it. All I've seen has been supremely professional."

"Thanks. I'll put it in the report, shall I, once we've swept the blood away?" asked Evans slightly sarcastically. "Your man here is referring to the *Guardian Orient*. In the truest sense, if she was important to you, that ship has well and truly sailed."

"Tell me about her."

"She's a large container vessel. En route to Singapore. She was originally heading to Rotterdam but those plans were changed yesterday by the skipper. It's now here to Singapore. You got something on board of interest?"

"Some*one* more like. The owner of that." He gestured again.

"Bloody Jesus Christ almighty!" said Evans, staring at the limb.

"You could have warned me."

"Apologies. Listen, who owns the *Guardian*?"

"Who owns that?" he asked, pointing awkwardly.

"Our primary target, which is why I need to know who owns the ship – we think he's on it."

"The Henry Tan Shipping Company." He looked away, then back at the arm. It was awful, yet he couldn't help but stare at it.

"Is that so? Tell me, do you log all crew who arrive here?"

"Absolutely, if they leave their ship, stand down here or enter the UK they need to be processed by Customs."

"If they remained on the ship?"

"Then, no. But we normally have the manifests long before they arrive."

Cade looked at Roberts.

"I guess we know where Mr Tan was calling from then, don't we?"

Evans looked puzzled.

"It's a long story. Look, we'll need to clear this mess up, but for now can you try to avoid the scene of the crime?"

"We can, Mr Cade, but the problem is we are a very busy operation, we can't just stop. From my days in law enforcement, you would want to lock down the scene; which seems to start here and travels along there, up there, across there and onto the bloody great exhibit that has since sailed half way around the world – quite some crime scene and a shed load of paperwork."

"Pretty much." He stood for a while. "Walk with me, Mike, I've got an idea."

# CHAPTER SIXTY-FIVE

"I hear you, Jack," said Evans, enjoying being what he considered to be genuinely operational once more. "The problem is Essex Police will be all over this place like chlamydia on a call girl."

"Not entirely. And I have plenty of antibiotics for you anyway, Mike."

They walked a few metres away from the blood trail, Cade taking in everything, logging it mentally.

"You can see here our missing man was bleeding heavily. I'm guessing this is where the container left the ground?"

"Correct."

"And the blood trail thins, which is obvious, but it's still a trail, which means he was alive when he boarded the vessel. Correct?"

"I'm not a doctor, Jack."

"Me neither, but just roll with this. If he was still alive when he boarded the *Guardian*, and importantly, when they sailed, then there was no murder committed here, on your site, or for that matter in Essex, or potentially even in British waters."

"Well, I hear you, but..."

"Buts are great, Mike, but now and then we have to look around them. This case is mind-blowingly complex and some of my colleagues are victims, as well as being accused of some horrid crimes. My job, my orders if you like, from on high are to make sure when we put the lid on this festering mess, it stays well and truly on."

"Sounds fair to me. Are you saying that other than a breach of some health and safety regs by a foreign crew, there are no obvious criminal offences disclosed? Isn't that the phrase we used to use?"

"Still do, I think. It's been a while since I hared around in a patrol car and chased people, but you've summed it up. Now, Mike, some of this may never come to light, may never reach the tabloids – and I need you fully on board with this, when I say never. The DCI over there has a lovely turn of phrase, he says 'I don't want my arse in a bun over this', and whilst you and I could argue for days over what that means, I think we'd both agree as men of the world we understand."

"Completely. Whilst we wait for the forensic folk to do their thing, we'll try to operate around you – the next twenty-four hours are looking good as we've got some foul weather coming in – and then we'll hose everywhere down and refer anyone who is wearing hi-vis and clutching a clipboard to you?"

"You have my word." He handed Evans a card. "If you ring that cell, I will answer day or night. And, Mike, thank you."

"My pleasure. Glad to help. This is the most exciting thing to happen here since a ship jumper arrived last year."

"Nice. Where did he land?"

"Just there actually. We had to hose that down too."

"Lovely. Hey this bad weather, when is it due?"

Evans licked his index finger and held it aloft. "Soon."

"Is that scientific?"

"Absolutely."

"Then I appreciate the weather report."

———

Cade was joined by Roberts, O'Shea and West, leaving Murphy to prove to the paramedics he was a miracle of modern medicine and that yes, actually, whilst his shoulders were very painful, his pride was the thing that hurt the most. He stood waiting, arm in a sling, drifting along in a ketamine haze and really needing to head to a hospital.

Cade was stood on the quayside, looking out towards the North Sea. The water was a darkening green and the sky a thunderous grey with streaks of fast-moving white clouds, rushing from north to south. A squall had arrived off Canvey Island, suggesting it would rain soon. They could almost see it edging down river.

"Time to go, I think," said Cade, pulling his collar up around his neck and walking to the car.

"What did you say to Mr Evans?" asked O'Shea.

"I promised him complete and utter support and a get out of jail free card from the prime minister."

"Really?"

"No, Carrie. She doesn't give them out. That's down to the Home Secretary." He flicked his eyebrows and grinned, which earned him a twist of the skin on the triceps, simple, but highly effective.

"Ow. Bitch, that hurt!"

"Us bitches can when we need to, don't you ever forget that. Where now, the Sanctuary, I guess, as always, drown our sorrows, raise a glass to the dead and head home?"

She knew the comment was too soon.

"I'm so sorry, guv."

"It's fine. Really, Caz, it's fine." He called her by his wife's nickname and hadn't noticed.

"Well, answer the lovely lady, Jack. Where to now?"

"To be honest, I'm thinking of just heading home, back to New Zealand, some running on the beach, a swim, perhaps drive the *Marlin* out to the Mercury Islands."

"You skipper a boat, Jack," said Roberts. "And I will take you up on your offer once I've sorted everything here. Perhaps next school holidays?"

"Can I come too, boss, bring the wife and kids?" asked West.

"Since when did you have a wife and kids?" asked Roberts.

"I don't, but it sounds more feasible."

Roberts looked at him. "These two lightweights aren't heading to the pub. You going to join me for a swift half?"

"Do you mind if I don't, boss? The girlfriend wanted to go out tonight and I'm way past that now, very much in the doghouse, this will be expensive to live down."

"Nope. Do what you need to do, Andrew. Not sure what's happened to our team, Carrie. There was a time you'd be dancing naked on the pool table and knocking back shots like it was an Olympic sport."

"Respectfully, guv, it wasn't me. The shots yes, but the naked pool was Nancy Warwick."

Roberts had a faraway look. "...it was, anyway I'm buggered if I'm going to go and sit with Roger the barman and talk about football all night, you know what Manchester United fans are like when they start going about Christian Ronaldson. I may as well..." He stopped himself.

They knew what was coming.

"...go home." He sighed loudly. "I've not been home since..."

Cade put his hand on his mate's leg. "Let it go, no shame, none at all. Come and stay with us tonight and for as long as it takes. We were moving to a new apartment, but no need now. We'll stay in town until the dust settles, then we can all make our minds up about where we head."

"And where will that be?"

"*Spindrift*. Fire up the F-Type and head out and find a deserted beach. But on the way I promised Andy Tsang I'd drop into Singapore and catch up − he's the new head of the Interpol Global Innovation Centre. Carrie has never been to Singapore, so I felt it was a chance to do both."

"Don't blame you. How long will you be there for?"

"As long as it takes."

"Then I'll wait before I head to New Zealand. I'd rather you were there."

"Of course. JD will be back then, too. And he runs a mean restaurant, so you won't be short of a great meal and a stunning sunset. You could even take the Jag."

"Bit of a dampener when the only single girl in the region sees me in it, then sees the kids."

"They are cracking kids, mate. Trust me, the girls will be flocking to meet you, when the time comes. And only then. Come on, let's go to the bloody pub, you've worn me down with your soulful Labrador eyes."

"Thanks mate. Really." He walked, head lifted slightly. His body bore the hallmarks of a broken man. But tomorrow was a new day.

———

They arrived over an hour later. Parked the car and knew a walk back to the apartment would be the correct thing to do. O'Shea had phoned ahead. The team, in their various guises, were waiting, minus one detective sergeant called Murphy.

He would have to wait a while, whilst Roberts decided just what to do with him. The reality was only the justice system could make such a decision. If Orion were to remain a respected outfit, they had to be above the law, where integrity was a byword. For now, another team would process Murphy, doing it all to the letter.

Roberts was mentally empty, physically pale, and obviously tired. But he managed to raise a glass to absent friends, loved ones and to someone special in his life who would never be replaced.

"To Cathy. My special girl." His voice broke as he tried to regain composure. "For putting up with me and for being my all-time perfect friend." He was crying as he took a huge mouthful of the malt.

The team quietly repeated her name.

"Until next time." Roberts finished the drink and placed the glass upside down next to a full one. He let out another long, audible sigh. "Until next time, my beautiful girl."

# CHAPTER SIXTY-SIX



"Captain, I am concerned about this weather front, we seem to be heading toward it, not away, forgive me, but is that wise?"

"I expect you to challenge me George, but trust me, we'll make good time this way and the Bay is not as bad as its reputation, you know the worst part of the region is a long way off, by then, looking at the radar and the forecast we'll be hours ahead."

He slapped him playfully on the back. "More time to celebrate when we get to port, and if you play your cards right, who knows, perhaps one day this beautiful lady will become yours to steer across the world."

"Perhaps. But may I go on record and lodge my concerns formally, sir? This doesn't look good. I'm only afraid of one voyage and that's my last, like yours, but I have a family and bills to pay. I recommend we sail due south west, get out into deeper water or slow down."

"Noted. But we maintain course. Do you trust me, George?"

"Absolutely. I just…"

"Just wanted to make it known. I commend you for your courage and honesty. The industry needs more like you. You'll go far, just like me, around the world a few dozen times or more." He laughed, but it was forced.

He left the bridge for a while, needed to think. He found himself stood on the port side of the bridge, watching out to sea from his second love, the Ultra Large Container Ship – he hated it when other sailors called them simply box ships. They were so much more.

He hoped his first love was waiting for him.

His ship was vast, but could still navigate safely through the Panama and Suez canals. She was an impressively stable vessel but had never been tested in the extreme weathers in the outreaches of the northern and southern hemispheres.

He'd been to both areas in smaller vessels and had no wish to ever sail the *Guardian* into those conditions. Yet here in the Bay of Biscay, with its infamous sea states, attributed to Atlantic Ocean storms and the power that is harnessed by the relative shallowness of the Continental Shelf, he normally felt at ease. Among the storms that created intense energy which became concentrated, manifesting as smaller, choppier seas, striking fear into the heart of many a mariner. Storms like the one he was staring down the barrel of.

He swept his eyes along the giant decks in front of the main superstructure that held the bridge, accommodation blocks, galley and administrative offices; she was a floating empire, almost self-sufficient.

But her sheer bulk did not make her immune.

He'd asked a lot of his crew. He asked if they truly trusted him and felt that whilst he had always known the answer before, now he wasn't quite so sure. Ambiguity could be the death of them all.

He'd asked them to press on, towards bad weather, reducing speed *when* they reached it. Just one knot made a difference of many days at sea and time, equalled money. Some of his most important cargoes were perishable.

Once he'd entered the Mediterranean, it should quieten down, then onwards to Suez, where if he had to, he could re-fuel. At seven-hundred-thousand dollars just to transit the canal he needed to save as much money for his owner as possible, whether the owner could afford it or not.

The *Guardian* had cost the owner's family thirty times that amount. Heaven help him if he so much as dented her, let alone put her at risk of running aground, running out of fuel, or worse, being hijacked.

He knew the game. He'd been playing it for a very long time.

The smoke from his French cigarette drifted away on the growing breeze. To the north, a brighter sky, east too, but ahead and to his west the darkening green-grey skies foretold a hazard for all sailors – a violent and uncontrollable storm.

He did a final visual check of the cargo. All looked just as it should.

He walked a short distance, brushed some rain from his coat, squashed the cigarette onto the deck, then flicked the butt over the side, watching as it spiralled towards the sea.

He checked his watch, had one last look around, then walked back onto the bridge.

———

In the container, the men had waited long enough. There was a sense that Constantin had abandoned them, but the man from Taiwan disagreed. "He is loyal. He has been a victim himself. He will be there for us. Not long now." He said, to no one in particular, a voice in the half light, convincing only himself.

The ship was definitely rolling now, the container stack creaked and moaned as the wind hissed and mocked, its whistling tendrils wrapping around the ship, smothering her and her cargo.

"I don't like that sound," said the bank executive.

"You don't like the sound of anything other than your own voice," replied the Nigerian, who had decided that if the opportunity arose, he would throttle the Englishman with his bare and sizeable hands, whether anyone was watching or not.

"Look, let's all agree that things are going to get a little rough, we'll conserve water and food. Another few days and we'll be there. Constantin said a week at the most. We'll know as the temperature will start to climb and that will herald the beginning of our new lives. Let's focus on that shall we?" offered the judge, trying not to live up to his title. Frankly, he was regretting every second of the journey.

The swell was developing. In the gloom and whistling wind, the ship pitched and twisted and groaned, to port, then back, downwards, as if they were riding a wave. Deep sounds, coming from the depth of the ship like spectres calling out for them.

What made it so much worse was the darkness, the lack of vision, the sense of being totally lost.

"I can't stand this a moment longer. There must be a way out of this bloody thing," said Judge Hector Barrowby. "There must be a way!" He kicked the door as hard as he possibly could. No one heard a thing.

"Of course there isn't, you bloody old fool, or every Tom, Dick and Harry would be free-riding across the ocean. We are in here until we reach the Mediterranean. Simple. Now let's try to get our heads down and ignore this God-awful swell," said his peer, Judge Carlton, an experienced amateur sailor in his spare time.

"Beastly."

The banker had heard enough. He has been desperately trying to think of a pleasant land where trees quietly grew and grass smelt freshly cut – a land of his childhood, his father's place in the English stockbroker belt, an Edwardian home in Surrey, with a grass tennis court and manicured gardens. He wanted to be there, rather than propped against the side of a cold metal box, discreetly wiping the sweat from his top lip, then shivering the next.

He'd tried to sit, but it just made him feel more vulnerable. He preferred to stand.

He'd swallowed bile for the last thirty minutes and knew he couldn't hold on much longer.

The Chinese businessman opened some food: fish or something pungent, the aroma drifted around the container until it reached the banker. He clenched his knuckles, swallowing saliva, trying so hard. Then it happened – up, violently, into his mouth, too much to swallow, too violent. Through the web of his fingers, everywhere, and it came in pulsing waves – over and over until his stomach was raw and his throat burned.

Then the man next to him started.

The ship crashed as it bottomed out from a large wave, then twisted and bucked and metal screamed in agony before two more men followed suit.

Fear was setting in, among the hideous, confined stench of semi-digested food, a sense of fermentation and acid pervaded. The warm liquid ran from side to side now, some of the men tried to avoid it, three had given up and let it swill around them. It succeeded in making another one sick. This was not in the brochure. Where was the Romanian bastard now?

If only they knew.

The Nigerian began to hammer his fist on the metal panel, praying someone on the ship would hear him. It was akin to dropping a marble in a bucket of sand when no one was there to hear it.

Futile.

"Hey! We need help in here," he yelled.

The merchant banker sobbed.

The judges tried to remain calm, listening to the rhythmic sound of something heavy scraping and banging on the outside.

———

Outside, their agent, their guide and host, hung lifeless in the wind – a forgotten scarecrow. His demise would have brought a wry smile to Jason Roberts' face, a long, satisfied smile that hid his true feelings, but went some way to easing his pain.

———

It took nearly an hour to reach the squall. Then the rain came in earnest. Driving, sheets of cold, semi-frozen rain, hammered against the metalwork like the devil's fingers tapping on the roof – *I'm coming to get you and you know why.*

The wind speed was increasing and the state of the sea had changed. Now it was primeval, wild, life-ending. The semi-dark nature of the container made the whole situation a thousand times worse. They had no idea where they were on the ship, let alone where they were on the ocean.

The sea grabbed hold of the *Guardian* and tried to rip her in two, twisting her like a giant flannel, trying to wring out the water.

"Brace!" called the third officer as a foaming, fizzing, hissing wall of white water smashed into the hull and rushed up and over the lower containers.

"Sir, we need to take action!"

"We'll be fine. We've ridden out worse storms than this."

"But we are fully laden. Our anemometer is broken. We have no idea what the true wind speed is. Think about what happened to the..."

"Are *you* going to give *me* a lecture on maritime history instead of guiding us to safety? You should be ashamed. Look around you. Nobody actually enjoys weather like this, but it's a part of our lives. We can't live with it, yet we can't live without it. Embrace it. Now shut up and get on with your job!"

"Sir! The *Rena*, she sank this close to the shore in New Zealand, she lost nine hundred containers. Five years ago. The *Comfort* snapped in two in the Indian Ocean and lost nearly six thousand. And the *Faro* sir, she was lost with her whole cargo in Hurricane Joaquin... all of their captains were prosecuted. Need I go on... *Captain* Ciobana?"

It was the use of his name and rank. He knew there and then his third officer was recording the conversation. Clever boy. He needed half an hour longer in these seas, that's all. Come on, you bastard blow, and with all your might. Then please let me start a new life and put all this behind me.

He squinted, staring out to the stern, fixing his gaze on the highest row of red and blue and white containers. Then he saw the scarecrow – a hideous, one-armed effigy. He swore if he'd had both arms, he would have been waving at him – with the smirk of the dead, a man who no longer feared anything.

Ciobana's crew was right. This was reckless.

"I want us to be ready to change course on my word. Call the coastguard and tell them we are experiencing heavy weather."

"Sir, this is more than heavy weather. We are in deep trouble."

"Adjust speed. All crew to avoid upper deck areas." He was listing things aloud, going through his time-honoured check list.

"All crew to avoid upper deck areas!"

He'd said that already, so it must have been important. "Secure the accommodation areas, secure engine room, galley and stores. I need reports from all stations. Take a radio. Go now!" He paced, desperate for what might be his last French cigarette.

He continued to bellow out instructions.

"Weather deck openings, ports and deadlights closed. Commence a visual check on all cargo. Please."

The engine room rang the bridge.

"If we take another wave like that, we will lose power."

------

The huge oil tanks were tilting so far, the inlet that fed the engine with its voracious appetite for fuel was temporarily starved, leaving the ship potentially helpless.

Ciobana screwed his eyes up once more, forcing himself to stare through the rain-lashed windows. Then the ship began to climb another wave before falling steeply, twenty, thirty feet, possibly more. As it had climbed the crest, the sky had blackened – no stars, no moon, no sense of horizon.

He tried to pinpoint the flags, checking their direction for a sense of where they were likely to drift, should the unthinkable happen. It was parallel to an astronaut, staring away from earth, deep into the solar system, not quite knowing where it ended, yet still feeling a driving sense of excitement.

Ciobana was a long way removed from what some sailors referred to as a stateroom skipper; someone who kept away from the decision-making during times of crisis, then emerged victorious when the sea had calmed. But he had changed. There was something different about the man. He may have been at the helm, but his mind was elsewhere.

## CHAPTER SIXTY-SEVEN

"SHALL I WAKE THE CREW, SIR?"

"No, not yet. We'll be fine. Won't we?" He turned to his chief mate, a sailor with forty years' experience who stood stony-faced and had no idea what to say. He had seen bad weather and atrocious weather and this was somewhere near the top of the chart.

The second officer spoke. "Captain, we can't keep taking on this storm, if the holds start to flood, or the load shifts, you know as well as I do, we are in serious trouble. May I activate the SSAS?"

Ciobana knew it was potentially the right thing to do. But his career had been seamless, not a black mark against him. Ever.

"No, you may not. Wait half an hour. This will pass."

—

Inside the container, the men were now at varying stages of panic. Some were shouting, hammering on the walls. Others were speechless, motionless, terrified. The vomit swilled up and down and side to side.

No one cared about the fineries of life now.

"When we reach port, I will do everything in my power to find Nicolescu and have him killed. He has betrayed us!" shouted the man from Guangzhou. "Do you hear me? When will you all understand we have been fooled? He has our money and he is now on board this ship dining like a king, drinking with the captain, he feels so far away from us that he is laughing. But I will not stop searching for him until I am close enough to hear and smell his breath."

———

On the outer wall, shackled to the container, Constantin's inert body was thrashing about in the wind, a kite by any other name. The wind lifted his body, then slammed it into the side, again and again, to the point where the occupants of the box had stopped responding to it. With each momentous crash, his limbs were weakened.

The man from Guangzhou had no idea just how close he was to fulfilling his goal. Just how close *they* were.

———

"Hold on everyone!" The second officer yelled his instructions, trying to make himself heard over the siren-like gale. Another pitch-black wave threatened to engulf them, driving them first upwards, then down, deep into the trough. He grabbed hold of the emergency beacon, clutching it tight, ready for the order to abandon ship.

The *Guardian* listed heavily to her right, almost beyond the point of no return.

"We need to right the ship!" called the captain. "Lifejackets on!"

The rear starboard side stack started to shift violently, effectively unlocked from its immediate peer, it let out a dark howl of steel against steel, the stack fighting against gravity and the sheer force of the storm.

The ship tried to hold onto its cargo, a mother clutching onto its chicks, staring at one of her young entering a whirlpool, but it was too little, and far too late.

———

"This thing is tipping! Please help me!" screamed the merchant banker, who would have given everything he owned and paid back every penny he'd stolen to escape his tomb.

The giant Nigerian was praying, quietly muttering the same line over and over again. He'd left it late to turn to God, but he was asking his forgiveness, anyway.

"This can't be how it ends. This is not the end. This is not how I end my days," said Judge Carlton.

His colleague sat and wept. "I'm afraid it is. We're done for. We are going..."

He slid along the container, scrabbling to stay upright, ripped into the darkness by the gnarled fingers of hell.

————

The red container was now at a critical angle, from which it would never return. It cracked and roared as it left the stack and crashed down, vertical, against the hull, dragging Constantin beneath it, his body being consumed by the waves.

"We've lost a container!" called the chief mate, scanning, trying to look at the whole ship through exhausted eyes. He pointed a powerful searchlight onto the chaos. "And another."

Five gave way; dominoes, one by one by one like a child's wooden block toy, tipped over by its mischievous owner.

The containers landed in the ocean, rapidly left behind by the vast ship.

The heaviest disappeared rapidly, deep into the sea. The lightest, stayed afloat.

————

"We've left the ship. We're dropping. Something has happened. We need to get out now!" shouted the normally quiet CEO of the UK high street bank.

"Come on, together, let's get out of here." He scrambled around the floor, trying to get to his feet as the waves threw him in every direction. His legs were simply not strong enough to withstand the onslaught.

Then, the waves changed, suddenly, like a pack of hunting dogs, sniffing around the container, insidious, searching for an entrance, funnelling in, litre after litre until the roof, where they now stood or sat was covered. Ankle deep, knee deep. This was happening fast and there was nothing they could do.

So much for riches. So much for power.

When it reached shoulder height, one man slipped below the water and held himself there. He'd had enough and wanted to be the architect of his destiny, not some bloody waves off the rugged coast of France.

The Nigerian tried to keep the man next to him above the water, his strength now apparent. The judges were both gone, drowning or drowned. In time, quick time, the only survivor was the man from West Africa who bellowed out his distress call – to no one. For they were alone and drifting, downwards. Rapidly.

The last person to remain on the surface was Constantin Nicolescu, the man from Craiova. He had no chance to think about his past; flashes of childhood, memories of his hedonistic recent life, the things he had done, the things he had ordered to be done, to others: his pristine white apartment on the Thames locked up, paid for, for at least another six months; all his money, the silver, the gold, dirty cash, laundered cash; the cars, the suits, the watches, the appointment next Monday to have his heroin decayed teeth implanted with new arctic white ones, now just a notation in a diary.

It was far too late for any of that. He'd left it all behind on the quayside.

The container plummeted beneath the surface and he followed, consumed by the waves, dragged down by a set of British police handcuffs to the bottom of a foreign ocean.

Summary justice, in any language. That they belonged to Detective Chief Inspector Jason Roberts only added clarity and the sense of sheer satisfaction that money could never buy.

## CHAPTER SIXTY-EIGHT

THE TV WAS ON, MORE AS A BACKGROUND, A DISTRACTION.

Jason Roberts wasn't really listening, wasn't actually watching. He was staring past the set and out into the city. He had been since the last news bulletin.

O'Shea quietly sidled up to him with a mug of tea.

"Pound for your thoughts?"

"You're flash with the cash, Catherine," he said, using her full name, which he knew she hated. "Where's that man of yours?"

"He's with the team. Four have gone back to the container port to support Essex Police, two are working with the local section and CID to follow up on the old music hall and the rest are racing all over the city trying to establish if what Del is saying is true."

"You mean he might have actually been telling the truth when he said that container was full of those bastards betting on my life?"

"It looks that way."

"Chance would be a fine thing. Quite frankly, it would be great if they all drowned. I'd want to know it was slow though. To one day find the container and see their fingernail marks on the metal." He gazed out of the window once more.

"You don't know how close you are to that coming true. Did you hear the news, Jason?"

"No."

"The *Guardian Orient* nearly sank in the Bay of Biscay last night."

"Is that a good thing?"

"Not if you were on it, no."

Roberts took a sip of the tea. "Don't suppose you've got any biscuits, have you?"

"Of course."

"And, Carrie..."

"I know guv... no gingernuts. Boss, how long have I known you?"

"Too long, some might say. Why?"

"No one will say this to you, but I think I can. You need to take some real time out, just you and the kids. What would Cathy do? Take 'em to Disneyland or something is what she'd do, the job will be there when you are ready. What would you tell your team?"

"I'd tell 'em to go to Disney World, it's better," he smiled a tired smile, but there was light there for the first time in days.

"With respect, boss... you can..." she paused. "Oh my God, look."

She pointed at the TV once more.

The BBC reporter spoke into his microphone as the tail-end of the storm lashed the local port deep in south west France.

"French Police are saying that a number of containers were lost overboard from the enormous cargo ship which got into difficulties during a Force Ten gale. Enquiries with British authorities have established the *Guardian Orient* had changed its course to Bilbao when it got into difficulties. What is yet to be confirmed is the suggestion that in one of the containers was an unknown number of people, possibly smuggled out of Britain, potentially bound for Spain or the final port in Singapore."

The reporter braced himself against the wind before shouting into his microphone.

"The ship's owner, Mr Henry Tan, was unavailable for comment but a spokesperson said that people trafficking was an endless risk for businesses such as Tan's and that his thoughts were with those lost at sea. Back to you in the studio..."

"Jason, I think Del was telling us the truth," O'Shea said holding her cooling tea.

"I didn't doubt that for a second. He's never put a foot wrong, Carrie. Just had a bad day at the office. I'll deal with him when I get back from Disney World. His time with us is over, but I'll do what I can for him. Worst case, I'll ensure his pension is protected. I guess he was loyal when it counted." He took a long drink, then placed the cup down onto the small round table. "I know people think I should be with the kids, I just can't, I feel so bloody responsible, I allowed Cathy to die."

O'Shea went to walk away then stopped. Looking down and across the Thames, she spoke.

"Seeing that bastard strapped to that container, pitiful and unapologetic, made me realise how much I hated him. It can never compare, but I understand your intense hatred. That day at the car wash, I was alongside you in heart and mind. I survived my time with Nicolescu and whilst I can't feel guilty, and Cathy wouldn't want me to, she would also tell us both to sort ourselves out and change what we can, when we are ready. I feel like I'm there now, you will take a lot longer. But please know I will be here – even if it's at the end of a long-distance phone call. I'll always be here for you, boss."

"Thank you. I know it's been awful for you, too. I really do." He joined her and looked out across his city. "Carrie, I can't sit here like a spare prick at a wedding. I need to do something."

"Jack will be back soon. Go and have a shower. Put on one of your famous ties, splash on a bit of Armani and lift your game guv. For me?"

"For you." He stepped forward and hugged her and sobbed. The kind of remorse someone displays when they have lost someone so dear to their heart. In Roberts' case, ripped from his fingertips: her smile, her laugh, the smell of her, the dent she left on her pillow, the dent that would be there when he finally summoned up the courage to walk through the door of their Surrey home once more; of casual glimpses of her in the mirror whilst she dressed, the smile and wave as she left home, praying silently she would return home every evening.

He cried for minutes, endless sobs, it was as if each tortured and exhausted sound was purging the past few weeks.

"I'm sorry, you don't need this, Carrie." He tried discreetly to wipe away the tears.

"I'd be offended if you didn't cry on my shoulder. I've cried on yours enough over the years."

"You certainly have. Listen, thank you. I'd be lost without good mates like you and Jack. I'll be back, but I agree I need some time out. I've got one more thing to do before I take a sabbatical though."

He went to shower and shave, then ten minutes later appeared in his grey suit with the hallmark orange tie.

Half an hour later, Cade arrived.

"Ding dong! I love the orange tie. Just look what the cat dragged in. Sharp DCI Roberts, very sharp. And you'll need to be. If you are up to it, we've got a date with a very special person. Then, if you are still running on eleven of your normal twelve cylinders, we've someone else to meet."

"I was born ready, Jack." He gave a tired smile; his eyes were surrounded by the colour of emotion; a hint of dark grey with reddened edges – he looked dreadful.

"I know, but we all need to take a break from that readiness now and then. Do me a favour..."

"Yes, I know, take the sprogs to Disney World. Been there, looked at the catalogue, gasped at the price of the tickets. But yes, me, the kids and their grandparents will go next month. And it's tangerine. The tie..."

"I know." He pulled Roberts towards him. "Give us a hug, you old tart."

"Don't start me off again, Jack. I've had enough counselling from Miss O'Shea here. So exactly where are we off to?"

"Secret. But you'll enjoy it. In different ways. Carrie, you coming?"

"No. I'll stay here and catch up on some more important stuff." It was obvious it had been rehearsed.

They drove from the apartment for about twenty minutes until they came to a familiar sight. The guard matched the registration number to his master list for the day, checked their IDs, then ushered them through and asked them to wait. Forty minutes later they were in a small room, in a large London property whose glossy black front door was as iconic as any other major landmark in the world; small, but famous.

A smartly dressed woman with a sincere smile entered the room. A conversation took place – swift, friendly, no time for tea and niceties. Cade stood; Roberts followed. He shook her hand warmly and she held it long enough to settle his nerves.

"I meant what I said, Jason. You've been through enough. The last thing you need is to be hauled over the coals and hung out to dry, when the evidence that's been gathered independently, fully supports your exoneration. Frankly, I don't know how you've coped. I don't know what I would do in your shoes."

He looked down. "Get someone to clean them properly." It was a moment of reckless, light-hearted relief.

"Yes, I probably would too. Now if you don't mind DCI Roberts, I've got work to do. Something about a vote of no confidence in a Brexit trade deal. See, you think you have problems." She winked and held her hand out to Cade.

"Jack, always a pleasure. Thank you for rescuing your colleague and for bringing the matter to my attention. I meant what I said last year. I would be here if you found yourself out on a limb."

"You have, ma'am, and for that, I thank you. I'm just sorry this time we've stripped your legal system of two of its most senior people."

"Well, to be fair, they were the architects of their own downfall. And last time it was my Home Secretary. Let's just decide that there won't be a next time or I'll soon have no one left."

"Are you disbanding Orion, ma'am?"

"Good heavens, no. Just asking you to go and give out parking tickets for a few weeks, or do other stuff, you know, police stuff, just for now, for a month, stop turning over stones. Agreed?"

"Agreed." He shook her hand. "And thank you for doing this."

"We owed you. You cashed in. Simple really. It's how it should work. I'm just truly sorry you lost your wife, Jason. I can't offer anything but platitudes, so I shall refrain. Would it be acceptable to send flowers? Is there anything we can do for you and your children?"

"She meant the world to me. Perhaps something anonymous for her favourite cause – she had plenty. Anyway, I must go it's getting dusty in here, ma'am." Roberts turned to walk out.

"Jason, I forget who said it first, but this too shall pass. Until then, and until it does, it's OK to not be OK. And yes, let me know which one of those causes is shouting the most."

He nodded and made for the door.

"Jack." Prime Minister Sassy Lane had something else to say.

"I'll be two minutes, Jason." Cade closed the door. "Ma'am?"

"I like you, Jack. A lot. There's always a place for you on my team, you know. However, I suspect you'd miss the thrill of the chase?"

"I would. It's ultimately all about the chase. There's nothing else like it. But thank you. Perhaps when I get nearer to retirement and the salt outweighs the pepper?" He pointed to his hair.

"I've got a few of those after you lot have rampaged through my bloody city. Two of my most senior judges and, God alone knows what carnage the city finances have been left in. I have people to upset, so off you go. Enjoy your next appointment." She winked again, which unsettled Cade slightly.

"Ma'am. Just one more thing, if I may. Just a seed to plant for now. You can water it, see if it bears fruit and if you could..."

"Go on."

"There's a team of ex-soldiers, airmen and sailors, all veterans, many have seen active service in some of the world's conflict zones."

"And?"

"And they are living homelessly under a bridge, minutes from here. Don't get me wrong, they don't live like your average homeless person, but they gave so much to the country, it seems only fair the country gives something back."

She took a moment. "I've always had a soft spot for the defenders of our realm. What can I do, Jack?" she asked, overtly checking her watch.

"I know you have to go, Prime Minister, but if you could see your way to pardoning a couple of them, I'd appreciate it. They were incredibly useful over the last few weeks, and we may want to use them again."

"Is that it, a few honourable pardons?"

"Well, that and a large helping of cash for them to build a purpose-built centre for homeless military personnel. I tell you what, I'll put up my salary from the moment I re-entered the country – tax free would be great!"

"We actually paid you?" She raised her eyebrows. "I'm guessing I have little choice?"

"Every choice, ma'am. Just make sure it's the right one. The public would lap it up."

"They would, wouldn't they? I should hire you as my speech writer, God alone knows the one I've got is truly awful. OK, leave it with me. In the meantime, get those names to my office and I'll arrange to have whatever was causing them grief erased from their records."

"Ahead of you." Cade handed a small envelope to Lane; it contained the names of all of the veterans who called the Embankment their home.

He thanked her and went to leave.

Her phone trembled in her hand.

"Jack!"

"Ma'am?"

"What do you know about the *Guardian Orient*?"

"The ship?"

"Yes, Jack, the bloody ship, what do you think I meant a football team? Don't play games."

"Only what I put in the ministerial briefing notes, ma'am. Foreign-flagged large container vessel, got into difficulties in the Bay of Biscay, lost a few containers, one you are very aware of..."

"And?"

"There is no *and*, Prime Minister. Am I missing something here?"

"The man who owns that ship is in bed with the British government. Knee-deep. Trade stuff, not your area of interest really, and this does not leave these four walls. If we'd lost the ship and its cargo, it would have been rather expensive for this country and cocked up an awful lot of backroom trade negotiations."

"But we didn't?"

"No..." she paused, looked straight at him."

"Ma'am?"

She noisily exhaled. "We had some intel from the NCA – off the chart sensitive, so seal those lips. I trust you with my life. There was a rumour the owner had agreed to scuttle her in the Bay – claim the insurance money and create a whole new set of trade deals between Britain and the East – just at a time when we need it with all this bloody Brexit stuff flying around and landing in the ointment."

"But it didn't happen?"

"No."

"Forgive me, but you seem almost disappointed."

"You're far too perceptive, Jack. Since when has any government deliberately got into bed with a high-level criminal entity and it not ended up splashed liberally all over the world's press?"

"No news is great news then? That what you are saying?"

"Sort of."

"Supply and demand. Sink a massive ship like the *Guardian* and you create a supply and demand situation. Especially so if the containers were all empty."

"Far too cynical. No, you fill them to the brim with high-end British goods and you create demand, then you cut off the supply chain – just one container ship can make all the difference – a bit like falling dominoes."

"Above my paygrade, ma'am. And I'm sure it will never happen on your watch."

"Of course, Absolutely. Now, go, get out and don't come back unless you've got me an egg and cress sandwich from Marks & Spencer and a double shot latte. Or alternatively, some new information about the country I'm trying so desperately hard to piece back together."

"Noted. And you'll ensure those service people are looked after?"

"Persistent aren't you, Mr Cade?"

"Very. White or wholemeal?" he paused. "Shall I go?"

"Please do." She shook her head, trying not to smile.

For the first time since they had met, Cade knew something

wasn't quite right. He was an experienced pawn in a box full of far loftier and more manoeuvrable chess pieces.

Know your place, John Cade.

———

Cade met Roberts at the car.

"Got a little date this evening, a nice steak and a bottle of Central Otago pinot noir?"

"Hardly, Jason, she was just saying how much she thought I deserved a pay rise."

"Bollocks, did she."

"She certainly does. I certainly wouldn't want to get on her bad side. So how does it feel to have those three pips back on your shoulder?"

"It feels good. Bloody hell, Jack, what a roller coaster. Nothing is as bad as losing Cathy, but those nights in prison were truly horrific. I can see why innocent people top themselves."

"Were you tempted?"

"No. I knew I was going to be sprung by my nemesis and strapped to the world's largest roulette wheel. I mean, who wouldn't want to try? Would make a great story, wouldn't it?"

"Right up until the part where he chose to use you as a prop for a bizarre game."

"Now that *was* weird. It's like the whole thing was a very bad dream. The sort you have when you have a high temperature. Have you ever tried ketamine, Jack?"

"Not for a while."

"Get lost, you are far too much of a goody goody."

"No, really, I once had it administered by a paramedic. Certainly made the pain go away."

"Did you see unicorns?"

"No."

"Just me then. Right where next?" He tightened the knot on his tangerine tie.

"This visit you'll enjoy. A great deal," said Cade, putting the car into first and joining the traffic snaking around the city.

"How are the team, mate? I really feel I need to meet up and see them soon?"

"Bridie and Dave W have been out and about hoofing doors in. Dave Francis has developed a taste for Coke, the brown fizzy type, not the white buzzing type you tried last week."

"You know, Jack, if I had to choose a drug of choice, it would probably be that. I felt good for a while."

"Really?"

"Yep. Even strapped to the Wheel of Misfortune and soaked in my own piss. I just forgot about everything. Like you do in a dream, one you wake from and then realise moments later it was just that, a falsehood. I spent time with Cathy and for me that made it worthwhile."

"Tell me you wouldn't?"

"No. Never. I've got the kids to think of now, Jack, and Mickey Mouse, and trust me the mice I saw last week were eight foot tall and riding a frigging whale. No, thank you. Never again. I need to see a doctor though, just to make sure there is no permanent damage."

"Agreed. We'll make it happen. Just say the word. When, not if."

# CHAPTER SIXTY-NINE

THE TEAM GATHERED AS THEY ALWAYS DID – SEEDS BLOWN ON THE wind. Dave Williams' team was there first, propping up the bar and commandeering the pool table.

Bridie's team was a close second, quoting a rare and hitherto, never heard of before rule, about the first team to arrive having to buy the first round.

She was an incredibly popular leader. A lighthouse smile and an enquiring mind, she was destined to go places, whereas Williams was content for now to stay in touch with the grass roots of policing. He still had a few foot chases left in him, but with the news Jason Roberts might not return, there would be the inevitable race for the line, among the many who felt they were suitable material for the much-prized detective inspector role, which had never been filled.

"Cheers, Bridie." Williams slid a Southern Comfort and lime, no ice, across the bar to his peer.

"Thanks, Dave. You going to apply for the acting DI role?" She took a sip, feeling the lime flirting with her tongue.

"No. So please go for it, B. You've earned it, whereas I am just too stunning a specimen to be wasted in a nine-to-five desk job!"

"Cheeky bastard!" She flicked a beer mat at him. She thought for a second. "I hope and pray Jason comes back one day."

"Yeah, me too. Whoa, talk of the devil and he shall appear!"

The team stopped what they were doing and were silent for a moment. The only sound was the eight-ball rolling slowly into the top left pocket.

"Welcome back, Jason. We've missed you. What will it be? On me this one. And the next until you tell me to stop, or Jack gives me the signal you've had enough."

Roger was more than just the licensee of the Sanctuary public house. He was a friend, ex-copper and blue to the core. He left the job when he witnessed the thin blue line getting thinner.

Roberts stared around the room. He felt like walking out. Could feel the tears building, his legs shaking slightly, his fingers tingling, his throat tightening.

'Breathe, man, breathe.'

"Hello, Roger. Team. How's everyone doing?" It was all he had.

A strong mumbling sound greeted him. People not sure whether to approach and shake his hand, give him a hug or just stand back and give him some space.

"Christ, I've never known you lot to be so quiet. Thanks, Roger, I'll have a large Coke please."

The room was silent once more. The boss had certainly changed. Grief did that to you, clung to you like mist to a cobweb.

"A large Coke coming up, sir. Anything else?"

"A triple Appleton's too please, Roger, and have one yourself!"

"Cheeky bugger – but seeing as though it's you, I'll join you in a rum and Coke."

They were clapping now.

"Cheers, everyone. Now listen, there's a massive elephant stood outside this room. A few actually, so let's either keep on ignoring them, or open the door and let them in."

Everyone nodded. It was the right time after all.

He took a long sip of the drink.

"Thanks for the flowers and the cards and whoever sent the bottle of Talisker, nice, I'll open it when we all gather at my place, when the weather's finally improved. Listen, guys, there's no getting around the fact that my dear, beautiful girl Cathy is gone. Jack put his boot up my backside and made me realise right now I'm not the only one suffering. I've two equally beautiful kids at home that need me. Cathy's parents too. I won't stop grieving for a while, maybe I never will. Perhaps I don't want to. It's my way of remembering her."

"You have had it more than rough, boss, and we'd understand if you needed some space," said McGee, holding his arm for support.

"Thanks, Bridie. Which reminds me, you will be the acting DI from tomorrow. There will be no appeals, I've already spoken to Dave and he's on board. We'll tread water on my role, as frankly, there's no one good enough to fill it and I *will* be back. One day. Soon."

"Where will you go, boss, if that's not a rude question?"

"Very rude, Andy. Disney World, seeing as though you asked and no you can't go. I reckon you are too small for half of the rides, anyway!"

The room lifted in unison as they all laughed at West's expense.

"Boss, respectfully..." West grinned.

He rated Roberts so highly that forgiveness came easily.

"You'll all know by now that I am also a confirmed junkie, so I'll need a bit of help to get off my eight lines of Charlie a day. Plus, before I go, I've got some paperwork to do. After all, it's not every day you stare up at a sea of faces, all willing you to die, so they can make money from your demise, is it?"

They nodded and shook their heads at the same time.

"They should have put it all on red..."

He took a long, slow drink of the rum and shuddered. "Bloody hell, Rog, that's strong. You'll all know there were probably up to ten men in the shipping container that went overboard. Between these walls, I'm glad. There, I've had my therapy and it worked. I'll be back in a few months. But first, I'll become a dad again, take the kids to school, make their tea, help with their homework. I realised whilst I was off my face in that old building there's more to life than fighting off a twelve-foot-high orangutan in a ballet dress."

"It's a tutu, guv."

"Yeah, thanks, Dave. Trust me, you don't make comments like that when it's there for real. And yes, it was very real. The last elephant is DS Murphy. Now we all know there's nothing a good cop likes less than a bad one. For now, the jury is out. Bear with me on this. Let he who is without sin and all that. His time with us is over, but he may still have a career, somewhere. Doing who knows what, but it may not be policing. For now, he needs time to heal. He may have life-changing injuries that stop him coming back at all."

"Any idea who might take over?"

"Yes, I do, Andy. And in good time, so will you. Set 'em up and let me remind you all why I am the undisputed king of the pool table. Bridie, you may hug me a little too inappropriately for a little too long. Everything else is off the table. Jack, anything to add?"

"Thanks, sir, and from me and everyone in this room, welcome back. I won't dwell on the past, but as elephants go what happened to you was a vast one and there will come a time when you might need some more time out. Carrie and I are heading offshore for a bit." A few cheered, like men do when they've had a drink.

"Calm down. We'll regroup, refresh and return if someone shines a light into the night sky. I'm content the last vestiges of the Seventh Wave team are at the bottom of the ocean, that the most despicable bully in the Met Police is languishing in a long-term hospital bed and soon to be unemployed, possibly imprisoned."

"What will happen to Mallory whatsisname?"

"He'll receive a caution and an anonymous bravery award. A shame we can't posthumously prosecute Nicolescu for his cowardly acts of violence. What was the last count, Dave?"

Francis scratched his head. He did that when put on the spot.

"Well, Dex Hodgkinson was collating all the unusual sudden deaths. As well as the ones we sent him, he reckons there were upwards of a dozen young homeless men who were admitted or dead on arrival having had major overdoses. Poly drug use was prevalent. In some cases, even weird and wonderful toxins that will take weeks to confirm. He can never prove it but he's happy to say unofficially Nicolescu was the man behind them all."

"He called himself The Chemist, you know," said Roberts. "Yet all he ever prescribed was misery. The world is well-rid of him. I'd like to raise a toast."

The team lifted their glasses. "To the captain of the *Guardian Orient* and all who no longer sail on her."

Roberts emptied his glass.

"And to Phillip Jenkinson. May the only place he ever walk be in hell."

————

Roberts and Cade sat at the bar, watching the team slowly unwind.

It had become a tradition. Many of them had changed in the time Cade had been with them. Some had divorced or separated. One had taken his own life. A couple had been brutally killed and now their leader had to contemplate burying his wife.

His job meant he had a clearly defined will; an outline of what he wanted in the event of his death, untimely, or otherwise. But Cathy was a free spirit. She had a will, but it simply stated that she wished to be buried where she could forever feel the warmth of the autumn sun and the sound of the birds in springtime. She wished to come back as a tree, and even talked about one of those coffins that turned into one.

Roberts promised he'd make her into a mighty oak, one that reached for the stars and provided a home to wildlife – whilst his last will and testament simply announced that he wished for his head to face the home of his favourite football club, and for a hundred pounds to go to Battersea Dogs Home and the same to go behind the bar at the pub he now sat in.

The rest would go to Cathy and his kids and he'd appointed Cade as his executor. He needed to change the will now.

"I've appointed you as the executor, Jack." He announced as he sat alongside a man he considered more than just a friend.

"Planning on going somewhere?" Cade asked.

"Not for a while, no, but after the last few weeks you never know."

"Well, I shall be delighted to look after you until that time comes, and when it does, rest assured you'll be in safe hands."

"And me you, mate."

"Actually, I haven't got a will," Cade replied, awkwardly.

"Then I suggest you get one written – who would you leave all your worldly goods to?"

"Honestly? I haven't thought about it. But I'd leave the *Black Marlin* to you, so you could drive her around the Pacific."

———

Dave Francis had arrived with JD. One was sipping on a Bowmore, the other an apple juice, as in the background McGee and O'Shea took on all comers on the pool table.

Cade turned to Roberts. "I meant what I said, Jas. We'll put in the hours between now and when we head away and if Cathy's funeral happens when I think it will, we will be there for you one hundred percent – anything you need get people to talk to me. I can give you some cash if you need it?"

"I'd rather borrow it, mate, you know, salvage just a bit of pride."

"Absolutely. Sorry, no offence meant. And I'm only ever a video call away. Day or night."

"Cheers. None taken."

Cade chinked his glass against Roberts' condensation-covered tall glass, which was begging to be re-filled.

"Cheers, mate. Been a wild ride, eh?"

"It certainly has. I'm sure we said that last time. Tell me, is everything OK with you and Carrie?"

"Of course, why do you ask?"

"Because I know her mate – and I know it isn't."

Cade emptied his glass. Leant into the bar, lowering himself to it. Roberts mirrored him.

"I feel the mysterious Cade is about to tell me something that will put my life into perspective."

"No, not really, Jason, nothing compares to what you've been through, you and those kids have a long journey ahead of you, but I know you'll soon have a map. As for us..."

"Go on."

"When Nicolescu took Carrie from me, I knew he did things that I could never forgive him for, yet Carrie told me that when he tortured her, something even more horrid happened."

Roberts looked at his friend. He could see his eyes beginning to redden.

"Mate, what did he do? Please talk to me. Can I help?"

"No. No, Jason, you can't, none of us can. Carrie was pregnant."

"Bloody hell." He looked around the room. "Did you know?"

"No. She hadn't told me. She carried on, somehow, but she thinks the treatment she endured and the shock was too much. She didn't tell me because it was going to be a surprise. A total shock actually, as I wasn't ready for kids – I'm far too old. Or at least I thought I was." He let out an audible sigh. "But now all I can think about is what he or she would have been like when I reached my dotage. Would I have walked her down the aisle, or been his best man? Who knows?" He stared across the bar at O'Shea who looked back and smiled.

"You told me she was a warrior the day we first met. How the hell can she carry on, mate? I just wish I'd known; I would have…"

"What? Punched his lights out? Shot him? Mate, trust me, I spent every waking hour in prison thinking about meting out my revenge, but in the end what good does it do? What can I do, right now?"

"You've listened, mate. Blokes don't do this very well, Venus and Mars and all that. This goes far deeper than physical. All I do is listen, or let her say nothing at all. I don't know if it's the right thing, or not. I guess there's no guide for the sense of loss, sorry, mate, this is all too soon for you."

"Jack, the difference is, you could try again, now you know how important this was. My future has been cut in two, who knows where I'll be in a year, navigating past birthdays and anniversaries, but you, you two, you've got hope, if that's what you want?"

"I have no idea when to even start that conversation. I've read up on this, quietly, away from her, we haven't discussed it since, but yes, there is tension between us."

"My sister lost a little one. I remember her husband really struggling. He told me later that there were no rules for how to deal with this, for either the woman or the man. Carrie will be experiencing raw emotions, anger, frustration and pain – and it's alright for you to have the same feelings, Jack. Tell me something…"

"What?"

"Would you consider naming the little one? You know, have

some sort of service? I think it's really important, so many couples just move on, society expects them to, but you could name the baby."

"It's a good idea. I thought so too. The problem is, I don't know what it was, a little girl or a little boy." It was becoming clear that this had created a deeper sense of loss than Cade had previously considered.

"Then go for a neutral name, mate. One you both like. Kim is one, Reese another, or Charlie."

"Charlie's nice. I might put it to Carrie later. I've told her to tell her folks, but she's fiercely private about this sort of thing. I guess the time will announce itself."

"My best advice is let the road open up before you." He put his arm around Cade. "Another?"

"No, but thank you, I'm already emotional, another of these and I'll be hugging everyone and buying the whole place a drink"

"So, tell me about your long-lost brother then. Carrie was mentioning him earlier. I had no idea."

"He's a cousin, actually. I keep him locked away for fear of frightening the children with his talk of politics and religion."

"No sex?"

"Hardly. Not in his line."

"Not with you?"

"He is, or was at last count, a priest or a vicar or something of that nature. Travelled the world after leaving some cloak and dagger mob in the navy, joined the police, got a secondment to Singapore, then suddenly, and to the shock and awe of the family he left, they say he took holy orders and ended up in British schools in Malaysia and Singapore teaching English and religious studies. After that, who knows?"

"I imagine a thin man with a receding hairline, glasses, wearing a linen suit and sandals. He must have lived a frugal life?"

"He made some money somewhere along the line. I never asked, and he never told me."

"Hang on, you are just going to rock up and knock on the church door. Any chance of some bread and wine, vicar?"

"Hardly. Not heard from him in years. Just how it is. Families, eh? You can choose your friends."

"What's his name?"

"He went by the name of Dick – he hated Dick Cade – said it either sounded like ten years or decayed."

"Dick the Vic though? Really?"

"Indeed, and I'm sure you'd agree that isn't a very good name for a priest. He changed it officially to Richard Bishop."

"Not so sure Dick Bishop sounds any better. I think the vicar that married Cathy and I was called Matthew, or Mark, or possibly Luke. But Rich Bishop, not many of those around? Apart from the corrupt African ones, anyway. A priest, though? I didn't see that coming. Is it wise to go and find him after all this time?"

"You know me, Jason. Why let peace and tranquillity get in the way of disorganised chaos? I swear if I led an expedition to conquer Everest it would sink when we were half way up."

"Promise me you'll never change. Promise me you'll stay in touch and please for the love of all things holy, that you'll look after yourself, Carrie too."

"Māori have a saying, and seeing as though we are heading to somewhere where it shines all year, it seems appropriate and I'd like you to get a copy and frame it for your home or even the office."

"Go on, I'm all ears."

"*Turn your face to the sun, and your shadows will fall behind you.*"

"I like it. There's a Roman one for you too."

"I am equally all ears."

"*Non omnia possumus omnes*. We can't all of us do everything. Seems appropriate for you. For both of us."

"Now, ain't that the truth. Another?" He pointed to Roberts' glass.

"Be rude not to. Send me a postcard, won't you?"

"Actually, Jas, can we come back later for one? Do you have an hour to spare? This lot will be fine on their own."

"Any clues?"

"No. But it's in your interest to come with me."

# CHAPTER SEVENTY

CADE AND ROBERTS DROVE FOR A FEW MILES UNTIL THEY REACHED the Schoen Clinic.

"Looks flash, Jack. I've just done a web search. They specialise in mental health issues. No offence, mate, but I'm not ready..."

"It's not for you. You'll note they also have spinal patients?"

"Yep. I've still got one of those."

"Follow me."

They signed into the hospital, famous for spinal and orthopaedic injuries.

Roberts felt good, to show someone his warrant card again was part of his healing.

"Room eight. Should be just down here."

They walked in silence. Roberts trying to work out why they were here in this prestigious private clinic.

Cade tapped on the door, more out of respect for the medical staff. There was no reply. He opened the door, and in front of him slumped awkwardly in a wheelchair, was a man Roberts had hoped to never see again.

"Well, well. Hello, Phil. How the mighty have fallen."

Jenkinson woke with a start. Tried to reach for his call button, but Cade had moved it painfully out of reach.

"Detective Chief Inspector Roberts meet Phillip Jenkinson, civilian of this parish."

The disabled man attempted to shift his weight in the chair, trying to gain the high ground, but failed.

"Chief Superintendent Jenkinson to you. And what exactly are you two doing here?"

"I was correct first time, Phil. You are past tense as far as the Met Police is concerned. You'll receive a letter in due course – you know how it is, once they've employed four new staff to run your old unit – and assign one senior enough to investigate you. The irony that DCI Roberts gets to serve these on you shouldn't be lost on either of you."

He handed Roberts two envelopes. "Open them if you like."

He slipped the brown one into his jacket pocket, then opened the white one. He stood and read the letter out aloud. It was a wonderful feeling.

Cade whispered something into Roberts' ear.

"Aren't I a little too close to the action?"

"Well, technically I can't do it, and now you are a proper copper again, by virtue of the meeting we just had with the PM. So over to you."

Roberts stared at the crippled man, trying to sit upright in his private room within a marvellous private hospital. Filled with amazing doctors, one of whom had told him that morning he would never walk again.

That Jenkinson had alopecia meant he was the brunt of many jokes. He blamed his father, who had also suffered. The smiling old fool that he was.

Often exacerbated by stress, it meant the loss of hair, in his case, all of it. On his head, his body, even his eyebrows, and it had never really grown back. They called him names, and rarely behind his back. When he had joined the police force, it stopped.

The occasional drunk had mocked him, but had swiftly felt the full force of the law.

Jenkinson hovered over the words with his infamous green fountain pen – he'd almost invented the term obsessive compulsive, if there was a section in the statutes, he'd find it. He knew them off by heart, line and verse, section and act.

Becoming the head of the directorate meant he had true power among the men and women of the Metropolitan Police. People stopped talking when he entered a room, because from constable to commissioner they feared him, feared what he could do. His lack of facial hair only added to his sinister, almost alien persona.

But just look at him now.

"Phillip Edward Jenkinson, I am arresting you on suspicion of false imprisonment, grievous bodily harm, possession of a controlled drug namely..." he listed every single one he could remember. "...with the intent to supply." Those five little words added huge impact.

"This is ludicrous. The job will protect me to the hilt. We both know it. *You* are finished, Roberts, not me."

"You see, the really weird thing is, Phillip, I want to feel sorry for you. But looking at you and what you have lost, I feel nothing. Not one thing. You see, you are still alive. Whereas the love of my life is gone, leaving her two kids without a mother and me to live a lonely life and never knowing whether I can ever love again."

"You can't blame that on me!" he said indignantly, without the slightest hint of empathy.

"No, sadly I can't. I wish I could. But there are a whole heap of additional charges coming your way as soon as you are able to face them, in court."

"None of them will hold up in a court of law in this country."

"You expecting some inside assistance?" asked Cade coldly.

"I have good contacts within the judiciary who will ensure I am treated with the utmost respect. I have cleansed this force of rats and they and the government appreciate that."

Cade laughed. "Actually, they don't. And when you say the judiciary, can we take it you are referring to the very top?"

Jenkinson took a sip of water, nodded, then replied, "We all know I am a protected man."

"Was, Jenkinson, was. Your senior contacts are ever so slightly damp at the moment, deep and very damp. Jason you might want to give Mr Jenkinson the other letter, he's looking tired, needs his rest, we should really go."

Roberts took the brown envelope from his pocket and opened it.

"That's addressed to me! How dare you open my mail."

"Let's call it a welfare visit. Mr Jenkinson looked shattered and unable to tear the envelope open, so I read it to him your honour... and trust me this will be as much of a surprise to me as it is to you."

He read the words slowly. Enjoying the moment. He finished with the last sentence, then tossed the letter into Jenkinson's lap.

"...with immediate effect you are suspended from your role with the Metropolitan Police, your final salary will be calculated, encompassing monies owed. Your pension will be temporarily frozen pending an internal disciplinary hearing." He raised one eyebrow, a victory of sorts.

"The Police (Conduct) Regulations of Two Thousand and..."

"Yes, I bloody well know which act and section, thank you very much, now get out. Both of you just get *out*!"

"We will. By the way, I've seen fit to bail you to court, I must warn you that if you fail to appear on the due date a warrant will be issued for your arrest."

"Go."

"And by the way, when the court clerk says 'all rise' you're forgiven."

"Is that supposed to be funny?" His face coloured, bloodred, Roberts had seen it before. Unbridled anger. This time it was the façade of a toothless tiger.

"I thought it was mildly amusing," said Cade. "Off the record, you deserve everything coming to you. You bet on his life. Knowing his wife had been killed. Think about it whilst you vegetate in here with your sudoku and daily physio. You allowed him to go to prison depriving two lovely kids of a father. You hung him out to dry and for what?"

"He undermined me in front of junior officers."

"That it? That was ages ago, what sort of child are you?"

"A badly damaged one. I blame my parents. I won't ask you again, get out." He was dismissive to the end.

"I'm sure they are very proud of you. See you in court. The bus routes are available online. We've seized your car as evidence and if lady luck smiles on us, we'll take your apartment, proceeds of crime, you know the score. Pension too if I have my way. Goodbye, I'll let you spend some quality time with Jason. I'll be at the car."

Cade walked out, leaving the door open.

"I supposed you are going to rough me up, a defenceless cripple, about your level nowadays, Roberts?"

"Not at all. I'm going to show you lots of pictures of my wife. I have them on my phone. About ninety at the last count." He started flicking through the screen. "And you are going to look at every single one."

"This was us very recently at a hotel. She looks so happy."

"What's the point of this? You achieved your aim, you gave me the letters, arrested me, bailed me, and don't you forget to create a custody record as I will be requesting a copy of it."

Roberts grabbed the handle of the wheelchair, spun Jenkinson around and pushed him towards the door. "And just what are you going to do about it?"

In the corridor, he quickly wheeled him towards the fire door. He opened it setting off an alarm in the reception area. He didn't care. He'd given up caring.

Outside, the rain was hammering off the road surface, large drops of water bouncing skywards, then gushing down the kerb towards the drain.

"That'll be you soon, Jenkinson. May as well start now – down the drain, everything you ever worked for in your shallow little life." He wheeled him quickly, away from the hospital, taking the delivery entrance roadway towards a small area of immaculate inner-city parkland, typical of many similar places in London; hidden oases, pockets of tranquillity in a frenetic city.

"It's bloody raining. I'm getting soaked. I'm a sick man. Damn you, Roberts, bloody well turn around and take me back inside, that's an..."

"Order? Those days are gone, pal."

"I'm sick!"

"Yes, you are. Very. Enjoy what's left of your lonely life, you despicable little runt. Those bastards burned the girl I adored. Burned her perfect skin to a fucking crisp. She would have been in hideous pain, just before the explosion which I'm praying ended her suffering."

"I told you, Roberts, I had nothing to do with it."

"But you knew *about* it?" He stared him in the eyes and waited for the tell. He'd seen it at meetings in the past and there it was, an almost indecipherable curl of the top lip.

"Thank you. That's the most honest you've ever been with me. You knew, and that is as good an admission as I'm ever going to get for a charge of aiding and abetting murder. I must remind you that you are still…" He pushed him as hard as he could. "…under caution and that anything you do say may be used…"

Letting the wheelchair freewheel into the park was cathartic. He hoped the bastard would know what total abandonment felt like. Jenkinson came to a halt under a tree, sat with no obvious way to get back, his arms weakened by the crash, he was marooned. Under a tree with heavy drops of rain dripping down onto his head and running down his back.

Roberts checked his watch, then looked at him for three minutes as the rain eased.

"Three minutes. That's what the pathologist told me. He reckoned the pain would have shut her heart down before anything else, but I knew my Cathy and she had more heart than anyone I've ever met. Let's just leave you here for one more minute."

He watched the second hand slowly sweep around the face of the Seiko his wife had bought him on their anniversary.

"See you around."

"You cannot leave me here!"

"I can. And I just did."

He shrugged off the droplets from his jacket and jogged back along the street to meet Cade. He felt like skipping through the puddles.

"Do you know what, I may not need Disney World after that. What a thrill. I hope the bastard sits there until his chair rusts. Thank you."

Cade tried to harness the sudden euphoria. "Right, there's a CID unit on the way to lock him up, I didn't think it was right that you did it, you know, impartiality and all that, but I could tell you enjoyed reading him the caution. What do you fancy doing now?"

"Well, I've got a custody record to fill out, then a bit of paperwork in the office, then I guess we could round up the team and head for another quiet one?"

"Leave the team to me. Listen mate, Carrie and I are definitely heading back to New Zealand, we need some serious quality time, away from chaos and drama, you know why now too. You do as well. The team is exhausted, give them all some leave. JD's heading back to the Land of The Long White Cloud soon. You've temporarily promoted Bridie to look after things in your absence."

"Sounds like you are never coming back."

"Never say never, mate. For now, it's a run home, mow the lawn, wash down the boat, swim in the Pacific, good food, great wine."

"Wish I was coming with you."

"Anytime, Jas, I've told you, just ring and say you are at the airport."

"It's a deal. I have to confess I've had enough of this year, already. The only good to come out of it is watching that bald bastard squirm, well the upper half of him anyway. I've met some amazing paraplegics in my time and he's definitely not one of them. I guess he'll go onto retrain as a defence lawyer or something."

"When he gets out of prison."

"You think we've got enough?"

"More than enough. The word of a legendary DCI, who let me remind you, stopped the city from chaos on a few occasions, against that nasty little man Constantin Nicolescu and his sideshow. Trust me, you'll be fine."

"Anyway, I'm still somewhat surprised that you have relatives. I always thought you were this mysterious loner, you know, like Reacher – rides into town on a cloud of dust..."

"No horse, just a cloud of dust," they both said in unison.

"Hardly, Jason. And besides, he only travels with a toothbrush, whereas I like to shower more than once a week and arrive in style."

"Smooth as ever."

"Always, and of course you know we'll stay until the shit has stopped dripping from the fan. Once everything is cleared up, stamped, dotted and signed off, then we'll head away for a few months, see how things pan out."

"Thanks. I wouldn't have survived without you. And the vicar I mentioned, he was called John."

"I'm sure you could manage. Now come on, before you get all emotional on me, let's go and paint the town red, or should that be orange, you know, to match the tie."

"It's tangerine."

"It's orange."

"Satsuma Sunrise."

"Orange."

"Nonsense. Anyway, what rhymes with orange?"

"No, it doesn't."

"You know I hate you, don't you, Cade?"

"Absolutely, and you wouldn't want it any other way."

"Actually Jack, I've changed my mind. I'd like to go home, see the kids, tell them how much I love them. I should have gone there straight away, but this needed doing. I'll be OK, won't I?"

"You'll be just fine. Kids don't judge us like adults do."

# CHAPTER SEVENTY-ONE



*GUARDIAN ORIENT*, SUEZ CANAL 3,300NM FROM BISCAY

HE COULDN'T BELIEVE HIS LUCK. HE'D WEATHERED THE STORM. Not one of the worst he'd ever sailed in, but bad enough to lose some cargo. A good job his owner didn't consider it valuable.

A few weeks had passed now and soon he'd be on a plane home, to meet with the builders and architects and other trades who would allow his dream to rise up out of the ground. He couldn't wait.

Three thousand and three hundred nautical miles, it had been an uneventful and relatively smooth transit from the Bay to the Port of Suez, Egypt. The highly organised motorway went from north to south and back, a maritime ballet, performed daily without a pause.

On a live map of the ocean, the ships resembled worker bees, toing and froing, vying for position on the starting grid, where around a sixth of the world's trade was channelled.

As strategic sea lanes went, it was arguably the most important on the planet.

"Sir, you have a call. Says it's Mr Tan." The ship's radio officer put the caller through quickly and without fuss.

"Hello, Captain Ciobana."

"Listen, do not answer. Make agreeable noises if you have to."

He knew the voice, recognised the tone, almost immediately.

"You got lucky in the Bay?"

"I did. Or rather, we did. The crew did well, sir. No news."

"Yes, I know. Except you did make the news, Captain, didn't you?"

"Yes." He felt like an errant schoolchild.

"Not to worry, you will make amends." It wasn't a suggestion.

"How will that be, sir?"

"Plan B. The one we discussed, should the need arise."

"And am I to assume that need is now?" He whispered as he walked off the bridge ensuring none of his crew could hear him. Outside, he spoke again.

"Mr Tan, this is not without great risk. It could cause an international situation – unprecedented. Can we really afford to risk this? On what might be my last voyage?"

"You assume correctly. It would cause an international situation and it *will* be your last voyage. And no, we or rather my company cannot afford not to. There will be blame. You will be prosecuted, but I will cover the costs. You will disappear and my company will rise once more, a phoenix."

"To the flame, sir?"

"To the flame. Goodbye, and Captain, please don't..."

"I won't." He stood for a while, looking out to sea, to the north Europe and within swimming distance, Africa. He spent five long minutes, an unlit cigarette in his mouth, trying to make sense of the conversation. He had two choices. He could either do as he was told, or do *exactly* as he was told. His decision made, he tossed the cigarette into the sea. It was time to quit.

# CHAPTER SEVENTY-TWO

Six hundred or so nautical miles further north, the Orion team had again made their way to the Sanctuary, another day, another reason to meet up, this time to celebrate Bridie's temporary promotion in style. It was Cade's last round before heading back to the Land of the Long White Cloud – New Zealand – his adopted home. This time, Carrie would join him and she planned to leave her demons behind.

"I wish Jason was here." O'Shea whispered to anyone listening.

They all agreed. They felt limbless.

He always said he was Ginger Roberts to Cade's Fred Astaire. He was the boss. The governor. Guv.

They missed him. But they knew he would walk back through that door one day, when he was ready, and not a day before.

"Acting DI McGee, can you shut your lot up for a second?" asked Roger, the bar owner.

"Right, listen in, you lot!" she shouted in her polished northern tone.

Roger pointed the remote at the TV.

"Thought you might want to see this."

Cade looked up at the screen to see a container ship. She was straddling a large body of water, with ships either side and a small team of engineers on the shore, busy scratching their heads, pointing clipboards at the vast hull, the bow of which was wedged fast into the bank.

Nothing could get past her. Like a British motorway during a French port strike, the ships backed up, to the north and to the south. Stock was at risk. Supply chains were already struggling. Financiers around the world were soon praying for a solution to this billion-dollar logjam.

"Experts here in Egypt are suggesting the *Guardian Orient* could be here for at least two weeks. After being grounded by a storm and talk of a mechanical failure, early attempts to re-float her have been futile."

The screen cut to some historical footage of a few vessels belonging to the Henry Tan Shipping Company, and a quick sound bite from an operations manager is Singapore.

*We are doing everything we can to avert this crisis. In the meantime, our new larger ships are able to quickly divert and navigate around the Cape of Good Hope, ensuring important supplies are delivered on time.*

The cameras returned to the live footage. The *Guardian* was roped and being pushed and pulled by a growing fleet of tugs. They looked for all the world like small children holding onto the leash of a Rottweiler.

*With port facilities in the Mediterranean already backing up and key supply routes into South East Asia completely hamstrung, some operators are resorting to diverting their ships around Africa – and with that comes the added financial pressure of higher fuel costs, sea time and the ever-perilous risk of piracy. Either that or they watch their ships sitting idle, burning fuel daily and their already tight margins cut back even further. There is a sense here that only the smart businesses will survive this. From Egypt this is Stuart Watson, BBC News.*

"Finished?" asked Roger.

"Yes, mate," said Cade.

He turned to O'Shea and McGee.

"So, she was right."

"Who?"

"It doesn't matter. Call it need to know. But what I can tell you is this was predicted. And the man who is making more money from this than anyone else is sitting in a high-rise apartment block a few thousand miles away to the east and let me tell you, he's smiling"

"New job for Orion?" asked McGee eagerly.

"Out of our reach Bridie. Way out."

"But aren't you heading to Singapore for some R and R?"

He looked at O'Shea.

"That was the original plan, yes."

"Could you make it a fact-finding mission?"

"Let's park it up for now. I'll have a think on the plane."

McGee knew.

O'Shea knew.

Jack Cade knew, too.

———

There were still questions. They had started with one person and his lies and brutal disregard for his fellow man.

Revenge had become such a bitter act and during it the Romanian Nicolescu had lost his way. Now he was drifting on the Atlantic currents until he rotted, providing food to a marine habitat that would probably consider him to be equally unpalatable.

His lies were readily embellished by the head of a professional unit that was supposed to police the police, to rid him of a layer of frustration, led by Cade and his team.

At the top of the food chain was another man and he needed the Orion people gone. Subtly, dealt with, but not at his hand. He'd paid the Romanian good money for that to happen too and he'd failed.

He'd paid the judges to release The Chemist, a man who genuinely thought he was in charge. Fool. The bankers, the African, all of them, fools. The businessmen. The Chinese warlord.

Now here he was, the young boy who had inherited an empire, a dynasty. The man with more ships than many companies put together. The man with logistical operations in all of the world's ports. The man with production facilities for all of the world's most desirable commodities.

*He* was in charge. No one else came close. He had it all, the warlord with the velvet touch of an international businessman, and the iron fist of a tyrant. He'd posed for society magazines, donated generously to children's charities, especially those in the United Kingdom who needed the greatest level of support.

In his home country, he had spread a web of fear and total respect. When people met him, they bowed, unnecessarily. Others shook his hand if he agreed to them doing so.

But he didn't truly understand the west. They ate the same, thought the same, even looked the same. None of them really understood the art of business, the art of money.

Now, as with all great businesses, he needed to expand his empire. He needed to fill the gap.

First things first. He had to manipulate the British, especially their government and particularly the Prime Minister. She was so easy. Wined and dined, she'd almost eaten out of his hand.

Then she had betrayed him, had gone against her word. She was smarter than she looked.

'You can trade with us when this happens. It would be our pleasure.' The fork-tongued smiling snake.

He hadn't misunderstood her. She meant every damned word. 'You close the major shipping lanes down. We'll support you as our primary logistical source.' A double bluff, so simply elegant in its execution.

Now, the lies were becoming very real, as his ships were stranded outside, or on their way to British ports, with their cargoes waiting for customers, whilst a major competitor sailed with naval escorts from Hong Kong, practically all the way up the bloody River Thames to Downing Street.

She had *lied* to him, and that bold decision was beyond forgiveness. You just didn't do such a thing in traditional east-west business.

When you dealt with Henry Tan, you did so only with the utmost respect.

———

Cade sat at the bar and used his phone to navigate towards the BBC website – his way of keeping pace with the world, wherever he was.

*And in breaking news it has been confirmed two senior members of the British court of appeal are listed among the missing stowaways, thought to have been in a container washed overboard in storms in the Bay of Biscay. Police are also appealing for any sightings of the following men. British authorities are refusing to comment at this time.*

O'Shea was watching the same article on the TV. Dated pictures of the city bankers appeared on the screen, alongside the most senior judges on the British circuit. The faces of men now lying entombed on the Continental Shelf off the coast of France.

All of the money won, traded and laundered at the old music hall was now safely locked away in a fingerprint identity safe, on the top floor of a stunning gold and glassy building, half way around the world.

But the real money, the smart money, lay elsewhere.

# ORCHARD ROAD

## Prologue

Henry Tan sat in his rooftop office, clicked a few cells within a spreadsheet, leant back in his cream leather chair and looked out across *his* city where hundreds of merchant ships jostled for position, waiting to dock and unload their cargo, the heat haze giving the impression they were floating in the sky.

It was another hot one: sultry, heavy clouds were rolling in, thirty in the shade, increasing the already unbearable humidity.

The large screen TV in his office, set permanently to Al Jazeera recounted the story of the *Guardian*.

The few million pounds he'd made from his gambling at the old music hall was hardly likely to make an impact upon Tan's business empire – small change, really. A bit of harmless fun. But it missed the point. It was the thrill of the chase, and he, too, had missed it. He had to hand it to Constantin, the idea had been a virtuoso performance with a seemingly never-ending stream of willing players.

It was just entertainment, and what he looked at now was purely business.

That's how he dealt with the faces of the dead and condemned, anyway. They were willing to gamble with their lives. The power brokers were willing to gamble on them.

He switched the TV off.

The *Guardian Orient* was scheduled to arrive in a few weeks, her captain would be rewarded for his role in sending a few of Tan's arch enemies and business opponents to the bottom of the ocean, and for bringing in ferociously profitable commodities that he would turn around quickly, doubling his profit in the process.

If he recalled the very specific wording of his contract, the captain would retire to his new beachfront home on the Black Sea and never be heard of again.

It was what Tan did, and anyone who prevented him from doing so, found themselves facing the most feared image in his country – a simple outline. Some mistook it at their peril.

The shape was easily recognized – a moth.

In Native American mythology, the moth was a symbol of rebirth, of change, of transformation. In Tan's country, it was often seen as a symbol of death. Just like the one on the top of the missing container, marking it out on the quayside.

The moth, or at least the fear of what it stood for, had been good to Tan. He'd used it to prey on people's minds for years, as a simple representation of death, whether death followed or not.

Whenever Tan had it added to a calling card, a letter, a shipping container or a front door, it tended to eventuate.

He liked truth.

If the information that Jack Cade was planning to visit Tan's city was correct, then the least Tan could do was lay out the welcome mat: treat him like royalty, meet him at the airport, direct him to one of his very best apartments, when he least expected it.

But would he take the bait, dangled temptingly in front of him?

The chase. It was what he enjoyed the most.

———

Cade would have no idea, of course. Why would he? To him, Tan was a relatively unknown quantity. He was a mystery man from the Far East – probably, it's what most Englishmen thought when they considered the great trading ports on the coastlines of South East Asia and along the Silk Road.

According to the booking agent, Tan's booking agent, Cade was travelling with the woman, O'Shea.

They were travelling in business class on Singapore Airlines, leaving London Heathrow, flight SQ317, in ten days.

A pity he wasn't travelling alone. Tan employed only the very best escorts and one or two could have made Cade a very happy man indeed. Plying him with drink and favours whilst emptying him of his deepest secrets.

The country was known for its hospitality after all, both by day and by night.

———

Henry had rid the world of Nicolescu, the repugnant Romanian thief.

The British police officer with the sneering upper lip, now sat in a hospital bed somewhere and was too busy wallowing in self-pity to ever be a nuisance. It served him right for what he had done to his nephew. Family was very important for Tan, a man who was well respected and much-loved by his nephews.

The two members of Jenkinson's corrupt police team had died at the hands of a heel-wearing host, about much of which he preferred not to know. He'd helped Roberts to escape, the man he had most admired in the whole sorry circus.

He had courage and would have made a marvellous high stakes bet – Tan was prepared to go to a million that Roberts would withstand any class A drug. A million pounds. There was a time it was considered an impossibly large sum of money. Now, some men and women were prepared to risk it on the journey of a ball, the throw of a dice, or the turn of a card.

The businessmen were dead, their personal accounts trawled and fleeced, the Nigerian oil magnate was at the bottom with them – shame, he could have been useful. The Guangzhou property tycoon, gone, too. The judges, so judgemental all the time, they were now swilling around in the submerged container, creating a foul human broth.

He found himself pitying Roberts when he had learned about his wife, actually admired his spirit. But he was a cop and Tan despised cops. Let no man forget that two of them had killed his father. A cold-blooded assassination in Chinatown one night. They told nothing but lies at the hearing. One even smiled at him, reassuring him.

Tan shouldn't have been there, but his mother insisted. She said it was right to look into the eyes of the men who had killed her husband and his father.

He'd only gone out to fetch their favourite treat, Hainanese chicken rice. He wouldn't be too long, he never was. Except on this occasion, he never returned.

His dear father, left dying in the street with people stepping over him, one man even taking the chance to steal his food. It was the best chicken rice in the city, so why let it go to waste? The consequence of arrest was that he would be publicly humiliated and sentenced to a greater term in prison than the two men who had killed Henry's father.

There was an inquiry, a full investigation. The man in charge had said all the right words, pressed the flesh, even came to their HDB flat and said how sorry he was, in their dialect. He shook young Henry's hand and said if ever he needed him, he only had to ask.

He followed up on that promise a few years later when his mother was run down by a drunk driver. But the call was never returned. So much for being a man of his word – a man for and of the people. That's what he had said. The Englishman with the heavy frown lines, bright blue eyes and a friendly smile.

Where had he been when he was identifying her in the morgue – barely able to stand tall enough to look into her eyes?

Henry hated many things in life, but dishonesty was equal first with disloyalty.

He was a little older now, and much wiser and very much richer.

He was the boy from the Housing Development Board flats and now the much bigger boy with an uncanny memory for names and faces and a ruthless head for business.

Tan lit a candle. He liked the smell. A simple scented affair, it soon filled the office with hints of apple and cinnamon.

"I will find you one day. It is an absolute certainty. I know you are still out there somewhere Richard," he whispered.

He stared at the orange flame, which wavered slightly in a rare breeze, then continued to burn brighter than ever.

"That you choose to remain alive after everything you have done, is either brave, or reckless. I've been busy for many years, but now my business empire is so strong I can employ the very best people, and revenge, as they say, is so much nicer served cold. Unlike Hainan chicken rice."

He threw his paper knife – a solid silver affair with a crafted tiger's head. It landed in the office door and quivered from side to side for a few seconds.

He licked his thumb and forefinger and squeezed the candle wick, hearing it sizzle against his skin.

"Come on, Jack, I need you to be the moth that cannot ignore my flame. And to then draw the other moths closer."

———

Tan looked back at the spreadsheet and calculations. Things weren't adding up. The trade deals in Europe were haywire. No one wanted to take a chance anymore, not until the dust had settled.

Whilst he had a huge fortune on paper, Tan's profit margins had shrunk and his cashflow was heading the same way. Even the corrupt had to have discussions with their bank managers or financiers.

Time for Plan B. Not a dishonest plan, just a necessary one, and with luck, no one would get hurt.

———

She had lied to him, the man who in whispered tones the people of Singapore called The Moth. Soon, if things went his way, his emblem would be carved on the door to her home – Number 10 Downing Street.

He had a particularly interesting plan of how to do it.

He took a sip of an expensive French red wine. He turned his nose up, then placed the glass back down on the desk.

He pressed a button on his desk phone. A male arrived. Immaculately attired, he'd worked for Tan for years, had known him since he was a boy, and had worked for his father before that. He knew exactly what to say and when.

"Sir?"

"Miller. Replace this hideous drink with something more fitting." He threw the glass at the wall, showering the pure white curtains in deep cherry red stains.

"Your mood, sir?" he asked skilfully.

"Angry. I have been betrayed by none other than a head of state and only I am ever allowed to betray people."

"Absolutely. Then may I recommend an aged Macallan – from 1968 to be precise? It's from your private collection."

Miller returned ten minutes later.

Tan smiled. "Is it obscenely expensive?"

"Hideously."

"Then you may leave the bottle. And order another three. It seems exactly what I am in need of."

His aide placed the perfectly cut glass onto the red leather Tan Shipping coaster, and the bottle onto another alongside it.

"Anything else, sir?"

"Have you found the other person that betrayed me, who robbed me of the right to a father?"

"No, sir, not yet."

"Then keep looking!" he yelled. Then controlled his temper. "Keep looking. I pay you handsomely, do I not?"

"You do, sir. But so far this man is one step ahead of us."

"So it would seem, Miller."

Tan stood, held his drink and looked out of the top floor office window, down onto the harbour where the merlion stood guard, glistening white, a majestic fountain and a symbol for the city.

"The man who betrayed me recently once asked me if I knew an old Romanian proverb."

"And did you, sir?"

"No."

"May I ask what it was?" asked his employee and lifelong friend – the man who had saved his business from a few predators. Miller was a quiet and assured individual who had been hired by Tan's father. He spoke the local dialects and understood its people. With a military background, he still walked everywhere with a purpose; places to go, people to see.

———

His full name was Harold C. Miller. Named after his father, a coal merchant from the Midlands. No one knew what the C stood for but those who had met him, either here in the luxurious offices of Tan Shipping, or down an alleyway late at night, knew better than to cross him.

He'd learned the hard way, boxing on the streets of Walsall, deep in the heart of the English region known as the Black Country. So-called after the coal, or the smoke from years gone by.

He had eyes as grey as a Walsall winter that watched the world like a cat watches a fledgling. His nose was slightly skewed, a legacy of a badly repaired injury, and his hands bore the myriad scars of youthful exuberance, before his father saw fit to send him to the local recruiting office. A visit from which he never looked back.

These days, his thick black hair was losing a battle with prema-ture greys, he was immaculately groomed, tanned, lean and capable. He spoke well too, considering where he hailed from. The English education system had taught him how to write, and the army had taught him how to right a wrong.

———

"I would only ask about the proverb out of interest, sir, and only if you chose to tell me."

"It asked if you would put your hand into the fire for someone – to vouch for them."

"Interesting. And would you?" he asked rhetorically.

"I think you know the answer. But would *you*? Let me remind you of a local proverb. *Those who speak aloud are boastful. Those who speak softly are unsure...*" He inhaled, then slowly let the air escape his lungs. "Care to complete it for me?"

He poured a glass of the malt and handed it to his most-trusted employee.

He nodded respectfully and took it before completing the saying.

"*Those who don't speak – are dangerous.*"

Tan emptied the glass. Harry Miller did the same.

"That's right. You are a man of few words. I like that about you. Now, I have some thinking to do and nothing much to say."

"I believe I understand, sir. And forgive me, but will that be all for today?"

Tan poured some more of the malt over the existing ice.

"This malt. You said hideously expensive?"

"Ridiculously so."

"Then here, take what is left and enjoy it. You have earned it these last few weeks."

"Thank you, sir. It isn't necessary, but I would very much enjoy savouring the taste. Sir, is there something else bothering you?" he asked, cautiously.

"Do you mean other than being betrayed by a foreign government, having one of my most modern ships stuck in one of the world's busiest shipping lanes and the man who I have spent a lifetime hating – yet who somehow eludes me to this day? No, nothing at all."

"I sense that it is the latter that is really troubling you. You have been so focused on expanding the business – and your father would be so proud of what you have achieved – but now perhaps with the problems in London dealt with you can take some time to relax?"

"I will relax when he is laying on the steps of the merlion with my paper knife sticking out of his heart."

"It's a beautiful knife, sir, perhaps something less tasteful?"

Tan smiled. Miller always knew what to say.

"Perhaps. But first we need to find him."

"Do I have your permission to start as soon as Cade lands?"

"You do, but why not now?"

"You are familiar with the saying, a sprat to catch a mackerel?"

"No. Why would you throw a fish away? In Chinese culture the fish is a symbol of good luck."

"I realise that, sir, but sometimes in order to catch the particular fish you are hunting you need to use the right bait."

"There is a Chinese legend – it refers to a carp that climbs the waterfall on the Yellow River..."

"Ah yes, I am familiar with that from my night school lessons. Legend has it the carp turned into a dragon. The moral of the story being that if you try very hard you, will gain great power."

"Great power is what I already have. But I am ready to leap up the waterfall and become a true dragon."

"But the people already know you as The Moth, a term which is feared among the community, why would you want to change that?"

"Which sounds better, Miller? Be honest. The Moth of Orchard Road, or the Dragon?" He looked at his old friend, a man who was more than just his aide.

"That's like asking whether I prefer to be called Harry or Miller. I feel you already know which you prefer, sir."

Tan raised his glass, then turned and looked at the large teak framed photo, hanging on the main wall, where it took pride of place against the deep red handmade silk wallpaper.

It was the photo of his dear father, a faded black-and-white image of him standing outside of the dockyard, the one Henry now owned. He wished he was in the office today, sharing some of the warming drink and telling tales of the past.

Tan gazed through the tinted glass, until the horizon blurred and he found himself staring at his own reflection, for just long enough that it frightened him.

"And Miller?" he asked without turning.

"Sir?"

"You don't mind if I call you Miller, do you?" He appeared to be genuinely intrigued.

"Not at all, sir. I feel it adds a certain something. A hint of mystery, perhaps. And after all, you look after me, reward me well, and frankly, that means you can call me whatever you like." He smiled a confident and warm smile.

"You are always so perceptive. I can change it to Harry, if you prefer?"

"No, sir, Miller is just fine. Will that be all for this evening?"

"Yes, Harry, that will be all." Tan smiled back, it was a rare event, and rarer still that he had called him by his first name.

The door was closing when Tan called out to his aide.

"Miller."

"Sir?"

"You will find him, won't you?"

"Absolutely. Good night, sir."

## ACKNOWLEDGMENTS

I have to start with my family. We've been on a few wild and unplanned journeys over the last ten years – but we've lived to tell the tale. Quite simply, without them I wouldn't be the man I am, or the author I became. Their love and the relationship we have is second to none. That my children have grown so fast and now provided me with three adorable grandchildren is both delightful and scary at the same time. I am after all, far too young.

In my professional life, I've recently dealt with chaos, natural disasters, terrorism and dare I mention the viral elephant in the room? The latter has seen me working from home – just as I did before The C Word and as a result of serious illness. For me working from home was a busman's holiday, during the long initial year of lockdowns and more, I told myself I had to do something with the 'spare time' – I tried the guitar again, I tried a little Spanish, but ended up poco loco, and I swore if I ever got invited to another zoom meeting, I'd turn up naked doing a handstand.

But, and it's a big one, my writing has entertained people, causing many to connect with me via social media platforms – the curse and blessing of any modern author – and frankly, I've loved the engagement. From the UK to Gibraltar, Singapore to India, Canada to New Zealand and back to the Plains of Texas, I've had emails and messages from afar.

Who in their right mind doesn't like praise?

I even received a one-star review from someone who decided that on the day we launched *The Angel of Whitehall* they'd rain on my parade – it backfired dramatically as so many major authors, among them Mr Peter James wrote to me to say 'Welcome to the club Lewis – *now* you are an author!'

I have loved writing this new novel, hopefully its authenticity rings true and the storyline captures people's imaginations. There are companies mentioned during the story and as with all of my novels I do this because I either like their products or admire their real-world operations. I am in no way affiliated to them. Nor do I benefit in any way.

In the latter stage of this book, you will read about the quite incredible and globally-challenging port that literally rose from the mudbanks of the River Thames – I chose DP World London Gateway not because they would ever allow such a storyline to develop on site, but because their systems are so damned good that it would never happen. Their brilliant web pages helped me to drive through the gates with a container and take it all the way to the ship – without ever leaving my writer's retreat!

To the team at DP thanks for allowing me to enter your world – a thoroughly modern organisation who keep the world moving whilst we sleep. You can find out more about them and take a virtual tour here https://www.londongateway.com/

To the characters who drift in and out of my life and add the real colour to the novels, thank you. You know who you are and I love you all dearly. Many are or were on the thin blue line, the people that some in society say we need to defund – yet are the first to call screaming for help when it's literally dripping off the fan. My aroha (love) and respect to Sergeant Matt Ratana, Royal New Zealand and Metropolitan Police who was killed in 2020 whilst working as a custody sergeant in London. A good mate and a formidable Māori warrior. Sleep well brother I hope you like your cameo.

To Mick Jenkins MBE – great leader, lovely man, questionable rugby team. May you always be climbing your next mountain. Rest easy boyo!

To Brian Price for challenging my mind, writing prowess and technical knowledge. And then some.

To Jeremy Batchelor for daring me to write a book about a chemist. I hope it captures your heart and mind.

To the doctors, nurses, frontline health workers, ambulance staff and firefighters, military personnel and frankly anyone that has put their needs second to fighting the first major global issue to affect us all in our lifetimes – thank you!

I have chosen to broach the subject of miscarriage in this story. I didn't do this lightly. It's a brutally sad fact of life and one that has affected my wife and I – we lost two beautiful sons in succession. Naming them, many years later, was the single best thing we ever did. I wanted to include this topic as it impacts upon men as well as women and should be discussed. To James and Michael, I hope this makes you proud!

In finishing *The Chemist* in much less than a year we've done incredibly well. I really should think about getting a life. I say we; I can't close without saying a massive thank you to my now one-year-long much-suffering publishers Rebecca Collins and Adrian Hobart – the powerhouses behind UK independent publisher Hobeck Books. Two Michael Caines walk into a bar...

One year on, we are friends and have a master plan to get Jack Cade and the team onto the 'To be read' piles around the world, into the charts, onto the prize-winning shortlists and who knows, even a script for TV one day (still waiting for the call Jed Mercurio!) Only the best will do. Aim for the stars son, aim for the stars.

On that note we've lost far too many loved ones to this virus since I started *The Chemist*, so do me a favour, hug a friend today, pick up the phone and ring your loved ones, smile at a stranger, lend a hand when no one else does. Never turn your back on a friend in need, and remember, it's very much OK to not be OK.

Above all, embrace life whilst you can. It's great. It's wonderful and if you are healthy, even better.

Either that, or become an author and end up like me! You have been warned!

LEWIS X

Lewis Hastings is a pseudonym. He was born in the nineteen sixties (a by-product of the long, harsh winter) in Kent, the Garden of England. By virtue of his father's role as a Prison Officer he became somewhat nomadic, moving from county to county during his formative years.

As quickly as he made friends, they became a distant memory.

His school life was a heady cocktail of fun, misery and abject failure explaining why he decided not to pursue a university career. Thrust into the world of full-time employment at seventeen he married young and forged out a highly unsuccessful and miserable career in sales; a way to pay the bills and provide a home for his growing family.

In 1988 a cathartic event changed his approach to life and he spent two frustrating years trying to forge a new career as a police officer. By doing this he would in fact continue a family tradition stemming back to the early 1800's.

His career commenced with the Nottinghamshire Constabulary at a time of enormous change. He was soon posted to some of the most beautiful and equally dangerous locations in the county where he learned the noble art of policing, including response, community, intelligence and vice work (the latter, whilst challenging, at least offered a secondary income).

In 2003, wearing a different uniform he found himself in a new country, soon realising the age-old maxim about familiar excrement and days of the week still rang true.

This is the fifth novel in the Jack Cade series. The Seventh Wave trilogy including *Seventh, Seven Degrees* and *Seven of Swords* was initially released between 2017 and 2019 to great acclaim, readers revelling in the 'highly realistic' and 'cinematographic' writing that fully embeds them in the story. *The Angel of Whitehall* a timely story about a retired naval officer with a terrible and dark secret followed in 2020. He is currently writing the new Jack Cade thriller *Orchard Road*.

Lewis is married with two children, a lake-loving Labrador and lives in a house.

# HOBECK BOOKS – THE HOME OF GREAT STORIES

We hope you've enjoyed reading this book by the brilliant Lewis Hastings. To find out more about Lewis and his work please visit his website: **https://lewishastings.wixsite.com/is-the-author.**

Hobeck Books overs a number of short stories and novellas free for subscribers in the compilation *Crime Bites*.

- *Echo Rock* by Robert Daws

- *Old Dogs, Old Tricks* by AB Morgan
- *The Silence of the Rabbit* by Wendy Turbin
- *Never Mind the Baubles: An Anthology of Twisted Winter Tales* by the Hobeck Team (including many of the Hobeck authors and Hobeck's two publishers)
- *The Clarice Cliff Vase* by Linda Huber
- *Here She Lies* by Kerena Swan
- *The Macnab Principle* by R.D. Nixon
- *Fatal Beginnings* by Brian Price
- *A Defining Moment* by Lin Le Versha
- *Saviour* by Jennie Ensor

Also please visit the Hobeck Books website for details of our other superb authors and their books, and if you would like to get in touch, we would love to hear from you.

Hobeck Books also presents a weekly podcast, the Hobcast, where founders Adrian Hobart and Rebecca Collins discuss all things book related, key issues from each week, including the ups and downs of running a creative business. Each episode includes an interview with one of the people who make Hobeck possible: the editors, the authors, the cover designers. These are the people who help Hobeck bring great stories to life. Without them, Hobeck wouldn't exist. The Hobcast can be listened to from all the usual platforms but it can also be found on the Hobeck website: **www. hobeck.net/hobcast**.

## PRAISE FOR LEWIS HASTINGS

### SEVENTH

'Emotions run high reading this thriller and I feel totally spent now.'
'Expect adrenaline surges, plenty of testosterone, deceit, empathy and extreme hate in this intense journey that is full of tension, suspense, action, drama and intrigue.'
'Clearly written from the heart.'
'I literally could not put it down.'
'Every page is a delight to read and the story takes you through an amazing journey.'
'A real page turner, I couldn't put it down.'
'This book is a must read.'

PRAISE FOR LEWIS HASTINGS

## SEVEN DEGREES

'A fast paced crime thriller with enough twists to keep readers guessing.'
'...gripping...'
'If book 1 of this trilogy blew me away, then this one blew me harder.'
'...edge of your seat stuff...'
'Fantastic.'

## SEVEN OF SWORDS

'Twists and turns in every chapter.'
'Had me gripped from the start...truly magnificent writing.'
'I didn't want it to end!'
'WOW what a read!'
'I implore you to pick up this trilogy.'
'Read it, this will not be a disappointment to you.'

## THE ANGEL OF WHITEHALL

'I would recommend this book unequivocally with no reservations, my one issue is that it will ensnare you and leaving it will not be an option until the last page. This is a story destined to be remembered as crossing a threshold of this specific genre. It is that good.'
'One of the most exciting new authors...another gripping, fantastic read from a master storyteller.'
'My first novel by this author but I find I now need to read whatever came before. What a tale.'
'Lewis Hastings has again nailed it!'

www.ingramcontent.com/pod-product-compliance
Lightning Source LLC
Chambersburg PA
CBHW060721190726
48285CB00001B/20